Acclaim for Ian Slater

WORLD WAR III

"Superior to the Tom Clancy genre . . . and the military aspect far more realistic."
— *The Spectator*

MacARTHUR MUST DIE

"A most satisfying what-if thriller . . . The plot [is] a full-speed-ahead page-turner. . . . Flashy, fast fun."
— *New York Daily News*

"Searing suspense . . . [A] rousing, splendidly told adventure."
— *Los Angeles Times*

"Taughtly written, this novel is loaded with scenes that will have you grasping the book so tightly your knuckles will turn white. . . . The final scene is a climactic hair-raising thriller."
— *West Coast Review of Books*

*Please turn the page
for more reviews. . . .*

SEA GOLD

"A first-rate, crisply told adventure story."
—*Toronto Globe and Mail*

"Thrilling, fast-paced . . . *Sea Gold* combines a high sense of adventure with excellent character and story development. . . . An out-and-out winner."
—*Hamilton Spectator*

"Full of furious action."
—*Quill and Quire*

AIR GLOW RED

"Provides page-turning thrills that should leave even the steadiest hands shaking."
—*The Toronto Star*

"One of the top suspense writers in North America. His plots are intelligent, well thought out, and have the eerie specter of reality hanging over them like a rain cloud on the horizon."
—*The Hamilton Spectator*

"One of the most riveting chase sequences in recent fiction."
—*Midland Free Press*

By Ian Slater:

Published by the Ballantine Publishing Group

FORCE 10

Ian Slater

BALLANTINE BOOKS • NEW YORK

A Ballantine Book
Published by The Ballantine Publishing Group
Copyright © 2000 by Bunyip Enterprises, Inc.

All rights reserved under International and Pan-American Copyright Conventions. Published in the United States by The Ballantine Publishing Group, a division of Random House, Inc., New York, and simultaneously in Canada by Random House of Canada Limited, Toronto.

Ballantine and colophon are trademarks of Random House, Inc.

www.randomhouse.com/BB/

Library of Congress Catalog Card Number: 00-107760

ISBN 0-449-00558-5

Manufactured in the United States of America

First Ballantine Books Edition: December 2000

10 9 8 7 6 5 4 3 2 1

For Marian, Serena, and Blair

I would like to thank Mr. D. W. Reiley for his expertise regarding small arms and associated subjects, and my friend and colleague, Professor Peter Petro for Russian phrases. Once again I am indebted to my wife, Marian, whose patience, typing and editorial skills continue to give me invaluable support in my work.

CHAPTER ONE

Washington State

THE MILLENNIUM.

The USMC—United States Militia Corps—needed cash. Fast. The cost of waging war against the federal government was high, and funds for new arms and recruits were low.

Like the storm raging over the desert of eastern Washington, there wasn't going to be anything subtle about their efforts. Time didn't allow it. Two days earlier, one of the thirty militiamen involved in "Operation Tax Rebate" had gotten into the foyer of the Rone building at Wills Creek wearing a FedEx uniform and carrying a parcel for a nonexistent employee. While the puzzled guards checked and rechecked their staff list, the militiaman took note of the laser ports on the ground floor above the protective steel-bar mesh wall. The ports were angled so that once the antiburglary circuits were activated at day's end, the resulting lasers would produce a crisscross thicket of beams through which no one could pass without setting off the alarms. He'd reported this to his major, Lucky McBride, who adjusted the operational plan for "Tax Rebate" accordingly. McBride was now on the rain-pelted highway driving a ten-wheeler Mack truck hauling a tarpaulin-covered wide load heading east out of the Cascade Mountains, toward Spokane. The Mack looked as if it was bleeding steam in the downpour, its tires spitting up a dirty cloud of rain and pebbles from the road's gravel shoulder.

McBride's co-driver, Neilson, saw a tricolored blur in his side mirror. "Son of a bitch!" he said. "Federals on our tail.

Looks like the state patrol." The militia referred to all police, state or otherwise, as "federals."

"I see them," McBride said calmly. Without turning his head, he told his three men in the adjoining sleeper cab directly behind him to keep their heads down.

The cruiser pulled abreast of the Mack's cab, its flashers on, the trooper's voice coming out of the miniature bullhorn on the patrol car's roof. "Where's the fire?" he asked McBride. There was an enormous streak of lightning to the east followed by an artillery roll of thunder.

"We're haulin' a Cat to Wills Creek," McBride shouted. "Local dam . . ." The thunder drowned out his voice momentarily. "—has sprung a leak. They want us to shore it up real quick 'fore she breaks. You want to give us an escort?"

"You betcha," said the trooper obligingly. "Move to the center line. Get off that messy shoulder."

"Will do. Thanks."

"Man," quipped McBride's co-driver, "you've got balls. I'll say that for you."

"Lucky McBride," said Brock, one of the three in the sleeper. "That's what he is. We're running behind time 'cause of a flat tire, and he gets a federal to run interference for us. Incredible!"

"Yeah," one of the other militiamen said. "But what're we goin' to do when we stop at Wills Creek and the fed asks where the dam is?"

"And," McBride's co-driver added, "what happens when he sees what's under the tarp?"

McBride smiled. "He'll be surprised."

McBride's luck held, however, and at the Wills Creek turnoff the state trooper wished him all the best and sped off, continuing east on Highway 90.

The lightning was getting worse, a long fork of electric-blue in the moonless night momentarily illuminating the high desert sagebrush as far as the eye could see. The landscape was scarred here and there by deep coulees, ravines that had been gouged out over the eons by ice and which up to now had lain dry after the long, hot summer. A moment later a barrage of thunder rolled over them, the wind picked up, and the edges of the tarpaulin flapped furiously behind them.

It made Norman Cawley, one of the men in the sleeper, nervous. He'd joined the militia, like so many others, because he was fed up—no, *furious*—with the federal government for caving in to all the damn global free trade treaties. An apple grower from around Wenatchee in central Washington, he'd seen the orchards in the biggest apple-producing state in the union go down the drain because the government was allowing the Chinese to dump produce below cost on the U.S. market, intentionally undercutting American growers. Independents like himself, who had worked hard all their lives, saw the price plummet from forty dollars a ton to ten. Farmers had gone broke all over, ripping out their trees, and meanwhile all they read and heard about was how the rest of the country, especially Bill Gates and all the other computer whiz kids on the West Coast, were living high off the hog. Biggest problem those yuppies had, so far as he could see, was getting their morning latte at Starbucks.

Cawley had eventually told his wife he'd had enough. For the first time in his life he publicly protested, joining the throngs in November '99 in the "Battle of Seattle," rallying against the World Trade Organization, another damn U.N. new world order bureaucracy. 'Course the protest had no effect. There were lots of arrests, and a fed in full black body armor at Sixth and Union fired at him, the bullet hitting him in the chest. He'd collapsed, thought he was dying. It turned out to be a huge welt caused by a new device, a plastic-coated pepper spray bullet that exploded on impact. But he thought he was dying. So when he heard about "Tax Rebate," he joined up. But there were things the militia hadn't explained, and it bothered him.

"Still don't see why we had to wait for a storm," he said now.

"It'll help cover our arrival," McBride answered.

Neilson laughed. "*Arrival*. Yeah, I like that."

Renowned for being able to maintain his equanimity as H hour approached, McBride smiled.

"Huh," said Cawley. "I thought it might be because of the cell phones."

"How do you mean?" McBride asked.

"Well, you know. Lightning might knock out their cell phones so they can't raise an alarm."

"No." McBride slipped the Mack into tenth gear. "Lightning has to hit the cell tower, the actual transmitter, to do that. But you don't have to worry about cell phones anyway. With the stuff they're working on, cell phones are verboten. Same reason you can't use your cell on an aircraft. It'd screw up the whole operation. They've got a shield built around the whole building. Stops any signals from entering or leaving."

"Huh," was Cawley's only comment. McBride had clearly done his homework, but then Cawley, known as "Worry Gut" among his fellow militiamen, thought of a flaw in McBride's plan. "Okay, but if there are no cell phones allowed, what about their regular phones? You know, land lines? They could raise the alarm that way."

McBride flipped up the brown leather cover on his watch. "That, my friend, will be taken care of in about six, seven minutes. Couple of our boys up ahead are going to cut the lines. The building'll be completely isolated, even more than it is now. That's what they get for being greedy, having situated so far out to get lower power rates from Grand Coulee Dam."

Cawley was only half listening, intrigued momentarily by McBride's watch. "Why do you have that cover?"

"What? Oh, that. I used to work at sea—fishing boat out of Seattle—before they gave the Indian fishermen—"

"Fishers!" put in one of the men in the backseat. "Not fisher*men*. Let's be politically correct here, boys."

"Before they gave the Indian fisher*men* more rights than us," McBride said bitterly, "like killing whales for ceremonial purposes. If we did that, we'd be put in jail."

"That's 'cause we're white," Neilson said pontifically.

"You got that right," McBride replied.

"So," Cawley pressed, "the watch cover?"

"Oh yeah." McBride smiled at his own lapse from his usual

good humor. "Well, the leather cover protects the glass face from getting all scratched up from drag cables and the like. And it cuts down on any reflection."

Cawley nodded. "Wish I had one."

"Tell you what," McBride told him. "We pull this off, Cawley, we'll have enough money to buy a watch cover for every militiaman in the country."

"That's over five million guys," one of the others said.

"A drop in the bucket," McBride quipped.

"Yeah," Neilson said, recalling the report—a militia mantra by now—in *Time* magazine in 1995 that talked about those who didn't have "a shred of sympathy for what happened in Oklahoma." The report stated that "if you include all the people . . . who respond to the patriotic rhetoric about a sinister, out-of-control federal bureaucracy . . . all the underemployed who blame their plight on NAFTA and GATT— then the count soars upward of twelve million."

"Well, maybe," Brock responded from the back, "but first we have to get it. Then we have to—"

"One step at a time," the ever-optimistic McBride said.

Another flash of lightning lit up the blue metallic sky.

"Why didn't you tell me about the cell phones before?" Cawley asked.

"Security," McBride answered. He simultaneously checked the rearview mirror for any of the four orange pickups that he'd had spaced at quarter-mile intervals behind him. The twenty militiamen in the four pickups, and the five he'd sent ahead of the Mack in two more pickups, were all wearing glowing orange Washington State highway workers' coveralls and well-worn white hard hats. He couldn't see anything, however, because of the spray being thrown up by his rig. The Mack's wipers were whining on full power, but the rain was so heavy—"like a cow peeing on a flat rock," as he put it— that all he could see was the intermittent ruby glow of a red taillight. The forecast had been for rain in the mountains, but he feared this would mean snow. But he couldn't worry about that now. He could only hope that everyone was in position and that the faint red taillight ahead was that of the forward road watch squad. Their job was to cut the phone and power lines leading to the Rone building and to reroute any traffic that might venture off the highway onto the Rone turnoff.

But it occurred to Cawley that the taillight they could see might be that of the highway patrol cruiser having been slowed by the rain. "What do you think?" he asked McBride.

"Don't know."

"There's our baby!" the co-driver said. He was pointing at the Rone building, about a mile off to the left. It stood out in the rain-slashed darkness like some huge, illuminated, up-turned bathtub, its shape dictated by the two semispherical ends of the SIGPRES, or signal protection shield that covered the entire building. The light emitted from its closed windows appeared like so many bright pinholes in its elongated beehive-shaped structure. Inside, only maintenance and security personnel and maybe a few scientists would be working the night shift.

Three minutes later, as McBride braked the Mack, the tarpaulin behind came alive with rivulets of water as McBride's four companions swiftly removed it. McBride, Neilson, and Brock then quickly climbed into the T-34 battle tank. Militiaman Neilson, as the driver, backed it carefully off the Mack's beam trailer, while militiaman Brock slid into his place as gunner. Cawley and the remaining militiaman would stay with the Mack.

"Something old, something new," McBride quipped. The *new* was the latest Generation IV PVS twenty-ounce NVGs, or night vision goggles, attached to his commander's "Fritz," or Kevlar helmet. The NVGs were capable of boosting ambient light several thousand times. The *old* was the upgraded and thoroughly reliable T-34, quite legally purchased, albeit through a front buyer or "collector," from Cold War Remarketing of Denver at the bargain basement price of $40,000, including state and federal taxes. The Russian T-34, weighing in at thirty-five tons, with 3.5 inches of sloped frontal armor glacis plate, its diesel engine capable of a very respectable thirty-four miles per hour, was still very much in use around the world; the legendary Russian tank had made its debut by astonishing the German Fourth Panzer Division at the Battle of Kamenewo halfway between Kiev and Moscow. It was there that Soviet General Katukov launched his T-34s, every tank mounted on the revolutionary American-designed Christie suspension, against the bridge at Lisiza. The Germans of Fourth Panzer, who had never seen the T-34 till then, fought bravely but were forced to withdraw, and that night the first snows of 1941 fell. For the Germans it was *der Wendepunkt*, the turning point, in the war against Russia, the beginning of the end of the Wehrmacht's "Operation Barbarossa."

McBride too was counting on the shock value of the T-34 as its tracks gathered speed across the storm-shrouded desert. He hoped to reach the Rone building before the downpour turned the volcanic soil to mud. Not that this would stop the legendary T-34, but it might slow it, and it was McBride's intention to hit the entrance of the Rone building at full speed, so he could crash through its outer SIGPRES aluminum shield and the extra-thick, twelve-inch Rebar-steel-reinforced concrete wall, then the steel bar door into the lobby, allowing the remaining twenty-five of his militia unit to pour through the hole and up to Room 501 to loot, or "*shoot* and loot" if necessary.

"Don't screw up my alignment," gunner Brock yelled. There was more lightning.

"Do my best!" shouted McBride, who was doing an Israeli, his head above the tank's cupola. It was a dangerous move, but he could see better even in the rain, his NVGs turning the rain-slashed night into a speckled green. Once they got closer, when the building, because of its lights, turned milky, the NVGs were in danger of "blooming." McBride flipped down the filter. The building now showed up more clearly, and as yet no one was coming outside. One of the reasons for waiting for a storm was that presumably no one inside would hear the tank racing toward the building, the throttling roar of the T-34's 500-horsepower diesel muffled by the barrages of thunder.

"Don't screw up the alignment!"

"Brock!" McBride shouted into the throat mike, then paused, knowing his voice would be drowned by the engine noise and the squeak of the twenty-inch-wide tracks as the tank dipped and rose sharply. It shucked off a minor mud slide and climbed out of a once-dry coulee that would soon be a raging torrent. Then he said, "If you say that again I'll shove one of those H.E. rounds up your ass."

"Don't screw up the alignment!"

It wasn't that Brock was concerned about the front- and cupola-mounted machine guns, but rather the alignment of his fifteen-foot-long, 85mm main gun. Too much of a shock could throw off the aiming mechanism, and he wouldn't have time to do an in field recalibration.

"Hopefully," driver Neilson cut in, "you won't have to use the .85. We've been through all that."

"Two hundred yards to go!" McBride said.

Then all the lighted windows went dark and quickly came alive again, telling him his forward team had severed the power mains, the building's auxiliary generator now kicking in. He spotted two figures emerging from the white square of the building's entrance. One of them was pulling something from his pocket, his other hand jabbing at it—a cell phone. McBride let off a long burst, the hot red tracer streaking white dots in his NVGs. The white figure he'd aimed at exploded like tossed confetti, while a long, white spurt shot out to the side, probably arterial blood. The other figure ran hell-bent back toward the building. Another long, sweeping burst and this second figure stumbled, fell, and was stilled. The last of the tracer, white on white, disappeared into the blotter of the white entrance.

At fifty yards McBride's NVGs started blooming, even the filter overloaded by too much ambient light. He whipped them off and was momentarily blinded, the entrance only forty yards away. He knew that by now twelve other militiamen, three squads of four in each assault team, should be covering the rear entrance-cum-delivery door and the fire escape door at each end of the building.

"Brace yourself!" he warned Brock and Neilson, and heard several pings—small-arms fire bouncing off the tank's shot trap above the glacis plate. Directly in front he saw a dark blur, the Rone's security vehicle, a Nissan 2000 Xterra, coming directly at him.

"Brave bastards!" McBride gripped the sturdy towel rings he'd had welded inside the top of the cupola. But there was no need, the sensation of crushing the four-wheel-drive Nissan nothing more than the faint tremor one might feel passing over a rut. Men were screaming, and he heard tires and windows popping, the Russian tank leaving behind sheet metal that seconds before had been the brand new Xterra, its pulverized carcass now aflame from a gush of its gasoline.

McBride buttoned up, slamming down the cupola's lid, the building's signal prevention shield shattering like a screen door as the T-34's thirty-five tons rammed through it before the three of them realized it. But the specially reinforced cement framing the four-foot-wide steel door offered much more resistance, suffering only a spiderweb of hairline fissures beyond the door frame. Neilson threw the tank into the first of the two reverse gears, backed out, shoved it into first, and hit the wall left of the door. A jagged four-foot-diameter hole appeared, through which McBride glimpsed three figures, Rone security personnel moving frantically back and forth like vaudevillians in panic. McBride felt the tank jerk in reverse again before Neilson bullied the monolith back into drive. Brock fired off 7.62mm bursts from the forward machine gun, clearing the lobby, filling it with the stench of cordite, though no Rone security were in sight. When the tank hit the doorway the third time, the wall imploded in a vomit of cement, choking dust, and dangling, fragmented wire reinforcement. The T-34, debris falling off it, was well into the lobby before Neilson braked. McBride, above the cupola once more, swung the swivel-mounted 7.62, firing through a glass-shattering 180-degree arc, dissuading any Rone security personnel from interfering, as several squads of his militiamen, eleven men in all, charged through.

There was the roar of a shotgun twenty feet left of the tank, and two militiamen fell, mortally wounded, writhing and screaming in dusty blood. McBride swung his machine gun about again, its bursts sending plaster flying as the corner from which the blast had come began to disintegrate. He heard the whine of the tank's turret turning, Brock bringing the main gun to bear.

"No, Brock!" he shouted. "Don't shoot. Don't want to take out the supporting beams. Whole damn building'll collapse."

Outside, six militiamen who had flipped up their NVGs in preparation for operating in the brightly lit interior of the building now rushed in through the rear and the two fire door exits, running toward the main stairway, three on either side of it. Another eight, who'd come in the front under cover of the tank, divided into two teams of four militiamen each, Alfa and Bravo, and, ignoring the main stairwell, went charging up the two exit stairwells at either end of the five-storied building. They choked back their bile as their noses were accosted by a sickly mixture of excrement, sweat, and sinus-clogging dust. The tank, its job done—unless it was called on by the road-watch squad—began withdrawing. The rumble of its engine shook the bullet-pocked walls, its nauseating coal-black exhaust spewed high above the concrete- and glass-strewn lobby, the latter crackling under the tank's tracks. Once outside, Neilson U-turned the T-34 in the darkness, the rain drumming on its roof as it headed back out toward the Mack, from where he would have a clear view of the road.

Despite the heavy downpour and moonless night, and the fact that Cawley had, as instructed, switched off all the Mack's lights, Neilson knew exactly where the Mack was because of the wrist-mounted GPS—Global Positioning System—each militiaman had been issued. It gave Neilson the precise vector he had to follow across the half-mile distance between the tank and the truck

"McBride!" Brock yelled. "You screwed my alignment!"

"Quit your squawking!" McBride riposted, buoyed by the fact that his EAC, or external assault crew—namely himself, Neilson, and Brock—had penetrated the building ahead of time. But he remained edgy because of the danger of snow in the mountains and the fact that the job was still far from done. It was now up to his interior assault crew, or IAC, led by Mike

Moran, to get to the goods on the fifth floor. His cell phone rang then. He'd turned the volume way up amid the ear-dunning noise of the T-34's diesel, but even so, his ears were still ringing so much from the machine-gun bursts that he barely heard the phone.

"IAC One," came Moran's voice, as clear as if he was calling from just outside the tank.

"What's up?" McBride asked as the tank struck the same ditch it had on the way in and lurched violently, throwing him hard against the cupola's rim, the thud of his helmet heard by Brock. "Son of a—" he yelled to Neilson. "Warn me next time!"

"Sorry, boss!"

McBride had almost dropped the cell. "Yeah, what is it?" he asked Moran again.

"We have a problem. One of our guys who busted in through the east end fire exit wasted a woman outside. She was having a smoke."

"So?" McBride asked sharply. Too bad they'd shot a woman, but hey, the fedcrals were using women now as security guards and combat pilots. Congress even mandated that they'd soon be serving on submarines. You couldn't expect a militiaman to tell whether someone who was braving the foul weather for a cigarette was a man or a woman, especially if he'd just removed his NVGs.

"So," Moran answered, "he found a cell phone in her hand."

"Jesus, was it on?"

"Powered up."

"Think she saw you?" McBride pressed. "Had time to make a call?"

But McBride knew the answer before it came. "Don't know, boss."

"Shit! All right, we'll keep watching the road. Grab the goods, soon as you can." They'd agreed to use "goods" in the remote event that their own cells were being monitored by the National Security Agency, or NSA—which the militia liked to call "No Such Agency." The NSA's massive scanners were sweeping the airwaves twenty-four hours a day, seven days a week.

Moran was shaken. Lucky McBride rarely used any kind of profanity. Always calm, the man was legendary in the militia. Even in the furious battle during the late eighties against General Freeman's Special Ops feds on Butcher's Ridge in northern Washington, he'd stayed calm. For a moment Moran had a flashback to the battle, when the militia was exacting revenge on behalf of Charlie Ames, a fellow militiaman who, like Randy Weaver, had run afoul of federal authority. Weaver had seen his ten-year-old son shot to death by the federals, his wife shot dead as she held her other child. The feds were so crazy they'd even killed the family dog. During the fight at Butcher's Ridge, the battle cry of "Waco" had also been raised, McBride and his militiamen remembering how David Koresh and his followers in Texas had been so savagely attacked by the federals, who'd killed over eighty men, women, and children, incinerating them in a massive fire *after* the FBI had sent in tanks against the compound.

Now, McBride, mad at himself for losing his composure, albeit momentarily, called Moran on his cell phone, but there was only the frying sound of static. Moran had gone back inside the shield.

No sooner had McBride's assault squads entered the building than automatic security cage doors descended, blocking off both end fire-escape stairwells, the main stairway, and the elevator. The militiamen ignored the elevator because of the threat that electrical malfunction in the damaged building could trap them if they used it. But the cage doors, consisting of four-foot-wide, eight-foot-high, high-tensile quarter-inch-thick steel bars, effectively prevented the team of five militiamen at the foot of each fire escape door and the team of six at the bottom of the main stairwell from proceeding any farther.

"Snakes!" Moran yelled, and three militia engineers who, as per custom, had previously taken up the rear, now ran forward with looped lengths of one-and-a-half-inch-diameter transparent green garden hosing. The men wore the hoses as bandoleers across their chests; the six-foot lengths of hose were packed with det cord and C4 plastique. Several militiamen fired M-16 "clearing" bursts up the stairwells as each of the three "snakers"—one at each stairwell—adroitly threaded his hose through the eight steel bars at the base of each cage door, while another militiaman played out more detonator cord.

"Stand back!" Moran ordered.

The militiamen took cover.

"Blow!" he shouted.

There were three ear-dunning "booms," one out of sync; the entire ground floor shook, filling the air with flourlike dust. The cement steps under the cage doors were blown asunder, leaving ragged trenches several inches deep below where the bars had originally met the concrete. The doors, though still visibly intact, were now decidedly warped, their structural integrity lost. A burly, bearded rifleman named Stanes stepped forward, grabbed the bars of the badly deformed main stairwell door and, grunting hard to make it look tougher than it was, performed what the militiamen would later refer to as a "Jesse Ventura," successfully tearing the door out of its sockets.

"There!" he grunted victoriously, but by then no one was paying any attention. They were charging past him. Moran, determined to be the first to the fifth floor, led, his Remington pump action shotgun at his hip. He knew that the cost-conscious designers of the Rone building had been so confident no one would get past the SIGPRES screen, reinforced concrete wall, and cage doors on the ground floor that they hadn't bothered to install cage doors on any of the other floors.

And so it was a clear run to the fifth floor, but here Rone's twenty-man security detachment, minus the two who had been shot outside, decided to make their stand. Moran saw that the entire floor was in darkness. From the frantic squeaking he could hear, Moran guessed, correctly, that the defenders were hurriedly dragging and piling furniture high against the doors of the fifty-by-twenty-foot Room 501. Moran knew—that is, the militia knew—that the Rone's owners had wanted only one double door for Room 501 to enhance security. But even the influential multi-million-dollar Rone board had to meet fire regulations and install three doors. Suddenly, a sustained roar of shotgun fire erupted from the darkened room, but the militia team, anticipating such a barrage, had already taken cover, dropping down onto the stairs as shot rent the air above them. Only three of Moran's men were hit, none seriously.

"Delta!" Moran shouted, and a four-man squad of militia dashed up from below, one man's helmet falling off, rattling back down the stairs. He made to retrieve it.

"Forget it!" Moran snapped, and the man, like his three comrades kneeling several stairs below the fifth floor level, undid the strap on his hip pouch, simultaneously calling out, "Masks!" Their voices echoed down the stairwell. As the remaining militia donned their masks, the four men of Delta, using their "pop" guns, fired a saturation barrage of fifteen tear gas canisters at the three doors. Their aim, inhibited by the fact that they had to lob the shots or risk exposure to 501 direct lines of fire, resulted—despite all their "barricade" practice—in only eight of the fifteen aluminum canisters actually entering Room 501. Three of the canisters were immediately tossed back. Five canisters, however, were enough, Room 501 quickly filling with the choking white gas. Despite the smell of singed carpeting, smoke alarms going off all over the place, and a woman in 501 screaming hysterically, Moran noted thankfully that the sprinkler system did not activate.

The Rone security team plus technicians and a scientist in white lab coats working night shift were rapidly overcome, coughing uncontrollably, frantically gasping for breath. The hysterical woman's screams remained unabated. Moran was conscious of the fact, as McBride had pointed out in the planning stages, that most people who have seen tear gas being used only in movies and on TV have no idea what a terrifying experience it is. Some middle-aged and elderly victims have died from the panic-induced stress of feeling unable to breathe. But as per McBride's instructions, apart from the gas canisters there'd been no shooting into Room 501. The usually laid-back McBride had been adamant on this point, warning that anyone who violated this order would have to answer personally to USMC C-in-C General Vance.

In less than two minutes the militia had smashed aside the furniture blockade and were in Room 501. Moran, his voice nasal from his mask, gave the order, "Loading dock." He ran back down the stairs, through the hole, pulled out his cell, tore off his mask—grateful for the cold, invigorating rain—and called McBride.

"IAC One to EAC One. We have loot. Repeat, we have loot." In his excitement, he'd forgotten to say "goods."

"Move it!" McBride said.

"Will do." Moran, his adrenaline racing through his veins, was disappointed by McBride's lack of bonhomie, but Moran had no way of knowing that while he had been securing Room 501, and ordering the scientist out at gunpoint, McBride had received a call from his roadblock team. Through their NVGs, they had just spotted a police car convoy approaching. They estimated time of arrival at the turnoff in two minutes.

The call that the now dead female Rone technician had made while having a cigarette outside had reached Wills Creek. It had also reached NSA at Fort Meade, Maryland, not during one of NSA's routine sweeps of the airwaves but because it had been routed through to them by Wills Creek Police Chief Hyson. Since the Rone project was initiated, Chief Hyson and his officers, like all the Rone employees, had been under the issuance of the strictest National Security Order, instructed not to report any "incident" at the Rone building, no matter how minor or serious, to anyone but NSA, which would then give explicit instructions on what to do. Most important of all, no report of any incident was to reach the media. If they violated NSA's edict, similar to that issued to the workers on the once unknown Stealth testing grounds in New Mexico, they'd lose their jobs and, just as serious, all accumulated medical, dental, and pension benefits.

"What a night!" Chief Hyson's deputy complained in the lead car. "Want to be crazy as a coon to be out in this weather."

"That's why the bastards are out in it, Stan. No one else is."

" 'Cept us."

"Yeah, aren't they gonna get a surprise?"

"Maybe we shouldn't put the flashers on?" Stan ventured.

Chief Hyson said nothing. He'd activated the flashers because he hoped it would disperse the militia before he got there. Hyson was fifty-three, too close to early retirement to get in a shootout. Last thing he wanted was to sneak up on 'em, whoever they were, surprise 'em, and find himself in a damn firefight.

"I figure it's militia," Stan said. "Grow like sage up here." By "here" he meant not only eastern Washington but the Idaho panhandle, home of the Aryan Nation, and Montana, where a group of rebels back in the mid-eighties in Jordan had declared their own brand of "just-*us*" and gone to war against the federals, refusing to pay any taxes and taking up arms.

Hyson's radio crackled. "Get that, will ya?" he told Stan. Hyson leaned forward over the wheel, looking for the turnoff through the waterfall that his wipers were barely keeping at bay.

"Two thousand yards!" the militia's roadblock team reported.

"All right," McBride said. "Get out of there. Go help EAC at the loading dock."

"Yes, sir." The two-man roadblock team needed no encouragement. They weren't cowards, both of them 'Nam vets, one having been in Tet, but three police cars, presumably fully loaded—twelve against two—were odds common sense couldn't endorse.

"Brock!" McBride said.

"Sir?"

"You have them in sight?"

"I do."

"Alignment fixed?"

"Think so."

Brock hadn't had time to improvise, either to tape dental

floss crosshairs on the muzzle and start monkeying with the breech or to rig up a marker board on the muzzle and begin correction firing. He was doing it by guesstimate, and from the experience of having fired off twenty practice rounds in the mountainous Sawtooth Wilderness west of the high desert.

"A thousand yards," McBride said. The turret made a short, sharp growl as it passed through the corrective arc, then a thump as it locked into position. McBride banged the cupola shut, buttoned up, and slid down to act as loader. Brock, having eschewed the normal optical reticles, crosshair sights, was instead crouched over the metal donkey sight, having double-checked the GELFOD—gun elevation for distance—card on the ammo crate, from which McBride extracted an H.E. round that contained a can of semtex.

When the first police cruiser was five hundred yards away, Brock pushed the button. The tank bucked, he saw the muzzle flash, sun exploded through the porthole, the T-34 filled with the acrid stench of cordite and ammonia, and steam rose in a fog from the superheated shell casing meeting the cold humidity of the tank's interior.

The H.E. round missed the first patrol car, landing ten feet aft of it, nearer the second cruiser. But with H.E.s, like grenades, near is enough. The patrol car blew sideways off the road like a boot kicking a paper cup, rolling afire through sage and sandy mud. The drenching rain had little or no effect on the flames, the cruiser's gas tank exploding. Only one deputy managed to get out, running madly, his fiercely burning body momentarily illuminated in a flash of lightning before disappearing from view. But all of Chief Hyson's attention was riveted on the road.

"Back up! Back up!" he screamed into his mike, his car's tires screaming in reverse.

"Jesus-H-Christ!" Stan said, transfixed by the sight of his fellow deputy's fate. "Who was that?"

Amid the noise and panic, Hyson thought Stan had asked, *What* was that? "Some kinda rocket," Hyson said. "I dunno.

But we're not stayin' to find out. Haven't got the equipment, Stan. We can't deal with that."

By now the remaining police car, having already made a U-turn, was in front of them, heading back at speed to Wills Creek, siren wailing.

"Goddammit!" Hyson said, thumping the wheel. "What's Luis got the goddamn siren on for?" Hyson clicked on the mike. "Luis, goddammit, turn off the siren. We're supposed to keep anything at Rone quiet. Among ourselves!"

"Roger, Chief," came the chagrined answer, "but who's gonna hear it out here anyway?"

"Well shit, Luis, then why put it on?"

"Got it, Chief. Sorry."

"*Sorry* doesn't cut it, Luis. Goddammit, you want to lose your job? Have those dicks from NSA climbing over your back?"

"No, Chief, but what are we gonna say?"

"I dunno but we'll—"

"Struck by lightnin'," Luis suggested. "An' their gas tank blew."

"It *has* to be militia," Stan opined. "You think they're still out there?"

"You want to go back and find out?" Hyson challenged, his eyes flitting nervously between side and rear vision mirrors.

"If it's a rocket," Stan said, "we ain't gonna see it comin'."

"Why don't you shut up, Stan—just, goddammit, shut up?"

Back on the highway, Hyson swung the car drunkenly from one side of the road to the other. If they, whoever they were—Stan was probably right, the militia—fired another rocket or whatever, maybe his weaving would throw off their aim.

"One of our guys got out of the wreck," Stan said.

"What are you talking about?" Hyson said angrily.

"One of our guys, back there. I saw him burning up."

"Yeah," Hyson said. "But no way he's still alive."

There was a long silence. Stan, craning his neck, looked back. "Guess not."

* * *

Euphoric in their success—at least in this, the first part of their mission—several militiamen, now changing back into their civilian clothes under a lean-to by one of the pickups, were laughing about Cawley, who was still waiting back at the truck.

"Cawley asked somebody if we got the *money*?"

"Bullshit!"

"No, honest to God. When the tank arrives back at the Mack, Cawley says to Neilson, 'Did you get the money?' Son of a bitch must've thought we were going for Rone's payroll."

A fellow militiaman shook his head, smiling. "I guess he thinks everybody still gets paid cash—you know, in those little brown envelopes."

"Guess that's the way he sold apples!" another said, laughing.

"Well," another militiaman interjected in Cawley's defense, "we told him sweet F.A. about Room 501. Lucky didn't tell anyone who didn't have to know."

"Yeah," put in another. "He's new—give 'im a break. We need everyone we can get."

Lucky McBride, having walked back from the truck, caught only the tail end of the conversation, but that was enough.

"Leave Norm Cawley be," he told them. "His job was watching the Mack. And that's what he did. Anyway," he added, putting his Fritz carefully into the pickup's cab to protect the NVGs, "we've a long way to go yet. I suggest you get moving."

"Yeah," one of the militiamen said, adopting McBride's mood. "Temperature's dropping too."

"Exactly," McBride said. "More snow."

CHAPTER TWO

THE FLASHLIGHT'S BEAM roiled with sea mist as the Oregon State trooper, his boots crunching on the road's gravel shoulder, walked from his cruiser toward the dark green '99 Humvee and peered in the window. The driver was a male, Caucasian, with brown hair, blue eyes, late thirties, weight about 150 pounds. Height near five-nine—a passing resemblance to Tom Cruise, only older.

The trooper's tone was polite, right hand on his holster, peaked felt hat coming level with the driver's window as he bent, careful from habit not to touch any part of the car lest it suddenly accelerate.

"Could I see your driver's license please, sir?"

"Sure." The driver was tempted to argue that he hadn't been doing more than sixty—well, maybe a tad. But he was too tired, and he had a promise to keep. The quicker he got the speeding ticket, the better. He glanced impatiently at the luminescent hands of his St. Moritz deep dive watch as he handed over his license. The trooper walked back through the salty sea air to the patrol car to punch in the computer check.

What the hell, Frank Hall thought. No use getting steamed. He switched on the radio for a little soothing music—instead he got hell and damnation, then a talk show, some kid shouting he had the right to burn the American flag. "Maybe," Hall told the radio, "but that doesn't make it right." Static rushed in and Hall turned it off, glancing at his watch again then at his rear vision mirror. "C'mon," he muttered. "Let's go."

He had crossed the five-mile-long bridge from Washington over the mouth of the Columbia and was now halfway between Astoria on the Oregon side and Seaside, fifteen miles south on the scenic Pacific Coast road.

An ex-SEAL team veteran, and now an oceanographer, he had just spent a grueling week with little sleep, refloating a tanker that had run aground in Washington State's Puget Sound. It had blocked the main egress channel from the Seawolf nuclear sub pens at Bangor. COMSUBPAC—Commander Submarines Pacific—and Greenpeace were both thankful for Hall's expertise. Unknown to the public at large, Frank Hall's reputation was legendary in the business of hands-on oceanographic and salvage work. The highlight of his career to date had been a highly classified salvaging of the U.S. nuclear sub *USS New York* from a submarine canyon over two thousand feet deep. With the pressure on his atmospheric diving suit 450 pounds per square inch, he had to get a line on her before she sank so far down that the sea would crush the hull and everyone and everything inside. The sub, already at a dangerous angle against a mud cliff, had rolled and nearly killed him before he'd managed to retrieve it. But that near disaster had taught him valuable lessons, which, along with his experience as a SEAL, helped him get the tanker afloat again. Not a drop of oil spilled, no one hurt, and no damage to sea life. All he wanted now was to drive to the house in Seaside that he shared with his partner, Bill Reid, pack a bag, then head the seventy miles inland to Portland and his fiancée, Gloria Bernardi, a biology grad student at Oregon State. Next morning they'd have a leisurely breakfast then flee the Northwest's fall mists, south to the sun for a few weeks during which they'd plan their wedding. "About time, after three years of dating," her mother had said. "In my time, the honeymoon used to come *after* the wedding."

The trooper came back from the cruiser. "You're the Frank Hall of Oregon Oceanics, right?"

"Yes." Frank's heart jumped. If the tanker had broken up under tow, the oil spill would have dwarfed that of the *Exxon Valdez*.

The trooper returned the license and with it a Highway Patrol card with a phone number scribbled on it—an out-of-state code. The trooper said he couldn't tell him any more, except that he was to call the number on the card. Extremely urgent.

"Can I use your cellular?" Hall asked. "My battery's dead."

The trooper shook his head. "Sorry, they want you to use a land line. More secure. There's a phone booth down the highway 'bout three miles. You can follow me."

Hall's heart was thudding against his chest. As he followed the trooper, all his senses were alert. He could hear the crumping of the surf in the darkness off to his right and was aware of the sharp, tangy smell of low tide. And he thought of his plan, or rather Gloria's plan, to drive south to California—Yosemite National Park, east to the Grand Canyon, then up to Wyoming and Yellowstone, and back through Idaho. "The Grand Circle Tour," Frank had dubbed it. It had been a compromise between his love of driving, of being on the move, and Gloria's wanting to stay put. For him the journey was always more interesting than the journey's end. It was the opposite for Gloria. She liked to settle into one place for a while, explore locally, get away from all the traffic on the interstate, and get Frank away from the dangers of his work.

"Every time you go to sea," she'd told him after the hazardous submarine job, "I feel like a miner's wife. Wondering if you'll come back. It's too risky, Frank."

"Living's risky."

"You know what I mean. You're not in your twenties anymore."

"At my peak," he'd answered, smiling.

"You've had too many close calls."

He didn't challenge that one. She was right. Instead he had patted the bed beside him. "Come here."

She'd tried to look determined and resisted.

"Come on," he said, patting the bed with more insistence. "I've got a surprise for you."

"Hmm," she said, her lips parting in a smile against her will. "I'll bet you have."

"Don't you want to know what it is?"

"I *know* what it is."

He stretched out a hand toward her. "No, seriously."

"Seriously, nothing. You want to make love."

"I always want to make love. You're irresistible."

"Don't soft soap me, Frank Hall," and in that moment he'd realized again how beautiful she was, the flash of her brown eyes, the quick shift of light of her brunette hair, the hourglass shape of her figure, and, most attractive of all, the sensuousness of her mouth. Whenever he saw her he was reminded of *Casablanca*—Ingrid Bergman.

"I'm not giving you soft soap," he said. "Come on—over here."

"You come over here," she countered.

He did and told her that she was right—one close call after another without a break was no good for anyone. Reaction time got slower, and aboard *Petrel*, the 150-foot U.S. oceanographic vessel from which he normally operated when working on government contracts, a second or two lost in reaction time while handling heavy underwater retrieval machinery could kill you.

"All right," he'd agreed. "We'll take some time out. Grand Canyon, Yellowstone—"

"You promise?" she'd said, still standing at arm's length.

He stood up and pulled her into him. "Scout's honor."

She'd chuckled. "You're so old-fashioned sometimes. I haven't heard anyone say that for years."

"As a matter of fact," Frank replied, "I was an *Eagle* Scout."

"Oh my!" she giggled, hands clasped and eyelids aflutter, affecting the tone of a southern belle. "Ah think ah'll jes' faint right away."

Slowly, he'd unbuttoned her blouse, feeling her nipples hardening, his fingers trailing along the edge of her bra to the softness of her throat, across her shoulder as she murmured in expectation. As his hand passed down her forearm, she tossed her head to one side and lay back on the bed. Next his hand moved up her thigh.

Her hand stopped his. "You promise?" she'd said. "A real holiday?"

"I promise."

"No matter who calls?"

"No matter who calls," he'd said, his voice dry and cracked, his breathing faster, pressing against her.

Suddenly she sat up. "How long?"

"Don't be rude," he shot back. "It's long enough."

She shook her head, her hair a sheen in the soft glow of the bedside lamp. "Men! I mean how *long* will the holiday be?"

Slowly, he slid his left arm beneath the small of her back, arching her body toward him. "As long as you want."

She pushed him away. "How long?"

"Two days."

"Frank!" She'd sat up on the bed, hands clasped firmly around her knees. *"How long?"*

"Oh, God," he said, grabbing at her. "A year! Two years . . ."

"You're hopeless!" she said, fending him off.

"But lovable," Frank panted.

"No, be serious."

"I am."

"Frank!"

"Two weeks."

"Three!" she insisted.

"Three."

"Promise?"

"Promise. Scout's honor. Cross my heart and hope to die."

"Don't say that," she said, frowning.

"What?"

"Hope to die."

Frank was thinking about it now and how they'd made love, the warmth together, two as one in a deep, dark cave away from the world.

Ahead of him he could see a call box.

Inside the phone booth Frank felt he was in another cave, dark but cold. The vandalized booth reeked of urine and tobacco smoke, overpowering the clean, salty air. There was no light to read the number the patrolman had given him. The trooper swung the headlights' beams into the booth. Instinctively Frank turned away from the harsh glare, broken glass crunching under his feet.

After the call, he came out deep in thought, zipping his windbreaker up to his throat.

"You look like a truck just hit you," the trooper said.

"I'm to leave the Humvee here," Frank told him. "You're to take me in your car to the nearest mile post and call in our position to the Coast Guard. They're sending a chopper."

The woods of scraggly ocean pine kept changing from a surreal blue and red to amber as the patrol car's lights continued to flash as a marker for the Coast Guard. Soon they heard the *wokka-wokka* of the helo approaching, then suddenly the world went mad in the hurricane beneath the helo's deafening, oily smelling, tree-shaking descent. Its spotlight etched out a long white wedge that sliced through sea air and brush until it found a clearing twenty yards to the right of the patrol car.

"Good luck," Frank heard the patrolman shouting through the roar that soon became a high-pitched scream. Frank crouched low, running through the mini squall, half blinded by clouds of water and stinging sand swirling about him in the spotlight's glare. The rotors' downblast continued, throwing up a drenching spray from what turned out to be a sodden cranberry field. The Coast Guard pilot kept the Sea King hovering a few feet above the marshy ground rather than risking becoming bogged. By the time Frank saw a hand extended from the sliding door of the big white-and-double-red-striped Coast Guard chopper, he was soaked through. His Nikes squished like sponges on the helo's metallic grid floor. It took him a minute to realize that the hand that lifted him so adroitly and unhesitatingly aboard belonged to a woman. And hadn't he argued once with Gloria that if he was ever in a fire, he'd want a fire*man* to help him, not a fire*woman*? Gloria would love it. By now she'd also be wondering where he was. But he'd been told not to contact her for another twelve hours, and as an ex-SEAL he knew it was as much for her protection as anybody else's.

At two thousand feet he glimpsed a cluster of lights several miles behind him where the Astoria Bridge crossed the Columbia heading north into Washington State. Heading south, the Coast Guard Sea King passed over the black expanse of forest before descending to a small airstrip. Within minutes, escorted by two men in Coast Guard uniforms, he was aboard a Learjet, heading south-southwest, the two men accompanying him disturbingly quiet. All he could hear was the steady roar of the jet's twin engines. The lighting in the plane's plush leather interior had been dimmed so low the only thing he could see clearly was the pulsating red beacon on the jet's port wing.

CHAPTER THREE

Southeastern China

THROUGH SWIRLING CLOUDS of steam, the Wuxi-Shanghai express picked up speed beyond Lake Tai. Green fields and ghostly two-storied commune buildings slipped by in the morning mist.

Four cars behind the Datong locomotive, an olive-colored carriage bearing the yellow "soft" class stripe was swaying as much as any of the "hard" class cars. But inside, where two bloodred and deep-set velvet lounge chairs of 1930 vintage faced each other, the sound of the train's wild yawing and hard clattering of steel on steel was decidedly muted. The springs and cushions of the party car better absorbed the shock. A young Chinese woman, Wu Ling, was the only other occupant besides General Chang, commander of Nanjing Military Region's 12th Army. The young woman was trying to keep her balance, her dark brown eyes as nervous as a doe's. The sensuous nape of her neck was the object of the general's stare as she struggled, against the swaying of the train and against her will, to unbutton her white cotton blouse. Her brassiere, Chang noted, was of cheap calico and looked more like a punishment, its cups far too tight, imprisoning her breasts hard against her body as if she was ashamed of them. Slowly, Chang took the lid off his white and blue willow tea mug, his gimlet eyes smiling, enjoying her shy beauty and awkward innocence.

Placing the tea mug's lid on the ornate mahogany table to his left, the general sipped the green tea slowly, elbows propped on the lace antimacassar of the wide, velvet armrests. He contemplated the sensuality he was sure lay hidden beneath her thin cloth of self-consciousness.

Shyly turning away from him, Wu Ling took off her blue cotton trousers, folding them neatly. Chang guessed they were probably her only pair; the care she took with her ill-fitting garb amused him. She did not realize that in a week or two she could have trousers by the dozen and slit-thigh *qipaos*, if she wished, made of the finest Suzhou silk. As many as she wanted, certainly more than she could ever afford in her old job as an English-speaking guide and part-time computer operator for Luxingshe, China's international travel service. But only if she pleased him.

Chang's military police had freeze-framed a picture of her brother Jun from an American TV report of antirevolutionary elements, passing it on to the Gong An Bu, the secret police in the Ministry for Internal Security. And it had been the Gong An Bu that had come looking for her brother at the family's house in one of Wuxi's *hutongs*. Not finding him there, they had arrested his sister, Wu Ling, and her parents instead, taking them in separately for questioning.

The general had put it quite simply to her: *"Ni yao fumu huan shi yao gege!"* Your parents or your brother!

"I am sorry, General," she had told him. "I do not know where—"

"Find out! If you do not, you and your parents will be shot."

She had given them the address of the import/export office on the Bund, Shanghai's main waterfront section, where her brother, a member of the "criminal antirevolutionary" Falun Gong sect, had been in hiding with friends while waiting to slip aboard a freighter for Macao.

Now, Chang gestured for Wu Ling to strip completely, and she did so, head bowed, hands clasped before her, face flushed. For a moment she appeared to him as quite ridiculous—her subservience from another century, before the Revolution had liberated China's women.

As the train rounded another bend outside Kunshan, Shanghai's sulfurous smell was already thick in the air, though the city proper was still an hour away. Wu Ling was thrown off balance, back into the deep embrace of the chintz-covered lounge behind her. Slowly, Chang put down his tea by the phone on his side table and ran a finger over the stubble on his top lip, which had been unshaven for years and which he now believed was a mustache. Her clumsiness was beginning to annoy him. It seemed purposeful, accusatory, a protest perhaps against the fact that she'd been brought here against her will. *"Wu Ling,"* he said derisively, mocking her name. "They should call you *Ben*—'clumsy,' not 'quick.' "

Wu Ling tried to smile apologetically but it would not come.

"Your brother will survive," Chang said, pushing the tea farther away. Taking out a packet of Lucky Strikes, he tore off the sales tax strip, scrunching it into a tight ball, lobbing it into the spittoon. "Fifteen years is nothing to a young man." He paused, flicking the gold Dunhill lighter. "I could have had him executed." He lit the cigarette, blew out, and inhaled deeply. "You're ungrateful," he accused her sharply. As he leaned forward, his row of ribbons, including the Tiananmen "victory" medal, and the bloodred collar tabs brightened in the bluish-gray bars of sunlight now piercing the carriage's smoky interior. "I could easily rescind the detention order— *today.* Have him taken out and shot like a dog."

"*Bu, bu!*" she pleaded frantically. No, no! "I am not . . . ungrateful, General."

"Then why do you have a face like the rain?" Chang said, sitting back.

"I—I do not know, General."

"I do," Chang said, heaving himself forward again to the edge of the lounge chair. Using his cigarette, held between thumb and forefinger, as a pointer, he jabbed relentlessly at her. "You are full of bourgeois liberalism—full of rubbish about the family. What did the leader say? The *state* is our only family."

She was still looking down at his feet, eyes averted with shame, confused, not knowing which leader he meant. Mao, Deng, Li Peng, Jiang Zemin?

"I am protecting your parents!" Chang proclaimed. "Is this not so?"

"Yes."

"*Dasheng dian!*" Louder!

"Yes, Comrade General," she said.

"Do you wish to see your parents again?"

She couldn't speak, her eyes bright with tears.

"Very well then," Chang said. He extended his hand to her, the gesture of a monk forgiving a penitent novice. His cigarette smoke rose like incense. "You can type?" he asked. It was more confirmation than inquiry.

She was nonplussed by his sudden change in tone but seized the question as a flood victim grasps for a reed. "Yes, General. At Luxingshe I have studied at—"

"Very well, then. You will be my secretary. I have an important mission." He had taken hold of her chin, his thumb pushing down hard on her bottom lip, moving her head side to side, looking at her teeth as if examining a horse. She winced, still kneeling on the carpet, her face taut, dried tears leaving streaks on her sallow cheeks.

"You will accompany me to Moscow and then on a journey." He paused. "I will need company at any time. Day or night. You understand?"

"Yes, General."

Chang glanced at his watch, sat back and smoked some more, but he was not at ease. The train roared through the rain, straining to make up for lost time. Soon they would be in Shanghai, and in the morning on the flight north to Beijing for final instructions. The general was afraid of flying in his own country, and had he had his way, he would have ordered his aide to reserve a "soft" carriage for a rail journey all the way north to Beijing. But Beijing had insisted he arrive tomorrow.

Like most senior officers in the PLA, Chang, following the Sino/Soviet border fighting in the sixties, had spent two years in the United States in the little-publicized military training exchange program, and while in America he had never been afraid to fly. But China Air was another matter—its maintenance, for all the party's haranguing, simply was not up to Western standards. There were crashes every week, all over China. But in a country of over one billion, a plane lost here or there was nothing—unless it was carrying a high-level cadre or Western tourists. This fear, together with the fact that he had not yet heard from his contact in Zurich about the American mission, so fed his anxiety that his need for physical release could wait no longer.

He looked down at Wu Ling, who was transfixed by the sight of his engorged member—her expression one of absolute horror.

"We will only have time for bamboo in the wind," Chang said matter-of-factly, sitting back. Wu Ling was staring at him, open-mouthed.

Just like a peasant, he thought, on her first visit to Shanghai Circus. Her stunned-mullet expression annoyed him anew, another sign of her abysmal ignorance. And yet it aroused him still further for it was now abundantly clear that she *was* a virgin. Unbuckling his belt and doubling it over, he slapped her hard on the buttocks, her yelp like that of a pup before slaughter, a welt quickly appearing on her skin. She gave off a warm, cinnamon-like odor.

The phone rang then, and Wu Ling hoped it might save her. Chang reached for it so quickly he almost knocked over his tea. He listened intently, and after a few seconds put the receiver down, then dialed the Beijing office of the Guo An Bu, China's counterespionage service, asking for a Colonel Yang. He was cut off. A typhoon had swept in from the South China Sea the night before, ripping up trees and power lines as well as taking out the microwave relay station in the hills west of the capital. Next time Chang dialed, his call rerouted via the southern suburbs, he got through, and was told, *"Yanzhi diao xia liao."* The swallow has fallen. Chang hung up and sat back, his manner instantly more agreeable. "We all serve the party," he said reflectively, gazing down at her with a thin smile. "My service will help China in the next Great Leap Forward." He paused, reaching for the tea. He asked with calculated nonchalance, "Do you know how I will do this?"

Wu Ling was shivering despite the fact it was warm and stuffy in the carriage, the smell of Shanghai's pollution stronger as they neared the city. Filled with panic, still trying to cover herself, she looked away in vain hope of escape, glimpsing fishponds flashing by like gray ice through the train's steam, the engine's long, piercing whistle exacerbating her fear. "I will succeed," Chang said, resting his head back and drawing heavily on a cigarette, "because the Americans are so stupid. Naive." He blew out a long, grayish-blue stream of smoke. "Like you."

He told her quickly how, at the turn of the millennium, the Russians had managed to install a highly sophisticated listening device deep within the inner sanctum of the American State Department. Extinguishing the cigarette, he waited for several seconds as the carriage rocked violently over some junction points. Then, motioning her closer, he opened her legs and told her to sip the tea to moisten her lips, her whimpering drowned in the feral roar of the train.

CHAPTER FOUR

California

AFTER FRANK'S HOUR-LONG flight, his biggest surprise wasn't the hacienda-styled Western White House—he'd seen enough pictures of that. Rather, it was the clutch of a half-dozen businessmen, heavy hitters, Wall Street bankers and the like from their appearance, any of whose suits Frank knew could have paid for his and Gloria's planned vacation twice over.

In the balmy California air of La Jolla, just north of San Diego, amid the potted plants and rattan chair decor of the reception area, the suits looked distinctly out of place. His impression was reinforced by the glistening aquamarine pool visible through the thick-plated and, Frank suspected, bulletproof glass wall that surrounded the pool and which now caught their reflections. The suits appeared to be standing on water, but they all looked worried, their expressions reminding Frank of a *New Yorker* cartoon of bird-sized executives balancing precariously on Manhattan's window ledges, following the stock market crash of '87.

Frank was still wet, his Nikes squeaking on the black-veined marble floor, when the President entered. Everyone stood up, and immediately Frank was introduced to him. The first thing the President asked his aide, Michael Brownlee, was, "Surely we could have given Mr. Hall time to dry out?"

"Sorry, Mr. President," answered Brownlee, a tall, thin man whose thick tortoiseshell-rimmed glasses made him look twice his age. "There wasn't time. But I'll have the staff hustle up a set of dry clothes. Meanwhile Mr. Hall can warm up with some coffee." Brownlee flashed a professional, concerned smile and offered Frank a cup from the gleaming pushcart festooned with pastries and bite-sized sandwiches.

One of the big suits, a man Frank now recognized from a CNN interview about the President's upcoming reelection bid, coughed impatiently.

"Very well," the President said. "Let's get on with it."

"Yes, sir," Brownlee answered. He immediately turned to a dark blue, cloth-covered map stand between Frank and the six businessmen, the latter sitting to the right of the President, Frank to his left.

Brownlee flicked over the map stand's cloth cover bearing the presidential seal. Underneath was a cutaway drawing of a rectangular white box, containing what appeared to be wafered circuitry.

"A Rone-II," Brownlee said, pausing, obviously expecting some reaction from the oceanographer, but Frank, though realizing all eyes were on him, sat silently, waiting.

"A Rone-II—mainframe super computer," Brownlee continued. "It's the fastest in the world. Faster than Intel's Paragon, capable of 1.9 teraflops—that's 1.9 trillion floating operations per second—which, in layman's terms, means it would take someone operating a handheld calculator over 57,000 years to calculate a problem that the Rone can compute in one second." Brownlee barely paused for breath. "It's the only computer, I repeat, the *only* computer, capable of rapidly handling all the calculations necessary to simultaneously detect, plot, and target previously undetectable submerged boomers and—"

"Boomers?" one of the big suits cut in.

"Ballistic submarines," Frank said. "SSBNs."

"And," Brownlee continued, "simultaneously computing multilevel air attack vectors and intercepts in nanoseconds, as well as coordinating all AirSeaLand operations—again simultaneously. And as you know, gentlemen, a split second lost in this business—a millisecond—and it's game over."

"What game's that?" Frank asked.

The bushy eyebrows on the tallest of the bankers, Morton Dalgliesh, arched menacingly. "He means nuclear war, man."

"I know what he means," Frank responded. "I just like to hear war called war—and not a *game*." He turned back to Brownlee. "Maybe I'm not getting something here. I take it this Rone is missing?"

"Missing?" Dalgliesh said, eyebrows rising. "The goddamned thing's been stolen! By the militia! Bastards blasted a hole wide as a bus in the building and killed ten people, kidnapped a scientist and— Didn't anybody tell you—"

"Calm down, Mort," the President advised. "We only found out ourselves a couple of hours ago—everything's been in a flap back there, and we couldn't go into detail with Mr. Hall on open line." The President turned around noiselessly in his soft, pillowed rattan chair to face Frank. "The Rone is a prototype, Mr. Hall. It was being designed in Washington State—your neck of the woods—and tested secretly. Or so we thought. These six gentlemen here represent the major civilian contractors involved—the owners, in fact, of the subcontracting companies." The President motioned to Brownlee. "Give Mr. Hall a few more of the details."

"Well," Brownlee said, "unless we go into all of the various specs of the machine, there's not much more to say at the moment other than it's the only thing we've got that can complete all incoming telemetry calculations, hold all the variables at once—in the case of an SSBN, surrounding salinity content, wave height variation, infrared heat patching on the sea's surface—as well as differentiate between hot patches caused by a sub's warm water discharge and warm water patching due to natural upwelling." He paused. "Anyway, the point is, this machine's so incredibly fast that whoever gets hold of it will turn the tables on us overnight."

Frank still didn't get it—that is, why they'd sent for him. Maybe he was too tired from all the rushing about—police cars, helicopter, then a sodden trip south. He put down his coffee. "Why are you telling me all this?"

The answer would have been apparent to him from the drawing, but Brownlee had been so preoccupied looking after the arrival of the VIPs, especially Morton Dalgliesh—a crucial backer for the President's hopes of a second term—that he'd forgotten to write down the scale of the penciled Rone on the map stand.

"I'm sorry," he apologized to Frank. "It's one inch to a foot. Biggest mainframe we've had for years."

Frank looked again at the sketch of the computer on the map stand and understood the implications. It was massive.

"Six feet high, six wide," Brownlee explained, "and twenty feet long. Seven hundred and twenty cubic feet. As you can see, it's far too big to get out by air, particularly with all our airports on continuous terrorist alert."

"By *unauthorized* air?" Frank proffered.

Brownlee shook his head. "Any unauthorized plane in NORAD air space will immediately be shot down." Frank remembered how they'd even scrambled fighters to chase that small civilian plane—the golfer, Payne Stewart—in '99. "Anyway," Brownlee continued, "Wills Creek—place it was stolen from—is smack within Spokane's SAC area. Air security's doubly tough up there. A rabbit hops, they see it."

"How about flying it out low?" Frank conjectured. "Beneath our radar screen?"

"No way," Brownlee countered. "Satellite surveillance picks up an aircraft soon as it's airborne."

"So you're telling me it has to go out by ship?"

Brownlee nodded. "Yes, that's where you come in. You've got an impressive SEAL record with us. And as an oceanographer with time on the research ship—"

"The *Petrel*."

"Yes, you'd have the perfect cover."

"Cover for what? Surely it's the military's job to—"

"No, no, no," the President cut in angrily. "No *official* action at all. If it becomes public that our technological lead has been stolen, we can say goodbye to any new arms limitation talks in Geneva."

Not to mention saying goodbye to any chance of you being reelected, Frank thought. Military action, like the Clinton administration's use of tanks against Koresh at Waco, would be a public admission that this administration had screwed up, having let the militia get away with the biggest heist in U.S. history.

"All right," Frank said, "you don't want to use the military. But even if the militia get the Rone through the mountain passes in all that snow, couldn't you simply have the Coast Guard watching the ports?"

"We *do*," an exasperated Brownlee said. "But do you know how many ports we have on the West Coast alone?"

"A lot."

"Hundreds," Brownlee said, unable to decide whether the oceanographer and ex-SEAL, so useful to the government in the past, was being deliberately obtuse, or whether he was simply too tired to think it through. "The thing is, Mr. Hall, if we don't stop the militia and they get it to one of our ports, we might have a little problem called 'freedom of the high seas,' if they get the damn thing out beyond our twelve-mile jurisdictional zone. We can't board them without sufficient evidence— not under the new millennium law of the sea."

"Unless we want to start a war," the President added.

"So you want me on call, as it were? To track them if necessary?"

"No," harrumphed Dalgliesh. "I'd like you to get the damn thing back *before* it gets to the coast. There's been a lot of snow and avalanches in the area so we figure the pricks are locked within a hundred-mile radius of the factory—or what's left of it. Problem is, if they get through the roadblocks and snow slides, there're so many places, as Brownlee's mentioned, that it could be shipped from. I was hoping," Dalgliesh added gruffly, "that being an ex-SEAL, as well as an oceanographer, you might have some ideas. They told me you were a man with initiative." Dalgliesh paused, then said pointedly, " 'Course if it's out of your depth— If you're no better than some private eye—"

Rude bastard, Frank thought. It was a challenge to his pride, nevertheless, and in the long silence, Dalgliesh knew the SEAL was thinking about it.

Frank smiled. "I'm not Superman. I'd need help."

"We know that," Dalgliesh growled.

"Who would you get?" Gold Rims cut in.

"Well . . ." Frank began.

The door to the poolside room opened softly and the President's press aide, Donna Fargo, a tall, striking blonde in a wine-red suit and clinging silk blouse, entered. "These digital photos of the damage just came in, Mr. President." She deposited a manila folder on the President's desk, smiled at Frank, and withdrew as quietly as she'd entered. Frank could smell her perfume. Plumeria. Hawaii. He and Gloria had often thought of it for their honeymoon. He also noticed something he'd recall later. Morton Dalgliesh, moving over by the pastry trolley for more goodies while the President was preoccupied with the folder, surreptitiously pocketed a souvenir—one of the silver presidential seal teaspoons.

"Well," Frank continued to Gold Rims, "I'd form a strike force. I've got some buddies who used to be in the forces but they've either retired voluntarily or been laid off, as it were, due to cutbacks."

"Fine," the President replied, ignoring the implicit criticism of his defense cuts. "As long as they're not presently in the forces. We have to insist on that."

"They're not," Frank reassured him. "But I've lost contact with a few of them. I'd appreciate it if the Pentagon could assist in giving me current e-mail addresses, phone numbers, etcetera."

"Names?" Brownlee asked, electronic notepad to the fore, as the President, receiving the latest digitally transmitted photos of the extensive damage done within the Rone building, sat down in his cushioned rattan chair to examine them.

"They're ex-SEAL and ALERT—Air Land Emergency Response Team—friends of mine," Frank told Brownlee.

"I've done Special Ops with them before under General Freeman, who—"

The President shot out of his chair "as if," Brownlee said later to Donna Fargo, "someone had jammed a stick up his ass."

"Freeman!" the President thundered. "I didn't hear you say that. I don't want to know any more. No details. No names. Brownlee, take care of it." With that, he strode out of the room.

"Ah," Brownlee began awkwardly, "the President and the retired general—how should I put it . . ."

"Hate one another's guts," Dalgliesh said. Frank could picture Freeman vividly as they spoke, a man so strikingly like the late actor George C. Scott, who'd played Patton, Freeman's hero, that he used to be referred to as "George C." among his troops. "Brought that cowboy out of retirement once," Dalgliesh continued. "Took over like he was Lord Muck."

"The President," Gold Rims added, "considers him a diplomatic disaster."

"Well," Frank commented pointedly, "I don't think they were diplomats who killed—" He turned to Brownlee. "—how many was it in the Rone building? Ten? And blew a hole you could drive a bus through."

"What we're saying," Brownlee replied, "is that Freeman doesn't know when to keep his mouth shut. He's been virtually exiled from Washington, D.C., because of his criticism of Republicans and Democrats alike. He calls the State Department 'Coma Gulch.' None of the politicians like him. So if you have any idea of him eliciting any help, albeit unofficial, from Washington, I'm afraid you'll be sorely disappointed. I admit he's able, brilliant at times, and he's won a lot of battles for us in the past, but that's just it—it's in the *past*. Anyway, I hear he's past it now, a worn-out war-horse. Better he be let out to pasture. Stew in his own juice."

"I'd still like to bring him in to coordinate," Frank insisted.

Brownlee shook his head. "As you wish. But we don't know anything about it. Understood?"

"Understood."

"Good."

"I'll need a computer to e-mail."

Brownlee indicated the study next door. "You'll have to be somewhat elliptical in what you say. We don't want to risk anyone—"

"I'm an ex-SEAL," Frank said, "not an idiot."

Donna Fargo stepped in diplomatically. "I'll get the e-mail addresses Mr. Hall requires." She turned to Frank. "If you'll follow me."

Inside the plush library, its decor more East Coast preppie than laid-back L.A., Frank glanced up at the security surveillance cameras in the room. "I'll want those masked, and the room swept for bugs."

The agent and Donna glanced at one another. "May I ask why?" she inquired.

"So any phone number I dial and my e-mail can't be seen." He saw Donna rolling her eyes at the agent.

"Look," Frank said, "you can think I'm paranoid if you like, but from what I've heard, whoever busted into the Rone building knew precisely what they were doing, where the computer was, the security setup, right down to the signal prevention shield. You don't pick up that kind of info in your local rag."

Donna remained incredulous. "You think they got it from the *White House*?"

"Miss Fargo. I don't know where they got it from, but you'll forgive me if I point out that it wouldn't be the first leak from a White House. Besides, I just saw one of our leading citizens pocketing White House silver."

"Sweep the room and mask the cameras," Donna instructed the agent tersely, handing a manila folder to Frank. "I thought you might like to see this. It's a photo of the kidnapped scientist." She paused, before adding sarcastically, "But maybe you shouldn't look at it until the cameras are masked."

"Thanks, I won't."

CHAPTER FIVE

IN MONTEREY, GENERAL Douglas Freeman, retired, though still in his late fifties, was watching TV while doing his midnight stretches—fifteen minutes three times a day, in addition to his two one-hour jogs along the beach and a half hour on the weights. If he didn't double up, he couldn't spend as much time as he wanted on the Net, where he was *re*-studying every battle from Gideon's offensive against the Midianites in 1100 B.C. to the Russian offensive in Chechnya in '99–2000. Along with his extensive field experience, his knowledge of war was encyclopedic, and it had paid off. His feats of arms from his time during the U.S./U.N. military intervention in Siberia to his fighting in Southeast Asia, the Gulf, and beyond were legendary. "An eccentric combination of Patton and Rommel," as he had once been dubbed by CNN war correspondent Marte Price. Freeman's reputation had been secured in a ferociously cold winter battle in the Siberian campaign during which he ordered his state-of-the-art 120mm main gun U.S. M-1 tanks to *retreat* before an onslaught of state-of-the-art upgunned Russian 130mm T-80 main battle tanks. For those who knew that the general's motto, like that of his heroes, Frederick the Great and Patton, was *"L'audace, l'audace, toujours l'audace!"*—"Audacity, audacity, always audacity!"—the speedy American withdrawal reeked of cowardice and out-and-out panic.

But what his critics didn't know was that Freeman, aware that "amateurs talk tactics, professionals talk logistics," and whose attention to detail was just short of obsessive-compulsive, knew that because of long-dead American chemists and engineers, whose names would never be celebrated but who had dutifully aspired to meet Department of Defense specifications far above those of the Russians' DOD, the lubricating oil for the Americans' M-1s would not freeze, should temperatures plunge below minus sixty degrees. Or, more accurately, he knew that because of American know-how, the waxes in the oil would not separate out, like cholesterol in the blood, and clog the vital hydraulic arteries of the world's best main battle tank. But in the more crudely refined Russian oil used in the upgunned T-80s, the waxes *would* settle out, clogging the T-80s' hydraulic lines, bringing the Russian behemoths of the Siberian Sixth Armored to a shuddering stop. And so when Freeman was informed by his met officer that the temperature had dropped to below minus sixty-four, he abruptly ordered a U-turn counterattack. The pursued suddenly became the pursuer, his M-1s wreaking havoc on the Russian armor. The American tanks, racing at over forty miles an hour, belching flame, sending APDS—armor-piercing discarding sabot—projectiles, smashed into the Siberian tanks at over six thousand feet per second. The T-80s bucked, snow flying off them like white flour, erupting in bloodred explosions amid the taiga. The Americans killed 119 enemy tanks in less than twenty-four minutes of unerring laser-directed fire in what, a half hour later, was revealed to have been the slaughter of the entire Siberian armored division.

Now on his Windows 2000 Plus, a buzzer sounded, and at the bottom of the screen a small tank belched flame, Freeman's personalized icon for "You Have Mail!"

The e-mail read: "Aunt Maude not well—am sure she'd appreciate a call from family asap."

Though a man renowned for his cool, as in the Siberian campaign, Freeman was so distracted by this unexpected message from one of his old ex-SEAL/ALERTs that for a second he'd unwittingly kept his finger on the TV remote's volume control.

"Who's there?"—his sister-in-law's imperious voice. In the past, until she moved to Cleveland, he had always visited *her* once a year—one of his late wife Catherine's requests should anything ever happen to her, a request he dearly wished she'd never made.

"It's only me," he replied.

"It's not that dreadful Patton film, is it?" Just like that. Out of a dead sleep she could come awake and go on the offensive. "Dreadful Patton film." He wished to God she'd stayed in Cleveland.

"Not Patton," he retorted archly. "It's that goddamned 'Sound of Mucus'!"

"You don't have to blaspheme, Douglas."

" 'You don't have to blaspheme, Douglas,' " he mimicked softly, while entering his computer's SEALER—SEAL ALERT Emergency Response—contingency plan.

Marjorie appeared momentarily at the door in her commiered dressing gown and rollers, glaring at him. "Did you say something, Douglas?"

"No."

She turned abruptly and disappeared back into her bedroom. By God, he'd rather go up against a T-80. Normally relentless, in rollers she looked damn near invincible. But now the general forgot all about Marjorie, concentrating instead on answering Frank Hall's e-mail, quickly taking down all the details Frank gave him concerning the militia's attack and theft of the Rone, including the e-mail detailed picture of the computer's motherboards. Then, by drawing on his prodigious memory, as well as his computer's, for details of members' families, he began contacting his old team of SpecWar warriors. From a list of twenty-four he hoped at least ten could go on such short notice. Besides asking the obligatory question, "How's the family?" or perhaps a solicitous inquiry about the family's pet, if necessary he'd use a little shaming by referring to their wives: "Of course if *Mommy* says you can't . . ."

"Sal?"

It was four A.M. in Brooklyn. "Who da hell—"

"General Freeman here, Sal."

"General?"

"Sal, the team needs you." The game, he advised Sal Salvini, would take place out of Seattle. Estimated time away from home "four days max."

For the next three hours, fueled by coffee and the urgency of Hall's request, the general networked with his other ex-SpecWar comrades, specifically those with "severe winter" warfare experience. Drawing on his logistical expertise, attention to detail, and, above all, his speed of organization, he apprised the team of what he succinctly referred to as the DOL, by which he meant the team's "division of labor," who was to do what, and when. Their old military clothing could be worn but, just as in their SEAL/ALERT heydays, absolutely no ID was to be carried. "Make sure *Mommy* hasn't sewn your name into anything."

Above all, there was one overriding question he asked of all of them: "Are you fit? No bullshit."

Four were not up to it. One admitted it outright—too much booze. Two hesitated but confessed that they were in lard land.

"By how much?" Freeman pressed.

One said, "Ten to fifteen pounds," the other, "Maybe five. But I could whip myself into shape."

"No time," Freeman told him crisply. "Game can't be postponed."

"Shit. Sorry, sir."

"Next time."

"Yes, sir."

In Portland, Aussie Lewis, though hung over after a bout with sixteen-ounce cans of Foster's lager, could truthfully say that he, just as David Brentwood, Sal Salvini, and "Choir" Williams did, was one hundred percent "good to go."

"How's your passing?" He meant his shooting.

"Perfect."

One thing about Lewis, he wasn't short on confidence. He had what the Aussies in Vietnam used to call "a ton of guts." Would have a go at anything.

"You practice every week?" Freeman inquired.

"No, sir. Every day."

"Good man. Game's in Seattle. Team's on its way now. Can you get yourself up there pronto?"

"I'm out the door." Lewis turned to his wife, Alexandra, a dark beauty whom he, as a part of Freeman's Siberian team, had rescued from the JAO—the Jewish Autonomous Region or Oblast—on the Chinese-Russian border. She looked stunned, peering at the silent alarm clock, shading her eyes from the bedside lamp. She saw him packing.

"Sandy, be a doll and get me a coupla aspirin, will you?" he asked her. "My head's killin' me. Have to go. Freeman. Four days max. Be back before you know it." He smiled at her. "Keep the bed warm, eh?"

"Are you crazy?"

"We owe him, sweetheart."

"*I* owe him."

"Same thing," he retorted with the engaging tone that had won so many of their arguments. "We were united as one, remember?"

"You like it, don't you?" she charged.

"Two as one. Better believe it."

"You know what I mean. The fighting."

Aussie tossed in a pair of thick woolen socks—last he heard, it was snowing like crazy up there.

"Don't you?" she pressed.

He forced a smile. "Is this going to be more Freudian 'my gun is my dick' crap?"

"Freeman calls and you all jump like trained—"

"SEALs? Guess so."

What he couldn't explain to her, what you couldn't explain to women, period, was the adrenaline rush of a SpecWar op, those moments when, compared to the humdrum of everyday existence, you were fully alive, every nerve in your body taut, awake, a hair's breadth from death. Nothing like it.

Ironically, it was ex-SEAL/ALERT David Brentwood, a Medal of Honor winner, who was most reluctant to go, dragged out of his Chicago bed by Freeman's call. But perhaps more than any of the others, he felt the tug of duty. He told his wife Georgina he wouldn't be away long, convinced, from what Freeman had just told him, that given the atrocious weather in the Northwest, the militia couldn't have gotten the Rone across the mountains yet.

As it turned out, he was only half right.

By early morning General Freeman had enlisted five of his best. The second five, yet to be roused, were to arrive in Seattle by the following afternoon. Thirteen hundred hours.

By morning, dried out but still tired from phoning and ICQing on the computer with Freeman and the other members of the team till three A.M., Frank sat in a limo on the way to San Diego Airport, with Donna Fargo giving him instructions on how to contact the Western White House. She was dressed in a form-fitting long black skirt and white shot-silk blouse. It was a treat just watching her breathe.

"Where will you start looking?" she asked, her mood more mellow.

"Most obvious routes between Seattle and Wills Creek," Frank told her, "before the highway department has a chance to clear the roads over the Cascades. Militia must have been as surprised as everyone else to see that rainstorm's turned to snow. Good break for us."

"Maybe, but be careful. People who take things don't like to give them back."

Hours later he was enjoying a free scotch and other unfamiliar comforts of first class. He was anxious to be airborne so he could call Gloria, the NSA waiting period almost up. Even so, all he'd be able to tell her was that he was on an urgent salvage job—lives at risk.

A flight attendant came to his seat. "Mr. Hall?" She flashed a plastic smile.

"Yes."

She gave him a message, a sealed envelope, from Donna Fargo. The state policeman who had stopped him on Pacific

101 and driven him to the phone booth, Patrolman Adams, was dead. His cruiser had apparently left the highway near Seaside.

CHAPTER SIX

SNOW FALLING HEAVILY as he returned with his deputies to the Rone site, Sheriff Hyson closed the cruiser's door softly, in deference to the dead being taken out of the building, the zip-up black body bags in marked contrast to the snow. Several injured Rone staff, including a hysterical female lab assistant from Room 501, had already been taken to Sacred Heart Medical Center in Spokane. Hyson took his hat off as a sign of respect, paused a moment by the ambulance, then started off down over the stretch of white bumps that were snowcapped sage between the gutted building, the abandoned Mack and tank about a quarter mile away. There, Luis, doing exactly as he'd been told for once, had driven four snowplow-height stakes around the two vehicles and strung yellow police tape around them in the highly unlikely event that someone might swing off the highway for a look-see, providing they could see the two militia vehicles through the thick curtains of snow. From where Hyson and Stan were, you couldn't even make out the Rone building, the snow was so heavy. "You haven't touched anything, have you, Luis?"

"Well, I climbed in and out of the tank pretty good—had a cup of coffee in the Mack." Luis's poor attempt at sarcasm nevertheless reflected the mood of the other seven cops. They were still mad with Hyson and at themselves for hightailing it earlier that morning after the explosion, obviously a tank round, that had blown their buddies' second car clean off the road.

"No prints outside in this weather," Stan said, indicating the truck. "May get some inside."

Chief Hyson nodded. "Maybe, but I'd lay ten to one these militia boys were using surgical gloves."

"Sometimes," Luis called over, "you can pull a print from *inside* the glove."

The chief mumbled at Stan, "Luis watches all those TV shows—you know, every sheriff carries an FBI forensic lab in his friggin' trunk."

"How 'bout it, Sheriff?" Luis called. "Have a look-see?"

"Might as well, Luis."

"The FBI in on this?" Stan asked.

"Yeah," Hyson answered. "NSA told me a woman named Linda Seth, from the Spokane office, is on it, and a guy, Bill Trey, from ATF. But they're gonna need more than that to track these bastards."

Luis started dusting in the Mack, but as Hyson expected, it had been wiped clean. All he found were Trident gum wrappers and empty Gatorade pop-top bottles with bilingual labels on them, English and French, which Hyson dismissed as insignificant, with so many Americans and Canadians crossing the line.

Before Luis cautiously lifted the top of the T-34's cupola, he drew his sidearm, which prompted Stan to chuckle to Hyson, "Like they're still in there."

"Nothin' much in here," came Luis's muffled voice. "More gum wrappers."

The tank exploded, an enormous flash of orange, its red-hot debris screaming into the snowstorm, the Mack truck rocking in the blast, its cabin/sleeper blown off its chassis.

Nothing of Luis was recovered, and Hyson and Stan were killed by the concussion.

"Jesus!" said one of the paramedics, stunned by the wanton savagery of the militia's booby trap. "Why'd they do that?"

His colleague, an immigrant refugee from Kosovo, took

one look at the burning hulk of the tank and resumed his grim work. "To show us," he said, "that there is no turning back. Militia see how U.S. Army was defeated in Vietnam and intend to do the same. Hit and run—and leave nothing. Yugoslavs did it against the Germans too. And won."

The radio in the ambulance crackled, a doctor at Sacred Heart asking to speak to the sheriff. One of the Rone factory's accident victims, a woman previously lost to hysteria, was demanding to speak to the sheriff.

Far below, Seattle was shrouded in rain, the Space Needle fleetingly visible through racing gray stratus. Boeing Field was obliterated from view; the kind of desolate sight, Frank thought, that might greet you after a nuclear war where the Rone had enabled the other side to have that split-second advantage that would mean winner take all, or rather, what was left. Suddenly, through gaps in the clouds, he could see the floodlit Boeing field, which tilted as the plane banked, making it look as if the brand new, gleaming, as yet unpainted 777s would all suddenly slide downhill.

The plane had to make pattern for a few minutes, and soon they were out over Puget Sound, black forests dotted here and there by a lonely pinpoint of light, the long, gray sliver of water that was Hood Canal visible beneath intermittent cloud, and, for a fraction of a second, the sharp cluster of lights around the nuclear sub pens at Bangor. By now he figured, if he knew anything about the general, Freeman would have thirty-power pixel SETRA—see-through radar—satellite shots of eastern Washington to see how much traffic there was between Wills Creek and the mountains. The latter, which Frank couldn't see on the way up because of the foul weather, was no doubt "chockablock," as Aussie Lewis would say, with snow.

In Moscow, snow billowed across the great square like powdered sugar, the long, black Zil limousine dwarfed by the majesty of St. Basil's onion dome as it passed several army officers in greatcoats and fur caps who were overseeing the long, drab column inching toward Lenin's tomb. Ironically, in the economic turbulence since Yeltsin, more Communists than ever before were lining up to see their saint.

In the Zil, General Alexander Androvich Kornon, new chief of POD—Pacific Ocean Department—glanced out at the shuffling line. The only sound he could hear was the Zil's defrosters, audible despite the glass panel separating driver and passenger. The snowfall was increasing, and in the co-coonlike warmth of the limousine, the smell of luxurious Georgian leather, the occasional tinkle of the car's crystal-equipped bar, and the knowledge that he had his own scrambler phone at his fingertips all coalesced to reaffirm Kornon's sense of power. What made it sweeter was that three years be-fore—these things still happening despite the new reforms—he had been abruptly "transferred"—"exiled" would have been a more accurate description—for the second time in his life to Gorky for a "reorientation" course, then to the wastes of Ulan Ude near the Chinese border. He had been in disgrace with the military for having been duped by the American oceanographer Hall into believing that the codes aboard the sunken U.S. sub *New York* had been irretrievably lost, when in fact Hall had salvaged them. In Ulan Ude, a mere dot in the vastness of the Transbaikal, Kornon, his wife, and teenage daughter Tanya had lived in what the government grandly re-ferred to as a "cottage." It was a shack. Beyond, there were beech, birch, and snow as far as the eye could see. Wolves bayed mournfully in the frozen night.

Then suddenly, in one of the political squalls that had broken out in the capital at the beginning of the millennium, he'd been recalled to Moscow, back in favor, to advise Presi-dent Putin, because Kornon was the only man in Russia who had been up against the U.S. oceanographer Hall. And be-cause Putin had been one of the architects of an extraordinary achievement in Russian foreign policy begun by Gorbachev. Despite all the ballyhoo in the Western press about the new "openness" in Russia, what the world at large did not recog-nize was Moscow's determination to expand its influence in the Pacific. Just as reported to the U.S. Congress by the CIA,

Russia, like China, had gained more territory in the Pacific since Gorbachev and Yeltsin than it had in the previous fifty years. Both countries had now acquired berthing facilities in Vietnam's Cam Rahn Bay, thus eliminating the long Vladivostok–South China Sea run, and had developed their Pacific flotillas into blue water deep ocean fleets. It all meant wider responsibilities and opportunities for Kornon. The Russian and Chinese strategy had been clear—first, acquire fishing treaties with the South Pacific nations, then docking rights for repairs and replenishment. In this they were aided by the newly independent status of countries such as Timor and Fiji.

Kornon, reflecting on his good fortune, caressed the velour drapes of the limousine. As sensuous, he thought, as a woman's skin. He had been reinstated as head of the POD at a time when the newly revamped KGB, now called the FSB—Federal Security Service—needed his services in carrying out its most daring coup since its theft of U.S. cellular and top secret U.S. super quiet sub technology in the 1980s. He heard the soft "burr" of his phone.

It was Colonel Ustenko, his POD/FSB liaison officer.

"What is it, Ustenko?"

Ustenko answered obliquely, knowing the American satellites could pick up all transmissions.

"Our American friend has been sighted by one of our European representatives. Our representative says you were correct. The U.S. Department of Agriculture is using his services."

There was a moment's silence as Kornon absorbed the news. The U.S. Department of Agriculture was the informal code between them for the U.S. government. So, he and the Americans were going to meet—or rather, be pitted against each other—*again*.

"General?"

"Yes," Kornon answered, his eyes losing their focus in the snow flurries coming at the Zil like tracer fire. He felt a surge of adrenaline in his eagerness to defeat the Americans. The bear against the eagle. The eagle flew higher and faster, but in any contest of strength—well, there was no contest—the bear simply crushed you to death.

"I have notified our colleagues in Reutov." He meant the FSB.

"Excellent," Kornon told Ustenko. "Good work, Colonel."

"Thank you, General."

Kornon sat back against plush leather, satisfied now that his Russian FSB and POD agents as well as his European reps from SRP—Swiss Rhine Petrochemicals—and their militia were all in place as the two arms of the bear's impending hug.

Kornon almost felt sorry for the Americans as he alighted from the Zil in the Arbat, an area known for its art and antique shops. He climbed up to Apartment 206 for his "meeting" with the new Tass "sports affairs" editor, a large but well-developed Belorussian blonde, Vanya Levosky. She'd broken more track and field records than he knew existed.

As he sat down on the bed, Vanya brought him a vodka, then took off his boots. Kornon closed his eyes to better relish his good fortune, letting the warmth of the overheated apartment, which he had procured for her, seep into him. Purposely, he dredged up bitter memories of his exile in Ulan Ude, of the bone-aching cold that made the luxury of his present post all the sweeter.

"Do you know," he began as Vanya, in her see-through chemise, refilled his glass, "that in America the eagle is all but extinct?"

Vanya made a face. "I saw a documentary that said America is taking measures to protect them."

"No," Kornon told her irritably. "They're finished."

Gently, she took the glass from him, placing it on her Norwegian pine dresser, above which she had arranged all the medals she'd won for Russia in track and field.

As Kornon roughly entered the woman his colleagues called the *udarnitsa*, "backbreaker," the thought of his impending victory heightened his pleasure.

CHAPTER SEVEN

FRANK HALL WAS late. "Most unusual," commented Freeman, who decided to use the time in the noisy Pike Place restaurant to give a situation report to Aussie Lewis, Sal Salvini, Choir Williams, and David Brentwood. The first thing he told them, as Frank had told him, was that if the militia were trying to get the Rone out of the country, they would have to use a ship. Aussie Lewis immediately faced a dilemma. On land ops, the ex-SEAL favored using Quik-Shok rounds against "Japs." It was a SEAL idiosyncracy to refer to all enemies as Japs.

The Quik-Shok bullet performs just like a conventional round en route, but then, rather than mushrooming on impact, its core breaks into three identical pieces which then "tripod" into the target. And without exiting the body, they inflict a one hundred percent "energy dump." Each of the three fragments penetrate up to one foot inside the victim's body, with the best handgun delivery coming from a .357 Magnum.

Fine and dandy, Aussie Lewis pointed out, if you're on a hostage-freeing situation and you don't want fragments to pass through the terrorist into one of the hostages. But at sea you would most likely be on an unstable platform, unless the Pacific was really being pacific, which, he concluded, was "highly bloody unlikely." It might be best, he argued, to go for the "piggyback," or duplex, two bullets packed into one cartridge. The up-front 84-grain bullet moves out smartly at 2,750 feet per second; the second, heavier, and hence slower, 85-grain bullet, canted at three to four degrees off, moves out at 2,200 feet per second. The two meant a combined whack of

169 grains hitting your target a foot apart. In short, two shots for the price of one, or as Aussie put it, "a fifty percent greater chance of hitting your Jap on a rolling deck."

"Doesn't matter what they're standing on," came Salvini's reply. "I'll take a shotgun any day. Bam, they're gone!"

"We're not fighting your New York family, Sal," Aussie quipped.

"H and K for me," chipped in Choir Williams, having always favored a muffled Heckler & Koch subsonic 9mm Parabellum. The sound suppressor prevented anyone from hearing the submachine gun firing from more than twenty feet away.

"Choir *would* choose the bloody muffler," Aussie said, winking at David Brentwood. "Any noise and Choir's afraid they mightn't hear his singing!" It was a crack at the Welshman's passion for competing in his homeland's eisteddfod competitions. "How about you, Davy?" Aussie asked Brentwood.

But Brentwood wouldn't commit to a weapon, never did until he knew exactly what they were up against, sea or land. All he said was, "What if they have a buyer here? In the U.S.? Shipping it down the coast in a container?"

"Highly bloody unlikely," Aussie responded.

"I agree," David Brentwood conceded, "but you never know. It'd be one way of avoiding state border inspections."

"Maybe."

"Hopefully," Choir put in, "we won't be on water at all, lads. I don't fancy all that rockin' an' rollin' on the stomach."

"All right, then," Aussie said, looking at each of his colleagues, his voice one of unshakable resolve. "We'll stop 'em in the mountains."

Outside mechanic Bill Reid's house in Astoria, which doubled as the office for Oregon Oceanics, his collie was barking furiously. The larger of the two men, emerging from the red Taurus, bent down to the collie's level. "Oh, c'mon. Say hi to Larry."

The collie woofed a few more times, half sidling toward

him but still barking. The shorter man was standing back. "Looks mean to me."

"Ah, beans!" Larry said. "Look at her tail. She's all bluff."

The front door opened and through the torn screen door they could see the figure of a man—Bill Reid, they assumed—standing ragged in T-shirt and pajama bottoms, yawning. Next the door opened. The squeak of its hinge momentarily penetrated the crash of the surf nearby.

"Hi," the taller man said, straightening up from patting the dog. "Sorry to disturb you but we're looking for Frank Hall. Oregon Oceanics?"

"He's not here," Reid said, obviously irritated at the intrusion so early in the morning, but trying, through the hangover of sleep, to be civil.

"Oh, too bad. My partner and I are in trouble. We need a salvage man, and fast."

The collie was standing by Reid, tail now wagging.

"Can't wait," the big man explained apologetically. "We've got a five thousand tonner—containers—badly holed off Cape Deception. Need someone to go down, fix a line to her. Tow 'er in fast before she goes down. We called Frank but only got a message machine. Said to contact you in emergencies. Tried your phone but no answer."

"He's on vacation by now," Bill Reid said.

"Shit!" the short man said.

"No way we could reach him?" the taller one pressed.

Reid shook his head.

"Uh-huh," the taller one acknowledged. "Can you recommend somebody else?" he asked, extending his hand by way of introduction. "My name's Larry Napoleon. No relation to Bonaparte." He smiled.

Bill shook his hand. "Well, there's Willoughby Salvage. I'll go get their number, if you like."

"Appreciate it," Larry said, his shorter companion, Dan, still keeping his distance from the collie, who kept up a face-saving growl.

* * *

Douglas Freeman produced a photocopy of TPC F-16A, a 1:500,000 Defense Mapping Agency Aerospace chart of Washington State. "I've got a call in to a buddy of mine for satpix of the Cascades, but it has to be one of these." He'd marked off Highway 20 through Cascades North, Route 2 in Cascades Central, and Interstate 90 in Cascades South. "Shortest route from Wills Creek is Route 2, but it's snowing there just like it is on 20 and 90, which means we have to be prepared to go to any one of the three." He answered everyone's unspoken question. "Yes, I know, gentlemen, but which one?"

"We have transport laid on, General?" Sal asked.

"Pave Lows. Unmarked, of course. Sanitized for the government's protection. On loan from Fort Dill via an old Fort Lewis colleague."

There was a murmur of approval. It would still be a highly dangerous business in this weather, but if you had to go, a Pave Low was the only all-weather day/night helo in the world. With its state-of-the-art "hover coupler," it could exactly and simultaneously counter pitch, roll, and yaw while maintaining precise altitude above a preselected drop point. Even so, going into a raging snowstorm the best Freeman's team knew they could hope for was a fifty-fifty chance of survival—with or without the militia.

"If any of you want out," Freeman said, "this is your last chance. I've got the other five members coming in this afternoon to join us."

Only Aussie responded. "Who's flying my Pave?"

Freeman smiled. "Old friend of yours, Aussie. Mort Riley."

"That old bastard." It was a term of affection.

"The Paves' block numbers taken off?" Brentwood asked.

"Think I've gone senile, do you, David?"

"No sir, just checking."

The old, easy familiarity of their Spec Ops was coming back, the differences between rank never having mattered as much as they did when Freeman was in command of larger, conventional forces. Besides, Brentwood's query pleased Freeman—showed him the "boy"—though Brentwood was in his thirties—was still on the ball, being coldly practical. If they crashed in the storm, they didn't want a traceable engine block to be found. Of course, in the wild fastness of glaciated volcanic peaks that made up the Cascades, all over ten thousand feet, men and machines, engine blocks and all, could simply disappear.

Sal glanced at his watch. "Where the hell's Frank?"

Freeman felt his cell vibrating in his pocket, rose from the table and went outside the coffee shop into the market to answer the call. He couldn't stand would-be big shots yakking on their cells inside restaurants and other public places.

It wasn't Frank calling, but his buddy, informing him, though careful not to mention the area covered, that the satpix were on their way.

Dan was stamping his feet, breath visible in the air. "Christ, it's cold!"

"Autumn," Larry said, tucking in his red scarf. "Season of mists and mellow fruitfulness, Close-bosomed friend of the maturing sun . . ."

"What the hell's that?" Dan asked.

"Keats," Larry answered. "English poet."

"Oh," Dan said. There was a pause. "Dead, then?"

" 'Fraid so."

"Never liked poets. All fruit."

"Horseshit."

Bill Reid returned to the porch as promised with a grease-stained business card for Willoughby's Salvage Co. Larry quickly punched in the phone number on his cell, thanking Reid as he did so. "Appreciate this. If I don't get a towline on that sucker I'll lose all my containers and— Oh, crap!" Bill Reid could also hear Larry's cell phone bipping, its screen flashing: LOW BATT! LOW BATT!

"Come in and use mine if you like," Reid offered, telling Daisy to be quiet, waving her off to the yard as he shut the door against the cold.

Inside, the bungalow smelled of fried onions. The cramped

living room that led immediately off to the right had a pile of fresh laundry in front of the TV, some of it already neatly folded, a Formica coffee table back from the TV near a low-slung brown velvet love seat stacked high with *Oceans* magazines. There were CD covers and DVDs atop the back of the love seat against a bland beige wall. Not a woman's touch in sight. Dan waited by the door, not far from Reid, and impatiently looked at his watch while Larry picked up the phone that sat on a pile of old white and yellow Astoria directories in the corner near the TV and dialed. He waited, looking annoyed.

"Message machine?" Dan asked.

"No. It's still ringing," Larry said, and asked Reid, "Any other number for Willoughby?"

Dan's fist crashed into Reid then, sending him reeling across the room into a lampshade, which rocked crazily, throwing frantic shadows up and down the wall. Dan walked across to the love seat and stood over Reid, who was on one knee, one hand on the edge of the love seat, a stunned look on his face. Larry had replaced the phone and taken off his coat and scarf, draping them carefully over an arm of the love seat. Daisy was barking furiously and they could hear her scratching frantically. Dan glanced back anxiously at the door.

"Forget the dog," Larry told him.

Reid was gasping for air, face contorted, his chest heaving, making a wheezing sound as he struggled unsuccessfully to drag himself up.

Larry took a gold-plated cigarette case from the inside of his jacket and sat down beside Reid. Extracting a Gauloise, he delicately tapped it on the lid before lighting up.

Bic lighter, Reid noted, though the man's face wasn't too clear, since he was sitting just beyond the penumbra of light that cut out at the edge of the coffee table. Even so, Reid could make out Larry's spiffy navy-blue blazer, light gray trousers, and what looked like an old college tie. A businessman, perhaps, but more like a model. Something too clean, too fastidious, about him.

"Won't waste your time, Mr. Reid," Larry told him. "We want to know where your boss, Hall, is."

"Told you before, I don't know," Reid answered, a knife-like pain in his chest. "He's not my boss, anyway."

Larry blew out the smoke, trying to direct it, but failed, eddies in the room dispersing it in all directions. The collie was still barking outside. "All right," Larry said, spreading his hands as if he was the most agreeable man in the world. "If you want to be pedantic, he's your *partner*. Will that do?"

"I don't know where he is," said Reid. "Told you—he's on vacation."

Dan moved closer.

"Look," Larry said, lips pursed, "don't be stupid, Bill. Friends of ours saw him at the Western White House. But they lost him at San Diego Airport. He must let you know where he is—or where he's headed. Right?"

"I told you—"

Dan grabbed Reid by the left ear, twisting it, lifting him, until it turned scarlet. He shoved him back into the love seat, creating a fall of CD covers about Reid's shoulders. "You want to fuck around? Is that it?"

"I don't know, for Christ's sake!" Reid answered, cupping his ear. "I *don't know*! I haven't heard from him since he finished the oil spill."

"Billy wants to play," Dan said.

Larry shrugged, sitting back in the love seat. "I guess."

Dan smiled, the first time he'd done so. "Want me to look around the kitchen?"

"Might as well," Larry said. He glanced at his watch. "This isn't working."

As Dan went to the kitchen, Reid's eyes followed him uncomprehendingly. Larry said nothing, the strong, pungent odor of the Gauloise filling the living room, overtaking the fried onion smell.

A minute later Dan reappeared. "Catch!" Reid instinctively turned his head away, his arm coming up protectively to ward off whatever it was. Ice cubes rained around him, the ice tray bouncing off Reid's arm onto the love seat. "That'll help," Dan said, tossing a tea towel after. "Your ear, dummy," he said, returning to the kitchen.

Larry dragged an old *Newsweek* off the coffee table. Putin, the Russian president, was on the cover. "Ex-KGB," Larry commented, flicking over the pages. "Old school. No results, and you're off to Omsk." Reid could hear cupboard doors and drawers being opened and slammed shut in the kitchen.

"Listen—" Reid said, sitting up, his voice conspiratorial, his hand clutching a few of the cubes against his ear.

Larry raised a finger to his lips. "Shush, have a rest for a bit."

Larry noticed several black and white photos on the mantelpiece, between a West Coast shaman's mask and a polished turquoise paua shell. He got up and walked over to look at the photographs, five-by-sevens. He pointed at one with his cigarette. "This you and Hall near the *Petrel*'s submarine?"

"Submersible," Reid said, his correction a vain attempt to show them they hadn't whipped him.

"The girl?" Larry asked, pointing to another photo.

Reid hesitated. He heard a rattling noise in the kitchen, and Daisy whimpering at the back door.

"The girl?" Larry repeated. "Hall's girlfriend?"

"Don't know," Reid said. "Someone he met at the pier, I guess."

Larry took another drag on the Gauloise, and, holding the cigarette behind him, leaned forward professorially, examining the black and white more closely. "Always poses with anyone he meets?"

Bill Reid felt frigid water, from the ice cubes, trickling down his neck. "Well, no, not every—"

"She live around here?"

"Don't know," Reid said.

Larry nodded. "So it's like that, is it?" Ash fell from the Gauloise.

Reid hesitated. "Like what?"

"Like Danny said. You want to play?" He took another suck on the cigarette, then stabbed it hard into the paua shell.

"I—" Reid began, and fell silent, not knowing what to say.

Larry picked up the photo of Hall and the woman and returned to the sagging love seat. Dan came in, his coat and suit jacket off, revealing a bull-like neck. The sleeve of his right arm was rolled up beyond the hairy forearm, the top button of his sky-blue shirt undone, his tie askew, a white plastic funnel in his left hand, a can of Drano in his other.

Reid dropped the ice, one hand shooting out protectively.

"What the fuck are you doing?" Dan asked him. "Making traffic signals?"

"He thinks you're going to put it down his throat," Larry said.

"Nah, I wouldn't do that. Wrong end."

Without looking at Reid, Larry pocketed the photograph. "We want her name, phone number, and address, as well as where Hall is."

Reid said nothing, praying frantically that someone would call—the captain of the *Petrel* making his weekly report, his mother, anyone he might solicit for help. But no one did.

"Did you hear me?" Dan said threateningly. "What's her fucking name?"

"Glor—" Reid began, his throat dry as sandpaper.

Dan shook the can of drain cleaner.

"I—I don't—"

"All right?" Dan asked Larry.

Larry had taken out another Gauloise, tapping Reid's head with the cigarette case. "Disappointed in you, Bill." He paused to light up and inhale. "You think you're being loyal. Want to know how long loyalty lasts?"

Reid shook his head.

"We'll show you."

"*I'll* show him," Dan said petulantly.

"All right," Larry said. "*You* show him. But let's go. Zurich's in a hurry."

For a completely irrational moment Bill Reid convinced himself that "let's go" meant they were actually about to leave.

"Gag him," Larry told Dan.

CHAPTER EIGHT

AUSSIE LEWIS THOUGHT he glimpsed Frank coming through the crowd at the Pike Place Market, and so left the group as the cloud penetration satpix of Washington State were coming through on the laptop.

"Where the fuck have you been?" Aussie asked him affectionately.

"And hello to you too," Frank answered, adding, "You ever see that old episode of *Seinfeld* where he tries to rent a car?" Before Aussie could answer, Frank continued, "Jerry tells the rental company that they can *take* the reservations, they just can't *keep* them. All the SUVs are gone."

"Hired by the militia no doubt," Aussie said, slapping his friend on the back. "Not to worry, mate. General's got Pave Lows laid on."

"Volunteers?"

"Yeah. Silly bastards. Like us. No ID, nothing. Just loads of personality."

David Brentwood grinned. "No Rone bonuses as incentives, I guess?"

"Filthy *lucre*? Not a word, mate."

By now they were in the restaurant and Freeman was extending his hand. "Good to see you, Hall."

"You too, sir." Brentwood was glad the general had selected the noisy, crowded restaurant. Ironically, it was one of the most private places to discuss a strategy in a world of listening devices and peephole cameras, against which the best defense was often the hustle and bustle of a public place like this. First he showed them the detailed pictures of the Rone's motherboards from Brownlee, telling them to "Read, peruse, and inwardly digest!" then called up the first satpix. It was a SNOOPER—snow-penetrating radar—overview of the state that, left to right, showed the thick, rugged, snowcapped wedge of the Olympic Peninsula, a dusting of snow on the coastal margins around Puget Sound between the peninsula and the snow-covered north-south barrier of the Cascade Mountains. Beyond the mountains there was a vast, undulating blanket of snow stretching all the way eastward to Idaho, north to Canada, and south to the Washington-Oregon border. The white expanse, the satpix showed, was relieved only by the dark, snaking courses of the Columbia and its tributaries, showing up on the satellite photo like the dark vessels of a brain scan. Here and there short black lines—bridges— appeared across the rivers, especially on the Columbia all the way along its 1,270-mile course from its source high in the Columbia Ice Field down to the shipwreck-littered sandbars of its five-mile-wide confluence with the Pacific at Astoria.

Freeman tapped the laptop's zoom icon for maximum pixel resolution, which now, in addition to the bridges, revealed small gray arcs across the Columbia and tributaries. "Dams," he explained to Hall. "Grand Coulee alone is 550 feet high. So they sure as hell can't float the merchandise down. It has to be somewhere on one of the three highways."

"One of *two*," Hall replied, signaling the waitress as he spoke. "Latest KOMO—local TV—report says the blizzard's still raging, and Route 2 through the central Cascades, from Wenatchee on the eastern side of the mountains to Seattle, has just been closed. Big snowdrift east of Stevens Pass."

"Good," Freeman said. "That narrows our search to either Highway 20 in the northern Cascades or Highway 90 in the southern part of the range."

"Still means we'll have to split our force in two, General," David said.

"I know," Freeman replied, tapping the computer again, bringing up the names of the other five SEAL/ALERTs who should have been arriving in Seattle as he spoke. "It'll be two teams. One team for the northern highway, one for the south.

Frank'll stay here with me on standby with his oceanographic ship in the *unlikely* event—" He paused and eyed each one of them. "—I say, in the *unlikely* event the militia get past you in the mountains."

Frank didn't like being on standby. Who did? Suddenly he'd become second fiddle to his comrades. But the general's logic was unassailable. Besides which, the general had put *himself* on standby.

"So," Aussie said, "we concentrate on routes 20 and 90."

"Dammit!" It was Freeman, realizing that if Highway 2 had only just been closed at Stevens Pass, the vehicle transporting the computer might still be on it. They were back to three possible routes through the mountains.

"How long did you say that computer was, sir?" Choir Williams asked.

"Twenty feet," the general answered.

"Then," Choir put in, "it has to be in a semi trailer. A truck?"

"We know *that*, you daft Welshman," Aussie riposted, indicating the satpix of the three routes. "But have you had a look at how many friggin' trucks are on those highways?"

"A lot," Salvini said.

"Yeah," Aussie said. "Well, what do you suggest? We haven't got time to stop and search every one. Don't have eyes in our bums. And never mind the bloody blizzard."

They were stymied.

The general closed his laptop and stood up. "Need to walk," he announced gruffly. "I'll meet you and the other five arrivals at the downtown helo pad in fifty minutes—1300 hours. All additional gear'll be aboard the helo except rolling SATs for Alfa and Bravo leaders." By "rolling SATs" the general was referring to the specially designed analogue/digital combination phones that would allow him to break radio silence if necessary and contact either Brentwood or Aussie during the op. "If anyone's late," he continued, "they stay with me, Hall and the other standby."

"Then I'll be early," Aussie quipped.

The general didn't answer. Confronted by the problem of the impossibility of being able to search all the trucks in time, he strode off, already in "mull mode," as his staff officers used to call it. It was a frame of mind like that experienced by drivers who, suddenly realizing they've arrived home, can't remember how they got there. A time during which his physical actions seemed perfectly normal but were in fact on automatic pilot, his mind so absorbed by a tactical or logistical problem that, in the days before his forced retirement, his aide, Colonel Norton, had always taken care to shadow him.

"I'll walk with you, sir, if you don't mind," Brentwood offered.

Freeman grunted, which Brentwood took as assent, the general handing him the laptop. The general strolled through Pike Place Market, head raised, hands behind his back. He paused now and then by a stall then walked on. Brentwood was conscious of how Freeman's idol, Patton, before his final push into Germany, had struck the same ruminating pose near the Rhine crossing while viewing the burning hulks of Tiger tanks and German dead scattered before him. The famed American general had been troubled by a dream he'd had the night before, especially by the recurring image of pushcarts, Patton telling his aide he couldn't get the carts out of his mind. Then everything clicked into place—the carts were there because the Germans were running out of gasoline, a crucial variable—perhaps *the* most crucial variable— in any general's logistical equation. Suddenly Freeman stopped at yet another coffee bar—the Pacific Northwest ran on coffee, not gasoline—the general struck by the sound of the rain drumming on the market's roof. "By God, it must be snowing hard up in those mountains." It was as if he was awakening from a reverie.

"Yes, sir," Brentwood answered, momentarily distracted by a shapely yuppie jogger nearby loudly ordering a "half-caf, half-decaf, eggnog, half-skim, no-foam latte with a dash of Irish cream to go."

"And cold," Freeman said, oblivious to the yuppie's exhibitionism. "You recall how cold they said it was?"

"Can't remember," Brentwood replied, recalling Freeman's obsession with the temperature during the U.N./U.S. Siberian "police" action. Some said the general was naturally lucky, like the militia commander McBride, but he knew differently. In Freeman's attention to the minutiae of military tactics and strategy, the general had built up such a wealth of knowledge that he was able to anticipate problems more than most, bringing him more successes than losses, an accomplishment always interpreted by the envious and less prepared as "luck."

It was by yet another coffee shop, the air acrid with the smell of scorched beans, that Freeman finally emerged from his "mull mode," staring at his laptop, which Brentwood had cradled under his left arm.

The answer, the general realized, had been staring at him in the form of his own laptop. "What's one of the first things you're told up here when you buy your computer?" Before Brentwood could think of a reply, Freeman was giving him the answer. "You mustn't let it get too cold—it won't work below zero. The militia," he hurried on, "can't let the computer drop below freezing. Unlike other trucks carrying perishables, etcetera, which must keep their trailers *cold*, the truck carrying the prototype computer will have to keep its trailer *warm*."

Brentwood had no problem seeing that, but surely this wouldn't pose any problem for the militia—most civilian haulage trucks, he knew, like those in the Army, had Peltier heater/cooler units to maintain the temperature needed—in the case of the Rone prototype, above zero. But Brentwood didn't see how this could help the SEAL/ALERT team.

"The roof of the heated semi trailer will be bare," the general said exuberantly. "No snow!" He reached for his laptop and glanced about the coffee shop for a vacant spot. "Feel like another java?" he asked Brentwood.

"No, General. I've had—"

"Grab yourself one all the same. We need a table."

By the time Brentwood had his decaf, General Freeman

had brought up the satpix of the three highways between Wills Creek and Seattle, zeroing in with high pixel resolution on the long, relatively flat sections before the mountains, searching for a "black roof," or, more accurately, one bare of snow. "Goddamn it! There's one on the central route that's just been closed because of snow near Stevens Pass, and *two* on the southern route, which is still open. Dammit!" He had expected to see only one such truck, not three.

"Maybe they've disassembled the computer?" Brentwood said. "Into three sections?"

"They're not that stupid," Freeman said brusquely. "Even if they'd had time to force those two scientists to do it, it would be tactically insane. If they lost any one of the three pieces, they'd lose the whole shebang."

Brentwood had to agree. Whoever the militia were selling the Rone to, the buyers would insist on an intact computer. "Then my money's on one of the two trucks on the southern route."

"Maybe," the general mused, "but why not the central route? It's the shortest to the coast. Well," he conceded, "it means two teams of five, one for each road." He glanced at his watch. "We've got seventeen minutes to get to the helo pad."

They made it in twelve, but it turned out that two of the extra five men he'd expected had been delayed by snow at O'Hare in Chicago, which meant there'd be two teams of four men each: Alfa, led by Aussie Lewis, Bravo by Brentwood.

The most disturbing thing for Freeman, knowing the militia as he did, was that he was sure they would have vehicles riding shotgun on whatever route their truck was hauling the computer. But which was the right route? The satpix showed that on the central highway near Berne, a small hamlet east of Stevens Pass, there were four vehicles in front of the lone black-roofed truck, and on the southern route a cluster of nine or ten vehicles, SUVs and pickups mainly, half of them in front and half behind the two black roofs. Some, of course, might be civilian, but it was possible, given the ruthless intent the militia had shown at Wills Creek, that *all* the accompanying vehicles were militia. If the computer was being hauled by either of the two trucks on the southern route, this could mean anywhere up to forty or fifty armed militia aboard the innocuous SUVs and pickups. And his ex-SEAL/ALERTs, good as they were, didn't "have eyes in their bums," as Aussie Lewis had so eloquently put it.

"Consequently, the key," Freeman told Brentwood and Lewis, "is to isolate the black roofs on your route from any possible backup asap."

To avoid confusion in their throat-mike transmissions, he forbade the use of the terms Highway 90 or Highway 2. The "nine" in "ninety" could easily be mistaken for a "mine," and "two" for "you." Instead he designated the roads simply "Central" and "Southern."

Watching one of David Brentwood's three men strapping on his Kevlar vest, Freeman hollered above the noise of the Pave Low's engine, "That hasn't got a neck flap!"

"She'll be right, General," Aussie answered.

"No!" Freeman thundered, handing Aussie his Alfa leader's SAT phone. "I ordered high collars. Cheap bastards!" He remembered losing a man in the Delta, a VC's AK-47 burst taking the GI's head off at the neck. Another inch or two of Kevlar wouldn't have saved him from massive bruising, but it sure as hell would have saved his life. Buttoning up his own vest, Aussie almost felt sorry for whoever it was who had screwed up the general's on-line requisition.

"Never mind," said Choir, who would be part of Brentwood's four-man team investigating the two black roofs on the southern route. "There'll be no shooting, General. In like Flynn and out like Bout."

"Bout?" Aussie inquired.

"It rhymes," Choir said, grinning.

"Silly Welsh bastard!"

The two Paves took off five minutes apart, Aussie Lewis's eastward from Seattle en route toward Berne seventy miles away in the Stevens Pass area, where traffic had been stopped amid the high peaks due to the blizzard and a huge buildup of snow east of the Cascade railway tunnel. Brentwood's team headed ninety miles southwest toward the foothills around Ellensburg on the eastern side of the Cascade range.

In each of Alfa and Bravo's Pave Low IIIs, or Su-JGs, Super Jolly Green Giants, the co-pilots had donned thermal goggles to ID any radiant heat from the target area.

Bristling with every kind of sensor, from the multimode radar and radar-warning receiver, to forward-looking infrared probe and infrared searchlight, each of the ungainly, boxlike helos, armed with a 7.62mm Gatling gun, was also equipped with starboard rescue hoist and detachable fuel tank. They were much quieter than many of the smaller, less powerful helos that Freeman's generation of SEALs remembered from 'Nam. The improved—that is, decreased—noise level was, ironically, due not so much to military considerations or modifications made as a result of the Gulf War as to muffling baffles developed in response to complaints by environmentalists and park rangers in Arizona, where noisy helo tours had been charged with disturbing wildlife and the serenity of tourists visiting the Grand Canyon. In the case of the Alfa and Bravo teams, the noise of the helos was further muted by the blizzard and abundance of packed snow in the Cascades.

Inside the helos, with pilot and co-pilot having no visual horizon—unable to tell, other than by their instruments, whether they were hovering or making headway in the horrendous blizzard whiteout—the zero visibility created in each man either a false, cocoonlike sense of security or a sense of increasing anxiety. The helos' TERTRA—terrain-tracking radar—alone kept the Paves on track, no more than a hundred feet above the ground. In Brentwood's Bravo Pave, this meant being no more than a hundred feet above the jagged mountain peaks as the helo range-hopped over toward Ellensburg. In the case of Aussie Lewis's Alfa Pave, it meant skimming above the Skykomish River, sheer cliffs at times rising on either side of the helo.

Despite the acute danger of flying in such conditions, however, Aussie Lewis, Sal Salvini, and the other two Alfa men, Michaels and Reese, had been on more than a dozen Spec Op insertions, and had learned to rest whenever they could, conserving energy that might be needed for the actual op.

In any event, although the journey to the Stevens Pass area, near Berne, was some distance by car through the rugged, snowbound terrain, it would take Alfa's helo, following the course of the Skykomish River and traveling at a reduced speed of just over one hundred miles per hour, no more than forty-five minutes to reach its IP, or insertion point.

Aussie, however, did take time to try to make book on whether the black-topped truck on the central route his team was headed for was in fact the "milch cow," as he called it—the truck carrying the computer. Michaels, a short, stocky Irish-American, was unsure—maybe it was one of the two black roofs on Brentwood's southern route, opining, though, that the militia would've had the pedal to the metal to make it to Ellensburg from Wills Creek.

"Yeah," added Reese, an ex-SEAL who, with a medium build and bull-like neck, had dispatched more than his share of Iraqis to paradise on "search and destroy" missions behind Saddam's lines. "They would've had to be moving."

"Shit," Aussie cut in, "they *have* been moving, I reckon, since the moment they grabbed the damn thing."

"Yeah," Reese agreed thoughtfully, zipping up his snow-camouflage battle jacket over his load vest. "On the other hand, Brentwood's route's still open. Ours isn't—stacked up east of Stevens Pass."

"Except," Salvini pointed out, "militia might have been committed to our central route before the forecasters announced it was closed." They knew they were driving Aussie nuts with their equivocating. The helo's lone crewman, who had helped stow the SpecWar gear thoroughly, was enjoying the verbal jousting, though.

Michaels's Irish brogue rose above the muffled sound of the Pave's three engines. "Looks like it's six of one, half dozen of the other, then."

"Never mind all the nattering," Aussie challenged them. "Let's see some money here!"

His three teammates declined. Aussie's obscene retort was

lost to the vibration of equipment. They carried everything
from rappeling ropes to vehicle puncture strips, several boxes
of 7.62mm ammunition, C4 plastique, time delay initiators,
and assorted rescue gear in the cargo hold of the big $21 mil-
lion super chopper. The Paves' all-weather day/night capa-
bility was designed from their inception to go deep into
enemy territory whatever the conditions.

Suddenly, their sinuses clearing, Aussie, Salvini, Michaels,
and Reese knew the helo had shot upward, as it took an ear-
popping hop in altitude of a hundred feet or more.

"Alpine Falls!" Michaels yelled above the noise of the
rotors.

"No way," Reese countered good-naturedly. "Deception
Falls."

"Well, whaddya know?" Sal said, winking at Aussie. "The
boys can read a map."

"No they fucking can't," Aussie replied. "We've left the
river. Driver's following the highway."

"Oh really," challenged the short, stocky Irishman. "And
seeing as you can't see any fucking thing outside, how do you
know that?"

"Rotor noise," Aussie shouted. "Different over packed
snow than water."

"Oh yeah," put in Reese. "What if the river's frozen?"

"It isn't," Aussie said, adjusting his vest load to accommodate his leader's SAT phone. "Skykomish doesn't freeze.
Edges maybe, but not the main flow."

"Bullshit," Reese countered, looking first at Sal, then at the
Irishman. "He's shitting us."

"Ten to one," Aussie challenged them, "we're following
the highway."

"I'm down for a buck!" Reese yelled.

"Whoa!" Aussie shouted. "Big spender—make it five."

"All right," Reese said. "Five bucks says we're still following the river."

"I'm down for five," Michaels chipped in. "Sal?"

Salvini shook his head.

"All right," Aussie said, turning to the lone crewman. "Ask driver Mort if—"

The yellow light went on in the cargo bay. "Three minutes to IP," the pilot announced.

Aussie Lewis's prediction that they'd left the river was confirmed by the Pave's TERFA—terrain following/terrain avoidance radar—computer. The helo was now following a big M-shaped section of the highway a mile or so north of the Burlington-Northern rail line, heading into the worst of the blizzard that was raging about the four-thousand-foot-high Stevens Pass.

"Hee hee hee!" Aussie Lewis chuckled. "Haw haw, fucking haw! I'm, let's see—" He gazed up at the ceiling of the Pave's hold. "—that'd be twenty bucks, I believe. Cash!"

They were all standing behind him now, one hand gripping the cargo net, the other their weapons.

"Don't carry cash into combat!" Michaels told him. "You know that, prickhead."

"A check'll do!"

"Fuck you!"

The crewman was amazed at the Alfa team's easy banter only seconds away from their insertion point, but then he guessed this was due not so much to high morale—for which such types were known—but because Aussie Lewis knew that with only one black—warm—roof showing, and the highway being closed at Berne, just east of Stevens Pass, the chances were ten to one that these warriors'd see no more action than falling snow.

The light turned red, IP imminent, and each of the four men snapped down the yellow antiglare snow goggles from the rim of his winter-camouflaged Fritz.

Fifty-five miles south of them, Bravo's Pave was coming out of the blizzard down into the Cascades foothills over a stretch of the Yakima River which, unlike the Skykomish, which flowed westward from the Cascades into Puget Sound, flowed southeastward from the western side of the Cascades into the Columbia. One moment they were in thick, cloying, gray cloud; the next, they were heading eastward into all but open sky, a few remnants of stratus remaining, and beyond, an endless, undulating blanket of deep snow. The Yakima River appeared as an astonishing ribbon of Prussian blue against the whiteness. Here, on the Freeman-designated "southern" route, the highway and rail route, as on Aussie Lewis's central route, followed the course of a river, as did transmission lines. The lines were a constant headache for the pilots, who, despite the help they received from the Paves' TERFA and supporting moving video map display, which pinpointed the helos' precise position at any given moment, still found themselves strained to the limit, the snow-coated transmission lines at times invisible against the background.

The sun had cast the vast Columbia Basin in a hue so pink that Bravo's pilot commented he wouldn't have believed it had he not seen it himself. David Brentwood, however, had little time for the beauty of the panorama before him. He double-checked that all was ready with his three SpecWar colleagues, two SEALs—Joe White and Art Wright, known as the "Wright Brothers"—and Choir Williams.

"We've got the two black tops up ahead," the pilot announced. "Big semis heading our way. Eleven other vehicles—two cars, two SUVs in front of the trucks—with six, no, make that seven, repeat *seven*, vehicles behind them. They your people?"

"Yes," Brentwood answered, amused by the unexpected Britishness of the phrase, "They your people?" an expression the pilot had no doubt picked up from working with Britain's Special Air Service or one of Freeman's other limey Spec Ops groups. Brentwood's amusement was cut short, however, by the realization that he'd most likely have to split his team of four into two to deal with the two black tops.

The pilot, having plotted the target's GPS location and speed at plus or minus thirty miles per hour, turned the helo a full 180 degrees. He informed Brentwood that the road looked shiny, ivory-colored rather than white, indicating that the snowplowed and traffic-hardened surface had no doubt started to freeze from the wind chill, a westerly, blowing toward the Cascade foothills below them at forty miles per hour.

The pilot, using his radar, backtracked a few miles along the highway north of Ellensburg until he reentered cloud that was hanging between the hills out of the line of sight of the twelve oncoming vehicles.

"This'll do," Brentwood assured him, and as the helo hovered, the crewman slid open the door. Brentwood braced himself for the rush of cold air, but it still shocked him. The frigid, nose-reaming draft snatched his breath away. The chopper descended off to the side of the highway at a point that Brentwood's wrist-mounted GPS unit told him was a quarter mile in advance of the string of traffic that contained the two black tops. The helo's six rotor blades blasted gritty, icy snow in a mini-tornado, momentarily obscuring the snow-blanketed highway as the four commandos jumped out four feet above the ground. The crunch of corn snow beneath his boots immediately told Brentwood that any recent powder had been blown away by the wind, and that the highway, as the pilot warned, would be extremely slippery.

"Box!" he yelled out to Choir as the chopper rose into the swirling oblivion above them.

"Got it!" Choir responded, the sound of the helo quickly receding.

CHAPTER NINE

THOUGH AUSSIE LEWIS'S Pave Low, over sixty miles to the north on the central highway, had a shorter distance to travel from Seattle than David Brentwood's, it had not yet reached its IP near Berne east of Stevens Pass. "How come?" Michaels asked Aussie, on hearing that Brentwood's team had already deplaned. "It's only seventy klicks to here as the crow flies."

"Well," Aussie answered, "we're not fucking crows. And we're in the middle of a fucking blizzard in the fucking mountains. Brentwood, the lazy bastard, could fly *over* the fucking mountains to get to his IP in the fucking foothills. We have to fly *through* 'em to get to our fucking IP. Takes longer, you boghead."

"Excuse me for asking," Michaels retorted.

"That's all right. Say three Ave Marias and no wanking for a fortnight."

It was harmless banter to reduce the tension, but Aussie sometimes put himself on thin ice with flippant asides regarding others' closely held beliefs. He got away with it because he didn't give a damn what anyone said about him. Except if someone called him a coward.

Incoming gusts up to eighty miles per hour coming from the south off Cowboy and Big Chief mountains, both over five and a half thousand feet, had further delayed Alfa's arrival. Now the radar's video display was showing high cliffs right and left of the helo, so close that the echo of the Pave's rotors sounded like another chopper. The pilot reprogrammed for an insertion point forty feet above the ground,

the Pave's state-of-the-art hover-coupler, inertial guidance
system, and radar altimeter enabling the chopper's pitch to
neutralize the effects of wind shear. The electronics effectively
took over the piloting, keeping the helo hovering steadily at
precisely forty feet above a point thirty yards north of the
highway. The snowdrift in the area had been too much for the
plows, so the pilot was unwilling to risk overriding the hover
coupler to take the 73,000-pound craft lower in the thick,
falling snow, lest the radar had misread surface fuzz from the
unknown terrain.

The red light turned green. The door opened upon a swirling world of white, the howl of the blizzard momentarily
swallowed by the noise of the Pave's three big General Electric turboshafts. Despite the baffling, their unified roar drowned
out all other sound, including the slithering of the two fifty-
foot lengths of one-inch-diameter polyethylene cord down
which Aussie, Salvini, Michaels, and Reese fast-roped into
waist-high powder behind an old, hard, ten-foot-high snowplow pile on the west shoulder of the highway.

The insertion was over in nine seconds. The Alfa chopper,
its echo reverberating loudly off the nearby cliffs, rose into
the blizzard to make pattern, like that of Bravo, until requested to pick up the four commandos.

Moments later the blizzard above the four turned orange,
followed by an explosion of such intensity that Reese's ear-
drums felt as if they'd imploded. He, like the other three, instinctively dropped flat into the down-soft powder. Fiery
debris and great chunks of snow rained down about them.
The air filled with the stink of diesel, a loud *wokka-wokka!* all
about them, reminiscent of the ubiquitous Hueys of Vietnam.
It was a single rotor blade from the Pave Low coming down
through the blizzard. It struck the ground at an oblique angle,
and rather than cartwheeling across the snow, the blade spun
through it, the *wokka-wokka* quickly giving way to a sound
like that of a bottle spinning on sand, then a chuffing noise,
followed by a tremendous thud as its edge whacked into the
tightly packed pile of snow on the road's shoulder.

Salvini, no longer hearing debris falling, stood and saw a

lump of burning debris a hundred yards off, its light glinting off propane tanks on a red snow-grooming machine parked by one of the Stevens Pass ski lifts. Then he saw Aussie Lewis getting up, his balaclava icing sugar white, only his blue eyes visible, eyebrows iced up. Ditto for Reese, who was also dusting himself off. Michaels still lay down, taking cover by the snowplow pile, or at least that's what Salvini thought the Irishman was doing until Aussie yelled, "Get up, you Irish bastard!" There was no movement. Michaels had been decapitated, his trunk twitching in spasm, bleeding profusely, the blood pooling and congealing in the depression where his head had been.

"Jesus Christ!" It was Salvini who found the Irishman's head in its balaclava on the far side of the mountain road.

Aussie Lewis was motionless, having signaled Reese and Salvini not to move. The sound he heard, like that of an angry hornet, grew louder until Lewis could discern a shape, about fourteen feet long, emerging through the thick curtain of snow east of him. It was two snowmobiles approaching at speed on the highway. Because of the acute angle, they appeared to be joined, both riders in canary-yellow snowsuits.

Aussie pushed the severed head into the road's shoulder. "Cover me!" he ordered, confident that while Reese and Sal were close enough to hear him, the snowmobilers wouldn't. Their training allowing them to momentarily push Michaels's fate out of mind, both Salvini and Reese were already in the prone position. Sal held his folding-stock pump action shotgun and Reese his scope-mounted M-16, a flash-bang grenade in the tube. Sal, closest to the snowmobilers, about seventy yards off, automatically put the first one in his cone of fire. Reese elected to use his iron sights rather than mess with the scope through what would have been magnified veils of snow.

Aussie could smell the snowmobiles' gas fumes, an odor he always found offensive, and he could now make out the name "Arctic Cat" on the first machine. He heard the first snowmobiler throttling down. The rider, in a yellow Day-Glo nylon snowsuit and matching visored crash helmet, had no doubt seen the stubby P-90 Bullpup which, not much longer than its nine-inch barrel, Aussie was holding nonchalantly by his side, its white canvas ammo-catch pouch on his hip all but indistinguishable from his white nondescript battle jacket and pants. The weapon was so small and unorthodox in shape that from farther away the snowmobilers had probably thought it was nothing more than a slab of wood.

"You okay?" the first snowmobiler asked. He was ten yards away, standing astride his machine, raising his crash helmet's visor, his buddy a few feet behind.

"Fine," said Lewis, whom the snowmobiler had seen kicking what looked like a blackened ball of snow into the road's shoulder.

"Heard an explosion," the first rider continued, his voice loud above the idling engine. "Sounded pretty bad."

"Yeah," shouted Aussie, who saw the second snowmobiler, visor still down, craning his neck, trying to peer over the road's high shoulder of old, plowed snow. Had he spotted Reese or Salvini? Aussie doubted it, but the rider would sure as hell be able to see the smoking debris scattered about.

"What happened?" the first snowmobiler pressed. The arm-length khaki tube mounted on his pinion seat was big enough, Aussie thought, to be a nylon-sheathed map case, if they were park rangers. Difficult to tell, since the yellow snowsuits might have been covering uniforms. If they were militia, the caselike tube and boxy protrusion attached could be a Stinger antiaircraft missile launcher, in which case the snowmobiler would know about the Pave Low's disintegration, despite the questions the snowmobiler now asked.

"You military?" the first rider inquired, his buddy still surveying the smoldering remains of the helo. There was a certain beauty to it, the warm glow of fires around the wreckage veiled by the blizzard's swirl of snow.

"You got it," Aussie replied. "On maneuvers. Search and rescue."

"Uh-huh." The rider waved at the debris. "Looks pretty realistic."

"That's the way we like it."

"Huh, so the road must be closed further west too? I mean, for your maneuvers?"

Too many fucking questions, and it looked as if the second rider, visor still down, was now staring at the P-90. Besides, the "search and rescue" bit wouldn't convince a moron.

"Turn off your engine," Aussie said, adding jocularly. "All this yelling, we'll start an avalanche."

"Right," agreed the first rider, throttling down further, turning to his companion immediately behind. The snowmobiles roared to life, coming straight at Aussie. A shot. He dove, heard two more sharp reports, felt one of the rounds punching him mid-vest, his SAT phone exploding. He hip-fired the P-90, beloved for its soft recoil, his second long burst through a thirty-degree arc unleashing thirteen rounds at over 2,300 feet per second. The first snowmobile's once clear plastic windscreen was now opaque, the Cat sliding on its side, treads kicking up snow like a wounded boar. Sal's shotgun blasted the second snowmobiler right off his machine, where he writhed, his right arm taken off at the shoulder. The man lay screaming in the powder, the bloodied snow like red popcorn, his helmet flying off into the base of the snowplow pile. Aussie saw that the first snowmobiler was up—assumed he must be wearing a vest—and was raising a sidearm. Reese's three-round burst from the M-16 smashed into the man's helmet, splitting it and the snowmobiler's head wide open, the man dead before he hit the snow. The second snowmobiler, they now realized, was a woman, long black hair having spilled out now that her helmet was gone.

Hardened as the three SEAL/ALERTs were, they were still surprised, but by no means shocked. They had heard of VC women regulars in 'Nam—if you were captured by them, you had more to fear than if taken prisoner by the men.

The woman was screaming as she continued to slither about. Reese tried to steady her, cursing the blood spattering over him. Salvini unzipped her buckshot-shredded snowsuit, expecting to see militia fatigues. Instead she was wearing what he guessed had been a white woolen turtleneck and jeans, the sweater sodden red and ripped by the twelve-gauge's blast.

"Give her a shot!" Aussie yelled as he pulled off her sweater, bunching it as an interim pressure dressing against the hemorrhaging hole that had been her shoulder joint. Reese pulled the hypodermic from his tactical vest's Velcro snap, flicked off the plastic tip guard, and plunged the needle into her jugular. But the trauma had overwhelmed her, her body convulsing so powerfully that Sal, his hands slippery from the blood, could no longer hold her. Her surge of strength knocked him off balance into the snowbank, his head striking a rock-hard clump of ice, momentarily stunning him. For a second all he was aware of was the strange printing above the ice-crusted taillight of the first Arctic Cat: NE VOUS ASSOYEZ PAS ICI, most of the English equivalent hidden by snow. The woman's left hand was frantically grabbing air where her right arm should have been, her chest shuddering in spasm. Suddenly her body arched, then collapsed. She was dead.

"Shit! Shit! Shit!" It was Salvini, standing up, his boot kicking the road's shoulder, ice splinters flying into Reese, who was dusting the snow off his knee pads. A foul odor filled the air.

"They want equality," Aussie said, having checked all her pockets and reloading the P-90's transparent mag. "They've got it."

Aussie turned to Sal. "Minox the silly bitch for possible ID and put her amid the debris. A PITAP might think she's part of the helo's wreckage." PITAP was slang for pain in the ass passerby. "We've got to go down the road and check out the fucking truck." He paused. "You got it together, Sal?" It was a myth that the hard men never minded killing a woman. It was a taboo too deeply ingrained in the American psyche. "Sal?"

"What?"

"Well, you've got the fucking Minox. Or can't you hold it steady?"

"I can hold it fucking steady."

"Then do it," Aussie said, chambering a round, "and let's go."

Sal push-clicked the Bic-sized camera, then, helping Reese, dragged her body over by what looked like a half-buried spoke, probably a segment from the Pave Low's steering rotor. By now Aussie had inspected the tube above the French lettering on the

Arctic Cat and discovered that it was indeed a plastic-covered map case that he'd seen, and walked east down the road, on point, as if nothing behind him had ever happened.

"He's a hard bastard," Reese commented.

"Aren't we all?" Sal said. "Besides, the Pave's pilot was a friend of his."

Already angry because of what had happened, including the fact that with his SAT cell phone now gone he had only his short-range intercom mike to contact Sal and Reese, Aussie found that the acrid smoke from the smoldering remnants irritated his nose, a distraction a man on point couldn't afford. It was possible that some of the fumes were coming from the vehicles out of sight down the road, beyond the snowdrift the satpix had shown was about a quarter mile away. There, Aussie guessed, the drivers of the waiting vehicles were no doubt keeping their engines running to stay warm in the intense mountain cold. He rolled his balaclava up over his ears, not wanting to muffle any oncoming noise, and concentrated on the task at hand, trying not to think about what had brought down the Jolly Green Giant and killed the three men aboard her.

"These two machines are still okay," Reese called out. "Why not ride down?"

"Yeah," Aussie said. "That's a good idea. Let every fucker within ten miles know we're coming."

"Grumpy prick!" Reese commented.

"He and Michaels were close buddies in the Gulf," Sal said. "Besides, he has a point. About the noise." Sal pointed to the two dead snowmobilers. "Might be more of these bastards around."

Sixty miles to the southeast, beneath the edge of the blizzard, David Brentwood, Choir Williams, and the two other members of Team Bravo had emerged into the cold, sunlit air north of Ellensburg and already had their targets in sight. The two black roofs were plainly visible in the line of ten vehicles approaching them from the east less than a half mile away. The trucks' high cabins towered above the vehicles before and after them, sun glinting on their tall cabin exhausts, one of which was spewing coal-black smoke into the frigid, pristine air. One of the trucks, Brentwood saw, was a pale blue, the other beige, making its container trailer more difficult to see against the snow-covered landscape, both trucks having shown up as gray on Freeman's black and white satpix.

The two-foot-square by six-foot-long "box" Choir Williams had quickly assembled from black plastic "flats" bore the cautionary "shamrock"—as the three-leafed "radioactive" logo was referred to in the business—on all its six surfaces. Lightly dusted with snow, it lay in the middle of the road. A yellow police tape had been placed around it and was flapping vigorously in the wind, a black puncture strip uncoiled across the road twenty feet in front of it. Brentwood and Williams held their HK MP-5K submachine guns close to the chest in a no-nonsense intimidating stance, fingers on the trigger guard. Art Wright and Joe White had taken up positions with their AK-47s in the snow-covered woods either side of the road. Brentwood, releasing his grip on the Heckler & Koch, fixed the lead vehicle, an old green '99 Grand Cherokee, in his binoculars. The sun's glare, despite the binoculars' filter, made it impossible to see how many people were in the four-by-four. Three vehicles behind the Cherokee were the two trucks, much closer together than the satpix had shown. But of course since then, Brentwood reasoned, the weather in the foothills had cleared, allowing the vehicles to travel closer together. Bravo's plan was to KISS—"keep it simple, stupid"—especially given the fact that even if only half were militia, they would be clearly outnumbered and outgunned. What made Brentwood suspicious was that the Grand Cherokee and the other three vehicles in front of the two trucks hadn't increased speed despite the weather having cleared in the foothills.

"It is odd," Williams agreed, his breath like short puffs of smoke in the clear, subzero air.

CHAPTER TEN

HEADING INLAND TO Portland from Bill Reid's place in Astoria, Larry was at the wheel of the rented Ford Taurus as they entered the bone-aching dampness of Clatsop State Forest along the less used 202. "What gets me," he said, recalling the mantelpiece photograph of Gloria Bernardi and shaking his head in amusement, "is that her number and address were in Billy's book all the time."

"Yeah," Dan growled. "Well, how'd we know he'd put her name in with his boss's?"

"What're you complaining for?" Larry said. "You had some fun."

"I'm not complaining," Dan replied. "It's a hoot." He was watching the side mirror. "You think she'll know where Hall is?"

"She's his girlfriend, isn't she? Going to marry him?"

There was a long pause as the rain-sodden woods flitted by, the snow having failed to materialize south of the Washington-Oregon border.

"You check everything?" Larry asked.

"No," Dan said. "Left my prints everywhere. Had a shit right in the kitchen so they can analyze it—see what I had for breakfast."

"I didn't see you wipe anything down in the living room."

"That's because there was nothing I touched. 'Cept him."

"How about the kitchen?" Larry asked.

"I used Baggies, for chrissake. What's the matter with you? How about your cigarettes?"

"The Gauloises? I tossed them out."

"I didn't see you."

"I tossed them out."

"How come you only smoke *them* when we're on a job—instead of Rothman's?"

"So if anybody finds a Gauloise there's no connection. Foreign bran—" He jammed on the brakes. A deer flashed in front of them and was gone in the forest. He saw a sign that read REST AREA AHEAD. "That'll do."

"What are you, nuts? It's a picnic area."

"Picnics in this weather?"

Dan shrugged sullenly.

"All right, where, then? We haven't got all day."

"Next river," Dan said. "Don't worry, I'll do it if you're all upset."

"You should have left the dog alone," Larry said.

"Fuck the dog. He'd've brought the neighbors out with all his barking."

"She," Larry said tendentiously. "The dog was a *she*, not a he."

"Since when are you the great animal lover? Eat hamburger, don't you?"

Larry lit up a Rothman's and accelerated out of the rest area, tires spitting up gravel.

Waiting for situation reports from Alfa and Bravo, General Freeman, at Scattle's mission control, was telling Frank Hall and the other standby, former Green Beret Ron Shear, to rest up, should they be needed, when he noticed the e-mail icon flashing on his computer. It was a message from a body armor manufacturer explaining why the general hadn't received collar-high Kevlar vests. "Temporarily out of stock, sorry."

"Sorry doesn't cut it," Freeman told the screen, proceeding to type out an order on-line for sixteen-pound Interceptor high collar body armor. Made of the new KM2 weave, the Interceptor vest was a full nine and a half pounds lighter than standard issue, capable of stopping not only 9mm handgun rounds but, with the addition of boron carbide inserts, M-16 rifle and machine gun fire as well. Freeman requested eleven units.

"Ten units, General," Frank corrected him. "Four each for Alfa and Bravo, two for Shear and me."

"Eleven," the general insisted.

It wasn't until that moment that Frank realized the general was anticipating going into action himself if necessary.

"What's the matter?" Freeman growled, seeing his surprise. "Think I'm past it?"

Past it? It was the very phrase Brownlee had used when talking about the general. "No—no, sir, not at all," Frank said, but there was enough hesitancy in his reply to fuel the general's anger.

"Suppose all you boys think I'm good for is sitting on my ass in front of this damn computer?" Before Frank could respond, Freeman added, "You know what it is to fly a Tornado in combat?"

Oh mercy, Frank thought, not the story of the Tornado pilot again.

"There was this Brit," Freeman began. "Son of a bitch was fifty-nine. Goddamn grandfather. Flew against Saddam—so low, to evade Iraqi radar, the mechanics said it looked as if the belly of his plane had been sandblasted. One hiccup, just one tiny thermal, would have driven him into the ground."

Frank knew he had to convince Freeman he didn't think he was over the hill—and quickly—or else he and Shear were never going to get the sleep the general wanted them to get. Instead they'd be regaled ad nauseum with accounts of how men who were thought to be "past it" had astonished their contemporaries, preeminent among them the retired nuclear sub captain. This "senior" citizen, while not as legendary as Freeman, had visited the boat school at Groton, Connecticut, got a young sub trainee to lie on top of him, and did twenty push-ups. Then the sub captain lay on the trainee and told *him* to do twenty push-ups. The kid couldn't move, the sub commander receiving—as Freeman never tired of telling anyone who would listen, or who couldn't escape—"a standing ovation."

"Hell, General," Frank said. "You've kept yourself fit. If

we have to go into those mountains and help out, I'd want you to lead." Freeman's ego, like that of his hero, Patton, could always be stroked by flattery.

"Me too, General," Shear put in. Known for his retiring nature, the former Green Beret had, as usual, just been sitting there, taking it all in, until he sensed the general's alarm at the mere implication that he was "past it." Shear was thinking of his dad—fifty-eight, about Freeman's age, an active, brilliant engineer—called in one day, Christmas 1999, to be exact, and told he was being "let go." Shear had seen what it had done to his father. "You're in great shape, sir."

"That's more like it!" Freeman boomed, another e-mail coming in, the Kevlar manufacturer confirming that eleven units of Specialty Defense Systems Interceptor armor had been located and were being FedExed.

He turned to Shear, who was in what the general described as a goddamn crocodile yawn. "Didn't I tell you and Frank to grab some shut-eye? Might need you later on."

It was to be the understatement of his career.

In Portland, Gloria Bernardi, sitting alone in the bay window of her Raleigh Hills apartment, was on a slow burn, half frightened, half furious about Frank, the storm-laden sky moving south from Mount St. Helen's offering no respite from her mood. She wondered when he would call again, and tried to ponder the imponderables behind his brief message on her machine that he would call later. All packed, and dressed in the clingy white Lycra blouse and jeans ensemble he liked so much, ready for their long-promised holiday in the Sierras and sunnier climes, she was now seriously considering whether she and Frank could go on like this. Frank could be called out at any time of day or night in any weather to salvage some ship or other, often of Panamanian registration, usually rust buckets that should never have been allowed out of port anyway. No wonder they sank. They deserved to.

She felt guilty about thinking that; no ship "deserved" to go down with the loss of life it so often entailed. But she was tired, damn it, tired of the unpredictability of their lives. What if they were to have children? Both had talked about it, both wanted them, but she didn't want to be another "sailor's wife" left behind for weeks on end as the sole parent, not knowing and, as now, not *allowed* to know, what Frank was doing. Oh, she knew that some women could handle it; she'd met some of them, mostly submariners' and current SEALs' wives, who preferred not to know the dangers their men were involved with. But she wanted to be an equal partner in everything, including the risks, yet how could she if so much of the time Frank was to be called off on hush-hush jobs that excluded her from so much of his life?

She couldn't sit still, and the more she thought about it, the more irate she became. She paced around the apartment, catching her reflection in the mirrored bedroom door, surprised at how grumpy she looked. She remembered Frank once giving her the old line about being beautiful when she was angry. "How can I possibly look beautiful?" she had shot back.

"I mean your body," he'd said. "You stand up so straight, like a dancer ready to go on. Shows off your figure." It had ended in a long, wonderfully dreamy session of lovemaking, without hurry and anxiety, devoid of all tensions except for those of passionate intensity. Now, slumping down in her recliner, tossing her hair back and closing her eyes, she tried to recall their intimacy, but she was too mad. Instead she was thinking of what she'd say when he finally deigned to call. She'd phoned Bill Reid. His message machine had kicked in and she'd asked him to call her asap.

There was a knock on the door. She started excitedly, got up and walked quickly to it, not bothering to check the peephole, unslipping the chain, fully expecting to see Frank standing there.

There was no one. Then she heard the rattle of keys in the next door up the hallway, which smelled faintly of stale smoke and disinfectant. It was Mrs. Price, an elderly widow given to a love of cats, though allowed only one in the apartment—and disposed to doing little favors for her neighbors, though often they were more intrusive than helpful.

"Mail, dear," Mrs. Price said, smiling back at Gloria and waving a large envelope, her long, orange cardigan looking more like a coat on her diminutive figure. It really was true, Gloria thought, that as people got older they actually did shrink. She knew the reasons from her training in biology, how disks in the spine wore down and so forth, but to actually see it was another thing. Would she end up like Mrs. Price, alone with an animal? Some of the poor old dears were outlived by their pets.

"The envelope, dear," Mrs. Price said. "It was too big for the postman to put it in your box, so I brought it up for you."

Gloria took the envelope from her, thanked her, and closed the door. She didn't bother with the chain lock, instead frowning at her reflection in the hall mirror. Being grumpy, Frank often said, would make you age before your time, and, quoting George Orwell, he'd told her, "Everyone has the face they deserve at fifty." She glanced around at the two cases she'd packed for the vacation and knew she had to make a decision. Either stay in the apartment, mope and feel sorry for herself, or go out and do something. The envelope clinched it. It was from a publisher's clearinghouse telling her that they were very sorry but they would have to drop her from the mailing list "and quite frankly, Ms. Bernardoo, we don't understand your reluctance to take advantage . . . *you,* Gloria Bernardoo, might have to forfeit the TEN MILLION dollars to SOMEONE ELSE!"

"Well," she said aloud, "when you can spell my last name right I'll take the ten million." Hastily she put on her big, down-filled, royal-blue overcoat and matching cap, grabbed her purse and threw the envelope in the trash can

"There's a river." Dan checked the rearview mirror; no traffic in sight. "So what are you going to do when we get Hall?" he asked. "If you're so upset about a dog?"

"Hall's not a dog. There'll be no problem."

"Man, you're weird."

Larry turned his head sharply, eyes bright in anger.

"It's okay," Dan said, conciliatory. "Just joking, right?"

"*I'm* weird!" Larry said. "You were the one with the funnel and Drano, and *I'm* weird? Listen—"

"Okay," Dan said quickly, "forget it. Sorry—okay?"

Larry turned back, looking out his side of the car at the misty blueness and deep gloom beneath the towering stands of spruce and pine. "It's these goddamn trees," he said, stopping the car. "Spooky."

"Don't worry about it," Dan said, dragging himself out from the passenger side. "Outta shape. Too many fucking jelly doughnuts."

"How long before we reach Portland?" Larry asked. "Haven't seen a signpost for miles."

"Half an hour maybe. Not that long if you give me a hand."

Larry looked ahead at the long black road dampened by mist. "Yes . . ." he said distractedly, but didn't move.

"I'll do the dog. You do the sore-ass," said Dan. He pulled out two packets of Glad garbage bags—extra strength.

CHAPTER ELEVEN

TWO HUNDRED MILES to the north, Aussie Lewis glimpsed a faint yellow light winking through the howling blizzard, then another. They marked the site where the snowdrift's height had overwhelmed the snowplows' capacity near Berne east of the seven-mile-long Cascade Tunnel, which ran beneath Big Chief and Cowboy mountains. Aussie raised his hand, giving Sal and Reese the signal to break their straight line down the highway, and while he continued ahead, Sal and Reese fell off to the left and right. Aussie momentarily removed his left hand from the P-90, cupping one of the grenades on his load vest lest the pin ice up.

He could see the four yellow lights blinking, and behind them, the huge snowdrift, at least twenty feet high. From somewhere beyond it he could hear the faint hum of unseen engines, which struck him as odd, given his expectation that such a high drift of snow would have completely absorbed the noise of the four vehicles that had shown up on the satpix. Perhaps the line had grown, due to vehicles whose Seattle-bound drivers hadn't yet heard the road was closed—the mountains having scrambled radio signals.

Thirty yards from the snowdrift, Aussie veered sharply left to negotiate its base into the surrounding forest. Within a minute or so one of the four yellow lights off to his right had disappeared from view, and now, what a short while before had been nothing more than a hum became a steady throbbing sound, the deep, pulsating noise punctuated by a throaty, stop-go roar. He figured the source was a front-end loader from the railway station at Berne a mile or so to the east attacking the drift from the other side. Then he, Sal, and Reese heard the angry growl of more snowmobiles coming their way. Aussie elected to use his walkie-talkie's throat mike. A hand signal would have been more secure, as no radio scanner could pick it up, but a hand signal might not be seen by Sal and Reese in this thickly wooded area beyond the road where the snowdrift had petered out. "Let 'em pass," he said quickly, and took cover in a copse of pine. He hoped the snowmobilers, who might simply be sledheads out for a fun afternoon from Berne, wouldn't see their footprints, which would soon be covered by the blizzard.

Aussie heard a gale of laughter, and saw a bright red Ski-Doo momentarily airborne, clearing a wind lip of snow at the end of the drift's apron. He lost sight of it momentarily, only to see it reappear thirty feet to his right, skirting a jumble of moguls then leaning hard into the drift, deliberately side-hilling, the machine at an acute angle to the hill. The maneuver was accompanied by more whoops of joy, and two other machines—one bright orange, the other royal-blue. From their maneuvers in the deep powder, Aussie could tell they were equipped with forty-inch-long, deeply lugged tracks, and their adjustable ski stance was set narrowly, no more than thirty-seven inches apart, for better side-hilling.

For a moment Aussie suspected they were friends of the two he, Sal, and Reese had just confronted, and was ready to open up on them, but then decided they were just a few of the droves of sledheads that come out at the first signs of deep snow. Taking his finger off the trigger, he recalled how once in Kosovo, when his SEAL team was patrolling Serbian territory, his point man—Choir or Reese, he couldn't remember— had almost opened up on a group of children playing. And so, conscious of the civilians up ahead waiting for snow removal, Aussie whispered in his mike, "Reese, nonlethal in the tube."

"Roger," came the confirmation in Aussie's earpiece. Reese unloaded the H.E. grenade from his M-16's tube and instead slipped in a bean-bag round. It gave them an option if a PITAP got in the way. The bean bag wouldn't kill anyone, except if it was a head shot, but its thump would stun without causing permanent injury.

Another loud "Whoopee" rang through the trees, this time from the third, blue machine, its rider in a wildly contrasting psychedelic-pink snowsuit. The snowmobile hit a dip, the machine skewing sideways and rolling, tossing its rider. "Can't handle it, Joey?"

The distraction caused Reese to trip on a hidden bough, Sal's quiet voice, from thirty feet, in his ear, "Can't handle it, Ree?" followed by a soft chuckle.

Aussie heard the exchange, and it didn't amuse him. SpecWarriors, "severe winter"-trained warriors, didn't trip. Christ, you spent hours learning how to make an approach in deep snow—could've been a goddamned mine. Fact was, they might all be in top physical condition and scoring top marks on the firing range, but like anyone else who'd been off the job a few months, they'd been off the edge, and the only way to keep on the edge was to stay on it.

The whine of the snowmobiles was fading in the blizzard, and up ahead Aussie could see a string of headlights, longer than previously indicated by the satpix—four vehicles, one pair a sharp bluish-white, probably a European make.

As usual, Freeman had left the two teams' cover stories to the initiative of Alfa and Bravo leaders, depending on exactly what they found. The general was renowned for letting his men-on-the-spot change their tactics as local conditions dictated. As Patton had advised, "Give your men room for initiative and they will astound you."

Aussie's approach was KISS itself—he and his two comrades, balaclavas pulled down against the severe cold, were a police SWAT team looking for escapees from the federal pen in Walla Walla. They would have had to inspect every vehicle. No one would ask for ID from anyone carrying a shotgun, an M-16, or P-90, and if they did, he'd tell them to get out of the vehicle or he'd shoot the crap out of their engine.

A front-end loader was attacking the snow pile with gusto, swiveling remarkably quickly for its size and dropping its load into a truck whose tray swayed precariously under the sudden thump of compacted snow. Other dump trucks waited in line, and the air, despite the blizzard's unrelenting assault, reeked of the fumes.

The front-end loader's operator braked, his machine's multitoothed mouth dipping like some prehistoric monster agape at the interruption, its operator having spotted Aussie emerging from the trees to the right of him.

Aussie waved. "How ya doin'?"

The operator said nothing, staring down at the P-90.

"Police," Aussie announced loudly over the diesel's roar.

The man took off his noise muffs. "What?"

Aussie heard a door shut down the line and saw someone walking away from the line of trucks in that studied, awkward way people do when they're not wearing waterproof footgear, heading off over the railway tracks on the southern side of the road into the trees.

"Maybe," came Sal's voice, "he's going for a leak."

"You find out," Aussie told him. "Reese, I'll take the first six vehicles, you check the ones behind them. Approach from the rear."

"Roger," came the quiet response.

"Police," Aussie repeated to the operator. "Looking for those escapees from—"

"Never heard about 'em!" the operator shouted. "Sure as shit aren't with me!"

"We're going to check the vehicles," Aussie told him.

The operator touched his hard hat in a perfunctory salute. "You betcha!" The front-end loader lowered its jaws, biting hard again into the white hill.

From Sacred Heart to Sheriff Hyson's empty cruiser, the plea of the earlier hysterical woman to speak to "someone in authority" had gone unheeded until it was passed on by the Wills Creek police dispatcher to NSA, then to the Western White House and by aide Brownlee to Freeman.

"Are we on scrambler?" the general asked.

"We are," Brownlee assured him.

"What's the message?"

"A woman lab technician from Rone says she thought she heard one of her fellow technicians telling her colleague, Dr. Healy, to activate the alarm."

Freeman was nonplussed. "Well, it didn't do much good, did it? The militias got the damn Rone, didn't they?"

"No," Brownlee said. "I mean yes, they got the computer, but the woman, the lab technician, wasn't talking about a general burglar alarm for the building but one set inside the computer. She says it sends out a beep."

"A locator signal?" the general said.

"So I gather."

"Why in hell weren't we told about this before?"

"Woman was out of it apparently, traumatized by the militia attack, et cetera. Half whacked on tranquilizers."

Without bothering to cup his hand over the phone, Freeman turned to Hall and Shear. "There's a locator beeper in the computer." He then asked Brownlee what the beeper's frequency was.

"She doesn't know," Brownlee replied. "All she can tell us is it was installed by the scientists as a safety pre—"

"For chrissake!" Freeman bellowed. "You don't know the

frequency and you don't even know if anyone had time to activate it?"

"No, but it's possible this Dr. Healy got to it before he was grabbed."

"Possible," Freeman repeated skeptically. "But not certain?"

Before Brownlee could answer, the general had put down the phone and, given the urgency of the situation, violated one of the SpecWarriors' holiest commandments by breaking radio silence.

"Alfa Bird, this is Mission Control. Come in."

No response, only a hiss of static.

He tried once more. Nothing.

"Bravo Bird, this is Mission Control. Come in."

More mountain static, then, coming through it, the pilot's voice. "Mission Control, this is Bravo Bird."

"Mission Control to Bravo Bird. Activate your Victor Fox Sierra." This was the Pave's variable frequency scanner. "I say again, activate Victor Fox Sierra for possible computer locator beep in your area. Notify Bravo team immediate. I say again . . ."

Twenty-three seconds later David Brentwood heard the information from the Bravo pilot via his SAT phone. He was also told that Team Bravo should take no action against the two "black top" trucks approaching on the southern route until the helo's radar operator had scanned the most likely frequency bands to see if the stolen computer was aboard either truck.

David Brentwood was unfazed, the general's request making perfect sense to a Spec Op warrior—namely, *never* to intervene in a situation unless deemed absolutely necessary. "Choir!"

"Yo?"

"Collapse the box."

Choir did so briskly, the "Wright Brothers" assisting him in removing the police tape. Within two minutes they heard the approach of the Pave, its subdued roar creating a furious wind of corn snow all but obscuring the chopper, peppering the four commandos beneath it, the snow crystals stinging their faces and sounding like hail on their Kevlar vests.

In another minute it pulled away, most drivers in the line of traffic heading past Ellensburg into the mountains understandably mystified as to what was going on. Except for the elderly woman, Nora Cleine, behind the wheel of a Chevy Tahoe four-by-four at the remaining vehicles.

"Militia," Nora told her twin sister. "Maneuvers. They're everywhere up here in the Northwest."

"I didn't know they had helicopters."

"Lordy, Liz'beth, don't you read anything?"

"What? I—" Truth was, Elizabeth couldn't keep up with half the magazines to which Nora subscribed.

"Back in 'ninety-six," Nora said impatiently, "*U.S. News & World Report* had a big piece on military surplus. Fella in the Midwest bought eighty-eight—I remember that, eighty-eight—Cobra helicopter fuselages. Another fella in Montana put rockets and machine guns on his Cobra—told investigators he went out shootin' coyotes with 'em." Nora saw the look of incredulity on her sister's face. "I'm not making this up, Liz'beth. You can go back and see the report yourself, 1996, *U.S. News &*—"

The horn blast behind her, a jeep, startled Elizabeth—again. "I wish they'd stop that," she told Nora anxiously. "Frightens the life out of me."

"Pay no mind," Nora said. "Assholes. I'm not speedin' on this ice for no one—too damn dangerous. An' I can't pull off anywhere. No room. They don't like it, they can lump it."

The horn blasted again.

"Screw you," Nora said, Elizabeth appalled by her twin's language.

Suddenly, the jeep's engine surged. The vehicle pulled alongside, its outside wheels crashing into the road's shoulder, tilting the jeep at a dangerous angle, forcing Nora to edge into the road's shoulder on her side. Elizabeth was petrified as she heard icy lumps scraping the Tahoe's passenger side. "Uh-oh—" She glimpsed the angry face of the jeep's passenger screaming at Nora, his middle finger clearly visible.

"Crazy!" Nora said, fighting to keep control, half expecting others in the line behind her to follow the jeep, but, happily, none did.

"Road rage," Elizabeth opined.

"You don't say!" Nora said.

CHAPTER TWELVE

"FOOL!" LUCKY MCBRIDE said, his snowmobile idling as he looked down at Al Barnes' body, the dead militiaman's corpse already stiff and blue. Barnes had been told to recon, and that was all—not get in a goddamn firefight. McBride pointed out the two bullet-riddled snowmobiles to his two companions. "You don't take on Special Forces until you know exactly how many and their positions."

"Jesus!" It was Brock, on the third snowmobile, the tanker's gunner, viewing the smoking wreckage of the helo and surrounding forest with renewed alarm. "Maybe they're still here."

"They've gone," McBride said.

"How do you know?"

"Use your eyes," McBride said sharply, still recovering from the shock of seeing Barnes. "No footprints," he told Brock. "They're gone."

"Oh shit—no!" He had discovered Barnes's companion, her face frozen in a grotesque expression of pain, edging on hysterical laughter. "Bastards!"

"Maybe the feds shot first?" Neilson, McBride's other comrade suggested.

"Doesn't matter," McBride responded. "Our two people are dead."

Brock continued looking about, seeing shapes through the falling snow that weren't there.

"Hope it was worth it," Neilson said.

McBride was silent, clenched jaw belying his usually calm disposition. "The pricks'll pay for this."

"We should bury them," Brock said, indicating the two bodies.

"No," McBride told him. "Let's head back."

A chill passed through Brock. "Christ—the feds probably saw us."

"Jesus, Brock," McBride said. "Why d'you think I had you and Neilson side-hilling, yelling like a coupla spaced-out sledheads?"

"Then the feds must be near Berne by now?"

Brock was a fine gunner, but sometimes he was slower than a wet week. "Well, hell, Brock, where would *you* be? Sitting here amid the wreckage?"

Neilson, as if seizing the initiative, had already U-turned his blue Ski-Doo, gunning the engine. Even so, he waited for McBride—Lucky McBride—to take the lead.

It had taken Bravo's Pave Low just over six minutes to get a hiccup on the scanner's oscilloscope, the beep coming in at 330 megahertz from the *second* truck, the cream-colored Mack semi, four vehicles behind the Chevy Tahoe. The pilot radioed the information down to Brentwood. The Bravo team leader immediately decided that there was no point in trying to use the spiked belt to halt the whole line. Besides, the Mack's driver, seeing any roadblock, would no doubt turn around and flee south, and what then? Bravo couldn't use the helo to give chase and rake it with the .50, the whole point being to retrieve the computer intact. No, he advised Freeman, though he could not reach Aussie Lewis, this would have to be a quick, straight-out ambush. "We'll go straight for the second truck." Even so, he asked himself, how many of the surrounding vehicles were riding shotgun?

* * *

"Well," Freeman told Frank and Ron Shear, "at least now we know the damn thing isn't on Lewis's route, but where the hell is he?" Neither Frank nor Shear spoke, their silence confirming what Freeman already suspected, that no contact with either the helo or Lewis suggested a fatal crash, everyone either dead or so badly injured they couldn't communicate with MC.

His boots crunching the crust-covered snow, Brentwood, his Heckler & Koch leading, closed on the cream-colored Mack. Choir, on the left flank, protected his back by watching the vehicles in front, while the Wright Brothers emerged from the maelstrom of the Pave's downblast to the rear of the truck, both their AK-47s off safety.

Aussie Lewis, still walking point in the blizzard over sixty miles to the north, realized that the truck he'd seen in his satpix line had gone, Sal noting, "Its tire tracks are faint, but you can see where he backed up and made a U-turn."

"Where the fuck to?"

"Dunno, Aussie. Maybe he got tired of waiting. Went back to have a coffee in Berne. He'd only be burnin' up gas waiting here for the highway guys to—"

"Aussie!" It was Reese, his voice sounding cracked in Aussie's earpiece.

"What is it?"

"There's no one in the other vehicles."

Aussie remembered hearing the sound of a door slam and seeing someone heading off the road into the woods—maybe to have a piss. But where the hell were the other drivers? And passengers—if there were any? What the fuck was—

"Aussie, you hear me?"

"Yeah yeah. I'm thinking."

"Out!" Brentwood ordered, shouting over the howl of the Pave's three engines. He had the Mack's door open, his submachine gun's front sight on the driver's chest. The cabin was full of cigarette smoke.

The driver, cigarette dangling from his mouth, turned white. "Yeah yeah, okay." He shoved the stick into neutral, jerked up the hand brake, and got out of the cab, the cigarette still dangling. "Whatever you say."

"Hands on the truck, spread your legs," Brentwood ordered.

The man hesitated. "My hands'll freeze. Stick to the metal. Need my gloves."

Brentwood nodded. The man reached in and snatched the gloves. Brentwood frisked him quickly. Thoroughly. "Open the back."

"Gotta release it from inside—the door."

"All right!" Brentwood said, feeling stupid. "Hurry it up."

The driver slipped on the icy step in his eagerness, cursed, and flipped the semi's rear door lever. "Now I can open it."

"Do it."

"You betcha." He'd tossed away the cigarette. As the two of them walked toward the rear, Brentwood glanced over his shoulder at Choir, then forward at the Wright Brothers who were now allowing the three vehicles—a four-by-four, a van, and Nora's Chevy Tahoe—in front of the Mack to drive on.

As the truck's driver pushed up hard on the rippled aluminum door, the first thing Brentwood saw was a wall of two-foot-square boxes.

"Unload them," he instructed the driver. "Enough so I can see behind."

"That's all there is," the driver said. "Boxes."

"What's in them?"

"Computers," the frightened driver told him. "Laptops."

"Laptops?"

"Yeah."

Brentwood was puzzled. It was the second time in as many minutes that he felt stupid, and he didn't like it. Or maybe he hadn't been so stupid after all? Maybe the militia, despite Freeman's assertion to the contrary, *had* disassembled the Rone and boxed it? "Open one of them," he ordered the driver, then had him open several more. Brentwood recalled the pictures of the Rone's motherboards. There was no way the contents of these boxes comprised a disassembled Rone. The driver was telling the truth. The Mack was full of laptops—IBM, Dell, Toshiba, and others—which explained the "black" warm roof to Brentwood, but not the beeper that the Pave Low had detected and which, such locators being no bigger than a cigarette pack, could have been secreted anywhere in the scores of boxes packed inside the Mack's huge interior.

"What's going on?" the driver asked, having to repeat himself above the Pave's noise.

Brentwood lowered his HK 9mm. "You tell me."

But it was clear that the driver, as Aussie would have said, knew "sweet f.a." Either that, Brentwood decided, or the man should have been an actor. He could actually smell the man's fear, a sour rush of body odor in the otherwise odorless air.

"Where are you taking this load?" Brentwood asked him.

"Seattle."

"From Spokane?"

"Yeah. Why?"

"Show me your manifest?"

"It's in the cabin."

"Go get it," Brentwood told him, instructing Choir via throat mike, "Watch the driver. He's getting some papers from the cabin."

"Roger," came Choir's calm, professional voice. "Should we check the black-top up front? The Kenworth?"

"Great minds think alike," Brentwood told the Welshman. "I'll do it. You stay here." Next, he ordered one of the Wright Brothers to go back with him to the other truck.

It too was full of temperature-sensitive computer parts and laptops, which, like those in the Mack, were being kept warm by a Peltier solid state unit.

"You guys use a beeper?" he asked the driver of the Kenworth, who was more frightened than the first.

"You mean a burglar alarm?"

"No, a beeper."

"Oh yeah," the driver said, trying desperately to be helpful. "You mean like when you leave your keys in the ignition?"

Brentwood's usual good humor had deserted him and he gave the man a long, hard look. "You have anything to do with the militia?"

"No, sir!"

SpecWar warriors stayed alive on their instinct, and Brentwood's told him that neither of the drivers was lying. Besides which, nothing he'd seen had even slightly resembled the pictures of the Rone's motherboards. "Sorry to have bothered you," he told the drivers, then ordered his three companions to board the Pave Low, and the pilot to catch up with the three vehicles that had been allowed to go ahead of the two detained trucks. There was a faint possibility, Brentwood told Choir and the Wright Brothers, that one of these vehicles had been gutted, including the passenger's front seat and even part of the floor/engine interface, in order to accommodate the Rone, the latter's frame removed.

But when the Bravo team descended in the Pave Low, the helo blowing snow over the vehicles of the terrified motorists, including Nora and her sister, there was nothing in their vehicles that resembled anything like a computer, let alone the big Rone prototype.

"Return to base," Freeman ordered Brentwood. "You've been suckered, goddammit!"

The general's outburst woke Frank from his catnap. Freeman turned to the wall map of Washington State. He stabbed his finger at Highway 20, the northern Cascades highway that had been closed for days and which they'd automatically disregarded as a possibility. "Frank, you know Washington State best. If you wanted to check to see whether anything got through on Highway 20, where would you go? Burlington?"

"But twenty's closed solid, General, and—"

"Where would you *go*?" Freeman demanded brusquely.

"Well, not Burlington—too many overpasses and interchanges. I'd go to Sedro Woolley."

"I'd like you and Ronnie to grab a rental, go up and check anyway. Do you mind?"

"No," Frank lied, glancing over at Ron Shear, who was in the middle of another crocodile yawn.

CHAPTER THIRTEEN

AUSSIE LEWIS WAS wishing he had his SAT cell when he discovered that the "black top" in his satpix's line of vehicles had vanished. The best he could do was run to the hamlet of Berne, hopefully to contact Freeman from there.

From where he was, near the junction of the highway and the Cascade Tunnel rail line, it was about a mile and a quarter to Berne. Running on the road—and this was where keeping in A-1 condition paid off—Aussie found the storm's cold wind invigorating, though it still seared his throat after passing through the filter of his balaclava. The adrenaline rush of the race for the Rone created in him the kind of high he hadn't experienced since Freeman had called on him to help run down a psychotic militiaman in Arizona's Canyon del Muerte. He could hear Sal about twenty feet behind him, Reese already up ahead with orders from Lewis to find out whether the missing truck had been seen by anyone at the Burlington-Northern station. Aussie, in the athletic high he was experiencing, his stride even, his breathing perfectly in sync, had to remind himself to stay alert for any surprises on the periphery. He needn't have worried. Dead ahead there was a warm, yellow glow in the blizzard's bluish light, a Norwest gas station-cum-café, the dark hulks of parked semis dwarfing it, and a cluster of tarpaulin-covered snowmobiles about twenty feet from the gas island.

The best way to enter anywhere, anytime, he knew, was to go in with absolute authority. It invariably held everyone in thrall for a few seconds. Whether or not they believed you were who you said you were didn't matter. You could flash a baseball card at them and they wouldn't contest your claim, not when they suddenly saw a fit, black-clad commando with P-90 and sidearm. The moment he burst out of the howling storm into the café, the noise hitting him along with the push of warm air, and he saw that the place was packed, he realized there was no mystery to the four vehicles up by the snowdrift being vacant. Rather than waiting hours for the front-end loader to clear the road, everyone had opted to be inside, warm and watching *Who Wants to Be a Millionaire?*

"SWAT team, folks!" he announced. "We're looking for escapees from the federal penitentiary at Walla Walla. Figure they might be in a container truck that was up at the slide. Anyone see it come back this way?"

Lewis saw the short-order cook, a thin, pasty-faced man with salt and pepper hair, poke his head through the service bay as Sal entered.

"Hey!" the cook shouted, his grease-stained chef's hat askew. "What the hell are you doin', bustin'—"

"I told you," Aussie said. "We're SWAT!"

"Don't give a squat who you guys are. Women and kids in here. And where's your ID?"

It was the first time it had ever happened. Aussie ignored him, turning to the dumbstruck clientele, seeing a woman desperately trying to hush her two-year-old, pulling him roughly into her booth.

"Any of you in the four vehicles by the snowdrift," Aussie said. "Do you know where the container went?"

The short-order cook was on the phone. Gutsy little bastard, Aussie thought. Not that it mattered. Lewis knew that he, Sal, and Reese would be long gone by the time anyone could reach them.

One of the customers, sitting in a booth, a nerdy looking type with a young wife and two kids, nervously put up his hand. "I saw the truck back up a ways and turn 'round. Heading back to Wenatchee, I guess."

"When?" Aussie inquired.

The man shrugged. "Twenty minutes, maybe half an hour."

Reese's voice, a little out of wind, was crackling in Lewis's ear, the static no doubt from all the electrical appliances in the café, plus the gas pumps. "Stationmaster said he saw three container trucks."

"When?"

"Last hour or so," Reese answered crackily.

Aussie left the café, his earpiece losing Reese's static. Well at least if the trucks were heading back toward Wenatchee, they weren't heading for the coast. "Did the rail guy say when it would reach Wenatchee?"

Reese's voice was remarkably clear, despite the howling of the wind. "They're not heading for Wenatchee," he told Aussie. "They're going to Seattle. Railway tunnel's free."

"Shit!" Aussie's brain was racing, his eyes peering through the blizzard southward across from the gas station. From the satpix, he remembered that the rail line was about two hundred yards from the gas station at this point, but in this weather it might as well have been two hundred miles. He pushed the balaclava high above his ears, but still couldn't hear anything except the wailing of the storm. "The train still here?" he asked Reese.

"Gone, ten minutes ago."

"Shit!" Stay calm, for chrissake, he told himself. You're a pro. He was looking at his watch. "Ask the rail guy how long the tunnel is and the maximum speed allowed."

He could hear Reese's question and the station master replying, "Tunnel's 'bout eight miles long. Maximum speed allowed is twenty-five, but in weather like this, with Jordans down, it's about ten miles an hour, even before it reaches the tunnel."

"What the fuck are Jordans?" Aussie demanded.

Reese was obviously very close to the stationmaster, letting the latter talk straight into his throat mike. "Jordan spreader wings. Snowplows. Have to clear the tracks before the tunnel."

"So how long will it take to get through the tunnel?" Aussie asked. "Twenty, twenty-five minutes?"

"No," the stationmaster said. "Longer'n that. See, the train itself is about a hundred cars. A mile long. In this weather it'd take, oh, 'bout half an hour at least."

"And that container you loaded would have gone on last, right?"

"No, the caboose last, then the—"

"Yeah, right." Pedantic bastard. "Bravo Three?" Aussie said, his voice nearly blowing the stationmaster's head off.

"Yeah, boss?" came Reese's response.

"They must have a—" Jesus, he couldn't think of the name. "You know, the vehicle they use to inspect the tracks?"

"A speeder." It was the stationmaster's voice.

"Yeah, that's it. Reese?"

"I'm here."

"Grab the fucker and go after the caboose. Tell the guard to stop the train. Just in case you can't reach him, I'll try for some insurance at the other end."

"Roger that," Reese said.

Aussie saw Sal coming out of the café. He was holding two cell phones.

"Atta boy," Aussie said. "Hope they didn't mind."

"They did." Sal patted his shotgun's stock. "I persuaded them. Should've got one for Reese."

"Wouldn't work in the tunnel," Aussie said abruptly. "Come with me."

When he reached the parked snowmobiles, he hastily removed one of the snow tarps that, though held down against the wind by hooked bungee cords, was billowing furiously in the gusts. He was lucky with the first one, or so he thought, a Polaris RMK 800, the key in the ignition slot. Most sledheads, he knew, didn't bother keeping their key with them. Lose the damn thing in the wilderness and you'd die of hypothermia before you found it again. But on trying to start it, he found the battery wouldn't respond. "Damn! A DieHard," one of the new batteries that could be deactivated by an owner's remote.

He jerked the covers off two more, one a Ski-Doo without a DieHard. "You warm up this one," he told Sal. "And call the general, tell him what's going on. And cover me if possible." "If possible" meant that while Aussie was leaving the Ski-Doo for Sal, he was still looking for something more powerful on which to travel back himself, to try to reach the other end of the tunnel beyond the Stevens Pass ski area in time.

Whipping off another tarpaulin that had been carelessly thrown over the front of the Ski-Doo, snow still blowing in beneath its visor, Lewis discovered what he told Sal was a "bobby dazzler," Australian for "top of the line, state-of-the-art, hunky-dory." It was a four-stroke 110-horsepower 950cc Redline with calibrated fuel injection. "And tell the general we're in hock for thirteen grand."

Plus the millions for the Pave Low, Sal thought.

"Keep up with me if you can, Sal!" Aussie shouted, shoving the bungee cords into his jacket. "I'm gonna do a fucking sight better than ten miles an hour on this beauty. Follow my tracks if you lose my light. First stop, Stevens ski area—maintenance shed. Remember it?"

"No."

"Then follow my tracks," Aussie riposted, and he was off, racing, back to the foot of the high snowdrift at over fifty miles per hour, a string of red dots, taillights from the four waiting vehicles near the roadblock, guiding him like tarmac beacons in the blizzard. Swinging hard right by the flashing yellows of the highway department's trucks and front-end loader, into the trail through the trees, he slowed to forty, then thirty, miles per hour. It put him on a collision course with Lucky McBride and his two comrades, no less than a quarter mile away on their way back to Berne, neither the militiamen nor Aussie and Sal aware of the other's approach because of the row made by their respective machines.

* * *

General Freeman was now on his "rolling" analogue/ digital cell, calling Aussie after Sal had made contact with his "borrowed" phone. Aussie didn't hear the ring above the Redline's four cylinders, but felt the digital phone, which he'd set on vibration mode in his load vest. Holding one of the handlebars, fishing for the cell, he almost lost control. "Alfa One to Mission—"

"Alfa One, this is Mission Control. Am routing Bravo's Pave from southern to you for pickup. ETA twenty minutes. You need anything?"

"Luck," Aussie replied, signing off. Twenty minutes would be too late.

The snowmobile he saw dead ahead was less than fifty yards away, closing fast. Its driver waved, Lewis returning the courtesy, the two machines' combined roar vibrating nearby boughs, snow plopping down like confectioner's sugar as they sped past one another, the other two militiamen following in suit.

In another two minutes, whereas it had taken him twenty on foot, Aussie, the wind hard on his face, was on the M-shaped section of highway on the westernmost side of the drift. Visibility was no more than twenty feet, the road rushing at him as he gunned the 950cc engine to seventy-five miles an hour. He side-hilled the high snowplow wall around the big curve near the Stevens Pass ski area. He sped past a hut, all but buried in snow off to his immediate left, then attacked the snowplow wall at about a thirty-degree angle, he and the Redline momentarily airborne, his butt high off the saddle, legs braced like a jockey's for the impact. He hit, felt the pinion seat smack him hard in the back, and let go of the handlebars—no point going "a over tit" with the machine. He disappeared into the powder, felt the P-90's stock jab into his gut, and heard the Redline's engine die. He was back up, covered in snow, his left side pushing hard against the snowmobile's right while he simultaneously grabbed its handlebars. He pressed the starter, the Redline roaring back to life, its engine spitting ice and fumes in his face. He twisted the throttle hard and was now heading up the second of the four ski runs he could discern through the curtain of falling snow. He bypassed the maintenance shed, headed straight for the red school-bus-sized grooming machine.

He pulled the Redline up in front of the groomer. Its Perspex door slid open, and a splotchy-faced youth with a ring through one nostril glared at him. "Hey, what the hell you think you're doing?"

Aussie had drawn his HK 9mm handgun. "Turn it off!"

The youth did so.

"Unhitch your propane tanks, and hurry!"

The kid had the dual, quick release ten-gallon tanks out of their cradle in less than three minutes.

"Put 'em on back of the snowmobile," Aussie told him, tossing him the two bungee cords.

As the youth strapped them on, curiosity momentarily overcame his fear. "Can I ask what you're going to do with these?"

"You certainly may," Aussie said, and he was gone, swinging back down the hill onto the road, racing against the clock. He figured he had eleven minutes before the first of the four giant diesel engines exited the eight-mile-long tunnel—if Reese hadn't already reached the caboose and stopped the train.

The putt-putting sound of the "speeder" the railway used to inspect its tracks was completely swallowed up in the Cascade Tunnel, one of the world's longest. It was ten minutes into the tunnel before Reese could see the diffuse glow of the caboose. Inside the car, the guard was probably relaxing, enjoying a coffee, reading the funnies, Proust, or whatever it was caboose jockeys did. One thing Reese knew for sure—it was a different world from being on a damned speeder in temperatures well below zero.

It took Reese, the ex-SEAL, only another two minutes to reach the caboose, the front of his speeder, he guessed, doing about thirty miles an hour faster. He braked then, slowing until the speeder bumped into the caboose's rear. One hand on the caboose's handrail, the other holding the M-16/23 combo, Reese jumped aboard the car's narrow platform.

There was a flash of light. The caboose's door opened, a shout—"Terrorist!"—then came the pop of a handgun, its bullet passing his cheek and a nauseating pain shooting up from his groin. Instinctively, Reese cupped his genitals from further attack. He fired the nonlethal weapon and his opponent stumbled. But the man managed to bring down a club of some sort on his head, and Reese fell from the train, glimpsing the oncoming speeder, hearing a cry—was it his?—its sound lost to the feral roar of the train.

Several miles beyond, driving the Redline off the road up the southern slope of the five-thousand-foot-high Windy Mountain to the right of the tunnel's exit, Aussie heard a piercing whistle, the train's warning to any wildlife on the tracks ahead. Stopping partway up the mountainside that rose menacingly above the treeline, Aussie, keeping the Redline's engine running, dumped one of the propane tanks into the snow. He worked quickly with the ball of C4 plastique, which he now held in his bare hands near the snowmobile's engine to make the C4 more pliable. He molded it from what had been a frozen lump into two six-inch-long sausages, one of which he flattened over the top of the tank. His hands were now so cold he fumbled momentarily as he extracted the two five-minute, time-delay pencil initiators from his load vest. Sticking one of the pencils into the sausage of plastique, he crushed the protruding end between his index and second fingers, thus breaking the acid-filled glass ampoule inside. The released acid would dissolve the "restrainer," a thin wire holding back the firing pin, in five minutes. The released striker would then hit the percussion cap, setting off the fuse.

With the Redline on full throttle again, he raced down through a line of fir trees to an open area a hundred yards below, and, shouting above the blizzard en route, he informed Sal what he was doing and to wait for him down on the road.

The snow, however, was deeper than he'd expected. He glanced at his watch as he stuck a pencil into the sausage of

C4 attached to the second propane tank, and saw that he had only a minute to spare before the first tank, a hundred yards above him, would blow. Hopping quickly on the Redliner, he gunned it to get clear. Fifty yards away, it coughed and died. He pressed the starter again. A cough, a sudden jerk forward, then nothing. He brushed the snow off the gauges. Out of gas. Jesus Christ. Lewis, you dumb bastard! he told himself, and was off the machine and running. No steady, deep-breathing, finding-your-pace run this time, as on the road to Berne. Now it was a sprint, if it could be called that, back along the shallow trench gouged out by the snowmobile, to get clear. He fell, throat mike and earpiece clogged with snow.

Sal, unable to contact Aussie by intercom, saw him trying to run in the chest-deep powder, and realized Aussie's machine must have packed it in. When the tanks exploded—two enormous blue flashes, simultaneously reflected and refracted by billions of snow crystals in the gigantic powder cloud—the ensuing sound was like that of a train. But it wasn't the train coming out of the tunnel, it was millions of tons of snow hurtling down in Aussie's man-made avalanche toward the railway tracks a quarter mile beyond the tunnel's exit. For a second Sal lost sight of Aussie in the roiling clouds of smoke-like snow.

A boiling whiteness enveloped Aussie, then a grayness closing to black, his body tumbling, the voice of a mountain warfare instructor from long ago screaming obscenities at him, telling him how random sieving in the guts of an avalanche, contrary to all logic, spews larger, heavy lumps of co-agulated snow up to the surface. It meant that the larger the area he could make with his body, rather than curling into the intuitively protective fetal position, the better his chances of survival. Even so, he knew that once the violent "clothes dryer" effect stopped, he must instantly bring his hands up to cover his face to prevent an ice mask forming. If he didn't, his air supply would be cut off in the primeval darkness, the loose, airy snow of moments before now compressed into tons of concrete-thick ice. He blacked out, came to still tumbling, fighting to stay calm but unable to breathe, snow turning to ice in his nostrils.

Stay calm, stay calm, stay fucking calm!

Sal glimpsed him once more, a black speck on the edge of the powder cloud, then lost him again, the avalanche's main stream funneling through the treeline at over eighty miles an hour.

In Zurich the air was cold too, but it was a clear, cloudless day as Herr Reinhard Klaus, the immaculately dressed head of SRP, Swiss Rhine Petrochemicals, walked by the lake with a stride worthy of a mercenary, owing no allegiance to anyone but himself. On Zurich's Bahnhofstrasse he was recognized as the undisputed king of the vast petrochemical conglomerate, which he had inherited from his late father. SRP's arms, some said tentacles, spread throughout the world, amassing such wealth that half a dozen national budgets from Paris to Pretoria could not be written without taking SRP's reaction into account. For years Klaus's corporation had ranked among the top four in Europe, along with Unilever, Phillips, and Royal Dutch Shell. But no longer. He was now on top and intended to stay there. To the world's public he was little known, for his pleasure lay not in being among the rich and famous, or infamous—these terms were purely relative to Klaus—but in wielding awesome financial power and in making other people miserable.

For Klaus, most of humanity were but timid flotsam to be brushed aside, to be used or discarded by capital. It was a view that the "nouveau riche" in Moscow understood and respected, President Putin's "reforms" notwithstanding. In Zurich the socialist opposition to the right-of-center government had sought for years to gain deeper admittance to Zurich's secretly numbered accounts. But in one of the great ironies of the millennium, the socialist candidates got no help from Moscow, not even from the old Communists like General Kornon. The Russian general and Swiss financier might have come from diametrically opposed political poles, but realpolitik, naked power—whether measured in Eurodollars, U.S. dollars, or Swiss francs—was their common currency.

In the détente—or was it chaos?—that had followed Gorbachev and Yeltsin, Swiss Rhine Petrochemicals had become one of Moscow's best customers in the purchase of raw materials from Russia's far east, and, in return, Moscow was an ever ready buyer of Western industrial secrets from Swiss Rhine Petrochemicals, providing the sale of such information was not contrary to SRP's own interests. There were, of course, many firms engaged, as fronts, in Russian intelligence's pursuit of Western technology, as in the case of Mitsubishi's sale of ultrasecret American Stealth submarine technology. But while Swiss Rhine Petrochemicals had certainly not been the only one involved with the Russians in the search for lucrative industrial know-how, it had also been a main player in the search for the lucrative deep-sea minerals known as sea gold.

It was in the race for these rich marine deposits that Klaus had first come into contact with the man he most despised and, though he admitted it to no one, the man he secretly feared: the American oceanographer, Hall. Frank Hall was in no sense a financial competitor—indeed, in Klaus's view, Hall's piddling little firm, Oregon Oceanics, though technologically on the cutting edge of submersible technology, couldn't even pay for the toilet paper Swiss Rhine Petrochemicals used in a day. But what had galled Klaus, a blueblood descended from one of the noblest houses in Europe, was the American commoner's persistence and success in finding several sea gold locations of enormous future potential, once land stocks of vital strategic minerals were either exhausted or politically inaccessible.

Normally the epitome of composure, Klaus increased his stride as he neared the bridge over the Limmat River. The very thought of Hall being up against him once more irritated what Klaus's private physician was pleased to call the "delicate sensitivity" of the Swiss financier's "gastric mucosa." This ulcer, the only one he'd had in his life, had lain dormant until erupting earlier this morning when his operatives in

America revealed that Hall, though they'd temporarily lost his track, was apparently involved, albeit unofficially, in trying to prevent the Rone from being smuggled out of the U.S.

Crossing the bridge, Klaus could smell the rich, sweet odor of freshly brewed coffee coming from the Bauschantzli restaurant. He resisted the temptation to indulge—it would only irritate his ulcer. Besides, it was now ten past five, and the two freelancers would be calling him again at five-thirty, hopefully with Hall's whereabouts. Klaus knew his American nemesis was small fry in the international arena of high finance, but the Swiss billionaire also knew that once the oceanographer, an ex-SEAL, got the scent, he was like a bulldog. And, as he had so curtly told the American freelancers he'd hired, there was only one way to release a bulldog's grip.

With a Herculean effort Aussie managed to move his jaw slightly. His mouth opened, swallowing ice crystals and a smidgen of air. Mother of God, was he hallucinating or what—his cell phone was ringing.

It was Sal calling, providing a beep for Bravo's Pave to zero in on. In the strange quirk of physics, wherein a buried avalanche victim can clearly hear his would-be rescuers calling but they cannot hear the victim, even if he or she has space to yell, Aussie could hear the loud voice of Choir Williams over the thudding *wokka-wokka* of the helo's rotor blades above him and the roar of an approaching snowmobile. That sound was followed by sharp, crushed-ice scraping of an entrenching tool, one of the commando's lightweight shovels striking the hard-packed snow directly above him. The Ski-Doo's engine stopped. He heard Sal call, "Hold tight!" then Choir's voice, clearly audible, yelling at Brentwood, who was presumably still aboard the chopper, to "get the helo out of here—'fore it starts up another slide!"

For a moment, when Choir and Sal reached Aussie, Choir ripping off a glove, placing his hand against Aussie's face to melt the layer of ice, no one spoke. Choir and Sal were winded from the sudden violent effort of excavation and not knowing if he was alive.

As they hauled him from what had nearly been his icy tomb, Aussie, his chest heaving, hungrily gulping in the blizzard's fresh mountain air, asked, "What took you so long? Stop off for pussy?"

"No gratitude," the Welshman riposted. "A terrible man you are."

Sal threw a fistful of snow at him—"Prick!"—and left on the Ski-Doo.

Aussie was on his back, eyes closed. "Where the fuck's Sal going?"

"Down to the tunnel, boyo, with Brentwood and Art Wright, while your slide holds up the train. General wants them to meet up with Reese and have a look at that container car."

As they spoke there was a teeth-grating screeching noise rising up from the foot of the mountainside. It was the sound of steel on steel, the train's wheels in a frantic reverse throwing up a long line of tangerine-colored sparks that danced in the blizzard's blue light before the wheels finally gripped. The train stopped with only meters to spare before a towering wall of tree-spiked ice rubble that marked the edge of the avalanche, hoarfrost rising from it as if from some vast subterranean fire.

While watching the train, its back half still in the tunnel, Bravo Pave's copilot advised Brentwood, Art Wright, and Sal, who were advancing toward the tunnel, that given the sea of electrical systems on the train, especially those emanating from the four giant diesel-electric engines in tandem, the Pave's scanner would find it difficult, if not impossible, to get a fix on any computer locator that might have been planted in the container car.

As Brentwood, Art Wright, and Sal entered the black, horseshoe-shaped entrance of the eight-mile tunnel in which a half mile of railcars still lay hidden, the yellow string of lights that ran along the roof and in the safety alcoves of the sixteen-foot-high by fourteen-foot-wide tunnel went out. Presumably, one of the huge, ice-sheathed praying-mantis-like hydroelectric transmission towers had given way under the weight of a long, broad finger of ice and debris that, racing ahead, had broached the rail lines as far as Scenic Creek.

Having to rely solely on their Fritz-mounted helmet lights, two men on either side of the train, Team Bravo moved forward. They tried to discreetly contact Alfa Three's Reese. Last thing they wanted was their fellow SpecOp warrior opening fire on them, thinking they were militia who'd been riding shotgun on the train. There was no answer from Reese, and for a moment Brentwood had to confront the possibility that he was dead. Then they saw a bobbing bright light coming in their direction. Again Brentwood and his three comrades resisted the temptation to call out—in case it was militia. Instead the Bravo team kept advancing, confining their inquiry to their throat mikes, Brentwood saying quietly, "Bravo leader to Alfa Three—come in!"

Still no answer.

"Who are you?" came a booming voice.

Brentwood and Sal stepped smartly into the nearest alcove against the northern wall of the tunnel, the Wright Brothers doing the same on the other side.

"Bravo leader to team," Brentwood intoned in a clear, quiet voice. "Douse your lamps."

Now the only light was the other man's—how far away was difficult to estimate.

"We're police," Brentwood announced. The light went out. Brentwood had assumed it was the caboose guard, but now he wasn't so sure, and in any case he estimated it was still over a quarter mile until they reached the end of the train. He adjusted his throat mike, again speaking softly, calmly. "Bravo leader to team. Easy does it."

Whoever it was, the tunnel was a perfect place to spring a trap, and with Alfa's Pave going down, plus Michaels, Freeman had already lost four men, over a third of his force. The Bravo leader had no intention of adding to the casualties.

He estimated it would take them at least fifteen to twenty minutes to reach the caboose and container car, while moving as lightly as possible from tie to tie so as not to give their position away, pausing now and then to listen in the pitch-blackness to the "clacks" and "clicks" that they hoped were nothing more than the metallic contraction and expansion endemic to railway rolling stock. To seasoned SpecOp vets, the sound was eerily like someone in the process of a "lock and load." Brentwood felt a rush of frigid air in his face, followed by a tremendous crash, ice shrapnel cutting his face as a huge stalactite dropped from the roof.

"You okay?" one of the Wright Brothers whispered into his mike, his voice shot through with increasing static.

"Fine," Brentwood answered, for a moment thinking of his wife, family, and disability insurance, which had a "null and void" clause, should he participate in "acts of war, declared or undeclared." He had won the Medal of Honor and had been celebrated, despite his requests not to be. It was a liability, a standard against which all his subsequent actions were measured and would be until the moment he died. Now, his near miss with the ice shard only inches from his face, the metallic taste of blood in his mouth from the lacerations, the clicks and clacks of the train—like some living thing in the stygian darkness—and the submachine gun he had been within a nanosecond of firing, were all playing on his nerves.

There was a screech in the darkness, the sharp clang of steel on steel as the rail cars' bumpers rammed into one another. The tunnel resounded with squeals and thumps as each car in the mile-long train made its own jarring adjustment to the four locomotives that were backing up from the overhang of timber-loded rubble which, though the avalanche proper was over, had shifted dangerously in response to changes in humidity, temperature, and snow density. The whole lot threatened to collapse and bury the engines.

The impact of rail cars on each other, as well as producing an ear-punishing din, also shook loose hundreds of icicles which till now had been suspended from the rail cars. The falling icicles sounded like a glass skyscraper crashing all around them.

"Jesus Christ!" Sal was unable to contain his fright, a fact he knew he would pay for if Aussie got to hear of it. Still there was no sign of the end of the train, or for that matter, the end of the tunnel. A hard, slithery object, presumably one of the icicles, moved beneath his boots as an ungodly bellowing and stifled thundering of hooves erupted farther down the line, where livestock cars had been spooked by the fall of ice. Moments later the darkness was thick with the stench of ordure and urine, the smell temporarily overwhelming the tunnel's ventilation fans. And then Brentwood's earpiece crackled with static, his Pave's co-pilot, barely audible, informing him that the variable frequency scanner still hadn't been able to isolate a locator signal in the train's mess of electronic overlay.

Brentwood shook his head disdainfully as he approached what he knew from the stink must be the cattle car or cars. Hadn't the Pave Low crew "twigged" yet, as Aussie Lewis would have put it, to what was going on? The militia clearly didn't have a beeper locator in the stolen computer. They'd obviously taken it from the Rone and planted it on the truck at the roadblock at Ellensburg, to dummy Bravo into searching the Mack whose driver was clearly oblivious that his truck had been used both as a diversion and bait.

Adding to the other hazards of the tunnel, the persistent wailing of the blizzard outside, invading the darkness through the ventilation shafts, made it more difficult for Team Bravo to discern what was in store for them up ahead.

CHAPTER FOURTEEN

Portland

GLORIA HAD PARKED her Datsun by Lovejoy Plaza and walked down to the rectangular maze of sculptures through and over which water ran and cascaded in a lively chorus. Although it wasn't late, she was conspicuously alone in the pneumonic cold of the plaza, her royal-blue overcoat in striking contrast with the pervasive gray gloom that hung over the city, making it seem night instead of day. A mother with two young boys—they looked like twins—came into the plaza, the youngsters yelling and running ahead along the edges of the pools and fountains, dodging out of sight behind one of the falls. "Come out of there!" the mother shouted. "Jason!"

They took no notice, and Gloria, not for the first time, pondered the awesome responsibility of raising children, of marrying Frank, of having a family. Being in her early thirties, she knew it wasn't wise to wait too much longer if she was to have children. But seeing the woman standing there, tired and drawn—"It never ends," her mother had told her—the prospect seemed so enormous an undertaking even *with* Frank, that the thought of *her* being alone with kids when he was at sea, for God knew how long, oppressed her even more.

"Jason! Mark! Come here!" The woman, lugging her shopping bag, went after them, the boys laughing at her. "Don't you ever—" she began, but Gloria didn't hear the rest above a squeal of brakes as a car skidded to a stop.

Hands deep in her pockets, feeling acutely lonely, she was walking slowly toward the Keller fountain, only peripherally aware of a jogger, several secretaries coming out from their offices for a smoke despite the cold, and two men entering the plaza to her right. She lifted her head and, realizing she was no longer alone in the plaza, felt even lonelier, recalling her sudden terror—that something awful had happened to Frank. She went to a phone booth on the south side of the plaza and called Bill Reid in Astoria, collect. He should be back by now.

He wasn't.

"Great!" she said aloud. "That's just great." She left the phone booth and immediately sensed that someone was following her. She picked up her pace, and he did too.

"Got a quarter, miss? Need a quarter to call home." His breath would have started a brushfire. Relieved, she gave him a dollar and walked quickly back to her car, navigating past the puddles of rain.

"Gee, thanks, lady!" the wino called out, his voice lost to the noise of traffic and the onset of another shower.

Portland had repeatedly topped the list of cities in which Americans wanted to live, Gloria recalled. She knew it had many advantages, including a relatively low crime rate, if you could put up with all the rain. It seeped into your very bones, and she resolved that the moment she got back to the apartment she'd take a long, hot shower—no, a long, hot bath—after she checked for messages. Reaching the Datsun, she gasped—the left rear window had been smashed, the miscellaneous contents of the glove compartment, including her registration papers, strewn over the passenger seat.

Out in Raleigh Hills, Larry had parked the red Taurus two blocks away from the Vista Apartments. It took Dan only a second to spot the number. "There it is. G. Bernardi. Ten twenty-three." They walked back to the Taurus and waited until they saw a middle-aged woman walking toward the apartment, fishing in her handbag for her keys.

Larry followed her, casual as he began patting his pockets, and then stopped. "Darn it—where'd I put them?" The woman opened the door. "Ah, found 'em," he said triumphantly, jangling his car keys in one hand, holding the door open for Dan with the other.

"I do it all the time," the woman said, smiling.

"Think we're in for more rain," Larry said convivially, glancing back through the glass door.

"Tonight, they said," the woman remarked.

Larry started up the stairs, Dan hesitating for a moment by the elevator, then following. Once the fire door had closed behind them, their footsteps echoing in the stairwell, Dan asked Larry, "Why the hell we walking up nine floors?"

"Ten," Larry corrected him.

"Why the hell we walking up ten floors?"

"So she couldn't get a good fix on us in the elevator. Besides, give you a good chance to work off some of those doughnuts."

When Larry knocked on 1023, Dan behind him, still wheezing from the climb, Mrs. Price, from the apartment next door, stuck her head into the corridor like some surprised and exotic parrot, her face covered with a glistening white-brownish concoction.

"She's not in. Gone downtown. Can I take a message?"

"Uh—no," Larry said. "Uh—I'm her uncle."

"Don't say?" Mrs. Price said chirpily. Her hair was done up in curlers. "The one from Salem?" she asked gaily.

"No," Larry called out. "We're up from Texas. Surprise visit."

"Oh," Mrs. Price said. "Then you can leave a message with me if you like."

"Uh, no," Larry answered. "We'll call back."

"Okey dokey," Mrs. Price said. "I'll tell her you called."

"You do that. Thanks," Larry said. They walked back down the hall toward the elevator and didn't stop until they heard her door close, then turned around and walked back to Gloria Bernardi's apartment.

Larry took out a credit-card-size piece of thin metal, masking tape on one end for a better grip. As he slid it down the tiny space between the door and its frame, testing it, Dan stood nervously behind him.

"Got the cutters?" Larry asked softly.

"Yeah yeah," Dan answered quietly. "Let's get on with it."

The lock was easy. The apartment, very neat, smelled of floor polish and flowers. From the bay window that overlooked Raleigh Hills, the gray sky was thick, as if about to split open with rain and lightning.

"It's in here," Dan whispered, hoarsely beckoning Larry toward the bedroom.

"Right," Larry said. "Stay by the door."

Larry sat down on the bed gently in case any of the springs creaked, moved a mangy-looking teddy bear away from the middle, gave a quick thought to how nice it would be to have her in here—naked, boning her up against the headboard, the room awash with the strong aroma of wildflowers, a small, heart-shaped lavender sachet hanging from the mirror, a fading Polaroid of her and Hall at the beach stuck into the dresser mirror's chrome edging. Larry pressed the playback on her answering machine, a voice on the tape blasting into the room. Dan stepped inside the door. "Jesus!"

"It's all right," Larry hissed. "Get back to the door."

But Dan came farther into the bedroom, hissing in reply, "Old bitch next door coulda heard that."

Ignoring him, Larry turned down the volume so it was barely audible. A pinhead-size red light came on and the tone sounded. There was only one message—from some realtor asking her to ring back if she was interested in moving to an affordable "upscale" rental.

"So what now?" Dan asked. "Thought you said she'd know where he was?"

"Don't worry," Larry said. "He'll contact her." He smiled malevolently. "They're in *love*."

"Yeah, but when?"

"Soon."

"Yeah? What d'we do till then?"

"Wait."

"What's the address, ma'am?" the Portland police dispatcher asked Mrs. Price. "Yes, ma'am. I got it. Uh-huh, now

you just stay right where you are, Mrs. Price. Don't go out in
the hallway. Just sit tight and we'll send someone over. Yes?
What's that—yes, ma'am, right away."

CHAPTER FIFTEEN

SAL, TO BRENTWOOD'S right, closest to the rail cars,
stepped into something soft by the cattle car. He could hear
the steers, cows, whatever the hell they were, moving rest-
lessly about in the fetid semigloom. Sal, following the fright
of his near miss of falling ice farther back, received his
second fright upon realizing that, rather than standing ankle
deep in cattle dung, he was standing in the mangled remains of a corpse—cold, but not ice-cold to the touch. Recent. Odds were it was the caboose guard or Reese. About to
crouch down for a closer look, he was stayed by Brentwood's
right hand squeezing his shoulder. The Bravo leader's other
hand gripped the Heckler & Koch as he detected movement
farther up the track. He and Sal froze, resisting the temptation
to use their throat mikes, hoping that, amid the noises of
the blizzard, dripping ice, and the moaning of the cattle, the
Wright Brothers had also seen or heard whatever it was. For
a moment Sal wondered whether it could be a wild animal
wandering into the tunnel, attracted by the smell from the
cattle cars.

Again, training would pay off, the ex-SEALs masters of
what Freeman called the "frozen wait," the ability to be absolutely still, not for a moment or two but, as their forebears
had so often done in harm's way, for hours if necessary. Sal
strained to hear whether the Wright Brothers had continued

forward, but couldn't tell. The cattle, sensing something was up, shuffled nervously about. It put everybody on edge. And, now that the train had been shunted farther back from the avalanche's overhang, it would be another twenty minutes or more before they reached the caboose and the container car in front of it. The wrong move now, the noise of a boot shifting position on the gravel between the ties, anything, could unleash a devastating blue on blue. Brentwood's eyes were fixed on a bump by the rail tie nearest Sal that looked suspiciously like an upturned guard's cap.

In Zurich, Klaus's secretary was ushering in General Chang, commander of Nanjing's Military Region's 12th Army, and chairman of China's PLACE—People's Liberation Army Computer Enterprises—accompanied by a strikingly beautiful young woman whose split-leg emerald silk *qi pao* at once restrained her ample bosom and teasingly revealed a shapely leg.

"This is my secretary," General Chang told Klaus. "Miss Wu Ling."

Klaus smiled, but only slightly. Ten years before, he would no more have thought of dealing with the Chinese than of canceling his membership in the exclusive Bahnhofstrasse's Billionaires' Club. But these "little yellows," as he referred to all Orientals, had come a long way in the past ten years. At one time, Swiss Rhine Petrochemicals would normally have expected a Japanese firm to be the natural leaders in Asia, but nowadays it was the Chinese who, via their increasing contacts with the West, were coming to the forefront of the computer world. But neither SRP nor PLACE had managed to match America's expertise or sheer speed in computer technology, as exemplified first by Intel's Paragon and now the Rone.

"Herr Klaus," Chang said, extending his hand in greeting. "Great pleasure to see you."

Klaus nodded, withdrawing one hand from behind his back, not to shake hands but to indicate the hard leather chair directly in front of his desk. Chang was flustered; jet-lagged, he had momentarily forgotten that the great Klaus seldom shook hands, especially with the "little yellows." During a meeting with Japanese officials he was once challenged about his refusal to shake hands. The Swiss tycoon had unblinkingly responded that insofar as Swiss Rhine Petrochemicals pharmaceutical division was in the business of ridding the world of germs, he saw no reason to be "spreading" his own. A rude but adroit response.

"Have you any more information on your end of our American project?" Klaus asked Chang curtly if vaguely. Any office, including his own, despite frequent electronic detection sweeps, might be bugged.

"Ah," Chang responded, "the American project is a little behind, Herr Klaus. The, ah, weather is very horrible for construction on the next factory."

Klaus rose from his chair, walking over to the tinted slash windows. Turning his back on Chang, he gazed down toward the lake, at the multicolored Chinese lanterns winking vigorously in the stiff evening breeze that rustled the deserted outdoor garden of the Bauschantzli. He loved the dead smell of fall. "You are telling me you have fallen behind schedule?"

"It, ah, could be so viewed. Yes, I—"

"It *is* so viewed," Klaus said, his back still turned to the general. "And I do not wish it to be so viewed by our partners in this venture." As Chang well knew, "our partners" were the Russians under the control of General Kornon's Pacific Ocean Department, whose job was to transport the Rone out of the country once it arrived—if it did arrive—on the American West Coast. The arrangement, despite its Byzantine financial complexity, was at face a very simple one. The Russians had offered the vital "transport" for the Rone together with some "internal assistance"; the Chinese, their labor costs being the lowest of the tripartnership, would do the actual manufacturing of the chips. After that it would be a straight three-way split. SRP would have Europe, Canada, the U.K., the United States, and Australasia. China would have all of Asia, and the Russians would have the chip to use in everything from advanced industrial production to upgrading the fire control consoles on each of their nuclear submarines. But at the moment Klaus was testy because he hadn't yet received the expected phone call about Frank Hall from the two American freelancers in the Portland area.

"Are our other partners assisting?" Klaus asked. He meant the Russians.

"Not as yet," Chang answered nervously, adding, "I'm sure once the weather clears, Herr Klaus—"

"We cannot wait on the weather," Klaus said sharply, staring out at the darkening lake. "Our prime subcontractors are Americans, are they not?" He was referring now to the American militia who had actually stolen the Rone and whom he was careful to keep at arm's length.

"Yes, sir," the Chinese general answered, not yet sitting in the chair, still standing and trying to preempt any more of Klaus's sarcasm.

"Then surely," Klaus said, "if they are locals, they are used to the local conditions?" The Swiss financier turned slightly, his glower that of a headmaster upbraiding a recalcitrant schoolboy. Chang deeply resented Klaus's treatment of him, but the PLA's Computer Enterprises, while a giant in China, had serious problems with what economists were pleased to call "international liquidity." Cash. And Chang desperately needed Klaus's financial backing.

"Yes, they are local contractors," Chang conceded, "but this is very bad weather, Herr Klaus. This La Niña current has gone, how do you say—'bananas'—again in the American Northwest."

Klaus turned around. Chang's forehead was beaded in perspiration.

"Would you care for our competition in Tokyo to be ahead of us in production?"

"No, sir. But this La Niña current is worse than El Niño. All the newspapers are discussing it, how the weather has changed because—"

"La Niña, El Niño. We are in a race!" Klaus cut in, his tone

stentorian. "A race, General, does not wait for weather."
Chang averted his eyes from Klaus's stare. Losing face in front
of Wu Ling would be an impossibility in China, for there he
was a king. But again Chang restrained himself, knowing that
if PLACE was to tool up quickly enough to produce clones of
the Rone before the Americans or the Japanese, SRP's liquidity was vital.

"My advice to you, General," Klaus continued in his stentorian tone, "is to bear down on the American contractors. If
they don't work well in bad weather, we might need extra
labor. Our old friends from Berlin may be of assistance."
Chang knew that Klaus was referring now to old Stasi
"friends" from what used to be East Germany.

Chang managed a confident smile. "I will do as you suggest, of course."

With that, Klaus sat down, pulled out the drawer of his
Louis XIV desk, and made out the check, postdated, to
PLACE for "services rendered."

"When everything is secured," Klaus instructed, signing
the check with a flourish, "you will advise me immediately
by sending me a message that 'production is proceeding as
planned.' " It was very Swiss, Chang thought, prosaic and
understated, for it would mean that together, Swiss Rhine
Petrochemicals, PLA's Computer Enterprises, and the Soviet
military would, in the American phrase, "clean up."

As they left SRP headquarters, Wu Ling told Chang, "He
was very rude. He completely ignored me."

Chang ignored her, calculating his cut in American dollars.

General Kornon was feeling good after a dinner of phea-
sant and roasted winter vegetables at The Hub, one of the
most expensive restaurants that had popped up in Moscow
during Yeltsin's reign and which, despite its chic Western mo-
torcycle decor, catered to the most conservative senior officers of the Soviet armed forces. And it permitted smoking,
Havanas filling the air with the rich aroma of Cuban leaf.
Vanya was not with him, for even in such discreet surround-
ings Kornon was careful not to be seen with her. He was

under no illusion, however, that his aide, Colonel Ustenko, knew of his affair with the "backbreaker," since it was part of Ustenko's job to know where the general was at all times.

As was his habit after dinner, the general was engaged in an earnest game of chess with a lieutenant colonel who had been a subaltern of his before Kornon's two years of disgrace in the wastes of Ulan Ude. The latter was thought by some to be beautiful, in its own frozen way, but in Kornon's case the memory of the place was imbued with such bitterness toward those responsible for his internal exile that the very sound of the Siberian city's name turned his stomach. And so, when his cell phone rang and Ustenko told him that a cable, originating in Zurich, had reached him via Beijing and Ulan Ude, Kornon completely lost his concentration on the Machiavellian trap he'd been baiting with his rook. The more he tried to keep the implications of the move fixed in his mind, the more it eluded him.

"What does the cable say?" he snapped.

"That we're behind schedule, General. Our American friend has not outbid us but his entry on the Vancouver exchange is annoying." Kornon knew instantly Ustenko was talking about the American, Hall. "If he holds up the bidding," Ustenko continued, "our shipment of grain might be delayed."

Kornon lost all hope for the rook. The cable meant Hall was somehow interfering with the schedule, and that while he had not yet "outbid"—that is, sabotaged—the delivery of the Rone to the West Coast, his very presence demanded countermeasures.

"When is our bulk carrier due to sail?"

"This evening by the latest," Ustenko answered. "We could possibly extend this to tomorrow morning if there's a delay in loading the grain in Vancouver."

"No, a change in the departure time of any of our bulk carriers causes chaos right down the line. Besides," Kornon added irritably, "winter production schedules for bread here have already been set. We must keep to our shipping schedule."

"Check!" his opponent announced.

Kornon pretended not to hear. "Are you at the office?" he asked Ustenko.

"Yes, sir."

"I'll be right over," the general said, and rose from his chair. "Sorry, Colonel. Matter of state."

"Of course, General. I'm sure—"

"Another time, perhaps."

"Yes, General. I could mark a sheet and we could take up where we left off."

"Don't bother. We'll start the game anew."

The general strode away, the cloakroom attendant ready with his coat, its bold epaulets contrasting with the bright red collar tabs. "That's the answer," he muttered. "We'll start the game anew."

The attendant smiled. He didn't understand the general's comment, but he would have smiled for the devil himself. He wanted to do all he could to please old party VIPs. Kornon had once been an alternate member of the Politburo before Yeltsin had abolished it, but since Putin's ascendancy, the "old boys" were on their way back.

CHAPTER SIXTEEN

GLORIA INSERTED HER key entry card to the Vista Apartments underground garage, heard the reassuring hum of the motor and rattle of the chain as the door rose. She thought of it as a drawbridge sometimes, its mouth swallowing her like Jonah in the whale, in her case affording her refuge from the hostile world. She heard a siren wailing somewhere and immediately thought of Frank.

Walking along the soft, red-carpeted hallway, she saw patches in the shag that were a darker red, where, like her, someone had obviously just come in from the rain. Unraveling the long white angora scarf with one hand, she used the other to shake her apartment key loose from her clump of lab and university keys and unlocked her door. Suddenly someone grabbed her, yanked her in, shoving her hard up against the vestibule wall, thrusting her hands up, her legs apart.

"Miss Bernardi?"

"Who are—" She saw a badge. "Yes."

"Sorry, miss." The policeman holstered his gun, his shoulders dropping with release from the tension of the moment. Gloria was ashen, shaking. She gasped as another policeman in plainclothes emerged from the kitchen.

"I'm Officer Norse," said the policeman who'd slammed her against the wall. "This is Officer Dybikowski. We got a call that someone was burglarizing your apartment."

"My God!" Gloria said. "What—What did they take?"

"Nothing, far as I can see, miss," Norse said. "But it was a break-in all right." He turned and pointed to the severed safety chain. "Unless *you* jimmied the lock."

"No—I—my God!"

"Your neighbor, Mrs. Price, phoned it in. She heard a voice in your apartment. Said she thought you were out."

They walked her slowly through the whole apartment. Maybe something was missing, but as the policemen well knew, a victim's shock, most of all the violation of her privacy, might prevent her from noticing whether anything had been taken.

"You have any jewelry, ma'am?" Dybikowski asked.

"No. I don't think there's anything—" She went into the bedroom, glad she'd made the bed. Her teddy bear was closer to the pillows than she normally put him.

"You have any idea what they might have been after?" asked Dybikowski, a tanned man with deep furrows across his forehead and penetrating blue eyes. She thought of her hiding place, a thermos in a kitchen cupboard, but the cash, a hundred, was still there. Next they checked the bathroom, letting her lead the way. Oh no, she thought to herself, seeing a pair of panties and tatty panty hose draped over the curtain rail to dry, a hole in the panty hose running right up to the crotch, and the bath needed cleaning.

Dybikowski asked her to check her medicine cabinet. "Any missing drugs—medications?" She hesitated. Unlike the rest of the apartment, it was so messy—and she wondered whether they'd already seen the K-Y gel and box of condoms Frank kept at her place, and whatever else she'd crammed in lately because she simply didn't have enough time off to clean it up. She moved a few of the bottles around, trying surreptitiously to push the condoms farther back, out of sight. "Everything seems to be here."

They questioned her a little more, strictly routine, asking her what kind of work she did at the university.

"I assume you're single?" Dybikowski said.

"Engaged."

"Congratulations, miss," Norse said, smiling.

"Thank you," she replied shyly.

"He's not a cop, is he?" Norse asked.

"I beg your pardon?"

"He's not a cop, is he?"

"No." She managed a brief smile. "An oceanographer, actually."

"Uh-huh," Norse said.

There was a pause before Dybikowski asked, "Would you like Mrs. Price to come in? Keep you company for a while when we leave?"

"Leave?" She didn't want them to leave—they couldn't leave.

The phone rang and she started in fright.

A moment later her face lit up. "Frank? Where are you? What—" The sound of traffic on what she guessed was a rain-slicked freeway was thunderous in the background, his conversation segmented by the electrical noise of windshield wipers and heater on full blast, or maybe the cell's battery was dying. Or both.

"Sedro Woolley," she said, adding quickly, "I'm coming up." It was said in a tone that brooked no argument, especially when she told him her apartment had been broken into and she was "freaked" out of her mind at the thought of staying alone. "What hotel?" she asked. There was a pause. "All right, when you know the name, leave me a message at Portland International."

He agreed, but she heard the reluctance in his voice. She didn't care, and hung up. *Damn.* In her haste she'd forgotten to tell him about her car being burglarized.

"Weather report says it's pretty bad up there around Sedro Woolley," Dybikowski informed her. "And as for flying, I wouldn't be surprised if everything's stacked up from Portland until—"

"I don't care," she said. "I'm going."

Norse was watching her breathing fast in the white Lycra blouse. "We can give you a lift to the airport if you like?" he offered.

As she thanked Norse, Dybikowski was shaking his head. "I'll just grab a few things," she told them excitedly.

Norse was making eyes at her derriere in the tight jeans.

"For crying out loud," Dybikowski hissed at him. "You're a married man."

"Well," Norse answered, "doesn't matter where I get my appetite—long as I eat at home."

Coming out of the bedroom, clutching her purse and coat, Gloria went quickly to the kitchenette and took the hundred out of the thermos. "Emergency money," she explained.

Heading to the airport, Norse, glancing in the rearview mirror, could see her fiddling with something, then saw it was a small crucifix. It hadn't been there before—must have been hidden under her blouse.

"Afraid of flying?"

"Sort of."

He turned to look at her through the wire mesh. "Weather'll probably clear," he told her reassuringly.

Dybikowski said nothing.

* * *

Behind them, but not too close, the red Taurus followed. This time, Dan insisted on driving, putting the heater on Defrost but opening his window to flush out some of the stinking frog cigarette smoke. "Dunno how you smoke that shit."

Closer to the airport, Larry told him, "I'll get out, then you park."

The police cruiser was pulling up outside American Airlines.

"For God's sake, wake up, Ronnie!" Driving the rental, a Montana minivan, into the Sedro Woolley exit off the I-5, Frank saw the rain turn to sleet then to snow that was sweeping down through the Skagit River canyon from the northern Cascades.

"How big is this berg?" Shear asked Frank, more to show signs of life than from any real interest, the steady whine of the wipers continuing to make him sleepy.

"Not very big," Frank answered. "It's an old lumber town. Last stop before the mountains."

"We're gonna have to stop soon if this snow keeps up. No wonder the highway's closed."

"Seventeen feet deep at the four-thousand-foot level," Frank said.

"Man!" Ronnie said. "And it's still snowin'. No way the militia'll—"

"You're right," Frank cut in, pointing up ahead. A ROAD CLOSED sign was flashing. Frank drove past it, explaining to Ronnie, "I want to check out the ranger station."

"Fine with me," Ronnie said accommodatingly. "I'm just along for the ride."

"So I noticed," Frank said jocularly. "That what you did in the Green Berets, sleep all day?"

Rounding the next turn, they saw the dim outline of an orange truck with Washington State Highway markings growling toward them in low gear, its elbow-bent hydraulic arm in the back and grader blade in front dusted with snow.

Shear sat up abruptly, pulling his shotgun, a Mossberg twelve-gauge Cruiser, from Frank's hold-all and cradling it in his lap. Frank could see the truck had chains on, throwing up hunks of packed snow behind it. The sound of the clumped snow on the undersides of the fenders sounded like a popcorn maker as he powered down the window on Shear's passenger side.

The truck stopped about forty yards away, and so did Frank. Through the curtain of falling snow two heavily clad men in well-worn hard hats hopped out from the jump seat, one of them pulling his heavy lamb's wool collar up, both men's breath condensing like smoke in the icy air, both wearing equipment holsters on their hips.

"What do you think?" Shear asked.

"Don't know," Frank answered. "You watch the truck's cab, I'll keep an eye on these two bozos."

"I'd like to get closer with the Moss," Ronnie said, climbing back to the seat directly behind Frank.

"Got it," Frank acknowledged, powering down his driver's side window. He had one hand firmly on the wheel, the other gripping the Colt 9mm automatic, snow blowing in, melting on his shirt.

The two men were walking slowly toward them, looking up at the ice-laden power lines sagging between the transmission poles that ran parallel to the road.

"Could be legit," Shear proffered. "Linemen?"

"Absolutely," Frank replied.

CHAPTER SEVENTEEN

DAVID BRENTWOOD, CONVINCED that whatever had been moving up ahead was now gone, whispered into his mike, telling Sal and the Wright Brothers to proceed. The pale gray light from the eastern end of the tunnel was becoming brighter, reviving his hopes of reestablishing static-free communication with those outside, though the blizzard's wailing belied any improvement. Suddenly, the tunnel lights came on again, and ahead they could plainly see the caboose, and in front of it, a container car. Joe White covered the rear of the caboose, Art Wright and Sal going in fast through the front.

It was empty.

"Where's the guard?" White asked.

"Where's Reese?" Sal added, becoming increasingly uneasy about whose corpse it was back down the track.

"Check inside the container," Brentwood told them as he stood watch, forcing himself not to think about Reese, the guard, or anything else but the task at hand.

"A huge friggin' crate!" White exclaimed. "We've got it!"

"Pry it open then," Brentwood said, still watching the tunnel.

"Might be boobied?" Sal proffered.

"No," Brentwood said, sure now that he saw something moving down by the cattle trucks. "Militia's not going to booby-trap its billion-dollar prize. Use your K-blades to open it. Easy does it."

By now all four men had switched their helmet lamps back on, the tunnel lights a help but not bright enough.

"Sal?" Brentwood called.

"Here."

"You stand watch. I'm going back down a bit. Have a look-see."

"Movement?" Sal asked.

"Possibly. Soon as you get the crate open, call me." Heading back down the tracks, Brentwood heard a sharp snap behind him and a "Shit!" in his earpiece and knew what had happened—one of the SEALs' legendary K-bar knives had broken, trying to pry open what was evidently a very tightly sealed crate. He continued on down the tracks.

While Team Bravo were in the tunnel, General Douglas Freeman in Seattle had been debriefing Aussie Lewis via his rolling cell. The conversation wasn't pleasant. Aussie heard various euphemisms used in and out of the service to describe a superior's dissatisfaction with a soldier's or employee's performance, but all were inadequate descriptions for what General Freeman was dishing out to him.

"*Excuse* me?" Freeman thundered. "You ran out of *what*?"

"Gas," Aussie said, still recovering from being buried alive by the avalanche.

"I suppose," Freeman retorted, "you didn't think to look at the goddamn gauge?"

"It was covered with snow, General."

"I see. Difficult to brush off, was it?"

Dammit. Aussie hated sarcasm from anyone but himself. "I was in one hell of a hurry, General."

"Obviously. Too much of a hurry to observe fundamentals. A moron knows to look at the goddamn gauge."

Moron? If it hadn't been the general who'd handpicked him for Special Services, Aussie would've told him to shove it up his four-star ass. So "George C. Scott" was upset about losing over a third of his force. Who wasn't?

"And," Freeman added, "I had to divert Bravo's Pave into a full-blown mountain storm, risk the team and their helo's crew, to pull your ass out of a snowbank, when all you needed to do was look at the goddamn gauge!" A pause. "You all right?"

"Yes, sir."

"What's the story with Reese? Is he okay?"

"Don't know yet, General."

"Probably nothing in that container," Freeman said suddenly, having no way of knowing that even as he spoke, Team Bravo were attempting to open the crate they'd found inside.

"You sure about that, General?"

"No," Freeman conceded, "but I've been struck by the fact that you met no armed opposition."

"Jesus, General, two snowmobilers came and tried to kill—"

"In Berne," Freeman explained. "Militia load a container on a train and don't guard it?"

"We don't know that yet, General. Maybe they did, maybe Reese ran into trouble."

"It's possible," Freeman agreed. "Anyway, I've sent Hall and young Shear up to Sedro Woolley—western end of that northern route through the Cascades—just in case. See if anything did get through." Before Aussie could object that the highway was closed by snow, the general anticipated him. "Yes, I know it's been shut down for days, but maybe those bastards found a way over it."

"What do the satpix say?" Aussie challenged.

"No traffic," Freeman had to admit.

"Well then?" A touch of insubordination there. "Could be there is something in the container. And—" Aussie couldn't resist it. "—maybe you've sent Hall and Shear on a wild goose chase—sir."

"Tell me about the two militia on the snowmobiles." Aussie had to give it to the old man—quick on his feet, changing tack with you barely noticing it. "You told me," Freeman continued, "that one of 'em was a woman."

"Yes, sir, a—"

Freeman cut in, telling Aussie there was an "override" transmission coming in on his rolling cell, that he'd have to get back to him. Lewis guessed, correctly, that it was a call from Team Bravo in the tunnel.

When David Brentwood proceeded farther down the tracks to check for possible movement, his HK MP-5's safety off, he saw what Sal had inadvertently stepped in earlier before the tunnel lights had come back on. It was Reese, or rather, what remained of him.

"How'd it happen?" Freeman asked. "Accident or shot?"

Brentwood went down on one knee to examine the god-awful mess more closely. "Hard to tell, General."

"His weapon been fired?"

"Haven't found it yet. Seems like he was dragged quite a way. I'll have a look—" Brentwood heard a hiss of static on his line, then "Bravo Four to Bravo leader." It was Joe White, and Brentwood put the general on hold. "Bravo leader to Bravo Four. What've you got?"

"Nothing. Nada. Zilch. Fucking crate's empty!"

Brentwood told the general, and all Freeman said was, "Get your ass back here. Fast!"

"Yes, sir."

"All right," Freeman said, switching back to Aussie, telling him coolly but grimly that the container was empty, and asking, "Anything that might give us a clue where she's from?"

"Who?"

"The militia woman you killed, dammit," Freeman said. "Anything to indicate where she came from?"

"Nothing."

"No ID whatsoever?"

"Zippo."

"License plates?"

There was a long pause, no answer from Aussie.

"Plates on the snowmobiles?" Freeman said.

Jesus Christ. The old man's passion for the minutiae of every incident, as well as for grand strategy, was putting him on the defensive. Perhaps that was its only purpose. "I never noticed, General."

"What *did* you notice?"

Aussie thought quickly, determined not to be outmatched. "Some French lettering on the rear."

"Whose rear?"

Oh, very droll, Aussie thought. "No one's, General. Above the license plates and—"

"French *and* English?"

"Yes. Both languages."

"My God, Lewis, a bilingual sign! Why didn't you tell me this before?"

Aussie was puzzled. What was so goddamn important about bilingual lettering on the back of two snowmobiles?

"It's Canadian!" Freeman shouted. "French and English. Goddammit, our sons of bitches are hooked up with Canadian militia. They're taking it north across the border, *then* west. I'll call back." Before Aussie could say anything, Freeman had hung up and was calling Frank Hall to tell him about the bilingual sign. Hell, he'd seen it in a flash, only angry that he hadn't seen it earlier—Canada and the U.S., the *border* between friends, the most porous border in the world.

As yet another icy blast from the blizzard swept through the Montana's window, Frank Hall was watching the orange truck. He angled his .45 against the heater's side vent to keep his fingers from freezing up. Ron Shear saw the two men from the truck suddenly running pell-mell at the minivan, one of them pulling something from what Frank and Ronnie thought were linesmen's holsters.

"Go!" Shear shouted.

Frank took his foot off the brake and jammed it hard on the pedal, the Montana surging forward. One man dove off the dry shoulder into a powder-filled ditch. Frank saw the other one throwing whatever it was at the Montana.

"Grenade!" he yelled at Shear, jerking hard on the wheel with his right hand, the power steering bringing it about in a wider arc than he wanted. He squeezed two shots off, but the geometry of the turn, the slippery surface of the road, were wrong and he missed. Unhesitatingly he reversed, spun the van through a 180, the roar of Shear's shotgun blast momentarily deafening him, after which all he heard was ". . . into the woods!"

"What?" he bellowed at Shear while watching the truck.

"He ran into the woods. Missed him." The orange truck was howling in a frantic drunken reverse on the icy road, disappearing into the whiteness of the blizzard. Shear glimpsed what he had thought was a grenade lying on the road. It was a lineman's "butt-in" phone. "Get out of here!" he yelled.

Frank's cell phone was ringing. A projectile came hurtling through the window. There was a grunt of pain from Shear, and the sound of something rolling on the floor. It was an ice-encrusted pinecone. Frank, driving hard with one hand, the other holding the cell, glanced at the rearview mirror and saw blood streaming down Shear's face. "You okay, buddy?"

"Something in my eye—that bastard in the woods. Oh, shit!"

"Hall!" Frank barked into the phone.

It was General Freeman, an angry George C. Scott. "They're shipping it out of *Vancouver*, dammit—not Seattle! Bastards have blindsided us."

"How do you—"

"Never mind. I know. Get your ass up to the Vancouver docks *now*! You know the port, don't you?"

"Yes."

"Thank Christ for that. First break we've had. Take Shear with you—"

"He's hurt."

"I'll be okay," Shear said.

"You're bleeding like a stuck pig, Ronnie," he said. Then to Freeman: "I'll go alone."

"All right," Freeman said. "I've booked you into Hotel California, Gastown. Only hotel available—others are full up with a travel agents' convention or some damn thing."

Hall's GPS unit told him that from where he was, just west of Sedro Woolley, to Vancouver was a tad over a hundred miles, eight- to four-lane highway all the way. He knew it would take less than two hours to get there—less time than to get a chopper to him and penetrate all the bureaucratic "fly over" red tape. Besides, the less the Canadians knew, the better. The Canucks, except for allowing the U.S. President's Secret Service to carry weapons on a State visit, had an absolute rule against letting firearms into Canada.

It wasn't until he was almost back on the I-5 near Burlington, where he intended to drop Shear at a doctor's office, that he realized his cell's battery was fading. The ex–Green Beret's right eye was bloodied and swollen almost completely shut.

"How's the eye? Frank asked.

"Can't see a darn thing. Blurry as heck."

The thing that struck Hall was Ronnie's use of "darn" and heck"—still the politest commando he knew. Frank called

Portland airport emergency. His message left for Gloria at Portland International was, "Hotel California, Vancouver. Not Sedro Woolley. Repeat, not Sedro Woolley."

For a bowel-chilling moment it occurred to Frank and Shear that the highway truck wasn't a decoy, that it might have been carrying the Rone. When things calmed down, however, and they had time to think about it, they realized they were wrong—that the hydraulic arm had taken up the entire back of the truck and there was simply nowhere else the truck could have hidden the big Rone prototype.

"So it *was* just another sucker ploy?" Shear said, pressing a bunch of blood-clotted Kleenex hard against his right eye.

"Guess so," said Frank, "but right now I'd better get you to a doctor."

"Damn militia's got us on the run," Shear said.

Damn. It told Frank that Ronnie Shear was getting mad.

He wasn't the only one.

CHAPTER EIGHTEEN

DAN RECOGNIZED GLORIA Bernardi at once, though she was muffled by the royal-blue overcoat and cashmere scarf, because in Seaside he'd had lots of time to study her photo in detail, while Larry held the picture of her and the oceanographer right in front of Reid's nose and he'd been having fun with the Drano.

Now, Larry was reading a British tabloid he'd bought at the Portland airport's newsstand. The front page featured a blonde, a "floozy," as the British paper referred to her, sitting up, bare-breasted, snatching a bedsheet from a startled and naked senior citizen by her side, the tabloid's four-inch-print blaring, COUNT'S NEW GIRL!

"She booked a flight to Seattle," Larry said as Dan sat down, "then changed it to Vancouver."

Dan was watching her. She was unbuttoning her coat, tossing back her hair. More relaxed.

"I'd like to eat her," he said. "Get right into her. Know what I mean?"

Larry was concentrating on the tabloid's crossword. Most of it was easy, but four down—eleven letters—was a "sporting position," the clue, "Unbalanced. Off center."

"Center," he mused. "Sounds like English football. Soccer?" He turned the page upside down and peeked at the answer. "Silly mid-off," he grumbled. "What the hell is that?"

"I mean," Dan said, oblivious to Larry's question, "I'd like to suck her dry."

"You'll get your chance."

Slowing as he approached Blaine, the small township on the U.S. side of the border, Frank could see the big white Peace Arch between the two countries, the Stars and Stripes and the red Maple Leaf fluttering side by side, injecting the only dash of color in the otherwise gray and gloomy afternoon. He pulled over to the lane closest to the Canada building, where the customs officer, a sprightly young woman in her thirties, smiled at him. "Hello. Are you a Canadian citizen?"

"No, ma'am. American."

"Could I see your driver's license please?"

He smiled as he gave her the card.

"You carrying any firearms or alcohol, Mr. Hall?"

"No, ma'am." He was a SEAL, yet his heart was racing. Why was it that border officials always made you feel guilty? Maybe this time it was because he had the Colt 9mm and the pump action Mossberg twelve-gauge Cruiser stashed under the backseat. Plus, he knew that, like Brentwood and Aussie, if he failed to retrieve the Rone, he'd have to face the wrath of Freeman—never a pleasant thought.

"What's the purpose of your visit, Mr. Hall? Business or pleasure?"

"Business. I'm an oceanographer. We do a lot of work out of Vancouver."

"Who's 'we'?"

"My partner, Bill Reid. Oregon Oceanics."

"You have a work permit?"

"Yes, ma'am," he said, and pulled it from his wallet.

"Where will you be staying, Mr. Hall?"

"Hotel California in Gastown."

It was the first time she showed surprise. Though the California had been renovated, it was far from plush; but considering his disheveled appearance, he thought, she should not have looked surprised. "Tried to get in somewhere else," he explained, "but apparently there's some Northwest travel agents' convention going on in Vancouver. Can't get in anywhere else."

"This is a spur-of-the-moment visit, then?" she said. "You look like you're in a hurry." He was. Christ, if the militia hadn't loaded the Rone by now, they must be damn close to it.

"Ah, yeah," he replied, as patiently as his impatience would allow. "Our research ship, the *Petrel*, is tied up there. We have to do a pollution prevention study." If she pressed for details and called Vancouver docks, he was dead, because last he'd heard, *Petrel* was somewhere off the Alaskan Panhandle.

She handed him back the permit. "Have a nice day."

Heading the thirty miles north on Canada's 99, he was soon slipping past verdant fields that stretched out south of the Fraser River delta.

Despite the catnap he'd had in Seattle, he was tired, a troubling collage of snow, the downed Pave, and the orange truck passing through his mind. The van dipped and he was out of the rain, swallowed by the roar of the Massey Tunnel under the south arm of the Fraser River, the yellow line of roof lights speeding above him like tracer. Then he was out of the tunnel back in the rain. He pushed the radio button for AM. It was twenty after three, the forecast from CISL for "increasing rain and gale force winds in the Georgia Strait" between Vancouver and Vancouver Island, thirty miles to the west. Overhead there was the thunder of planes taking off from Vancouver International, Canadians heading south, like geese, for the winter.

Slowed by a long traffic jam that had begun shortly after the exit from the tunnel, Frank's fingers were drumming the steering wheel. "C'mon, c'mon." Glancing in the rearview, he could see the fishing fleet in Steveston, the ships' masts black lines scratched against the gray sky. Soon everyone was bumper-to-bumper, the sky darkening even more, thousands of ruby-red taillights stretching ahead like an endless red snake slithering toward Vancouver. On the news, the lead story was how American, Russian, and Chinese negotiators—though still some distance apart—were approaching a possible arms agreement in Geneva that would further reduce the number of American MX, Russian SS-20, and Chinese Long ICBMs. Hopes were high in Switzerland, but commentators were warning against excessive optimism, pointing out that any incident between the three countries could easily scuttle the delicate negotiations. After the news they played Johnny Cash singing "The City of New Orleans"—and Frank Hall never felt so far away from home. Fifteen miles in front of him, Grouse Mountain and its neighboring peaks disappeared in gunmetal cloud.

A while later, driving north down Vancouver's Main Street, Frank could see the gray city spread out before him. A glorious city in the sun, like Seattle, it was one of the most dismal in the rain, its grayness a nightmarish precursor, in his present mood, of the terrible grayness that would follow an enemy's super-computer-guided missile hit on America's Northwest, the awesome sub-launched ICBMs of the U.S. hidden in the forests only a few supersonic seconds away to the south.

He stopped at the red light at Main and Pender. Suddenly there was a different smell—no longer gasoline and rain sucked in by the minivan's heater, but odors that made every tastebud stand to attention. Nerves alert, his brain processed the sensation at twice the normal speed, this double exposure giving him a sense of déjà vu. Then the smells told him where he was: Chinatown.

Gaudy signs and lights were everywhere, enlivening the gray, the crowds dotted here and there by drunks and junkies straying up from Skid Road a few blocks farther east, where the railway tracks from the eastern seaboard four thousand miles away finally reached the Pacific at the Vancouver docks.

Exceeding the fifty kilometer speed limit, Frank swung the Montana left from Main onto Powell, to the California Hotel. Its odd, narrow triangular shape, once run-down, had been tarted up as a tourist attraction, though it still wasn't much to look at. It was located in Gastown, the part of the city's waterfront where modern brick cobblestone lent an ersatz old-worldliness to restaurants and jewelry and souvenir shops. In one of these, Bill Clinton had bought the infamous scarf he'd given Monica Lewinsky.

After he'd parked the van, shoved the Colt 9mm into the glove compartment, and registered, Frank asked for one of the few rooms in the California with a private bathroom, trying not to appear as hurried as he was. He gave the old woman, the hotel's sole clerk, a twenty to look after his bag, which contained the Mossberg, left a note for Gloria, then hurried quickly across Powell Street to the cyber café near the old fake steam-powered clock. A group of tourists sprouting umbrellas were huddled around it, one of them regarding him suspiciously. He'd forgotten his appearance, and the mirror of the café's window reminded him—his shirt wet from his run-in with the orange truck, his unshaven and bleary-eyed appearance emphasized by his rumpled, snow-stained khaki shirt and trousers. With no time to waste, he grabbed a coffee and sandwich to go, went to the nearest computer terminal, gave a teenager ten bucks to give up his spot, and clicked onto www.portofvancouver.com. There were six impending arrivals in the next twelve hours: four U.S. vessels, one Swedish, and one Italian. The two impending departures were the *Vasilliy Kolesnichenko*, a bulk wheat carrier, and the *Burkhanov*, a container ship berthed at Centerm 5.

Speeding into the container terminal's parking lot at the foot of Clark Drive, Frank barely missed one of the gate posts. The rain was pelting down so hard now it obscured the lines of freight bays, their yellow borders all but lost in the downpour. To his right he could dimly discern columns of unloaded factory-fresh Toyotas, but little more. The immediate problem for the militia's thieves, as he saw it, would have been to get by the inspection booths on lanes 4 to 8, above which a huge neon board informed all incoming truckers that their vehicles must stop for customs inspection before clearance receipts could be issued. Only then could they proceed, after which the enormous green Taylor lifts would close their jaws around each container, moving it to the various piers for loading aboard waiting vessels.

Racing up the stairs to the terminal's fourth floor observatory, he looked out on the docks and the big grain silos that fronted the rain-curtained slate of Burrard Inlet, and at a vessel tied up at Centerm 5, the berth listed for the container ship *Burkhanov*.

He ran back down from the observation room along the overpass walkway to the Vanterm information office. Inside, a plump woman, well-dressed, late fifties, was peering over bifocals, explaining the big silver and green aerial map of the port and environs to a group of Japanese schoolchildren.

"Excuse me," Frank cut in. "Can you tell me where the *Burkhanov* is berthed? It's a Russian container ship."

"I'll be with you in a moment, sir," she said archly, turning back to the map. He flashed his U.S. driver's license at her. "Frank Hall. Interpol. I need to know where the *Burkhanov* is. *Now!* It's a kidnapping case," and he realized he was telling her the truth—or at least half of it. The scientist.

The school kids seemed impressed. The woman, frowning resentfully, waddled over to her computer. "Nothing secret about it," she said curtly, tapping out the ship's name and swiveling the screen so he could see for himself. "*Burkhanov:* Container ship—Departed Centerm Five."

He asked whether there could be any mistake. Could the *Burkhanov* have changed berths?

She was alarmed by his intensity, the sleep-deprived, un-shaven face. "No, I—"

He was out of the office in a second, tried his cell. Dead. Remembering the public telephone booth nearby, he went in and dialed Vancouver vessel traffic control, as he'd done so often when leaving in the *Petrel* on oceanographic work. He got a recording—weren't there any people left in the world? It told him the same story, with one additional piece of infor-mation. The *Burkhanov* had departed at 0430. Shit! Then he did the math in his head, and realized that if the *Burk-hanov* had left twelve hours ago, it couldn't possibly be the ship slated to carry the Rone. The distance the militia would have had to cover from Wills Creek in Washington wouldn't allow it, unless there was a semi that could do 300 mph. In a blizzard.

He swung hard left away from the dock, his brown hair flattened, black from the rain running down his face. There was a scream of brakes. The bumper of a car dipped inches from him, a voice yelling, "You jerk! Look where you're going!" The guy was right. Time out.

He sat in the van, wiping his face, trying to figure it out. Where did the Vanterm office get their info about arrivals and departures from? Was it a mistake, a clerical error, a mix-up in names, passed from one to the other? God knew, Murphy's Law was alive and well in cyberspace as elsewhere. It had happened before. He remembered one time they'd listed *Pe-trel* as having departed when it was still tied up loading emer-gency seismic gear. Was the *Burkhanov* still here at some other berth?

He returned to the phone booth, called information, and got the number of the *Burkhanov*'s shipping agents, an outfit called Morflot located on Pender Street. They sounded busy, impatient. Could they call him back in a few minutes? He gave them the number, 666-6129, having to repeat it over the drumming of the rain. He was worried. If the militia had aver-aged forty to fifty miles per hour, the Rone could have arrived in the last hour or two. He waited impatiently. Waiting motionless in an ambush for six hours, the kind of thing he and Aussie had done often enough in 'Nam, was one thing. Waiting for a phone to ring was something else. That was civilian duty.

Five minutes later, it rang.

"Who is asking about the *Burkhanov*, please?" A different voice now.

"John Doe," he said.

"Hello?" Another voice. "Who is this please?"

"John Doe. I'd like to send something out on the *Burkhanov*. Can you help me?"

A voice, Russian accent, told him, "Ah, I think—wait a minute, please. I am finding out." The voice came back two minutes later. Enough time for them to have pressed Star 69, consulting the NULOC—number location—index. But it would take them at least ten minutes in the heavy traffic along Pender from downtown to reach him. He'd be long gone by then. The voice returned. "The *Burkhanov* has departed."

He was leaving the booth when the phone rang again. At first, given the noise of the rain, he couldn't hear anything. It was a whisper, barely audible, sounding parched but definitely English. A frightened voice. "Mr. Doe?"

"Yes."

"I don't have much time. There is a German ship—just arrived. She will be loading quickly with grain and leave in the morning for Vladivostok from Pacific Elev—I must go."

"Hello?" Dial tone.

A disgruntled employee of Morflot, the missing computer scientist who had maybe managed for a few seconds to get to a phone? Whoever it was, Frank silently thanked them. Even on the worst days sometimes you got a break. No German vessel had been listed on the website as coming in, but if she'd been diverted to Vancouver in the last twelve hours, there was a good chance she wouldn't yet be listed.

Driving fast toward Pacific 11, a pier adjacent to the grain silos farther along the waterfront, he was trying to put it all together. A grain ship? Well, you sure as hell couldn't pour a computer aboard through a pipe. But you could *cover* it, pour tons of grain on top, providing you had an airtight seal, otherwise the grain dust, which he'd often seen loaded when *Petrel* was in port, was so fine, like talc, that, depending on the humidity, it would gum up a computer, as well as a person's lungs, in seconds.

As he passed block 000 at the foot of Salisbury Drive, toward Pacific Elevators, it was almost nightfall, and there was the mixed smell of grain dust and salty air. Ahead stood the high, castlelike cylindrical concrete grain silos, or elevators, towering left and right of him. Three-by-four-foot crawl doors and air intakes at their base looked like tiny mouths, the harsh, weathered exteriors of the elevators pressing in on him as he got closer and drove on into the narrow canyon between them. There were only two exits: straight ahead and along the dock, beyond which lay the pumice-colored sea; and back through the silo canyon. The rain had abated, and ahead he saw a dozen or so Canada geese and glaucous-winged gulls walking impudently back and forth over the railway tracks that crossed the road, the birds taking all the time they needed, pecking at grain that had fallen from the rail cars moved into position for unloading alongside the elevators. Gloria would have loved it, so despite his sense of urgency, he slowed for them. "Why the hell aren't you in Florida?" he asked the geese. "All right, don't answer."

When he saw the dark blue pickup filling his side mirror, he knew he'd made a mistake. He couldn't make out the faces of the two men—all he could see were two blobs behind the wipers, the latter swishing slowly back and forth, giving the false impression that the pickup was in no hurry. Frank flipped open the glove compartment. He grabbed the Colt 9mm, stuck it in his belt, and swung the Montana hard left at the end of the elevator canyon along the dock. There, in the harsh glare of arc lights, its V bow aimed straight at him, was a bulk grain carrier, the MV *Ernst Mann*, the high-security fence of cyclone-strength mesh running across the dock at a right angle from the ship's stern.

He was trapped. Two men in blue coveralls and dust masks were coming toward him from the mesh gate, another pair, behind him, alighted from the pickup. One of the latter, dressed in a heavy red-check logger's shirt, waved to Frank and said something. The way he did it it looked friendly, but Frank, now out of the van, couldn't hear what the man was saying because of the din of wire gyred pipes and conveyor belts carrying the grain from the elevators to the ship's tarpaulin-sheltered hold. The four of them were closing on him.

There was only one way he could go, and he moved quickly, scuttling through one of the crawl doors he'd seen coming in. Now the roar of the grain-sucking pipes was deafening, the dust in the enormous dimly lit elevator filling the air like a sandstorm. He made for a long flight of metal steps in front of him. Grasping the Colt in one hand, hauling on the rail with the other, he made his way up through swirling grain dust. The steps stopped at a landing smack against the inner cement shell of the elevator. A dead end.

Five feet above him was a lightbulb, a tiny sun in the storm of wheat particles. He steadied the Colt and fired. The bulb died, the sound of the shot and imploding glass lost in the rushing noise of the grain belts. Now, thirty feet down, only a dimly lit patch of grain dust was visible near the crawl door through which he'd come in. He felt for the steps' guardrail by his side and, steadying the Colt on it, aimed at this patch. To get to him they'd have to cross the space between the foot of the stairs and the crawl door. Waiting. He saw a blur in the space, fired and dropped. There were two or three flashes in return, tiny gritty particles of cement stinging his neck as bullets struck the cement wall behind him. Using the covering noise of the grain belts, he quickly descended the stairs, one hand sliding down over the guardrail, the other gripping the Colt. He could feel his cordite-singed shirt sticking to him, his breathing becoming difficult in the fine dust. Reaching ground level, he glimpsed, through the crawl door, the lower half of the pickup, visible about fifteen feet beyond the silo's opening. Whipping off his shirt, holding it in his left hand like a matador's cape so it would hide the flash, he fired three more shots, at least one of the bullets hitting home, gas peeing from the pickup's gas tank. Someone—armed—jumped from the back of the truck. Frank fired twice and the man was flung back against the pickup, his left leg shuddering in spasm, his moans audible even above the rattling of the elevator's machinery. Backing away from the crawl door, Frank made his way cautiously through the ground level darkness, his left hand finally feeling the crevice of a doorway, then its handle. Testing it, he could tell it wasn't locked.

He went in low and wide, the gun preceding him in a 180-degree arc. No one. Another door, also unlocked. He stepped outside, could hear water lapping beneath the dock.

Two men were running at him from around the base of the silo. He fired twice. They ducked back behind a winch on the dock and he heard zinging sounds hitting the mesh fence behind him. There was only one way to go now—toward the fence. Running parallel to the ship, the big feed pipe above him disgorging grain into the *Ernst Mann*'s hold, he knew that if he could reach the end of the stern before they reached him, he could dive off before hitting the fence and hopefully swim to safety among the forest of barnacle-studded pilings.

Someone shouted from behind, sounded foreign, and two men at the ship's stern, chipping rust, suddenly looked up, dashed to the rail, and leaped the short distance onto the dock in front of him. Frank fired. Nothing—a dud round, or had he lost count? Without hesitation he ran back a few paces, then left, across the gangplank, jumping down onto the *Mann*'s well deck behind the retracted hatch top of a forward hold. Twenty feet across from him he could see the other side of the ship, from which he could dive into the harbor. There was a blur of blue coveralls, a German voice to his left, its owner charging at him, swinging a pinch bar. It missed, then a fist hit Frank so hard he was knocked off his feet. But he'd grabbed the man who struck him, both of them tumbling along with the iron bar, a sound like hail all around them, both men caught in a torrent of wheat. Struggling awkwardly to his feet in the quicksand of grain, Frank turned on the German with his Colt, the German frantic, yelling at him in broken English not to shoot, at anyone or anything; it would be very bad for everyone. What he meant was that the grain dust was an explosive mixture—all it needed was a spark from the Colt to blow the ship apart. Frank saw a walkie-talkie's aerial sticking out of the German's coverall pocket.

"Get a rope down here!" he told the German. "Quickly!"

"*Ja! Ja!*"

Grain stopped raining down on them and became a trickle, and after a few minutes a rope ladder with wooden rungs—metal would have posed the risk of a spark—was thrown over into the thirty-foot-deep hold. With the German in front, Frank's gun jabbing his ribs, the two of them began to climb. At the top the German lost his balance momentarily, the rope beginning to swing under his weight. Frank could hardly breathe in the dust that was still rising, his instructions to the German sounding hoarse, almost inaudible, but the German could sense his determination, his focus of purpose, despite the pain he had to be feeling from the punch to his face and the fall.

Frank shoved the Colt harder against the German's back. "All right, Hans, we're going back past the silos. Slowly. Fuck up and I'll take your head off. You understand?"

"*Ja! Ja!* Of course," the German answered.

"Okay. Let's go."

After the darkness of the hold, the glare of the loading lights was temporarily blinding as the two of them reached the top of the thirty-foot hold, but Frank nullified any temporary advantage this could have given his pursuers by keeping a firm grip on the German's coverall collar as he stepped out onto the deck, quickly steering the German erratically, left, right, then right again, as if in a maze, denying anyone a good clear shot. The downward incline of the gangplank ahead was steeper now, the fast incoming tide having lifted the bulk carrier's hull higher against the wharf's pilings. In the outer ring of the halos formed by the dock lights in the salt air, he glimpsed seagulls dipping, disappearing and reappearing again with unsettling rapidity. The German's weight going over the aluminum gangway shifted slightly and Frank almost lost his balance. He jabbed the gun harder into the man's ribs, swinging him about sharply, knowing hostile eyes were watching them from the darkness among the scattered islands of heavy equipment on the dock and the monstrous legs of the huge, praying-mantis-like gantries towering above.

Frank knew that up ahead the stretch through the rail-serviced silos would be the toughest part. The Germans and/or militia probably hadn't risked a shot anywhere near the volatile air of the hold, but the farther away he and his unwilling German got from it, the better chance they had for a steady shot. As he approached the first silo, passing between crates on either side, he told the German they'd go through fast, then veer hard left. "To my van. You get it?"

"*Ja, ja!* The van."

The van was gone.

One of the crates came alive. He glimpsed a lumberjack-shirted figure, a rain of blows pummeling him in the darkness, but with all the ferocity of a cornered man he lashed out in every direction and got two shots off. Thankfully, his gun was working again. There was an ungodly scream, and in a second he was through the confused bundle of bodies, running as hard as he could along the rail tracks, into the shadows of the elevators for protection. He heard frantic voices behind him and the sound of an approaching train, its electric horn and clanging bell a hundred yards off front right. Running across the tracks then swinging hard right, he was moving parallel to the train along the waterfront, the train separating him from his pursuers. Throwing all his strength into one last burst, he caught the edge of one of the train's open cattle cars and hauled himself aboard.

Another quarter mile and the train slowed, but didn't stop, merely braking as it approached Gastown. Impatient to get back to the hotel, which he figured was about due west of him, and spotting a patch of grass coming up, he jumped. Misjudging his leap, he slipped, striking his head on a hidden stone, losing consciousness.

CHAPTER NINETEEN

IN MOSCOW IT had stopped snowing, gone into a melting sludge, then dropped well below zero. *"Chorny lyod,"* black ice, Moscow's met officers warned, the coldest October day in six years. For Kornon, pushing the bell on Vanya's apartment, the night was special. Vanya's birthday. He had brought her a special gift, one of the finest of Swiss watches, a Blancpain, wrapped, or rather concealed, in a negligee of translucent silk, "the color of pearls," he told her—to match her hair—and which he expected her to model for him as soon as possible. Now. Vanya hugged him, her rose perfume engulfing him as she kissed him passionately, then pushed him abruptly away. "You'll have to come back later, Androvich. I'm off to the studio. We're doing a bit on that boy, the swimmer, thirteen-year-old from Vladivostok. Well, he did it. A world swimming record broken for the hundred meters."

"Really?" Kornon said, trying and not succeeding to keep the anger out of his voice. Sports bored him—about as interesting as watching ice in Ulan Ude. The only athletes he was interested in were women record-breakers in bed. He slumped into the living room chair, his coat still on.

"Yes," she said triumphantly. "By two-hundredths of a second. That mightn't sound much but it's a lot in sport. I'm sorry, darling, but I won't be home till midnight."

"Kchortu!" Damn!

"You can stay here," she said as if it was a consolation prize. "Don't get drunk." One of the most powerful men in the Soviet Union slouched sullenly like a petulant schoolboy deprived of sweets. She went into her bedroom and closed her door, the slit of light under her door only tormenting him further.

When the door opened, her movement toward him was as graceful as any ballerina's, the athleticism of her body at once evident in the firm rise of her breasts beneath the gentle swish of the silky negligee.

"My God!" he said, sitting up abruptly.

"The studio can wait!" she cried happily, laughing at her general's gullibility.

Quickly he began undoing his coat, one of its polished brass buttons flying across the room.

"Be careful," she said. "You'll lose them."

"To hell with them," he said excitedly. "I can buy more buttons. A hundred buttons. A thousand buttons . . ."

"I didn't think you'd come," she said teasingly. "Too busy at work."

He was transfixed by her figure, half hidden yet half visible through the gossamer of silk.

"It's all fixed," he said distractedly, like an automaton. "I've arranged a big surprise for that American bas—" Abruptly, he stopped. "I don't want to talk about work. I want to—"

"I know what you *want*," she cut in playfully. He pulled her roughly toward him. "First, Cossack, a little vodka."

"I don't want to drink," he said. "Not now."

"I do," she said slowly, seductively. "But not from a glass."

Kornon fell back into the chair again. "Promise," he said. "Don't torment me, Vanya."

She unscrewed the bottle, pouring the oily liquor into a shot glass, put it down on the carpet, unzipped him, then, dipping her finger in it, knelt before him.

"My God," he told her, "you're beautiful." He closed his eyes and lay back to enjoy it, clearing his mind of delayed schedules, confident that the American revolutionaries—the militia, as they called themselves—were keeping one stop ahead of their opposition.

* * *

It had stopped raining over Vancouver, the Pacific front having blown over the mountains, and from the plane the lights of the city were like glittering jewels in the cold, brittle air.

Gloria gripped the armrests. The plane's tires skidded for a heart-stopping moment on the runway, replaced instantly by the roar of the engines in full reverse thrust, her anxiety giving way to excitement, her mood buoyed further when she deplaned and entered the stunning beauty of the Northwest rain forest motif in Vancouver International.

"California Hotel," she told the cabbie.

"First visit to the city?" he inquired in a thick East Indian accent.

"No, but—" She hesitated; you tell them you're not from the city and they give you the grand tour—and a price to go with it. Don't let on that you have scant knowledge of the city's layout. At least that was the way Frank always told her to play it. But she suspected cabbies could always tell anyway.

"It is a very beautiful city," he said in a singsong voice, his turban moving in rhythm.

But when the cab pulled up outside the California on West Cordova, she didn't see anything beautiful. The "hotel" was a dump, albeit newly painted, and in the glow of its neon, the rain-slicked cobblestones had taken on a patina of dried blood.

Behind the counter in the dimly lit, stale-smoke-and-beer-stained foyer, the old woman was sitting low behind the counter, only the top of her head visible, her hair gray and stringy. When she stood up, Gloria saw that her face was like creased leather. She took a sip of green tea from a dirt-veined mug marked No. 1. Outside, another cab pulled up, and Gloria saw two men get out.

"Wanna room?" the woman asked her.

"I believe one's already been reserved for me. My name's Gloria Bernardi."

"Bernardi," she muttered, reaching lethargically for an envelope in the mail slot for Room 503. "There's a message here for you." Gloria felt a surge of excitement—it was in Frank's usual scribble:

I'm in 503. Take the spare key and wait for me. Shouldn't
be too long. And don't answer the door till you see it's me.
Luv you!

"Wanna room?" the old woman asked the two men behind
Gloria.

"You betcha!"

"No phones. Just TV."

"No problem."

"She'll fight," Larry said as they followed her up.

Dan saw him pulling out his packet of Gauloises. "I
thought you couldn't smoke in the hotels up here—only in
bars?"

"You have the lock pick?" Larry asked.

"I lost it."

"Very funny."

Frank walked unsteadily up from the waterfront to West
Cordova, still groggy from his concussion. His immediate
concern was to clear his throat of a persistent choking cough
brought on by the grain dust, and to do something about the
pounding headache that made it difficult to think. Amid the
throng of tourists passing through Gastown and the down-
and-outs from Skid Road, his ragamuffin appearance and the
blood on his sleeve didn't rate a second look. He slipped into
the beer parlor next to the California to settle the dust. The
pub's band was working into hard rock, as if intent on worsening his headache. Through the thick blue haze of smoke
pierced by the pulsating strobe and disco lights, the stripper
was about to pull the "shower" chain. It had been a long time
since he and Gloria had— Jesus! He felt his pocket. His cell
phone was gone, buried under tons of wheat or in the long
grass where he'd fallen. Or ripped from him in the rumble by
the silo.

He downed a beer and left, eager to get to a call box across
the street, away from the din of the beer parlor. His cough

started up again with a vengeance. He figured it must be an allergy—maybe it hadn't been wheat. Barley? He didn't know, but as the red pedestrian light changed to green, the one thing he did know for sure was that the Rone had to be aboard the *Ernst Mann*. If it wasn't, then, as Aussie Lewis would say, he'd eat his hat. He called General Freeman and told him.

"You sure?" the general demanded.

"Positive, sir."

"Outstanding!" Freeman declared. "Outstanding!" and Frank knew you couldn't expect better than that from any general. "All right," Freeman continued. "I'll ask Brownlee to contact Ottawa. Have the Mounties sweep the scow and get that damn computer back where it belongs. Meanwhile, you grab some sack time."

"Roger that, General."

"I'll call you later at your hotel."

"Yes, sir."

The old woman was asleep when he entered the California, and he saw his message envelope for Gloria was gone. As he put his hand around the back of the counter to get his bag, he could feel another coughing fit coming on, his face going beet red with the effort to stifle it. He heard a snap, felt a searing pain in his finger. "For crying out—"

A mousetrap was dangling from his hand, and as he was pulling the spring back, the old woman awoke, upright in the chair. "Aren't the first one," she chortled. "Put it there for the punks. You all right?"

"I'll survive." He grabbed the bag and walked toward the elevator, his sodden shoes squelching on the bare carpet.

"Your girl, Gloria's, here."

"So I see," he said, indicating the empty mail slot.

"You been in a fight?"

"Yes." He pressed the elevator button.

"Be careful," she advised. "Coupla fellas came in after your girl. They were watchin' her. Bad eggs."

Frank paused and turned. "What did they look like?"

"Thick-set fella. Other one was better dressed," she said cryptically, "taller."

"One of them in a lumberjack shirt?"

"Nah. Sporty looking."

"Thanks," he said. "Appreciate it."

Larry was sitting on one of the two chairs in the far right corner of Room 503 so that if anyone came in he'd be hidden by the opening of the door. They'd made her undress and put her things on the bed, and turned the bath tap on. That way when Hall came in, first thing he'd see was her clothes, and he'd hear the water running. Dan had a little fun helping her undress—he liked to mess with their hair—but now he was outside the room, around a corner halfway down the hallway so he'd be out of sight and to the left of anyone who came out of the elevator and headed toward the room.

While he was waiting, Dan thought about the Swiss guy Larry said was paying the shot, and he wondered what it was like over there. He had a vision of a little village, snowy Alps, and a guy in funny leather shorts blowing a long horn, hawking cough lozenges like in the TV commercial. He glanced up at the elevator light. The bulb was missing but it didn't matter—he could tell from the clump sound that the elevator had started on its way up. He'd wanted to stay in the room and just wait—the hallway reeked of stale cigarette smoke and booze—but Larry always wanted insurance, in case any pain-in-the-ass guest got in the way.

Dan had his Beretta behind him as he leaned unconcernedly against the wall. He'd done it so many times, his first time as a kid in L.A., whacking a crack dealer in the Ramparts. He shook his head at the memory—he'd done it for a hundred bucks. It cost more than that now for the ammo. He checked to make sure the safety was off. He'd known a couple of guys who had really screwed up; not nervous, just got bored to death—started flicking the safety on and off for something to do, and when they'd gone to fire, it was still on. They weren't around anymore.

The elevator clunked to a stop. The door slid open. No one. At the far end of the hallway, behind him, the fire door squeaked. He swiveled, and Frank dropped, firing, the Mossberg's "boom" and smoke rolling back, filling the stairwell, Dan's shot wild, taking out the Exit sign above Frank. Dan sprawled wide-eyed, his intestines spilling out. He hadn't made a sound till he hit the floor, a soft bump, his hand still holding the Beretta. He'd fallen partway into the elevator, the door's two panels sliding back and forth against him, unable to close.

Frank pumped the Mossberg, walking quickly toward 503, stepping over the fallen man, who'd defecated, the threadbare red carpet squishing beneath his shoes. The California's bloodred neon sign pulsated beyond the hallway's far window. He glimpsed a door opening a crack farther down than 503. A nosy guest peeking out quickly withdrew, the hallway resounding with the sound of chain locks frantically slotted into place.

Larry had heard the Beretta fire *after* the shotgun, which told him his partner might have downed Hall. Still—a shotgun blast?

Flat against the dirty hallway wall, the Mossberg in his left hand, his right edging along the wall, Frank quickly inserted and turned the key, kicking the base of the door. Before he stepped back, he heard the chain bust loose and a bang—wood exploding above him, the door slamming back at him under the impact.

"Your partner's dead," Frank called out. "Give it up!"

"I've got your woman, Hall." A pause. "You think I'm bluffing?"

Frank's finger was on the trigger. He could hear the elevator, twenty feet or so behind him, still bumping monotonously back and forth against the dead man's arm.

"Now you just put the scattergun in front of the door, then back off against the wall where I can see you through the peephole. Where she can see you." The man's tone was unhurried and deadly. "Stand against the wall, your hands out, or I'm going to open this little one right up, Frank."

"How do I know you'll let her—"

"You don't," Larry said. "You've got five seconds." A pause. "You think I haven't got her?" Frank was listening intently, then heard a faint tearing noise and a gasp of pain. "Say hello!" the creep was telling her.

"Frank . . ."

Jesus, save her.

"You're one second down, Frankie. Four to go."

Frank put the shotgun down in front of the door, hands out to his sides to show he'd obeyed the instructions. He knew he'd be at point-blank range when the guy inside came up to peer at him through the hole, but he had no choice. To shoot through the door would be unreliable anyway, possibly fatal for Gloria, for he was no doubt using her as a shield. Frank was watching the door's peephole, alert for the slightest flicker of movement.

After he called out twice, asking what he was supposed to do next, Frank realized he'd been had. He kicked in the door and went in wide with the Colt, saw a shape to the right and spun. Froze.

She was taped to a chair, naked, mouth taped, her face ashen—so cold she was shivering like a terrified puppy, the grime-smeared window behind her open, flimsy drapes, once white, now pollution-brown, billowing over her. The duct tape had been bound so tightly around her that it had raised welt marks all over her body. But it was her eyes, turning away from him, sobbing, not wanting him to see her like that, that constricted his throat with rage at what they'd done to her. Not content with using her as a hostage, as meat for the trap, they had brutalized her. He would find out later that her head had been repeatedly pushed under the bathwater, which was why her hair now hung moplike and hacked, lying in clumps about her feet. He shut the window that led out to the fire escape, a dull reflection of the beer parlor's neon sign below turning the spiderweb of steel pink and black and pink again. When he knelt down beside her and took off the tape, she folded her arms over her head, trying futilely to hide her debasement. Slowly, softly, repeating her name, telling her he loved her and lying that everything was all right, he touched her, only to feel her stiffen and recoil from him.

"Gloria," he said gently. "Honey—"

She was crying but he could barely hear her over the steady thump of the heavy rock from the bar across the street. Having untied her, he handed her clothes to her and saw parts of them bloodied. His rage now shot through him like bile, his head pounding, and he had to control himself before he could talk to her in anything like a normal voice. "Honey, did they—"

"No," she said, with sudden bitterness. "It's all right. They just played a little. I'm safe for you."

He had never felt hurt like that.

She turned, burying her head in his chest. "I'm sorry. I *did* fight. I scratched the one who left by the fire escape—"

In all, it had been less than five minutes since he'd shot the slimeball by the elevator, but already he could hear sirens approaching Gastown.

After he steered her through the hassle of the hospital emergency entrance and police questioning, complicated by the fact of her American citizenship, and she was taken to one of the bays in the emergency ward, Gloria was still shaking. He made another call to Freeman then, this time to tell Brownlee that it was over, that having given them the name of the German ship, he and Gloria were going home. Period.

Freeman was extraordinarily understanding, given the fact that spouses, girlfriends, and relatives were never supposed to be involved in Spec Ops. Then again, the general was renowned in battle—whether it was a local firefight or a major offensive—for turning an apparent deficit into an advantage, and now he cunningly pointed out that "it's always the same, isn't it, Frank? The lowlife that does this sort of thing to your girl—well, sometimes we get them. I'm sure we'll get this bastard too. Of course we're only chopping off the tail of the snake, aren't we? These are just the message boys. The ones we really want are those who gave the orders, the ones who get off scot-free." Anyway, he added, the U.S. Consulate officer in Vancouver would be instructed to give Gloria all possible assistance. Two Secret Service people would be with her all the time. One of them a woman. Even accompany her to the bathroom if that's what she wanted. But he was sure that the bastard wouldn't bother her again. He'd blown it. "It was you they were after, obviously. They suckered you."

Frank bristled—they'd suckered Aussie and Brentwood too. They'd suckered the general!

"Well," Frank said, exhausted, the only thing keeping him awake being the raw tension of the last two hours, "you got your ship."

There was silence on the line.

Frank pressed, but was too fatigued to be angry, "You *have* boarded her?"

"She's gone. Left port."

"Jesus—"

"Don't get your balls in an uproar," Freeman advised him placidly. "I've sent Brentwood's team, along with Aussie and Sal, with Coast Guard assist, to intercept her. We'll use a drug search as cover—as soon as she's in U.S. territorial waters, which'll be in about an hour's time—soon as she passes through the strait between Vancouver Island and Washington State."

Good, Frank thought; that gave him some satisfaction.

"Meanwhile, you get down to the consulate and get some shut-eye like I told you."

"Let me know the moment you get the merchandise."

"Absolutely. Frank?"

"Sir?"

"You did a fantastic job up there."

"Thank you, General."

One of the nurses was signaling to him to come back into the emergency bay. "Dr. O'Reilly says you should have that head injury and shoulder attended to, but I'm afraid we can't wait for you much longer. There's a lineup. Weekend traffic."

It was the first time Frank was conscious it was Sunday. "Miss Bernardi should be kept overnight for observation." Frank looked across at Gloria. The Valium had taken effect and she was asleep.

Overlooking the harbor from the twentieth floor above Georgia Street, the consulate office smelled of leather and stale cigar smoke. Despite the presence of the U.S. Marine guard, Frank locked the door and jammed the chair against it. He was sure that the guy from the Hotel California hadn't tailed him, but it was best to play it safe. Stretching out on the leather sofa, he checked the Colt and slid it under the pillow. At least now he was out of it.

CHAPTER TWENTY

IN THE ROILING darkness off Cape Flattery, Aussie was watching the *Sea Hornet*'s radar screen as the Coast Guard patrol boat plowed into heavy swells.

"Bit bloody crowded out there, isn't it?"

"It's crowded, all right," agreed the *Hornet*'s captain, pointing at the 3001 marine chart where a dotted east-west line marked the invisible water border between the southern tip of Canada's Vancouver Island and Washington State's Olympic Peninsula. "Juan de Fuca Strait," the captain explained—pronouncing it "Warn de Fooka"—"is one of the most heavily congested waterways in the world. Each of those amber dots you see sprinkled across the screen is a vessel, either coming from or going to Vancouver or Seattle."

"Which one's the kraut?" Aussie asked, meaning the merchant vessel *Ernst Mann*.

"Not sure," the *Hornet*'s captain said. He glanced uncomfortably over at his first mate, Mueller, a man who had served with him on this, the Coast Guard's latest state-of-the-art, 109-foot-long SES, or surface effect ship, for the past five years. Mueller, however, his face barely visible in the glow of the radar, showed no sign of offense at Lewis's use of "kraut." Spec Op types, it was known, especially SEALs, were like that. It was still *de rigueur* for them to refer to their opposition as "Japs." Though why these characters—Lewis, Brentwood, and company—had been virtually given the run of the *Sea Hornet* to execute a drug interception search in Juan de Fuca Strait was a mystery to the seventeen officers and crew. It was normally the job of the *Sea Hornet*'s crew, and no one else, to intercept drug runners, illegals and the like. But apparently Douglas Freeman had buddies in the Coast Guard as well as in other branches of the armed services.

"Guess the fog doesn't help either," Aussie said.

"Sure doesn't," the captain responded. "And it's the weekend. Every pleasure boater is out there on anything that'll float. Added to that, you've got Canadian and U.S. ferries crisscrossing through our San Juan and the Canadians' Gulf Islands, plus all kinds of cruise ships heading out on the South Sea, Alaskan, and Mexico routes. It's rush hour out there."

Brentwood, standing on the other side of the radar console and taking a good grip on the roll bar as the *Hornet* rolled over an invisible wall of water, had counted as many as fifty-eight dots on the radar screen, and that was only a quick tally. He also saw from the chart that some of them were tiny islands and/or intertidal reefs. "How can you tell them apart?"

"Sometimes you can't," the captain confessed. "Have to watch them very carefully. We've had some pretty bad collisions up here. Few years back a Russian freighter cut a big Canadian ferry clean in half. Went through her bulkhead like a knife through butter. Lot of people drowned. Semis and cars parked 'tween decks toppled into the water like dinky toys."

"*Mann*'s changed course, Captain," Mueller informed the

captain. "She's bearing two-six-niner, if I've got the right one."

"Very good," the captain responded, displaying full confidence that Mueller had the right ship. "Hands on. Steer zero-three-four. Intention to intercept."

"Hands on. Zero-three-four. Intention intercept. Aye aye, sir."

"The computer can take us on automatic pilot," the captain explained to Brentwood and Lewis, "but when it's heavy traffic out there, I like a man on the wheel in the event we have to go to override. Never know what some of these drivers'll do."

Brentwood appreciated the captain's explanations. They demonstrated a professional courtesy, even warmth, which was in marked contrast to the sullenness of most of the crewmen. The latter had done little to disguise their anger at having to host him, Lewis, Sal, Choir, and the Wright Brothers, and with sailing at such short notice from their Neah Bay base near Cape Flattery without any explanation from above other than to "provide all possible assistance" to Freeman's commandos. Those instructions included handing over the *Hornet*'s two prized drug-busting "sonar guns," handheld units whose shape bore a remarkable resemblance to hair dryers and whose sound waves could be used to penetrate bulk cargo to detect any foreign object of a different density.

Below, forward of the wheelhouse, two of the *Hornet*'s seamen, buffeted by the stiff westerly, stood in the spray-drenched darkness, bundled up in heavy wet gear. They held long, aluminum-handled steel pikes and bitched to one another about orders coming from on high that never made any sense.

"Fucking cowboys take over our ship. How come we didn't get a tip-off about this *Ernst Mann*?"

"Political," the other seaman opined. "Fucking political. Always is. Some fucking congressman up for reelection wants to make a big splash on CNN. Drug bust of the year."

"Uh-oh, here we go!" It was his buddy reacting to the

sudden rise of the bow as the *Hornet*'s two 1,800 hp diesels went to full power. The patrol vessel's two forty-inch 350 hp lift fans simultaneously created an air cushion below the forty-foot-wide welded aluminum hull, allowing the patrol boat's side walls to form a shallow draft, slicing through the water at over thirty-one miles an hour. The Coast Guard captain was taking a decided risk, pushing his boat at such speed under such conditions of zero visibility, but the bulk carrier had abruptly changed course to the southwest—if Mueller was tracking the right blip—and they knew they had to reach her before she either was lost in the fog or crossed the twelve-mile territorial limit.

"ETA," came the captain's voice over the ship's PA system, "is 0914. Eleven minutes. Repeat, ETA 0914. Eleven minutes. Boarding party ready."

"That's us," Choir said, slapping Sal on the back in the large holding cabin immediately below the wheelhouse. "Feel like a swim, laddie?"

"I do not. Gonna board this tub dry."

"If we can bring you close enough," the bosun said. "Otherwise we'll use the rigid inflatable, in which case I suggest you slip some Baggies over those sonar guns."

"No sweat," Aussie said optimistically. "Ten bucks we go in dry?"

Sal thought about it. As SEALs, they'd done it many times in the past, but not for a while. And if they had to use the rigid inflatable, they'd get wet, even in a light dew.

"What d'you mean, wet?" he pressed Aussie. "Wet or really wet?"

"Really wet," Aussie said.

"You're on."

"Anyone else?" Aussie inquired cockily.

The Wright Brothers took their cue from Sal. He'd seen more sea duty than they had. "Okay, we're in!"

"Choir?" Aussie pressed.

"Can't afford it, laddie."

"Cheap Welsh bastard. Davy? How about you?"

Brentwood, via the intercom to the wheelhouse, asked the

captain for his opinion. Would it be dry or wet? It was silly, but good for morale.

"The swells are moderate," the captain answered cagily. "But the wind's picked up. Difficult to say."

"Yes," Brentwood said. "But if you *had* to say?"

"I'd say . . ." He paused. "Fifty-fifty."

There was laughter below, each of the six SEALs bracing himself against the rolls, checking weapon and pack. Once aboard the *Ernst Mann*, things would move fast, its crew already alerted by their run-in with Frank.

"Could be dicey," Aussie said.

"Really?" Choir riposted.

"And fuck you too," Aussie joshed.

"Promise?"

Were they always this jocular so near to what was sure to be a dangerous mission? the *Hornet*'s captain wondered. Or was it just Spec Op swagger for the benefit of the men on the *Hornet*?

"Crudest lot I've ever heard," Mueller commented.

"Yes," the captain conceded. "But they get the job done."

"Maybe," the first mate said. "But during a boarding anything can go wrong."

"True, and—" With the nationality of the target vessel in mind, he was about to say, "Germans are never pushovers," but decided to let it ride. "Range?" he asked Mueller.

"Five miles."

Moving astern for some fresh air, Aussie didn't find any, the wash of the *Hornet*'s diesel exhaust enveloping him. One whiff was enough to shut down his sinuses, and already he felt nauseated. He stuck his head over the side into the slipstream created by the 150-ton vessel as she approached maximum speed on her catamaran hull, but couldn't evade the fumes, and he longed for the operation to be over and done with. He could see the fog thickening through his infrared goggles. The constant blaring of foghorns, which he normally found comforting ashore, irritated him, exacerbating his sudden mood change.

"ETA, nine minutes," the captain announced. "Repeat, nine minutes."

Aussie told Choir he could use a Gravol from his medipak but knew that to take one would make him drowsy, and you didn't need that against the freighter's crew of at least thirty men, presumably ready to do battle.

The *Hornet*'s radio operator, transmitting as per regulation on 156.7 megahertz, was instructing *Ernst Mann* to "heave to." There was no response.

"Try again," the captain ordered.

They waited three minutes—a long time in the crackly static of the strait's heavy traffic.

"Still no response, sir."

"She's not stopping," First Mate Mueller informed him. "Still proceeding on two-six-niner."

"Very well, Mr. Mueller. Inform boarding party to stand by the boat."

"Boarding party to stand by the boat. Aye aye, sir."

Unhurriedly, clearly, the captain spoke to the crews manning the *Hornet*'s two M-2HB .50-caliber machine guns. "Forward gun ready?"

"Forward gun ready, sir."

"Stern gun ready?"

"Willing and able, Captain."

"By the book, if you don't mind, Petty Officer Neil."

"Stern gun ready, sir."

"Very well."

On another ship, the *MV Petrel*, three hundred miles away in the turbulent North Pacific, another radio operator was trying to evoke a response, in this case a much less urgent one, from Bill Reid, as part of *Petrel*'s weekly status call to Oregon Oceanics. But instead of being answered by Reid, the *Petrel*'s operator found herself talking to a police detective out of Astoria who, in response to a "Block Watch" complaint about two strangers in the area, had discovered that Bill Reid was missing, despite the fact that his pickup was still parked out front.

"How about his dog?" the *Petrel*'s master, Captain Tate, had inquired. It struck the Astoria detective—not an animal lover—as a flippant aside, until it was explained to the detective that Reid and his collie were inseparable.

"No sign of it," the detective replied.

"Her," Tate corrected him. "Where's Frank?" Tate asked. "Frank Hall. His partner?"

"Don't know. Neighbors tell us he's got a girl in Portland. We're trying to track him down." There was a tone of suspicion in the detective's voice.

Tate hadn't meant to cast any suspicion on Frank, something he was immediately at pains to explain to the detective.

"Yeah, well you never know," the policeman said. "Partnerships go sour."

"But damn it, Bill and Frank are like—like brothers. I'd look—" Tate's voice was unintentionally cut off by the *Petrel*'s bosun, who was working astern on the Swann winch. "I'd look elsewhere if I were you," Tate advised the detective when he came back on.

"We are. A red Taurus sedan was seen leaving the premises. Two men. Caucasian. One thickset, the other one tall. A smoker apparently. You know any of Reid's friends, acquaintances, who own a red Taurus?"

Tate turned to ask his Scottish first mate, again his voice fading due to more interference, but this time because of the unusually high sunspot activity in the high latitudes. "No," Tate told the detective. "We don't know much about their private life—only when they're at sea with us."

It was after this conversation that Tate told *Petrel*'s radio operator to try to contact Frank, see if he knew anything about Bill's whereabouts.

"Maybe," the Scottish mate said in an accent still intact after thirty years as an American citizen, "we shoulda given them Frank's cell number."

"Maybe," Tate said, unsure as to why he hadn't, but they were a close-knit bunch on the *Petrel*, and Frank himself had often spoken of the "unit integrity" that in the SEALs superseded everything else.

* * *

In Portland, the police department was taking a call from a hunter who said he'd spotted a red car the day before, pulled up by Rock Creek, in Clatsop State Forest. It looked like somebody was burying something, he told them. The hunter wasn't sure, but he suspected it was something "pretty bad." The desk sergeant asked the man why he hadn't reported it earlier, and the hunter hemmed and hawed. The sergeant explained in his report that the man had apparently been hunting without a license and hadn't wanted to get involved until his old lady made him make the call.

CHAPTER TWENTY-ONE

THE *SEA HORNET*'S radar told First Mate Mueller that the *Ernst Mann* was less than a mile off to starboard, but at least three other vessels were in the way, and Mueller knew if he took his eye off the radar blip for a second, he'd lose it amid the others. The blip suddenly made a sharp turn to the southwest, bearing two-five-five.

"They'll say of course," the *Hornet*'s captain said, "that they couldn't hear our transmission because of the noise." He meant the heavy radio traffic in the strait.

"You can bet on it," Mueller said.

"Reduce speed to ten knots!"

"Reduce to ten knots," came the helmsman's confirmation.

Immediately the *Hornet*'s speed slackened, the air cushion collapsing, creating the impression that the *Hornet* was wallowing when in fact it was still proceeding. It came around parallel to the 10,000-ton freighter's port side, which would soon be towering above that of the 150-ton patrol boat.

"Slow to two-five-zero," instructed the captain.

"Slow to two-five-zero, sir."

The *Hornet*'s captain, though his vision was inhibited by the pea-soup fog rolling in from the Northwest Pacific, did everything right. Allowing for cross current flow, wind speed, swell height, and swell power, and knowing that a swell's height, like the size of a boxer's fist, is not always the true indicator of its punch, the captain gave a virtuoso performance of seamanship. Toggling his engines on override, he demonstrated why he'd earned his master's ticket as he coaxed, then, in a particularly eccentric trough, bullied, the *Sea Hornet*'s diesels into doing precisely what he wanted. He brought the patrol vessel abeam of the bulk carrier that they believed, by calculating its time of departure, fully loaded tonnage, and currents, to be the *Ernst Mann*. The halogen beam struck out from the *Hornet*, sweeping up and across the bulk carrier midships. She was low in the water, weighed down to the plimsol line, but was still massive. The swells rising and falling between her and the Coast Guard vessel created a rough, localized sea between them that slopped and slapped against its sides. Weighed down as she was, what would otherwise have been the merchantman's towering port side was now more or less level with the starboard side of the *Hornet*'s bridge. Several dim figures appeared on the big ship's bridge as the Coast Guard's bullhorn opened up with the captain's instructions to "Heave to." Both of the *Hornet*'s machine guns were cocked, ready to pour raking fire fore and aft if she disobeyed.

"Yes! Yes!" came an equally loud report through the fog. "We heave to."

"Accommodating," Mueller said.

"Sounds Oriental," the captain said. "Bit odd, isn't it? A German ship?"

Brentwood, steadying himself in the chop against the outer bulkhead, searched the deck and high points on the ship through his infrared binoculars for possible snipers. "Nothing visible," he told the *Hornet*'s captain.

"Means squat!" Aussie cut in. "Could hide a fucking company behind the railing."

"Check its letters," the *Hornet*'s captain instructed the spotlight operator. The beam's long, white finger, diffusing in the fog, swept down the side of the fog-shrouded ship, settling on the vessel's forward nameplate.

"Ernst Mann!" the operator confirmed.

Now that the ships were closer, the *Hornet*'s captain had a change of heart, the swells, increasing in frequency, threatening him with a collision. "Use the rigid," he instructed the bosun, telling the merchantman captain to lower a rope ladder for the boarding party.

"Looks like you're going to get wet," Choir joshed Aussie.

"What a wuss," Lewis responded.

"Weapons on safety!" Brentwood ordered. "Eyes open. Something wrong about this." As the boarding team wound down the rigid inflatable via the ship's stern bridle, Brentwood advised, "First sign of any movement, and it's flashbangs onto her deck. Understood?"

"Roger," Sal said, unclipping his vest pack pocket for ready access to the grenades.

When Ronnie Shear called the general to report that his eye was patched up and that he was ready to go again, Freeman thanked him and gave the ex-Green Beret a shock, namely that Shear and Frank Hall had caused "one hell of a row between Washington State and Washington, D.C.!"

"How's that, General?"

"You damn near killed two linemen, Ronnie, that's how."

The scene was replaying itself in Ronnie's mind, and he told the general how the two men had suddenly started running at the van, one of them reaching for his holster.

"They weren't running *at* you," the general corrected him. "They were running *toward* you. Transmission line was iced up, snagged, and came zooming down at them, carrying seven thousand volts. You'd run too."

"But one of 'em drew a—"

"A 'butt-in'—phone to dial their HQ—warning them what was happening. You guys must've thought it was a weapon.

The Washington highways department said you fired at them. Did you?"

"Yes."

"Frank as well?"

Ronnie mumbled from embarrassment, feeling his face going beet red.

"Frank as well?" Freeman repeated.

"Yes, sir."

"Well, thank God your aim was off, which I must say was the thing that surprised me most. I thought you guys had been keeping up with your target practice?"

Shear didn't answer, the full implication of what he and Hall had almost done hitting home. No wonder the guy had thrown a pinecone at him. "Guess when Frank saw the highway truck," Shear told Freeman, "he remembered how the militia used one when they attacked the Rone building."

Freeman had been reasonably understanding until now, but he couldn't abide excuses. His Spec Op men got the job done—they didn't screw up and they didn't offer mealy-mouthed rationalizations for having fouled up.

"Ronnie, you and Frank screwed up at Sedro Woolley. Fortunately, Frank got a lead on the *Ernst Mann.*"

"Mann? Who's he?"

"It's a ship, and right about now the rest of our outfit is about to board her. You better get your ass back here to Seattle. I want a specialist to have a look at that eye of yours."

"Not necessary, General. The doc up here says it's—"

"Bush doctor!" Freeman cut in with the bluntness that so endeared him to the diplomats at State. "Have to go, Ronnie. I'm about to be patched in to our boarding party."

The rigid inflatable rode the dark, fog-shrouded swells between the two ships as gracefully as could be expected, and for the first fifty yards there was a minimum of spray. But at the seventy-yard mark, just before reaching the port side of the *Ernst Mann,* the bow of the fiberglass boat fell precipitously down the glissade slope of the next swell. On rising out of the dark trough, it slapped its nose into the crest of a breaking wave, soaking the six ex-SEALs. Aussie Lewis, for once in his life, stifled a rising surge of obscenities for fear of unduly alerting the *Mann*'s crew as the bosun turned the inflatable smartly to port, bringing it parallel to the Jacob's ladder that the *Mann*, upon the *Hornet*'s instruction, had lowered down her port side. For a moment the Coast Guard's lookout, caught by the unexpected motion of a cross swell, allowed the spotlight to sweep across the ladder.

"Get that light out of there!" snapped the *Hornet*'s captain. "You know better than that. Keep it for'ard—steady on the hold."

"Sorry, sir. Yes, sir."

"See any of them?" the captain asked Mueller.

"Not a one. Don't like it."

"Neither do I." With that, the captain spoke softly into his mike link to the *Hornet*'s bosun. "Advise boarding party—no one on deck as yet."

"No one on deck," came the bosun's soft reply, the sound of water slapping hard against the rigid inflatable. "I'll tell the boarding party."

"Could anyone by the ship's rail hear him?" Mueller asked.

"No," the captain answered confidently. "I can barely hear him." The captain was struck by Mueller's uncharacteristic nervousness. Everything about the operation felt wrong, and for the first time he was genuinely glad his orders from Washington, D.C., via Neah Bay, had been to let the commandos do the boarding instead of his own men. Below him, forward of the wheelhouse, Ralph and the other seaman stood by with their pikes, not needed now that the inflatable had been launched. They could feel more relaxed, at least until the inflatable returned, when they would have to help man the stern bridle to bring her aboard. All Ralph could see was the *Mann*'s portside light, a hazy blob in the fog.

Having gone over the drill in the *Hornet*'s holding cabin, the black Nomex-suited and Kevlar-protected SEALs had agreed that David Brentwood, with his Heckler & Koch MP-5, would lead; Aussie second, his field of fire left front quarter;

Choir, a southpaw, third man, his FOF right side with a Remington 700 bolt-action shotgun; the Wright Brothers in positions four and five, left and right FOF, armed respectively with an M-16 and M-203 with 40mm grenade launcher. Sal would be tail-end Charlie, his 180-degree weapon of choice a short-barreled CAR-15 with collapsible stock, a rifle with a mild recoil and which, because of its smaller .223 caliber round, would allow him to hump more "ammo for weight," around two hundred rounds, than that carried by an M-60 machine gunner. Sal also favored the CAR for its precision, high velocity, and a hydrostatic punch that, if it didn't kill the opposition outright, would take them out for the duration.

As they climbed the Jacob's ladder, the *Hornet*'s two machine guns ready to provide covering fire, Brentwood was glad he'd forbidden the use of Kevlar shin and elbow pads. Favored in other operations, these protective pads, though flexible enough for most missions, were far from ideal for moving fast up a ship's side, where movement was already inhibited by the pendulumlike motion of the ladder.

Brentwood was first over the bulk carrier's side, the smell of grain dust mixing with the fog creating a musty smell shot through with the thicker odor of the stack's dieseline exhaust. The first thing Brentwood saw as he entered the fringe of the spotlight beam was a soft, crumpled, peaked cap on one of *Mann*'s officers, his hands raised as he maintained his balance against the swells by his feet alone. "No shooting," he implored Brentwood in an unmistakably European accent, though not German. "There has been, I think," he said, staring at the Heckler & Koch, "a big misunderstanding." It was a high-pitched voice, like a woman's, and very nervous.

"Where's the captain?" Brentwood asked.

"In his cabin. He is ill. Very bad coughing. I am officer on watch. Kazinski." Brentwood saw from the lone chevron on the man's shoulder board that he was the third mate.

"Where are the first and second mates?" Brentwood asked.

"There was a problem with load spreading," the third mate replied. "They are checking the holds."

The other five SEALs were now aboard, two on either side of Brentwood, Sal back of them at the rail. "Aussie," Brentwood said, "check out the captain. Five minutes!"

"You got it," Aussie said, at one with his colleague's suspicion. There was something very odd about the master of any vessel, particularly one so large, relegating the egress of his ship through the myriad navigational hazards of so many islands, at night, in fog, to his most junior officer.

"Choir," Brentwood instructed the Welshman, "I want you and the Wright Brothers to take your detectors and see what's going on in the aft and for'ard holds."

As the three SEALs moved off to the forward hold, they switched on their flashlights, which sliced through the fog, Choir's sonar gun momentarily visible through its Glad bag. Brentwood reminded the *Hornet*'s captain to keep his two .50s trained on the two exit doors to the deck on either side of the *Mann*'s superstructure, in the event of a sudden rush of crew. It had happened once in the Gulf, resulting in three SEALs killed before they took down thirteen of the Arab crewmen, bringing the rush to a bloody standstill before they could search the ship and find six big multipronged contact sea mines stashed belowdeck.

Suddenly, the *Ernst Mann*'s deck became an island of light as Aussie, having ordered the arc lights switched on, emerged on the bridge's portside wing, his figure in the black Nomex suit and the Heckler & Koch cast in silhouette. The third mate, Kazinski, proceeded down the portside ladder to the deck. Brentwood watched Art Wright, accompanied by the first mate, disappear into the bulk carrier's forward hold. Joe White stood by the hatch ready to provide cover with his M-16. Then, glancing astern past Aussie and the diminutive third mate, Brentwood saw Choir approaching the aft hold with the second mate. Why hadn't either the first or second mate been the officer on the watch? Why Kazinski?

"What's the story with the captain?" Brentwood asked Lewis, who answered in an Aussie slang, the only lingo his longtime comrades like Brentwood and the other SEALs, certainly not Kazinski, could understand.

"Seems fair dinkum," he said, meaning he thought Kazinski's report about the captain being bedridden was genuine. "Looked bloody crook to me, mate. Coughing his guts out. Surprised they'd leave port without having a quack in."

Brentwood turned to Kazinski, whose nervousness was emphasized in the floodlit grayness of fog. "Didn't a doctor see the captain in port?"

"No, Colonel."

Aussie grinned at "Colonel." Well, Brentwood thought, that explained why the *Ernst Mann*'s master was not on the bridge. It still didn't explain the absence of the two other senior officers. And another thing, neither of these officers, unlike Kazinski, seemed even slightly perturbed by the boarding. Cool? Or used to it? Brentwood heard his earpiece crackle.

"*Sea Hornet* to Brentwood. How's it going?"

"Fine."

"Good. Take your time. We've got all night, nearly all day, if you want to go through her with Chemsniffs."

"Roger." But despite the Coast Guard captain's reassurances that he was in no hurry, Brentwood got the distinct impression that *Sea Hornet*'s captain didn't think the SEALs were working fast or efficiently enough if they hoped to find whatever it was they were after. He probably thought they were giving the suspect crew too much time to dump. Brentwood turned to Aussie. "What are Chemsniffs?"

"Chemical odor detectors. Poison gas or drugs. Doesn't matter how well the shit's packaged and sealed, it still gives off trace odors. Almost as good as my nose. I can smell diesel more than—"

"Davy!" It was Art Wright, waving Brentwood up toward the forward hold. "Big Brother's got a reading on the sonar gun." When Brentwood gazed down through the hatch onto the mountain of golden grain, he saw a sine wave hiccuping across the detector's green two-by-four-inch screen. "He's registering an anomaly," Art confirmed.

"How big?" Brentwood shouted down at Joe White.

"Can't say. Detectors don't give you size, only density of the anomaly. But they're covering up something, boss."

Brentwood told the first mate accompanying White that he wanted the cargo dug up. Inspected. The mate looked puzzled, gabbling away in German.

"Get Kazinski here!" he called Lewis.

Kazinski explained the mate didn't understand English.

"Well," Aussie advised Kazinski, "tell him that if he doesn't start shifting the fucking wheat I'm gonna take the mother astern and he's gonna accidentally drown."

Kazinski was panicky. "Mother?"

"The first mate," Brentwood explained. "Or the second. Or you. We don't care."

"I will tell them," Kazinski said.

"Good," Brentwood said.

The first mate quickly climbed up from the wheat pile and stopped, halfway out of the hatch, bellowing at them in a guttural Bavarian, via Kazinski, that this was an outrage. The *Ernst Mann* had a tight schedule to keep, and any delay in delivery of the ship's cargo could cost the company thousands of Eurodollars a day. And he wasn't afraid of *amerikanischen gangsters*. If any unprovoked incident occurred against the *Ernst Mann* or any of its crew, there would be international repercussions. The vessel—did they know?—was partly owned by Russia.

Aussie's right hand shot out like a snake, grabbed the first mate by his right ear, twisted it, and dragged the Bavarian out of the hatch. The German yelled, his arms flailing about ineffectually as Aussie marched him aft out of the floodlit fog into the darkness behind the bridge housing. "Shut up!" Lewis bellowed in return. "Shut the fuck up! Now listen, Adolf. You listening?"

"Yes, yes."

"I don't care if President Puke-Teen personally owns this bucket. I've just lost four of *my crew* in the fucking Alps and I'm in no mood for any wanking around. You're hiding something under that fucking wheat and we need it so we can meet our delivery schedule. Understand?"

"Yes, yes. Let go of my ear."

Aussie twisted the man to the fog-slicked deck and didn't like the effect it had on himself—he was enjoying it.

"Tell your crew to start shoveling."

"Yes, yes."

Though Aussie released him, there was still defiance in the mate's voice as he rose from the glissade deck, cupping his ear. "Shovels would take forever. We will have to use the sucking pipes, redistribute the grain from one side to—"

"Just do it!" Aussie shouted. "Now!"

Within minutes the deck was a hive of activity as the huge two-foot-diameter flexi vacuum hoses were run out from the foc'sle spools, and cables plugged in to receive power from the ship's engine room over seventy feet below the well deck.

Choir Williams, returning from the stern hold with a negative reading on his sonar gun and seeing the ship come alive, observed wryly, "So they understand English after all?"

"Which is more than I can say for you," Aussie joshed.

They felt the ship turning, rolling less, pitching more, as she headed into the wind at right angles to the modest swells, Kazinski explaining that this would "maximize" the effect of any horizontal shift in the cargo.

"Minimize," Brentwood corrected him.

"Yes, exactly, minimize."

Brentwood made sure the *Sea Hornet* was turning with the bulk carrier, anxious that the Coast Guard patrol boat stayed parallel with her for maximum use of her .50s, should they be needed.

"It's possible," Choir suggested, "that these poor bastards don't know they're carrying the Rone."

"I know," Aussie conceded. "I've already thought of that."

"*Someone* knows," Brentwood countered, his patience wearing thin after twenty-seven hours straight duty, as one of Freeman's teams, without a break. "And we'd better be on our toes in case whoever it is panics. How much did Frank say it was worth? A billion?"

"Or two," Sal said, behind them by the rail, vigilant, despite his fatigue.

"Not to worry, lads," Choir assured his Spec Op comrades. "The *Hornet*'s two .50s can be brought to bear."

Brentwood ignored the Welshman's optimism. Things could change, go wrong, with lightning speed. Any predisposition he once might have had toward the glass-half-full theory of life had been forever shattered by his memories of 'Nam, one in particular in the South China Sea, where he and a team of six SEALs, as now, had boarded a Chinese junk suspected of ferrying ammo to North Vietnamese regulars. Same modus operandi as the *Mann*—they pretended not to receive the SEALs' radio message. Initial prevarication—"no understand English." But then they heaved to, following a bull-horned command. The junk, said the captain, was carrying rice. "Okay," Brentwood had said. "Let's have a look." Two crewmen—the junk's cook and his helper—had made two trips topside to throw over galley slops. Both times one of the SEALs—a kid from Ohio—had checked the slop bucket, just to be on the safe side. Third trip topside, the cook pulled out a stockless AK-47 from beneath his tunic, likewise his helper and a dozen others who'd had their weapons carefully hidden—stashed, waiting, knowing that once the Americans were aboard, the SEALs' heavy machine gunner on the riverine craft, standing off from the junk, would be unable to fire without hitting his own men. Which was why, now that Choir had returned from the aft hold, Brentwood kept all six of his present team "tight" together near the forward hold, giving *Sea Hornet*'s gunners a wide, unobstructed arc of fire, should they need it.

On the junk, in confined spaces, it had been a firefight, the likes of which the Medal of Honor winner had never seen before and hoped never to see again. Two of his SEALs were taken out in the first nanosecond of fire, three others wounded, one mortally, the SEAL coxswain on the riverine craft literally disintegrating in a shuddering blur of flesh and bone before his body parts hit the brown water that was churning with enemy fire. Brentwood and the three remaining members of the boarding party had jumped off, the riverine craft

calling in an F-4 Phantom while fishing the other SEALs ig-
nominiously out of the sea.

Brentwood switched on his throat mike. "SEAL leader to
Sea Hornet."

"Come in, SEAL leader."

"You tell those boys on those Gatling guns to keep alert.
This could turn ugly real quick."

"I know," the captain replied. "They've been here before,
Captain."

It was the first time the *Sea Hornet*'s captain had called
Brentwood by his formal ex-Navy rank, a moment of pique,
evidencing for the first time the *Sea Hornet* captain's resentment that his Coast Guard crew hadn't been given the jobs.
But then, they thought it was a drug bust.

While Frank Hall slept, troubled by dreams of endless hotel
corridors awash in blood and filled with Gloria's screams,
down at the St. Nicholas Mission on the waterfront, the usual
disconsolate crowd of out-of-work seamen and longshoremen
gathered for free coffee, day-old doughnuts, and the chance
to grumble. Like their fellow unemployed in American ports,
they complained about the stupidity of the government, not
only the government in Ottawa or Washington, which, thousands of miles away from the problem, made crazy immigra-
tion policies, but what the unemployed North Americans
regarded as the real world government of the International
Monetary Fund, the World Trade Organization, the North American Free Trade Agreement, the APEC, and all the other
conspiracies of globalization that had opened the floodgates,
allowing cheap labor and "illegals" into North America—
Asians and Hondurans into Canada, Mexicans into the
United States. The mission was a de facto recruitment center
for the militia in both countries, and many of the militia, as
U.S. congressional committees back in 1996 had discovered,
were composed of former Special Forces mercenaries. These
soldiers-for-hire had simply applied the Special Forces "mul-
tiplier" program to militia recruitment and training. One man
trains ten men, those ten each train ten more, and in very

short order you end up with a cadre of thousands of highly
trained individuals.

But tonight at the mission there was a respite from the usual
hate sessions against the agencies of globalization. There was,
in fact, an air of celebration, and contrary to mission regulations, the coffee was spiked with liberal shots of hard liquor,
since the word on the docks was that the boys from across the
line—the American cousins—had pulled off a big one, right
there in Vancouver.

A "big one," however, wasn't sufficient enough description
for one young Canuck who called himself "John" and who,
excited by several cups of coffee, was pressing for details.

"You a narc or somethin'?" one of Lucky McBride's men
in civilian garb asked.

"Shit, no, man. Just want to know how it went down, eh?"

"It went down. That's all you need to know."

"Well, not exactly *down*," chortled a red-bearded long-
shoreman who, like half a dozen others, had helped the
cousins—not, as usual, for a bribe, but because the cousins
had said that whatever was in the crate would swell the
militia's antigovernment coffers "tenfold, twentyfold. More!"

"Then it didn't go down?" John said, eyes bright with the
booze and with the knowledge that he was privy to something hot.

"I meant it's afloat," the other drinker joshed.

"That's enough, eh?" a fellow Canuck cautioned. "Loose
lips sink ships."

"Hey, I like that," John said. "Loose lips—you make
that up?"

"It's from the war, eh?" grunted an ancient mariner who
could barely stand but could still drink, and, like most
working-class Canadians, tacked "eh" on the end of everything he uttered.

"That's right," McBride's man said. "It means keep your
mouth shut."

"I figured that out," John said, clearly offended, and
walked off.

"Can't handle his piss," someone commented.

"Yeah, but he's a good deck man."

"Sure he's not a narc?"

"Even if he is," the red-bearded Canadian said, "who's he know, eh? We don't even know what was in the crate. Took it to the ship. Crew loaded it."

The doughnuts had run out, and by now the mission coordinator, more hurt than angry that his no-booze rule had been violated—a lot of the men were alcoholics—told everyone to go home.

"Home? Where the fuck's that?" someone shouted.

The disgruntled unemployed filed out into the chilly fog-shrouded night, and one of them saw John floating facedown by the cannery dock. The story was that he was half-pissed. "Must've slipped, eh? Hit his head when he fell in the water." A warning.

The wheat dust rose into the *Mann*'s arc lights like brown rain, combining with the fog to form a sticky mixture that adhered to metal and men alike. Kazinski seized the moment to explain that this "pollution," as he called it, was precisely what had incapacitated the captain with such a severe attack of asthma. Brentwood had difficulty hearing him because of the noise of the pipes sucking up the grain above where Art Wright's sonar gun had detected the anomaly. Several of the crew were clearly enjoying his discomfort as he stood, with mask and goggles, a few feet from the pipe's intake in a storm of wheat husks. The goggles did little to help him; the dust required him to constantly wipe the plastic lenses and the small iridescent green screen. The sine wave's hiccup was only faintly visible. The wheat particles swirling in the air of the hold were so dense that his Nomex suit was soon covered in a fine talc that gummed up his hair, ears, and the space around his throat where his suit ended. Suddenly there was a loud metallic crash in the vacuum pipe, followed by a rattle akin to handfuls of coins in a clothes dryer.

"Halt! Halt!" It was the first mate, waving his hands frantically at the operator, but the crewman had already shut everything down, the danger of a spark generated by metal on metal—at least that's what it had sounded like to everyone— more important than wrecking the million-dollar machinery.

The hiccuping on Art Wright's oscilloscope ceased, and in its place there was a straight line.

CHAPTER TWENTY-TWO

FRANK THOUGHT THE ringing was in the dream, and it wasn't till the sixth ring that he woke in the darkness of the consul's office and another few seconds before he found the light switch and saw the ivory-colored phone on the con- sulate's desk.

It was General Freeman contacting him, as promised, the moment the boarding party had completed their mission.

"Nothing," he told Frank tersely.

Frank sat there stunned, his head throbbing as if catching up with the shock. "Nothing at all?"

"The merchandise wasn't aboard the *Ernst Mann.*"

Frank didn't believe it. Oh, he believed the general be- lieved it, and no doubt Brentwood and the team did, but as an oceanographer, he knew how easy it was to hide something on anything bigger than a lifeboat. That's what had made him laugh when he'd seen that movie, one of his favorites, *The Usual Suspects,* three guys taking all of four minutes to search an oceangoing vessel for contraband and concluding there was nothing on the ship. "Balls, sir!" he told the gen- eral. "They didn't search it properly."

"Yes they did, Frank." The general's tone was surprisingly forbearing. "It's over seven hundred cubic feet. You can't tuck that away in some corner." Before Frank could respond, Freeman told him that Brownlee wanted a word.

Brownlee wasted no time with civilities. "The shit's hit the fan, Frank. We're in the middle of delicate arms limitation talks and we're being accused by Russia in the U.N. of committing 'piracy on the high seas.' China and Libya are supporting the accusation."

Frank laughed incredulously. "*Piracy?* The bastards are in our waters."

"The point is," Brownlee riposted, "the President doesn't like it. Not with our election race heating up. Opposition's already calling him reckless. Besides, he doesn't like being made to look the fool, like some private eye who's kicked in the wrong door."

The "private eye" reference rankled Frank, taking him back to his meeting with the President in La Jolla. Was it Dalgliesh or one of the other five pinstripes or Brownlee who had called him a private eye? He couldn't remember.

"Already the heavies in Moscow are calling for the arms limitation talks to be scrapped," Brownlee continued. "Suits their hawks like Lebev just fine. We haven't heard bitching like this since the cold war." Brownlee paused for a second, then gave it to him with both barrels. "You blew it, Frank. You've got us in a lot of trouble, my friend. The White House is calling your guys the Sea Air Land Screwups. You were suckered to that grain ship while whoever is running this operation—the same people who set the two creeps on your trail—are laughing, and—"

"General," Frank cut in. "Did they search the wheat?"

"Yes." It was Brownlee butting in again, and the general didn't like it, especially after his SEALs joke.

"Dammit, Brownlee. I'm not one of your White House stooges. I'll answer for myself, and you make a crack like that again, you turd, and I'll personally come down there and smash your goddamn head in!" There was a long pause, and Frank could hear the general still breathing fire. "I've lost good men up in those goddamn mountains. Good, brave men."

"My apologies, General."

Freeman ignored him and spoke to Hall. "Yes, Frank, they searched the wheat—found a pinch bar."

"A metal rod bar," Brownlee said, unfazed. "Apparently it's a crowbar of some sort."

"He knows what it is," Freeman growled.

Frank remembered the German rushing him, swinging something at him, then dropping it when they both fell into the hold. He should have told Freeman earlier to tell Brentwood, but he'd been preoccupied with Gloria, a case in point if there ever was one of why wives, kids—anyone close to you—had to be put out of mind. He was tempted to confess he knew about the bar, but what was the point? Brownlee was right—he'd blown it.

"There's something else you ought to know, Frank," the general said, uncharacteristically gentle. "Your business partner, William Reid . . ." From the general's tone, Frank knew that Bill Reid was dead, even before Freeman spoke the words.

For once Brownlee sounded genuinely empathetic. "The police suspect it's the same pair who were stalking your fiancée. Thugs for hire."

"Was it clean?" Freeman knew Frank was addressing him, not Brownlee. A civilian wouldn't understand the question. A Spec Op warrior did.

"No," Freeman answered unequivocally. "It wasn't."

"Jesus! How 'bout Daisy?" For a moment he thought neither the general nor Brownlee understood who he meant. "Bill's dog," he added.

"You want the details?" Freeman asked softly.

"No."

There was a long silence before Brownlee came back on the line. "We have to press on, Frank. We owe it to your partner, those boys killed in the mountains, and that research scientist they've kidnapped. And your fiancée, Brenda . . ."

Jesus, he can't even remember her name, Frank thought. Earlier he hadn't said a damn thing about anyone; everything had been about how much flak Washington was getting at the U.N. and the arms limitation talks.

In the end, however, what swayed Frank wasn't Brownlee's appeal on behalf of his dead comrades, or, however callous it might have seemed to anyone else, any overriding concern about the missing researcher. It wasn't even his need to avenge what had been done to Gloria, though that played a part. Rather, it was his own penchant, bordering on the obsessive compulsive, for confronting an enigma. It was the *angst* of not knowing how they—whoever *they* were—had beaten him. He was still bothered by the *Ernst Mann*.

"Twenty-four hours, Frank?" Brownlee pressed, sensing the moment. "That's all I'm asking. Freeman's ready to help. Right, General?"

"*If* Frank agrees."

"I thought you said I'd screwed up," Frank told Brownlee. "Now you're asking—"

"That was to spur you on. Besides, you were right about them going to Vancouver."

Frank was about to remind the presidential aide that it was Freeman who'd come to that conclusion after his teams had drawn a blank on the three roads through the Cascades, but Brownlee's impatience—which meant the White House's impatience—didn't allow for any tendentiousness.

"And you're right about them having to get it out by sea. Plus you're the man on the spot."

What was this, suck-up time at the White House? Well, Frank conceded to himself, we all have our moments, like him assuring the general he wasn't "past it." Besides, what Brownlee said made sense.

"Twenty-four hours, Frank? After that they'll probably be out of our territorial waters anyway."

Brownlee was right again.

"All right," Frank said. "But you'd better get the *Petrel* down here. I might need her, and she's probably somewhere in—"

"Done," Brownlee said.

Damn it! Didn't the man let anyone finish a sentence?

"What else?" Brownlee pressed.

"I don't know," Frank replied. "I'll have to have a look around the port. Soon as I have something, I'll let you know. Meantime, I want Gloria watched twenty-four hours a day."

There was silence.

"His fiancée," Freeman cut in.

"Yes, yes. Of course."

It took Frank a full fifteen minutes on the phone to get the consulate official who wanted authorization from Brownlee to give him the password for the consulate computer. Once he had it, it took Frank only seconds to log on to the port authority's list of impending departures that Sunday. With the *Ernst Mann* ruled out and the *Burkhanov* container ship gone long before the Rone could have reached the West Coast from Wills Creek, there was only one possible contender: a Russian cruise ship, the *Southern Star*, which had entered Vancouver harbor the night before, due to depart for Fiji at noon. He called up the record of ship's provenance and saw it was operated by Russia's Pacific Ocean Department, director A. A. Kornon. A cruise ship, bound for Fiji, was the last thing you'd expect, but "Russian-owned" changed everything. And it struck him that it was precisely the kind of thing that Kornon—if it was the Kornon he remembered from the salvaging of the *New York*—would do.

Noon was four hours away. He called Freeman and Brownlee, telling them he intended to check it out. Hopefully, using the happy confusion of the usual bon voyage parties for passengers as cover, he could slip aboard and get a look at the cargo bays. "I've lost my cell," he told Brownlee. "If I find anything and can't get to a land line, I'll send a fax or something." He thought for a moment, then added, "I'll sign it Frank, spelled F-R-A-N-K-E for security."

"Fine," Brownlee responded. "Good luck."

It went more smoothly than Frank had expected. He got out of the cab in front of the Pan Pacific's big white Seiko digital clock showing the time in various places of the world,

except Moscow—maybe they wanted to keep it a secret?—
and moved through the understated opulence of the foyer.
The hotel of choice for every visiting luminary, from Prin-
cess Diana to the Hollywood elite, the Pan Pacific formed the
stern end of the cavernous clipper-shaped Canada Place Convention and Cruise Ship Center, which jutted out into the
harbor. There was so much hustle and bustle beneath its enormous white Teflon sails that it provided the best cover he
could have hoped for.

He walked past the Hertz rental car booth and the Royal
Bank ATM to his right, onto the brownish-pink marble floor
where the sound of passengers and well-wishers smothered
the more pleasant sound of the sculptured waterfall that cascaded beneath the enormous skylit dome. There was a momentary alarm as an elderly passenger, a plump woman too
busy admiring the architectural grandeur about her, rather
than looking where she was walking, slipped on the marble
floor while heading for the down escalators to the cruise dock.
Frank made his way down to the luggage area where suitcases
and trunks were being put on a conveyor belt that fed the aft
bay in the stern of the ship, from which, he guessed, luggage
would be distributed to the cabins.

Many of the passengers were already aboard, exploring the
chandeliered luxury liner with all the bubbling excitement of
schoolchildren. Frank made his way onto the ship via the
midships gangway by infiltrating a party of raucous revelers,
one of them so drunk he had difficulty negotiating the slats on
the gangway, temporarily distracting the officer beneath the
security camera, dutifully smiling and welcoming the passenger and authorized guests. Most of the passengers, Frank
noticed, were fellow Americans, obviously taking advantage
of the dirt cheap fares the cruise line could offer because, in
one of the great ironies of the post–cold war world, the Russians used only nonunion crews.

In the train of the revelers, Frank descended the plushly
carpeted central stairwell that spiraled down through the top
three of the seven decks, then made his way farther below to
the loading deck. Here he could hear the shouts of the crew

and the clattering of pallets being unloaded toward the ship's stern. Ahead he could see grubby green swing doors, their "No Admittance" signs in Russian and English flaking in parts, their brass push plates dulled from years of use. And he could smell the odor of cabbage and other perishables that formed only a fraction of the hundreds of tons of food it took to feed the 450 passengers in the pampered world above. Down here it was a sweatshop, everyone from dishwashers to sous chefs rushed off their feet to provide the kind of meal that would cost the average crew member a month's wages.

"Pardon please." It was a junior officer, smartly turned out in dark blue uniform with white cap and a single gold ring around the sleeve. "Not permitted here for passengers. Dangerous machinery."

Frank smiled. "Sorry, I got lost."

The young officer was pleasant, and explained in halting English that the first day of a cruise at least a dozen or more lost souls were found wandering the labyrinth of seemingly endless corridors, connecting passages, and multiple decks. Some of the older lost "madams," he said—Frank guessed he meant "older women"—were found "crying buckets."

What he didn't tell Frank was that he was also on the lookout for stowaways who had come aboard looking for a free cruise.

"I will be leading you out. Yes?"

"Fine," Frank said, following him through a passageway leading toward the port, dock, side of the ship. They passed several Chinese crew members carrying armloads of freshly ironed linen and went through several more sets of swing doors. One of the rooms was lined on either side with huge, wicker-cane laundry baskets, now empty but lashed firmly to the bulkhead with yellow polyethylene rope. Frank caught a whiff of acetone, as in a laundry. Over in less than a second, he felt an astonishingly cold, sharp jab in his jugular vein, a rush of pins and needles through his body, and was blinded by a brilliant light.

The young officer turned briefly, saw him fall, but kept walking because when one of the squad of KGB, now FSB, agents aboard told you to do something, you did it and you didn't linger. Only later, when he was sure he was alone with the ship's doctor, would he ask why they had injected the American spy in the throat.

"Carotid artery," the doctor explained. "Very fast-acting."

CHAPTER TWENTY-THREE

Zurich

GENERAL CHANG BEGAN to speak, but Klaus indicated silence with the same dismissive authority a headmaster might use with a schoolboy. Chang had not brought Wu Ling along this time, having no desire to have her witness any more of Klaus's condescension toward him. If the PLA had not needed the financial partnership of Swiss Rhine Petrochemicals, Chang thought, he would be quite happy to shoot the Swiss capitalist. Klaus was sitting at his desk, stirring a decaffeinated cappuccino until the chocolate had surrendered and sunk. "You assured me, General Chang, that your people would take care of any interference."

"Yes. I'm very sorry, Herr Klaus. This has of course been unpredictable. But never to worry, the merchandise is now sound and safe."

"*Is* it?"

"Yes, yes," Chang assured him. "It is well on the way. This I can guarantee. Absolutely."

"Our contract with you is contingent, General, upon delivery. Only then do I regard it as *safe*."

Klaus saw that Chang was visibly disturbed, or was it

angry—and was made even more uncomfortable by Klaus not inviting him to sit.

"Uh, Herr Klaus, I cannot control our other partner." He meant the Russians.

"Quite," Klaus retorted, "which is why I strongly suggest you amortize the risk."

"Ah . . ." Chang hesitated. "I do not understand this word." Chang knew Klaus had used it as a deliberate intimidation.

"Reduce your risk, General." Klaus sipped his coffee. "It's not merely this pest Hall being in Vancouver that I'm concerned with, but what if our Russian friends get it to Vladivostok via Suva then claim something happened en route—that the Rone has been 'irreparably damaged' or some such thing? They would have had your help and mine in arranging the procurement of the Rone and getting it to Vancouver for them. And then they report an unfortunate accident. Where would SRP and the PLA be then, General?" Before the general could answer, Klaus went on, "No doubt in six or twelve months we would read of an astonishing breakthrough in Russian computer technology." Klaus let the point sink in before he continued. "My loan has been extended to you, General, I repeat, solely on the condition of *delivery*. Nothing else. *On delivery*. If I were you, General, I'd get myself and," he added knowingly, "your companion to Fiji without delay. There's nothing like direct supervision at point of sale. Wouldn't you agree?"

Chang nodded as the thrust of Klaus's comments came home with nail-driving clarity. It wasn't simply that the Swiss Rhine Petrochemicals loan might be lost should there be an "accident," but that all the money Chang's own PLA Computer Enterprises had put into the project on his recommendation would have been for naught. He would have to answer to the Central Committee in Beijing for any such disaster. "You do not trust the Russians," Chang said.

Klaus's arms spread like a benign prophet's. "General. Did I say that? I am merely talking about insurance. I'm sure our Russian colleagues would welcome any assistance you could provide."

It was obvious to Chang that Klaus must already have his own "insurance" man aboard, watching the Russians, and his suggestion about going to Fiji made sense. But did the Swiss financier really think that the little "yellow," General Chang, who had survived so many purges in China, was so stupid, so incredibly naive, that he would not have already placed some of his own people on the ship transporting the supercomputer? But why tell the pompous "big nose"? Chang thought. Instead, Chang thanked him for the suggestion, adding, however, "I think there will be enough Russian security aboard the ship in question, Herr Klaus, to take care of this Hall if he appears. The American will be completely outshot."

Klaus was nonplussed at first but then allowed himself a wry smile at the general's fractured English.

"Outgunned," Klaus corrected him, his tone that of a tutor with infinite patience.

"Yes," Chang said. "Outgunned!"

"Of course," Klaus explained, "the American might already have been waylaid, in which case there will be no problem."

Once again Chang was confused by an English word, in this instance "waylaid," but he suspected it meant to be led in the wrong direction. In any case, he certainly wasn't going to ask the "big nose" to explain.

Washington, D.C.

"Without a trace?" Brownlee's voice was seemingly unmoved by the news from General Freeman that Hall hadn't been heard from for over seventy-two hours. Aide Donna Fargo suspected Brownlee was bothered more by having to be the bearer of bad news to the President. At least Brownlee was practicing what he preached, namely, that if you allowed yourself to get too close to operatives, official or unofficial, you'd be a nervous wreck within three months. "Remember

Director Casey," he would caution her, referring to the CIA chief who had to listen to the Iranian tapes of his friend being tortured. It was essential, Brownlee warned his fellow aide, that you created a buffer zone.

Hall's disappearance, however, had distressed her. She was feeling guilty about her own part in having induced the ex-SEAL into taking on what everyone at the White House had known from the start was a highly dangerous business. Now, by way of atonement, she kept asking Brownlee awkward questions; for example, was he looking after the oceanographer's girlfriend?

"Bernowski?" Brownlee said. "Yes, she's being taken care of."

"Bernardi," Donna corrected him.

"Yes, Bernardi. We've had her taken back to Portland. Giving her round-the-clock protection. Can't do much more than that."

"Round-the-clock protection isn't going to do her a lot of good when she comes out from under that Valium haze."

"It was Hall's own decision to leave her," Brownlee said testily.

"For twenty-four hours," Donna reminded him. "Not *three days*. And what about that creep in the hotel?"

"I don't know," Brownlee answered impatiently, completely missing the thrust of her question. "After the shooting at the—" He glanced down at his pad. "—the California, we were able to get the Vancouver police's cooperation without compromising any information about the stolen computer. Far as the local press are concerned, it was a simple, straightforward rape, and he was shot."

"What's a simple, straightforward rape?" Donna asked archly. "Anyway, I wasn't talking about the creep who was shot. I mean the one who escaped."

Brownlee shrugged. "Who knows? He might still be after her. You can't tell with those guys. Psychopaths, half of them. That's *why* I sent Andrew and Shirley—"

"Who?"

"Oh," Brownlee parried, "don't you remember their names?

The two Secret Service people. I told them to take her back to Portland. And stay with her until—" The buzzer sounded from the Oval Office. "Yes, Mr. President?" Brownlee asked promptly.

"This memo you've sent me, Al, about this ship, *Southern Star.* It doesn't sound Russian."

"It is," Brownlee assured him. "I've checked it on the Net. It was to be called the *Brezhnev*—until his son-in-law was sent upriver for crimes against the state."

"Embezzlement," Donna interjected.

"Whatever," Brownlee said irritably. He was late for a press briefing on the arms reduction talks. "We could have the *Petrel*—the oceanographic ship Hall requested—shadow her."

"All right," the President agreed. "But for God's sake, don't do anything else until we have proof positive. One more *Ernst Mann* incident and we could start World War Three!"

"Yes, sir," Brownlee responded. "Ah, there is one other thing, Mr. President." Brownlee was fingering the flexistrap of his watch, a sure sign to Donna Fargo that he was considering whether to drop a minor bombshell, to whit, a case of him having acted on his own initiative without presidential authority. Strictly forbidden under the Constitution, but in the practical affairs of the State, necessary at times, or so Brownlee saw it.

"What is it?" the President pressed.

"I took the liberty of suggesting to the Secretary of the Treasury that it might be prudent to put one of our Treasury people on board the ship."

"Treasury people," Donna knew, always sounded less contentious, unless you knew that the Secret Service had begun life under Treasury.

"I don't remember signing any order to that effect," the President said.

"You didn't, sir. But I had to act quickly. By the time I'd've gone through normal channels the ship would have sailed."

"Your memo said it's bound for Fiji?"

"Yes, sir."

"Why in hell," the President pondered aloud, "would they take the Rone to Fiji? Surely it'd be a lot quicker straight across to Vladivostok on one of their freighters."

"Originally that's probably what they figured on doing," Brownlee agreed. "Out of Seattle. But once Freeman and company became involved, they fouled up the militia's time-table. Then they used the *Ernst Mann* as a ruse. That gave the militia time to switch the Rone to the nearest Russian ship available, *Southern Star.* And by now she's in international waters."

"I think," Donna Fargo cut in, "that if they show their hand, start any rough stuff out there, Mr. President, we should be prepared. Have Freeman standing by at Boeing Field with a team. Just in case." The phone in the aide's office kept bipping and it was driving Donna crazy. She wanted to snatch it up, but you didn't interrupt the President of the United States.

"Very well," the President said. He sounded exhausted. "One more thing. You mentioned here in your memo that Mr. Hall didn't agree with you about the *Ernst Mann.* He thought it was still dirty."

"Yes, sir?"

"*Why* did he think that?"

"I don't know, Mr. President," Brownlee answered. "Just a hunch, I guess."

"Hmmm . . . Keep me posted."

"Yes, sir."

"And Donna, would you please have someone tell Morton Dalgliesh not to keep sending us encoded e-mail asking what *the situation* is. When we know what it is, we'll tell him, dammit! At the moment, we're all only guessing."

"Yes, Mr. President."

"You're sure Frank Hall's on that ship?" Donna asked Brownlee.

Brownlee was about to answer when he spotted young Lawson, his harried, bow-tied assistant, coming excitedly toward him, a fax flapping in his scarecrow hand. "There's been a murder in Oregon," Lawson announced.

"There's a murder a minute, Lawson," Brownlee said

snarkily, taking the fax from him. "What's so special about this one?"

"It's that oceanographer's assistant—his technician or something. They found him in some picnic place. Buried. And his dog. Pretty gruesome, apparently. That Hall sure left a trail of wreckage behind him."

Donna Fargo flushed with anger, upset more by Lawson's use of the past tense when talking about Frank than by his excitement. "Who else have you blabbed this to?"

"No one," Lawson said, taken aback. "Mr. Brownlee here told me to keep an eye on Hall's assistant and—"

"What she means," Brownlee cut in, "is that we already know about it, but if it leads to a news leak about us suspecting the Russians of heisting our top-of-the-line computer, it'll take more than a presidential memo to keep it under wraps."

"And," Donna told the hapless Lawson, "apart from dooming any further arms reduction talks, Dalgliesh and his pals will lose a billion or two overnight and you'll end up a lighthouse keeper in Adak."

"I haven't told anyone—" the aide spluttered, looking at Brownlee for support. "You told me to keep an eye on Hall's assistant and—"

"All right," Brownlee said, "what about the oceanographic ship I told you to contact?"

"The *Petrel*? On her way, but there's a snag."

"A what?"

"It's over a hundred miles away from the *Southern Star*, doing some kind of survey work with a Dr. Shalit and—"

"She's pissed at having the *Petrel* diverted."

Lawson was open-mouthed. "How did you know?"

"I know everything, Lawson. Now I want you to continue to keep me posted on the position of the *Southern Star*."

"Yes, sir," Lawson said, and scuttled away.

"How are we doing that?" Donna asked. "Keeping surveillance on the cruise ship?"

"SOSUS. Sound Surveillance System. We've got strings of hydrophones, underwater microphones—so have the

Russians—all along the major sea routes and then some. Every ship gives off its own sound print. Trouble is, since the Walker spy ring, the Russians know where most of our hydrophones are located. They tamper with them from time to time."

"Then how about satellite surveillance?"

Brownlee shook his head. "No way. You request time on a spy sat, you need to give all the reasons. Anyway, the Russians can jam our signals." As they neared the press office, Brownlee returned to his notes for the press briefing on the arms limitation talks. "Bit hard on young Lawson, weren't you? Lighthouse keeper in Adak!"

She was smiling at the *Washington Post*'s rep who waved from the hallway.

"I mean," Brownlee continued, "Hall's assistant *is* dead. Nothing we can do about that."

"And Frank'll be dead if he's on that cruise ship and your assistant blabs. The press'll put one and one together and the Russians will dump him over the side."

"He might be dead anyway."

"I feel responsible," Donna said. "We asked him to go and he went."

Brownlee said nothing. She was right, but what could you do? In the big power game, someone somewhere had to be on point, and Hall was it—or had been. In either case, Brownlee knew his most pressing problem was to have the *Southern Star* shadowed until he could ascertain whether Hall was on the *Star* and until the *Petrel* could arrive and take over the job. He called Freeman, who in turn asked Ronnie Shear to come see him immediately after the ex–Green Beret had left the ophthalmologist.

"What did the doc say about your eye?" Freeman asked.

"A-okay, sir. Read everything on the chart. Swelling's going down."

"Doesn't look like it," Freeman said, his fatherly concern camouflaged by his brusque tone.

"Well, I got everything right on the chart, sir."

"All right. Ronnie, you're probably the most rested, so I want you and Art Wright to go up to Neah Bay and do a job for me. Coast Guard has an undercover boat up there. Crappy-looking trawler but lots of power, and deep-sea capable. Has a crew of six. We want you to tail a cruise ship, the *Southern Star*. We've got an oceanographic ship, with all the bells and whistles, coming down from up north, but until she gets down south we want you to shadow the *Star*. Can't have the Coast Guard or Navy do it—otherwise we'll have another goddamn incident. I've told the trawler's skipper not to get too close, just act like any other of the trawlers that ply the coastal waters. But keep her in radar range. You take the first watch. Let Art get some sleep."

"How about Brentwood, Aussie, and the others? Can they help?"

"No. They're on the way to Boeing Field." The general paused. "Don't worry, Ronnie, they're not on vacation. As you might have guessed, this whole thing is not going well. These bastards that have stolen the Rone have got us behind the eight ball." The general looked again at Ronnie Shear's eye as the commando was doing a last minute check of his gear. "You sure that eye's all right? Looks like hell. You're not lying to me about that eye chart, I hope."

"No, sir," Ronnie lied. One of Shear's heroes was the Luftwaffe air ace, Adolf Galland—not because the man flew for Hitler, but because, against all medical odds, he flew with only one eye functional, the other being a glass eye as a result of a childhood accident. Like Galland, Ronnie had memorized the eye chart.

"Just monitor any traffic that goes near the *Southern Star*," Freeman told him. "Personally, I think Frank, if he is aboard, is barking up the wrong tree, to mix metaphors, but we might as well cover it. If the Rone gets away on us, we're in deep shit. I mean the whole country, not just our team."

"I know, sir."

* * *

In Portland's Good Samaritan Hospital, Gloria Bernardi was being given five-milligram injections of Diazepam to combat the post-traumatic stress caused by the assault on her, and now by Frank's disappearance. Andrew and Shirley, the two Secret Service agents, who were not privy to the specific details of Hall's mission, tried to tell her that it was no fault of hers that Frank had vanished. She didn't believe them. Shirley tried to reason with her. Gloria asked her if she'd ever been in love.

"Nothing you could have said would have stopped him. Some men are like that. Some women too."

A few minutes later, outside Gloria's room, Andrew told Shirley that whatever the hell was going down, the Bernardi woman should "pull up her socks."

"And when was the last time you were stripped naked and assaulted?" Shirley challenged him. "And had your wife disappear?"

"I only meant," Andrew said, "she should face facts."

"Oh, and what are they?"

The two agents heard Gloria's buzzer and within three seconds were back in her room.

"He's there," Gloria said, her face pale and drawn, hand quivering as she pointed out her second story window across the street at a clump of cedars. The two agents saw nothing but the wind moving in the trees.

"I know it's him," Gloria said, her voice trembling. "He's out there watching."

Maybe it was the Valium making her paranoid, but to make her feel better Andrew went outside and walked over to have a look.

"There's no one there," he assured her when he returned. "You're safe."

CHAPTER TWENTY-FOUR

THE DARKNESS WAS impenetrable, the ache in his head a crushing heaviness that permeated Frank's body, as if every part of it had been weighted down. Even the simple act of breathing became a monumental task, the pressure he felt reminding him of the creatures the *Petrel*'s grabs periodically brought up from the sea's depths, their bodies exploding through sheer decompression. His mouth and throat were so dry, his tongue literally stuck to his palate.

The pain and the blackness had been invaded now and then by fleeting lighted images of a plastic pouch swinging slowly above him, a long plastic tube running from it to his arm, the images broken periodically by a sensation of cold steel piercing his arms, crushing through taut skin, his head reeling inside but kept still, immobilized by giant paws, reality and unreality blurring into one another, a voice, questions about what he'd been told, whom he'd spoken to, and, repeatedly, who else knew where he was? It wasn't a harsh, bullying voice but calm, persistent—and white sheets and faces, always above him looking down. But how many, he had no idea. Craving water, he was feeling hot, the slight moistness on his lips not blood or water, from its taste, but his sweat.

Gradually he became aware that the pounding in his head was in part coming from *outside* him. The deep, throbbing rhythm of engines penetrated his whole body, or what was left of it—the reek of diesel filling the stygian darkness that engulfed him. Now he remembered the ship, the young officer, the large wicker laundry baskets, so vivid in his mind that the very memory of them momentarily obscured everything else like a flashbulb in the dark—and now a soft moaning that seemed to come from far off but which he dimly and slowly realized was the sound of wind howling. He felt for his watch, hoping for a glimmer of fluorescence, some notion of what time, what day, it was. It wasn't there. Neither was his wallet.

He felt about him in the darkness for the sheets and the bedding he had fleetingly recalled, but there weren't any on the cold steel. Slowly he turned onto his side and began to sit up, feeling a steel bulkhead, cold but not so cold as the floor. Was he on the cruise ship, or had he been moved to another vessel? He became aware of more vibration and a sense of motion. His head throbbed so badly that he pressed it against the bulkhead, relishing its chill, the rest of him feeling warm and clammy. All he could concentrate on, all that mattered, was his desperate craving for water. Feeling his way along the wall in the darkness, he came to a corner, then moved at right angles along another bulkhead. The windowless cabin cell, he figured, was about eight by ten—how high, he had no idea. Then his foot touched something metallic and he heard a clatter by his feet. It felt like an overturned bucket, the air suddenly filled with a sickly combination of ordure and powerful antiseptic.

"For Christ sake, sit down! There's crap all over the floor."

Frank swung about toward the sound of the voice, staring intently, seeing nothing. The voice sounded like a limey's. "Sit down. It isn't the bloody promenade deck."

His head pounding even more with the surprise, Frank felt his way back into the corner which he figured must be diagonally opposite the other voice in the cell. But there wasn't a skerrick of light and still he could see nothing. "Who are you?" he asked hoarsely.

"Prince Charles. My bloody 'oliday this is. Love it. Being pounded by these bloody Ivans. If this is glasnost, mate, they can shove it and spin. I'll take the cold war any day."

Frank tried to speak again but couldn't, his throat so dry that his attempt came out in segmented syllables. "How . . . lon . . . been . . . ?"

"Four or five days, I think," came the reply. "You were in bed like us for a couple of days—on IV drip and lots of Pentothal—but you didn't do 'em much good. Kept throwing up and saying rude things. I think this is phase two. They kept telling you the old Pentothal was the easy way but if you persisted it'd be the hard way."

Frank licked the sweat on his lips. "Who's *they*?"

"Well, there's Boris—not his real name. We call him that."

Frank's brain was still not clearing as fast as he wanted it to, but he realized the other man was also a prisoner and that gave him a clue. "You're the scientist?" he rasped, his tongue working hard against his teeth to produce enough saliva that he could talk.

Immediately the other voice cut in. "You know Henry Morse?"

Frank felt as if he was coming awake with a hangover in an unknown hotel, in a foreign country, only this one was moving. "Henry Morse?"

"Yeah, you know, Camptown Races all day long, doo-dah, doo-dah day? Dot dash?"

Frank, quickly switching the subject now that he'd realized through the curtain of pain what the Englishman was getting at, Morse code, asked, "You have any water?"

"Two cups a day, mate. That's all. Here. Put out your hand—feel it? Don't spill it. Boris won't give you any more."

Frank reached out through the darkness toward what he hoped was the middle of the cell, then heard the man groan, the first indication he had that despite the other's defiant banter, the man must be badly hurt—perhaps in as much pain as he was. Frank reached out again in the darkness and his fingers felt something rubbery, rough.

"My shoes," the man said. "Stay where you are. I'll—" The man gasped, and Frank sensed the other was dead still for a moment or two before he could move again. As Frank's outstretched hand felt the metal mug, about the size of a measuring cup, the other man gripped his forearm. Instinctively, Frank withdrew but the man gripped harder, breathing hard from the effort. "Steady," he told Frank, "or you'll spill it. Only two cups a day, remember."

"Can't live on that," Frank said.

"Tell me about it," came the man's reply, sounding now more pained than before from the effect of having moved, the man's sweaty palm gripping Frank. "Relax. I'm not going to kiss you."

Frank could feel the other man's fingers tapping, the nails jagged, bitten to the quick probably. The man kept tapping Morse until Frank got it—"m-i-c-r-o-p-h-o-n-e." Frank gulped half a cup of water, fighting with everything in him not to finish it off. "We get any more today?"

"Not today, Fred," the Englishman answered.

"What's your name?" Frank asked.

"What's yours?"

"Frank Hall."

"I'm Bill Healy."

"Where you from?"

"Kilburn. Suburb of London. Originally. Last few years I've been in the States. Yourself?"

"Astoria, in Oregon."

"Were you shanghaied?" Healy asked.

"Yes. Were you?"

"Yes, but no shilling."

Frank tried to make sense of the "shilling" but couldn't. Was Healy trying to tell him something else in addition to having warned him in Morse about the probability of a hidden microphone? "Royal Navy," Healy explained, his breathing loud and uneven. "When they needed men, they used to go out with press gangs—recruitment drives. Bash you on the fucking head, give you the Queen's shilling, and you were in for the duration." It was said without any humor, as if Healy had come smack up against the reality, or rather the hopelessness, of his imprisonment.

"This Boris," Frank said, "will he be back?"

"Don't know," Healy answered. "Boris told us they've had it with us. You and me. Apparently we haven't cooperated enough. That is, tell them what they want to hear."

"Which is?"

"I don't know," Healy answered, pausing, stopping and swearing. "Bloody leg. Bastards twisted it. They seem to think I've been involved with some super-duper defense computer. I told them it's all a crock. They didn't believe me."

Frank couldn't see anything, even his hand that he was holding in front of his face, but from the way Healy was speaking, punctuated by his groans of pain, Frank imagined him crumpled in the opposite corner, head back, unseeing eyes looking upward, utterly exhausted but still fighting, as if the very act of speaking through his pain was itself an act of defiance against those who had brought him to this. "And you," the Englishman continued. "Old Boris is very annoyed with *you*. Called you 'recalcitrant.' Speaks very well, does Boris— Oh, Christ—"

"What's wrong?" Frank could hear Healy breathing now in short, sharp gasps.

"My leg again. They had some fun with it. I—" He stopped and didn't talk for another few minutes, and for a moment all the bravura—his attempt at levity—was gone. "I'd get ready if I were you, Frank. Said they were going to show us something that would make us more cooperative."

"What?" Frank asked.

"No idea. But I don't think it'll be high tea. They've been asking me about you, who you told, who knows."

"Knows what?"

"Knows you're here. They're very upset about some computer they keep on about. A Rone. Never heard of the damn thing."

"Neither have I," Frank said, trying to make it sound as natural as he could, if Healy was right and there was a microphone planted.

"Well, there you are," Healy said. "Looks like we're in the same boat." He tried to suppress any laughter as he repeated the pun, "In the same boat." The laughter no doubt hurt him but he couldn't keep it in, and it came out with a frenzied edge to it—very close, Frank thought, to hysteria. The fear caused Frank to feel about his waist for his belt. It wasn't

there either, and his shoelaces were gone. Steeling himself
for the effort, he forced himself up against the bulkhead,
making his way slowly around it until he felt the crack in the
metal that marked the door. Healy had gone quiet now.

"You okay?" Frank asked.

"No, mate. Feel bloody awful." *Mate* reminded Frank of
Aussie Lewis.

Frank felt urgently about the doorjamb.

"Don't waste your energy," Healy said, hearing him.

Frank worked his way back to the corner, exhausted. From
feeling where the hinges were, he'd been able to deduce that the
door opened toward his corner. Catching his breath, he realized
he needed to husband his strength, relax as much as possible so
that when this Boris came in, expecting two exhausted prisoners, he and Healy might be able to do something. It was
worth a try. He sat down and thought of Gloria and of them
making love, of the beautiful beaches of Oregon, not now in
the cold, wet fall but in the sun of high summer, when all along
the rugged coast the rocky black monoliths stood up like
mountains in the sea mist, halos of seabirds around them
sparkling in the sunlight against an endless blue of hope.

"We aboard the *Southern Star*?"

"The what?"

"*Southern Star*. Cruise ship."

"No fucking idea, mate. Kept me blindfolded."

Unbuttoning his shirt, Frank took off his T-shirt and quietly
tried to tear it, but drained of energy, he couldn't manage it.
Instead he used his teeth to rip the hem and then slowly tore it
in half and made a tight knot for a garrote.

He would have to get to his feet as soon as he heard them
unlocking the door. It would be his only chance—and Healy's.
He would crouch, mustering all his residual strength, and
charge through the door. He doubted if they would expect any
attack. He felt his way through the darkness until he bumped
against Healy's shoes again and, using Morse, asked how
many would likely come.

Two, Healy replied. *Possibly three.*

Without anything by which to gauge movement or time,

the two men waited, speaking only once when, as if from another world, they heard the faintest sounds of a stereo playing carefree Polynesian tunes. Now, with time to think of how it might go wrong, Frank was seized by a fear so swift and deep that it momentarily left him breathless. His chest tightened painfully, sweat breaking out all over, his pulse racing. What if Healy was a plant? Well, he would soon know if, when the door opened, Healy merely sat back—or, worse, helped the Russians subdue him. But perhaps Healy was thinking the same thing about him? Utter darkness was meant to disorientate and prey on one's fears. It was working. Using Morse, he arranged with Healy that if either of them heard anyone approaching, they would tap lightly. Twice—on the bulkhead. Sitting there on the cold metal floor, Frank thought he detected the smell of wheat flour.

CHAPTER TWENTY-FIVE

NIKOLAI MENDEV, RUSSIAN, was cruise captain of the *Southern Star*, Alexander Valery, an Estonian, the staff captain. Valery, a medium-built and self-effacing man in his early fifties, was just as qualified in seamanship as the more worldly looking Mendev, holding his International Masters ticket and with more than twenty years of seagoing experience behind him. But in the hierarchy of captains, the staff captain—a heartbeat away from the cruise captain—had the most demeaning and boring job among all the ship's officers, to Valery's way of thinking, from having to welcome the wealthiest and most influential of the 450 passengers aboard, to overseeing the "cattle yard," the lifeboat drill that had just given him a ferocious headache. He also had the unenviable responsibility of troubleshooting anything from complaints about the menu to a major failure in the engine room, from re-assuring first-time passengers about the safety of the ship to making sure that crew members—from the Chinese firm hired to do the laundry below decks to the Belarussian stewards—were not exceeding their alcohol allowance. And from time to time he was called upon to deal with amorous widows who blatantly propositioned him and other officers, and make sure they were neither accommodated nor rudely rebuffed.

Valery had discovered that, like airline passengers he had met while flying from port to port to relieve another staff captain, passengers aboard cruise ships often abandoned their most cherished shorebound inhibitions, saying and doing things they wouldn't even contemplate, let alone actually do, in their normal day-to-day lives. But after all, who could blame them? Every glossy brochure in the business promised escape. At times Captain Valery felt as if his mouth had been taped into a perennial smile for the hordes of travelers who demanded and paid handsomely for levels of service hitherto undreamed of aboard ship, save for the grand days of the *Titanic* and the other luxurious leviathans of the Blue Ribbon Atlantic Run.

The job that the tall, fair-haired Estonian disliked most, however, was that of having to go through the long roster of 450 names and to choose a list, not necessarily of the most wealthy but of the most *vliyatelyne industrialisty*—industrially influential—and deliver it to whoever was the KGB, or rather FSB, liaison officer on the cruise. For any cruise ship carrying in excess of four hundred passengers, this meant someone above the rank of major, in this case a Colonel Sergei Orloff, a thickset but nevertheless agile Georgian and one-time SPET-SNAZ commando in his mid-forties. Orloff, in turn, would carefully peruse the list, paring it down to embrace a spectrum of professions whose trade secrets might be of interest to FSB's Directorate One, whose prime function was to gather vital information relating to Western defense industries.

Using the cover and uniform of "assistant purser," Orloff would study the list intently through his stylish half-moon reading glasses, deciding to tick off those cabins that were to be bugged. The ship's listening room or monitoring station was an annex to the radio room immediately aft of the bridge. There, a half-dozen FSB rank and file, on three eight-hour shifts—sometimes with help from a member of the MVD, the strictly military intelligence arm—monitored conversations. And all this while, passengers lounged in the wind-protected fiberglass bubble that swept gracefully back from the bridge to the rakish angle of the double stack, the latter overlooking the kidney-shaped pool that was kept at a balmy eighty-three degrees Fahrenheit.

On occasion, to break their boredom, the FSB and MV eavesdroppers would select the most unlikely candidates for bugging: for example, a pair of ladies from Des Moines whose anatomical descriptions and rating of the most desirable bed partners among the officers would have the FSB rank and file guffawing—with the exception of Colonel Orloff, who had to provide a detailed intelligence report to both General Kornon's Pacific Ocean Department and FSB HQ.

Orloff, like so many other post–cold war warriors in Russia, claimed he was "*ex*-Communist"; nevertheless, his reputation among his colleagues as an old party member, and a particularly humorless and straitlaced individual at that, stayed with him, unlike other "ex-party" members who had risen to prominence in Georgia through the usual course of bribery and corruption. And despite all the revisionism in vogue in the post-Yeltsin era, Orloff's hero had been and always would be Stalin, another Georgian likewise not known for his sense of humor. For Orloff, a man brought up in the hard days of the Great Patriotic War of 1941–45 and on revolutionary dogma, a cruise ship was an anachronism, a quintessential example of vulgar capitalism on display—decadence and class distinction wherever you looked. He viewed his cover as yet another ship's officer enjoying the lavish menus and entertainment as being strictly in the line of duty.

But if Staff Captain Valery, like some other officers, was struck by what he saw as Orloff's self-deceiving hypocrisy, he was equally impressed by the colonel's professionalism; the ex-KGB man certainly knew his job. It was said, for example, that Orloff had spotted the American Treasury agent the moment she came aboard, even before the computer had matched the security camera's image with the photo of her from FSB's file of known American operatives. She was single, brunette, brown eyes, about five feet eight inches tall, plain-looking yet attractive in an athletic kind of way. A runner, Orloff thought, his assumption verified by the printout. In fact, however, it wasn't the security camera image of her that had first tipped him off, but the videotape of the terminal, which he'd been watching after being warned by the *Ernst Mann* about the American spy, Hall. It was sheer luck, because alone there'd been nothing to distinguish her, as single women formed a large contingent of the passengers. Orloff cued the shot for later zoom analysis as her luggage had been placed on the conveyor belt after it was examined by Canada customs. And after battling his way through the throng of passengers crowding the rails, he moved to take Valery's place, officially welcoming the woman aboard, noting she was traveling under the name Sheila Moffat. Five decks below, her luggage was thoroughly searched by the chief steward before being delivered to her cabin, midships on the port side. He found nothing suspicious, reporting only that she seemed to have a passion for red shoes, formal and casual, and "Jockey for Her" underwear. Practical.

Five minutes before the ship sailed, amid the usual rush of last minute Interflora deliveries, a bouquet of carnations and maidenhair fern arrived for her at the purser's office. Orloff was notified and asked if he wanted it searched also.

"No, I want nothing disturbed. Her luggage has passed through customs, so she will expect some minor rearrangement in her suitcase. The flower arrangement is something else. We must be careful. Take it aft to the ship's doctor. Have it X-rayed."

In the bouquet's green sponge foam base, they saw the outline of a .22 caliber HiVel.

"A very quiet weapon," Orloff told Captain Valery in the chart room, upon receiving the report from the chief steward. "The choice of most American *ubiytsy*"—assassins—he smiled wryly, "and the U.S. Treasury. They've moved away from the bigger, noisier .45s." It was the first time Valery had seen evidence of a firearm on the ship, apart from the cache of antiterrorist AK-74s, assorted small arms and grenades that were kept under lock, the keys to which were held by Captain Mendev and Orloff.

"Well," Valery had said, "she certainly seems serious about it."

"What do you mean?" Orloff asked, looking up quickly over his half-moon glasses.

"I mean, if you're not good enough in bed," Valery explained, "she'll shoot it off!"

Orloff ignored the vulgarity. Sex and drink were all that seamen talked about.

Later, when they were well under way, Valery pointedly asked Orloff: "I hear we have stowaways on board? Your FSB assistants wouldn't tell me much." Valery's tone had a sarcastic edge. "They merely *informed* me as staff captain, which I thought was nice of them. All I could get out of them was that these *stowaways* were in the 'basement'! I assume they meant beneath the waterline?"

Orloff was smiling for a change. "You mustn't let my men rile you, Captain. They know very well what to call it. It's their little joke."

Valery wasn't amused. They disliked each other intensely.

"How long will your *stowaways* be aboard?" Valery pressed.

"Oh," Orloff replied, "not long."

The FSB colonel clearly enjoyed Valery's uneasiness at having two foreigners as prisoners on the ship. "I will tell you something, Captain Valery, that should dispose you more toward cooperation between your POD and my FSB." He paused, using his folded glasses as a pointer, tapping Valery's chest. "You may not realize it, but this is the most important cruise of your career. When we deliver our special cargo, I would wager my pension that—" and here the colonel tapped the four and a half staff captain's rings on Valery's sleeve "—you will have five of these. And then there is our new cruise ship, *Gorbachev II.* Over 145,000 tons, four thousand passengers. Bigger even than Royal Caribbean's *Voyager of the Seas.*"

Beyond this, Orloff didn't elaborate. He didn't have to, for Valery knew that though he was officially far below him in rank, the colonel, as FSB "station chief" aboard the *Southern Star*, had the power to recommend or kill his elevation to bridge captain, which was among the highest-paid jobs in Russia's maritime service. Valery had dreamed of being appointed captain of the *Gorbachev II*, the most prestigious command in Russia's eighty-two cruise ship fleet. Along with the sheer status of the job, there was a score of special privileges attached; as master he could bring his wife aboard, though the joke was that some saw this as a penalty.

Of course, even if Valery became bridge captain, like Mendev, he would have to accept the anomaly of the Russian system whereby the FSB "station chief" aboard could supersede both the cruise and bridge captain's authority in matters of "national security." Nevertheless, the vision of himself as bridge captain of the new super cruise ship held Valery captive. What Colonel Orloff was telling him, however, was that this was only possible if a "correct political report" detailing his "cooperation" was forwarded to POD's General Kornon and his FSB counterpart.

Bridge Captain Mendev had ordered several changes in the course, at one point sailing due north. But the dot on the radar—a trawler, from its size—stayed with them. Mendev informed Orloff, who immediately upbraided him for not telling him sooner. "We cannot afford to take the slightest chance." With this, Orloff encoded a message, disguised as a request for updated sea conditions, and had the radio operator in the communications room immediately aft of the chart room send it to the container ship, MV *Burkhanov*, via the Vancouver office. He also sent a message to a Mr. Raymond Delware, 5081 West Seventeenth Avenue, Vancouver.

When he heard the message coming through on the fax in the Vancouver safe house, Raymond Delware, aka Lucky McBride, together with co-driver Neilson, Gunner Brock, and "Worry-Gut" Cawley, was unwinding after the long haul from Wills Creek, watching a television documentary on secrecy in the U.S. government. It included everything from evidence of the illegal surveillance of U.S. citizens to reports of how JFK's long string of affairs while he was in the White House had been kept secret from the American public.

"Rotten to the core," commented McBride, who, despite his legendary easygoing manner, became incensed by any evidence of malfeasance in government. He reserved a special hatred for the Internal Revenue Service, which, he claimed, had driven his sister to suicide over back taxes. "Hounded her to death for a measly two grand," he was telling Brock. "Put a garnishee on her wages. She was a waitress, for chrissake. Two kids. Husband—a *cop*—left her and they put a garnishee on her wages."

Brock was only half listening, using a militia onetime pad to decipher the incoming fax, which was couched as a mundane message from a "Mrs. Delware," a passenger on the *Southern Star*, to her husband.

"Who's it from?" McBride asked, turning down the TV sound.

"Orloff."

"Trouble?" Cawley asked.

"Hang on," Brock replied. "It's still printing."

Now the documentary was showing the reenactment of the Waco siege, each side of the dispute claiming that it vindicated their interpretation of what had happened.

"Waste of taxpayers' money," Neilson said. "It's obvious the damned FBI fired first."

"Looks like *Southern Star* is being tailed," Brock reported. "By some trawler."

McBride killed the TV. "Where's the trawler hail from?"

"Doesn't say or doesn't know," Brock replied.

"He give you lat and long?" McBride asked.

"Yep. About a hundred miles sou'west of Cape Flattery." McBride was tapping the remote and accidentally hit the On button. "Shit! Do we have anyone nearby on the coast?"

"Not near the cape. Nearest is La Push. Around and down a bit. Forty miles south. Better positioned, if you think about it."

"Better for what?" Neilson put in, looking for support from Cawley, who wanted to get back to Spokane.

McBride and Brock ignored him. "Is there an airstrip nearby?" Brock asked.

"Yep," Brock answered. Cawley and Neilson didn't like Brock's "Yep." He seemed altogether too keen.

"How long to get there?" McBride pressed Brock. "La Push, I mean."

"By air," Brock mulled, "a four-seater charter—about fifteen to twenty minutes."

"All right," McBride said. "Book it."

"I hate boats!" Neilson said. Cawley looked worried.

"Want to know what I hate?" McBride said. "I hate losing a billion dollars because someone's scared of getting a bit seasick." Neilson and Cawley said nothing. McBride turned back to Brock. "Who's our guy in La Push?"

Brock pulled out his Palm Pilot.

"I hope that's not in plain language," McBride said disapprovingly.

Brock refused to answer—of course the entries weren't in fucking plain language. Did McBride think he was an idiot? The truth was, everyone was on edge. That Freeman fucker and his team had really put everybody on overtime.

"Here it is," Brock said, reading the name off his Palm Pilot; it was listed under Car Dealerships. "Captain's name at La Push is Fowler. Has a fishboat called *Push 'n' Shove*."

"Clean record?" McBride asked.

"Arrested once for protesting against the federals giving special fishing rights to the Indians. A lot of the guys on the West Coast have—"

"You ever met him?" McBride asked.

"No."

"But no one knows he's militia?"

"No," Brock answered.

"Sure about that?" Neilson said.

"Absolutely. We've got him flagged as a sleeper."

Cawley looked worried.

"A sleeper," Brock explained, "one of our guys in place—until we need him."

CHAPTER TWENTY-SIX

VANYA HAD BEEN complaining, tired of her apartment, rare as it was for an individual Russian citizen, even post-glasnost, to have four rooms all her own with a small kitchenette thrown in. She yearned to go out more, to be seen with General Kornon. It would give her job as sports announcer with Radio Moscow added influence. What the Americans called "clout." Kornon told her they were going to the Kosmos, the huge, curving, glass hotel in Moscow's outskirts, where he had reserved a booth and they could enjoy a quiet dinner of baked sturgeon with chilled Tsinandali, white wine from the Caucasus.

Kornon couldn't quite quell a feeling of guilt as his shiny black Zil eased to a stop at the hotel's gate, where passes had to be shown in order to keep ordinary Muscovites from entering the island of Western-style decadence. He could see the resentment in the faces of ordinary Russians walking past the gate. But whenever the general felt an attack of inequality coming on, he thought of Ulan Ude in the grip of winter, fifty below, when skin exposed longer than fifty seconds froze. He had paid his dues in the white wilderness. Now it was time to enjoy. Besides, much lower ranks than his, such as his POD agents aboard cruise liners like the *Southern Star*, enjoyed Kosmoslike luxury for ten months of each year.

Vanya disapproved of the short skirts of the girls in the

hotel's five opulent bars. "Where do they think they are? In the Bolshoi?"

Mention of the ballet reminded him of how well his daughter Tanya was doing. She was now dancing with the Kirov, and although he found the short skirts exciting, he went along with Vanya's disapproval, eager to get her upstairs to one of the penthouse suites which he had booked for "official business"— having filled in the POD authorization chit as "debriefing of a Western agent." Among commoners, it was one of the most naive assumptions of the millennium's post–cold war era that Russia and the West had reduced their spying on one another. In fact, under Yeltsin and Putin it had increased dramatically, with so much at stake in the global marketplace.

Kornon looked across at Vanya, willing her to hurry up. He knew, however, that if she was hurried, especially after drinking, she would become petulant, even uncooperative, whereas if she was left to linger over a few more glasses of wine, she would be more accommodating, her performance more uninhibited. In the artificial twilight from the bar, Vanya dipped her finger deep in the white wine and, her tongue curving about her finger, sucked it dry.

"Now!" he said.

"Finish your paper," she said playfully.

He had been glancing at the *Financial Times*—no sign of a market drop for Rone in New York, Tokyo, or London. This gave him a sense of deep satisfaction, confirming his view that the U.S. government would not dare admit to having lost the world's most modern defense computer, terrified in fact to admit it, for fear it would presage a massive market panic in the West. It was a delicious conundrum that Kornon, the Swiss financier, and Chang had created for them. But the oceanographer Hall had walked into a trap created by the Americans themselves when the interference of Freeman's teams in the mountains had delayed delivery of the Rone to the *Burkhanov*, which had been especially equipped for the straight run to Vladivostok. Kornon was proud of the way in which his POD had reacted so promptly, first employing the *Ernst Mann* and now the *Southern Star* in his contingency plan. He smiled, knowing that once the FSB's Orloff had finished with the oceanographer, he would, as the American mafioso were so fond of saying, "be sleeping with the fishes." His nemesis would be destroyed, after all these years, and not so much by his POD's planning as by the American's own stubborn refusal to give up the chase.

"I've finished my paper," he told Vanya. "Let's go upstairs."

She pouted but was drunk enough that it wasn't a serious rebuff. "Are you big?" she asked.

He turned and signaled frantically for the bill. He paid cash, never using a POD requisition chit in the bar. The Kosmos waitress leaned over and he saw deep cleavage.

"Bitch!" Vanya said easily as the "hostess" walked briskly away, her short, white skirt barely covering her derriere.

"She's just doing her job," Kornon said self-righteously. The situation was touchy, and he knew it could go either way. He leaned forward. "I love only you, Vanya." For a moment she seemed downcast, withdrawn, staring into the wine, but in its dim reflection she saw the ring he'd given her. He could just as easily have chosen a hostess. She smiled, indiscreetly taking his hand beneath the table, thrusting it between her legs, gripping it so tightly he felt the blood draining from his fingers.

"When I'm finished," Vanya promised, "you'll be so sore you'll be unable to walk." She giggled, then suddenly releasing his hand, sat up and tossed her long blond hair back over her athletic shoulders, her tight beige blouse in dramatic contrast to her coat's collar of jet-black mink. "I'll eat you alive, Alexander Androvich."

Glancing outside as they waited impatiently for the elevator, Kornon saw it was snowing again. For a moment it took him back to Ulan Ude, and a surge of anxiety, a sudden fear that he was still not safe, assailed him: Vanya could be an FSB agent. And if she was? he asked himself. No matter, he had told her nothing. In the elevator they were alone. That fact aroused him further.

*　　*　　*

McBride, sitting near Brock in the back of the rental on their way to Vancouver International, briefly saw the mountains immediately behind Vancouver, then they were lost again in the rain. "Is the boat ready?" he asked Brock.

"Not yet. It will be by the time we arrive."

"We'll need close-in stuff," McBride said. "We're not going to start shooting at any distance. That'd give this federal boat tailing the *Star* too much time to send an SOS. We'll have to get in close, so we should have shotguns, a couple of AK-47s, and the disposables. Will there be any problem with that?"

"Are you kidding? This is the Northwest. The wild Northwest. They have access to all kinds of stuff. Plus these guys were brought up hunting—bear, deer, moose—"

"This Fowler's boat," McBride cut in. "Diesel or gasoline?"

"Didn't ask."

"You should have. If it's gas, then that's all right. But if it runs on diesel, you'd better make sure this Fowler has a can of gas aboard for Molotovs. No plastic bottles—glass only. I want shrapnel as well, and plastic pop bottles aren't worth a damn."

Neilson, driving, was trying to get himself up for it. "That's why he's lucky, right? Pays attention to detail."

"Uh-huh," Cawley said unenthusiastically. "They say that's what that federal, Freeman, does too. How come he knew we'd come up through Canada?"

"What's the matter with you?" Brock asked Cawley. "Lord, you're a worry gut."

"He doesn't want to go on the boat," Neilson said, now trying to redeem himself with McBride.

"Have you ever *been* on a boat?" Brock asked Cawley.

"Yes. Once—on Pend Oreille, in Idaho, up near the Aryan Nation HQ."

"Pend Oreille?" Brock said. "It's a fucking *lake*!"

"A big one," McBride put in. "Over ninety thousand acres. Deep too. Can get pretty rough. Was it rough, Cawley?"

"Yes, sir."

"We'll get some Gravol. Gets too rough out there, you can take one."

"That'll make him dozy," Brock said.

"He's fucking dozy already," Neilson quipped. "Aren't you, Cawley?"

Cawley didn't appreciate the ribbing, but he was glad McBride mentioned the Gravol. Truth was, he didn't much like the idea of a close-up firefight. At the Rone building, he'd been allowed to stay out of it, looking after the truck.

"You figured out how long it'll take us to reach the federal snooper from La Push?"

"Two, three hours max. Fowler's boat is one fast craft. Have to be these days. Lot o' competition out there for less and less fish."

"You can say that again," Neilson said.

"Lot o' competition out there for less an—"

"Very funny," Neilson retorted, swinging left, away from the main terminal and toward Strait Air Charters.

Cawley looked worried. He hated planes, and with all the fog, he knew it would be instrument flying to La Push. It was going to be a long twenty minutes. It never occurred to him that beyond the coastal mountains and the fog hugging the sea's coastal shelf it might be clearing.

Aboard the *Southern Star*, Orloff sent a radio message to the container ship *Burkhanov*, ordering her to turn about and make speed back toward the *Star*.

"May I ask why?" Valery had the temerity to ask.

"Because she was the vessel specially equipped to carry the Rone, and would have if it hadn't been for Hall and his cohorts upsetting our timetable."

It was obvious that Orloff had no interest in elaborating beyond this. He turned to the officer of the watch, telling him brusquely, "The *Burkhanov* should reach us in a few hours. I want to be informed the moment we have her on radar."

"Yes, Colonel."

"Something's up," the OW said as Orloff left the bridge. Valery shrugged. He felt humiliated and simultaneously relieved that he wasn't privy to the FSB's plans. On one hand, he wanted to know what they were going to do with the *Burkhanov*; on the other, he didn't want to know what they were going to do with the "stowaways."

The rugged coastline around La Push was stunningly beautiful, with stunted pines growing atop the rocks beyond the sandy ribbons of beach. It was among the most dramatic scenes any of the four militiamen had seen, the spray flung high above the rolling breakers sparkling here and there as the sun fought to penetrate the fog bank that still lay like a dove-gray blanket several miles out to sea. The whole scene, especially the strong salt smell of the ocean, invigorated Cawley in a way he'd never known. His next surprise, and one for McBride, Brock, and Neilson as well, was the discovery that Captain Fowler was a woman.

"You look like a stunned mullet!" Brenda Fowler told them, smiling broadly and shaking hands with a grip that told them that anyone who tried to take advantage of her would be in for a fight. "So," she continued, "we gonna fuck these federals for a change 'stead of just waitin' around?"

McBride took an instant dislike to her. He didn't hold with women swearing. If she was trying to be one of the boys, this wasn't the way to do it. Brock and Neilson, however, were obviously quite taken with her. Cawley looked worried. He'd never heard such a good-looking woman talk like this, except some of those Hollywood types. He thought of his wife; she definitely wouldn't approve.

"We're going to run a little interference," McBride told her. "Against another trawler. You up to it?"

"Try me."

He definitely did not like her, but he wondered if this was more contrived on his part than real. Maybe he was only distancing himself from her because he knew what they had to do.

Neilson wasn't distancing himself; he believed in love at first sight. "She looks like that actress," he confided to McBride in a schoolboyish whisper. "You know, Meryl Streep."

"You're married," McBride said.

"I can still window-shop," he replied.

"Yeah, well some other time. Keep your mind on the job—which is to stop that trawler from shadowing the *Southern Star*."

"No problem."

"And keep an eye on Cawley. Ever since I told him to load those Molotovs, he's been looking shaky. He was all right guarding the Mack, but that might've been his limit."

Neilson, whose hatred of federals was as intense as McBride's, had no sympathy for any misgivings Cawley might have. "Leave him behind," he told McBride. "You, me, and Brock can take care of it."

"Yes," McBride agreed, "but I don't want him hanging around by himself. Bad security. Best we have him with us."

"Okay, I'll watch him," Neilson said, then, grinning, added, "if I don't run into Meryl's headlights!"

"Well, she's perked you up," McBride said. "Thought you hated boats?"

"I do, but we'll only be out a couple of hours, right?"

"I hope."

"Will ya look at those clouds, Martha! Piling up like ice cream. Must be twenty, thirty thousand feet high. Just an hour ago we were in fog."

Martha Lynch was dozing in a deck chair on the *Southern Star*'s sun deck, thinking of her grandchildren a thousand miles or more away back in Los Angeles, where another of the earthquakes that seemed to plague California had been reported the day or so before they'd left Vancouver. Their son-in-law had bought a condo not far from the San Andreas fault because he said it was going for a "real good price" and he wanted to "flip" it to easterners. As if any easterner would be as dumb as he was and live right on the fault line.

"Martha? You hear me?"

"Seen one cloud, George, you've seen 'em all." Her eyes were still closed.

George, a portly retired insurance salesman, moved his deck chair back into the shade offered by the ship's stack. "You stay too long in that sun, you'll start to broil. Get skin cancer."

"Doesn't bother me. I like it."

"Well that's stupid, that is."

"George, I'm seventy-eight. Seventy-nine Friday. I got varicose veins and one kidney. I'm entitled to a little sun. Hell, that's what we paid for isn't it?"

"Have it your way. You always know best."

"Well you just go ahead and enjoy your clouds."

George struggled to sit up in his deck chair. "Goddamn sun'd fry a chicken," he said. "I'm going down to the bar."

"Don't you get pickled now."

"If I want to get pickled, I'll get pickled."

George was still mumbling to himself as he ambled awkwardly toward the bridge. There was a NO ADMITTANCE BEYOND HERE sign on a chair, but even from where he was he could see three officers, one of them Captain Valery, looking as if they were having a ding-dong row. A seaman appeared from behind one of the lifeboats where he'd been chipping a spot of rust from the scuppers, the foaming sea slipping by fast a hundred feet below.

"Can I help, sir?

"Yeah. Which way's the bar?"

"Which one, sir?"

"The one I was in yesterday."

Captain Mendev, one of the three officers George Lynch had seen—the other was Orloff—considered himself too near retirement to risk a confrontation with Orloff over the colonel's "request" to increase the ship's speed from the average cost-efficient twenty-four knots per hour to thirty knots. In fact, Mendev had no problem with Orloff's rationale. He well understood that since POD had reported that the U.S. oceanographic vessel *Petrel* was heading their way, the *Southern Star*'s speed en route to Suva should be increased. The problem for Mendev, however, and one that he quickly computed, was that the increase in speed would mean docking in Suva in the early hours of the morning rather than in daylight.

To Orloff's childish taunt that perhaps the great *Southern Star* wasn't up to it, Mendev had answered coolly, "Of course we can do it. Though I doubt whether the chief will be pleased. More speed will use up much more fuel, and—"

"Comrade," Orloff had cut in. "You are senior to the chief. In any event I will take full responsibility. We must reach Suva—"

"Responsibility for what?" Valery interjected, despite knowing that his sharp-edged question was hardly the kind of interdepartmental FSB-POD cooperation Orloff had indicated was vital to his career advancement. But Valery simply could not bring himself to kowtow to Orloff's, and FSB's, slightest whim. *"We—"* Valery indicated Mendev, who was busying himself with an unnecessary inspection of the myriad dials on the space-age bridge. "—we have a direct responsibility to the passengers. Quite apart from the increased and very expensive fuel consumption, this would mean a serious setback for the reputation we have taken so long to build for an efficiency and punctuality that rivals any of the Western lines."

Valery knew this was an exaggeration; how could one ever be as punctual as the obsessive-compulsive Scandinavian lines? They were born with clocks in their heads. But he was correct in asserting to Orloff that the improved reputation of Russian cruise ships had been achieved after a long, sustained battle with a bureaucracy painfully slow to answer Yeltsin's call to raise standards. "To tell over four hundred passengers," Valery continued, "that our timetable will be eight to twelve hours in error and that we will be docking in Suva not when they expect but—"

"Ah," Orloff said dismissively, "they will not object. We are not talking about being late, but early, Captain."

"Early or late," rejoined the tall Estonian, "it is . . . it is bad manners. . . ."

"Poof!" Orloff replied contemptuously. "Manners? You

are worried that 450 pigs stuffing themselves day in and day out will object to an early arrival? It will give them something to talk about other than who is bedding whom, who is winning at deck quoits . . . which officer they danced with . . . who sat at the captain's table."

Valery looked to Mendev for support. He wasn't going to get any. In an uncharacteristically cowardly move—what did the FSB have on him? Valery wondered—Mendev had retreated to the far side of the bridge. Valery turned back to Orloff, knowing the FSB man was probably right—the passengers wouldn't mind that much. After all, they were on vacation. But it was Orloff's presumption, the idea that the FSB could simply snap its fingers and everyone had to jump, that galled Valery. The KGB's initials may have changed to FSB, but they were the same old bullying mob of fanatics. What had become of Putin's reforms among the "guardians of the state," his injunctions that even the secret police had to "humanize their efforts"?

"All right," Valery conceded, "but I must caution you, Colonel, there will be many complaints. Some of these 'pigs,' as you call them, have worked as hard, most of them harder, than any worker in the old Soviet Union for this cruise. I think you are mistaken if you believe Americans will stand for—" Valery hesitated, searching for the American expression he wanted. "—yes, 'screwing around.' There will be more cell phone calls to the head office than you think and—"

"To the head office," Orloff said, who, despite his dour disposition, allowed himself a smile at Valery's naiveté. It was obvious that Staff Captain Valery knew next to nothing about cell phone technology. "There are no cell phone relay stations at sea, Captain Valery," Orloff pointed out tendentiously. "And we are in satellite shadow way out here. The only possibility for transmitting such complaints is by the ship's radio telephone."

"Then," Valery responded, in an effort to salvage his original point, "there will be more *radio telephone* calls than you think to the head office on our radio-telephones complaining that—"

Orloff frowned, but it wasn't in anger. Was it possible that a man of Valery's long experience at sea honestly believed that an old KGB "head of station" had not done his homework before being assigned to this floating city?

"Certainly there will be radio-telephone calls," Orloff said. "Has Captain Mendev not told you?" Mendev was now making his way slowly back toward them, ostensibly inspecting the huge and immaculately clean bridge, the ship's steering levers and control panels that spread in a wide-angled apron of shining green pastel-painted steel and hard plastic consoles before him. But Orloff saw at a glance that Mendev, probably embarrassed to show he was bending to the FSB, had not explained the strategy to his younger colleague. Orloff did it for him. "Yes, there will be many radio-telephone messages but I am afraid not all will get through."

There was a silence for several seconds. *"Atmospherics,"* Orloff explained. "Sunspots. Like the northern lights, Captain, they play havoc with ship-to-shore and satellite communications. You know this surely. Of course, some of the calls will get through—the ones we don't smother with atmospherics."

"You mean," Valery charged, "just enough to lend credence to your story?"

Orloff spread his arms philosophically, clearly proud of his stratagem. "Your radio room's cooperation is appreciated."

Valery, disgusted, turned to leave the bridge.

"We will, of course," Orloff called after him, "make no announcements to the passengers about our increase in speed."

Valery glanced back. "We'll have to tell them something," he said, and added scornfully, "or don't you think they'll notice?"

"Yes, but it might be necessary to *stop* the ship for a while as well." Now Valery was totally confused. "I mean," Orloff continued, "that what we gain with increased speed now might be offset, though I sincerely hope not, by what we lose during the stops."

"Stops? When?" Valery asked. "Where?"

Orloff had an irritating habit of using his tongue instead

of a toothpick to clean his teeth, unconsciously exposing his gums.

"Stop where?" Valery repeated.

Orloff was examining what appeared to be a small particle of food on his finger before brushing it off on his well-ironed "assistant purser's" uniform. "What for?" he said, looking up at Valery. "Burial at sea."

Valery walked over toward the Russian, Mendev. "Is this true, Captain?"

Mendev was busying himself inspecting the bow thruster panel. "It's not uncommon," he said quietly. "You know that. Many of our passengers are elderly. They overdo everything once they get aboard. Drink, food, exercise."

"Yes," Orloff said, "accidents."

"That's why we have a ship's doctor," Valery shot back.

"Yes," Orloff conceded. "But some accidents are fatal."

Valery stormed off the bridge, the sun's glare blinding him for a moment before he could look out over the cerulean-blue stretching as far as he could see, the tips of the long, languorous Pacific swells twinkling silver, visible, alive one moment, gone the next.

CHAPTER TWENTY-SEVEN

FRANK HAD FALLEN asleep until he heard boot steps approaching again. As his head jerked up in the pitch-black, windowless room, he heard a faint scrabbling sound, like some small animal or insect racing across paper. It came from Healy's corner.

"What's that?" he whispered to the Englishman.

"They're not coming," Healy said. "It's the storeroom guy. Comes down three, four times a day. Must be a linen room or something nearby."

"No," Frank said, "I meant that scratching sound." He had a morbid fear of rats.

"Probably a rat," Healy said.

Frank felt clammy cold all over. He had to get out.

Shortly after, there were more footsteps, in unison, heavier, at least three or four men, whispering to foil any hidden mike.

"Not now!" Healy cautioned. "Boris is bringing the boys with him. We don't stand a chance—"

The footsteps stopped. Frank could hear the metallic rattle of a key. Quickly, he stuffed one end of the knotted T-shirt garrote behind him, into the waistband of his trousers, and shifted away from the door. He was glad he did—it flew open with such violence that anyone behind it would have been smashed against the cell wall. The next second the cell exploded in light—from what he guessed was one of the ship's emergency lamps—so bright he found himself forced to look away.

"Listen to me," said a no-nonsense voice. It was Orloff, his tone sharp, bullying, and totally uncompromising. "You two have one hour to tell me. You—" He wheeled on Healy, whom Frank saw only now for the first time as the Englishman scrambled awkwardly to his feet. Healy was taller than he'd imagined, over six feet, spindly legs, unshaven, a dirty white shirt caked with dried blood. He was barefoot; his belt too had been taken, and to Frank's dismay, he saw that the Englishman looked much worse than he had thought. The Russian poked Healy hard in the chest, a big steward in white coat and bow tie beside him, the steward's hands folded neatly in front, waiting. Another steward, one of two with Orloff, was holding the lamp, which cast gorilla-size shadows of Orloff onto the walls. "The exact circuitry and configuration of the chips," Orloff ordered. "The information you gave us before—we had difficulty with it."

"What—" Healy began.

Orloff nodded and the big steward hit Healy hard in the

stomach. The Englishman fell, clutching his solar plexus, his face contorted in pain.

"It didn't *work*!" Orloff shouted. "When we first asked you, we thought you would be sensible, but no—you want to play the circus imbecile. If you do not want to tell us, things will get much worse for you."

Healy looked up and away, as if staring through the impenetrable steel ceiling, defiant even though he was barely able to talk.

Orloff crouched down and poked his finger hard into Healy's throat. "When the Rone reaches Suva, I will expect a full operating manual from you." To Frank's surprise, he picked up a pad of paper and pen beside Healy. "That is why I gave you these materials to work with."

"I can't bloody see," Healy said.

"I gave you a flashlight."

"Wouldn't work," Healy said defiantly, but his body cringing at the same time.

"Give it to me!" Orloff ordered, and pressed the pen-sized flashlight. Nothing happened.

"Russian-made, I suppose," Healy said. "Not worth a—"

Orloff stood up and started berating the chief steward in a torrent of Russian. The steward was trying to apologize but Orloff would have none of it. He swung back and looked down at Healy. "You are right. The batteries are dead. You will be brought new ones." He looked around to his left to face Frank. *"You!"* he said, with the stern command of someone in absolute control. "You will tell me who else on this ship are American spies." He paused. "Whoever they are, they are better than you at their job. You are a bumbler. I saw you the moment you came aboard."

"I don't know anyone aboard," Frank said.

"Who are the CIA agents waiting in Suva?"

"I didn't know there were any," Frank said.

"I think you are lying," Orloff said.

Frank didn't see any kind of signal, but the big steward advanced on him, the man's face not at all implacable, as Frank had first thought, but wearing a twisted grin. It told his potential victim that he enjoyed this much more than shaking cocktails in the glitzy, obsequious world he normally inhabited above.

"I'll ask again," Orloff said. "Who are the other agents aboard the ship?"

"I don't know anything about agents," Frank repeated.

Orloff's face clouded. "Don't be playing the fool, Mr. Hall. We know who you are. General Kornon knows who you are."

"Really?"

"You don't deny you know General Kornon?"

"Oh no," Frank said. "I know General Kornon. We're old friends."

"Da!" Orloff said, and nodded to the steward. Frank fell for the feint, covering his stomach, the big man's right fist crashing into the side of his face, sending him reeling, thudding hard against the bulkhead. His face went numb and he could taste warm blood.

"I'm not playing silly interrogation games with you two," Orloff said, looking from Frank to Healy. "The Rone *will* be delivered intact. And with full instructions." He turned toward Healy, who was still sitting on the floor, arms dangling by his side, eyes staring at the ceiling as if by refusing to look at the reality immediately about him he might somehow avoid seeing the brutality visited upon his cellmate. "An operations manual," Orloff said, looking down at Healy, *"and a troubleshooting guide."* Then he turned back to Frank. "You will give us the names of the agents aboard this ship and in Suva. Or else Miss Moffat will die." Orloff held a picture of her in front of Frank's face. "You see, we have you all on file."

Frank had never seen her before. "Who is she?" he asked.

Orloff stared down at him with a forced smile. "Oh, she's the Queen of England, as you well know—or maybe she's a U.S. Treasury agent?" With that, the Russians left.

"Listen!" Healy called out to Frank frantically. "He'll probably send the two goons back with the batteries. That's our chance." It was only then that Frank realized just how clever the cheeky Englishman had been.

"You screwed up the batteries?" Frank asked.

"Right!" Healy said. "All due respect to you, mate, we couldn't have handled the three of 'em." He grimaced. "Christ, my gut hurts! That bastard!"

"Well, what do you plan to—" Frank began, then suddenly stopped. He quickly felt his way through the pitch-blackness to Healy, whispering, reminding the Englishman of his own warning about the possibility of hidden microphones.

"No," Healy answered in a normal, if pained, voice, "I know all about that stuff, mate—hidden mikes—and I got a good look 'round when the bozo with the emergency lamp was showing you the wine list. This cell is plate steel all around. Not a sign of a bug."

"Couldn't it be in the bulkhead?" Frank pressed. "Vibration mike?"

"In the U.S. embassy in Moscow maybe," Healy said, "but not here. Vibrations from the engines would white it out. Smother it."

"He opened the door too fast for us to surprise him," Frank said. "We'll have to wait and pull the two goons in when they hand the batteries to us."

"Yes," Healy said, "the doorsill will act like a trip wire if we grab 'em in quickly— Christ!"

"What?" Healy was obviously having doubts.

"Maybe they'll just toss the batteries in."

All Frank could hear was the hum of the ship's engines in the darkness, and all he could think of was whether he and Healy would be able to escape. "Eventually," he told Healy, though as much to comfort himself, "someone's going to wonder where the hell we are. Right?"

"Right," Healy concurred. "But I can't wait for 'eventually,' mate. Boris is in a big hurry. Probably figures the quickest way is to thump us 'round a bit—show us they mean business. Tell us the woman they showed you will go for the high jump if we don't cooperate. Much more effective."

"High jump?" Frank asked.

"Kill her," Healy said. They were both silent for a moment, then Healy asked, "You know her?"

"Never seen her before," Frank said, the horror of the Russian's threat against the woman finally sinking in through his own pain and worry about Gloria—who was a million miles away. God, what she must be going through, not knowing—

Frank could hear Healy gasp again from his stomach pain. "We'd better get out," Healy said, "before 'eventually' comes. Maybe she's not an agent at all. Maybe the bastards just pulled someone's photo out to bluff you."

Frank was grateful for Healy trying to make him feel better but saw at once that it didn't matter whether the woman Boris referred to as Moffatt had been pulled at random. If he didn't tell them what they thought he knew, she'd die anyway. Unless it *was* pure bluff. But there was no way he could take the gamble with the woman's life, since the FSB was ruthless in such matters.

"I'll stand well back from the door," Frank said. "Soon as the first goon comes in, you yank him through. I'll get the second one with the door."

"What if they don't come in?"

"Well hell, then," Frank said. "Might as well go for broke. Run at 'em!"

"Yeah," Healy said without conviction.

In the darkness the Englishman's voice was now taking on a more desperate tone. "I hope it bloody well works, or else—"

"Wait a minute," Frank said. "Listen, you stay where you are and I'll—" They could hear footsteps again. Two men. Then the steps receded.

"Damn storeroom again!" Healy spat.

"Just trying to wear down our nerves," Frank said.

"Well they're succeeding. Much more of this and—" They noticed a sudden change in the overriding hum of the ship's engines, a tremor passing through the lower decks.

"We're picking up speed," Frank said.

"Think we'll make it to Suva?" Healy asked grimly, clearly meaning the two of them, not the ship. It seemed to Frank that the Englishman was losing his nerve. He heard footsteps approaching again, or were they once more coming to the storeroom? Quickly, he shifted in the blackness, his back to the bulkhead, the door to his right. The footsteps came closer, then stopped. There was the rattle of keys, then a ray of light cutting the darkness like a blowtorch. At the end of the ray, sitting, bunched up in the far corner to the right of the door, Healy was cowering, arms protecting his head, eyes avoiding the light.

One of the two goons, both in stewards' uniforms, stepped over the sill, his right fist clutching the batteries. "Here," he grunted, his accent sounding heavier than before. Perhaps he wasn't the same one. Healy showed no sign of stirring. The steward gave him the boot. Healy groaned, looking up, frightened, squinting in the glare.

"Here—take them," the steward instructed, thrusting out the batteries at Healy. The second man muttered something in Russian, his tone impatient. He leaned in the doorway, sticking his head into the room, looking around at the far left corner for Frank.

Frank hit the door hard with both feet. The man pulled his head back but not quickly enough—knocked unconscious, his torso was wedged hard between the metal door and its steel frame. His partner whirled around, but Healy pulled his feet from under him. The Russian's hands instinctively flew out in front of him to break his fall, batteries flying. Frank, up now, took one step, kicking the Russian in the ribs, Healy already scrambling up as quickly as he could. The Russian should have gone down but he didn't, and in a remarkable feat of fitness and agility, as he fell he pivoted to his right, striking out as he hit the deck, kicking Frank on the thigh. But Healy was now up, and his foot flew out like a disembodied limb, but in the sliver of light from the partially open door, it found its mark. The Russian fell, clutching his scrotum, cursing, the cell's waste bucket clattering onto its side, its lid rolling about like a metallic Frisbee.

Frank kicked the Russian in the head, then, dizzy from the effort and lack of food, unsteadily helped Healy drag the second man into the cell as well.

"Get his keys," said Healy, who had slipped the batteries

into the flashlight then kicked the big Russian again. "Tie their hands behind 'em with their belts. The bastards."

Frank found a six-inch switchblade on the other man, who he thought was hemorrhaging badly until he saw in the flashlight beam that what he'd thought was blood on the man's shirt was urine from the spilled bucket. Frank felt relieved as well as exhausted, for no matter how bitterly he felt against his enemy, it went against the grain to leave a man to bleed to death, unless he was a terrorist or had attacked first. The stench of urine and feces enveloped him as he suggested they try to use the other steward's uniform.

"Don't think so," Healy said, sounding reinvigorated by the fight. "It's covered in piss too. Bit spotty for the dining room! I'll take his pen, though."

"Listen," Frank said, then paused, feeling so woozy he had to grab the door frame to steady himself. "I've got to get some food. Can hardly stand."

"What do you know?" Healy said, pulling out a switchblade from the pocket of the first Russian. "A pair!"

Frank was so dizzy he thought Healy had said a "pear," and asked, "Where?"

They laughed about it, but it was the mad laughter of fatigue as they checked to see if the bare, austerely painted passageway outside was clear. They spun the cell's wheel lock closed behind them and clicked the big Yale lock shut.

Frank cautioned that it would be just as dangerous from now on, and Healy, as if to underscore the point, told him that the crew alone probably numbered over two hundred, and that among the passengers there were sure to be plants.

"What kind of plants?" Frank asked, pausing for breath outside one of the storage rooms but high on their momentary victory. "Indoor plants? Cactus?"

"Ah, the bloody laughing oceanographer," Healy said, flushed as well with the excitement of their escape from the cell. "You're in worse shape than I thought. You need a drink."

Frank detected a whiff of acetone in the air. "The laundry's ahead," he said.

"What laundry?"

"Last thing I remember before waking up in the cell was the smell of a laundry. Chinese."

"Right!" Healy said, his sudden optimism overcoming his pain. "Then we're in luck. Freshly starched uniforms coming up. What d'you want to be—wine steward?"

"Crew," Frank answered, leaning on the bulkhead to steady himself. "If we look like crewmen, we'll have the best chance of anonymity. Problem is getting past the laundry staff—"

Healy caught Frank as he began to fall, everything ahead of him momentarily blurring. "Don't worry about the staff," Healy assured him, steadying him before they moved on. "They won't ask questions—not if we look as if we know our way around. Long as we have *some* uniform on."

Now Frank could smell acetone again, and they could hear the Chinese staff talking to, or rather yelling at, one another farther down the corridor above the hiss of steam irons and rumble of dryers that were situated in this almost deserted netherworld of the big cruise ship.

"Stay here," Healy said. He steered Frank off into a doorless compartment the size of a horse stall, where laundry was piled high.

Frank felt humiliated by his physical weakness. Healy had been beaten up but was able to go on, while he, lowering himself to the floor, knew that until they got something to eat and drink, his condition wouldn't improve. He was grateful for the temporary respite among the hills of dirty linen. It was soft and warm, too warm, in fact, for, like the *Petrel* and most other modern ships he'd sailed on, the *Southern Star* was fully air-conditioned, at times preventing fresh air from getting into circulation. From somewhere in the pile of used bedding he got a whiff of perfume and thought of Gloria. What a mess he'd created for her. Somehow he had to get a message to shore. Exhausted, he fell asleep.

The next second, or so it seemed to him, he was being shaken violently awake, and looked up at a tall, uniformed seaman, the blue *Southern Star* patch on his shoulder.

"Hey, Frank!" It was Healy, having returned with enough

uniforms to outfit a squad of able-bodied seamen. "You awake?" As Frank sat up and got his bearings, Healy was grinning. "Are we in luck or are we in luck?"

Frank's eyelids closed.

"Don't nod off again, you twit," Healy said, pulling out a pair of crewmen's trousers from the used but still presentable pile he had brought back. "What waist size?"

Frank tried to stifle a yawn, unsuccessfully. "Thirty-six. What are we lucky about?" he asked, shaking his head, trying to throw off the fatigue.

"We're down among all the goodies," Healy said. "Food lockers. All locked, unfortunately, but I can smell baking up ahead somewhere. We'll scrounge something somewhere."

"We've got to get out an SOS," Frank said.

"You're right," the Englishman replied. "Once they find us missing, they'll go ape. We can send a message out if we can get into the radio room. Trouble is, it must be five, six decks up. Have to run the gauntlet."

"Uniforms should help," Frank said.

"All right," Healy said. "What's our message. Who to?"

"Just send out an SOS," Frank said. "Say 'Merchandise aboard *Star*. Send help.' "

Frank was about to give Healy Brownlee's number when the Englishman stopped him. "No, wait till we get to the bridge. If I get caught before we get there—what I don't know I can't tell them. Okay, now—"

Someone was coming down the passageway toward the laundry bins, Chinese voices, loud laughter—now one going off somewhere, the other coming closer. Suddenly a Chinese— in a stained white jacket, his collar open, tobacco-stained teeth, a spike of stubble on his chin—was staring at them.

"What you do here?" he demanded. "You no allow—"

Healy kneed him in the groin, and they both fell into the pile of laundry. Healy's fist came up into the air and there was a stifled cry, then silence.

"You're pretty good at that," Frank complimented him, while tearing up a pillowcase to gag and bind Healy's victim.

They had to pass through the Chinese laundry where the passageway widened to accommodate the big washers and dryers. Healy told Frank to take a deep breath and tough it out, and the two men in their stewards' uniforms strode in as if they owned the place. Halfway through, Healy paused, picked up a shirt, examined it haughtily, and pointing to the worn collar, berated a sullen-looking Chinese worker through a cloud of steam from one of the big press irons. "No good," Healy said. "Lookee awful. You do better. Understand?"

The Chinaman looked up at the tall Englishman, turned away and very deliberately spat.

Frank knew Healy's audacity came in part from the euphoria of their escape, a "high" of the kind he'd seen before on missions with his SEAL comrades and other SpecWar types. It was the product of the release from high tension, a kind of reverie that for a while hunger and exhaustion actually increased. He'd seen it in Aussie Lewis on Eagle Island and at one time off the Aleutians, a sudden invigoration when the body is in fact approaching collapse. Healy wasn't in as good shape as he thought.

"Bread!" the Englishman announced, as Cortez might have declared, "Oro!"—fresh golden loaves being wheeled out by one of the Russian stewards from a bakery fifty feet ahead of them, on the way to diners in the other world, four decks above.

"Slow down," Frank warned Healy. "If he turns and says something in Russian we're dead."

CHAPTER TWENTY-EIGHT

THAT NIGHT WHEN Captain Tate, master of the *Petrel*, now two hundred miles to the north, received instructions from Brownlee via Washington's Department of Oceans to abort his oceanographic cruise and proceed "at full speed" to shadow the *Southern Star*, described by a security-obsessed Brownlee as being "in possible distress," Tate noted in his log that the DoO scientist aboard, Dr. Sheila Shalit, was "less than enthusiastic." In fact, as both he and the *Petrel*'s tall, deceptively dour first officer, Scotty Redfern, well knew, the head of the four-"person" oceanographic geology team was furious. She was a bossy woman, and when her five-foot-two-inch frame appeared on the bridge amid the islands of indicator lights to "have it out" with Captain Tate, a man twice her age and experience, Redfern expected a verbal punch-up. It was much worse. Dr. Shalit wanted it put "on record" that she was "outraged . . . insulted . . . and furthermore humiliated" at the "arbitrary and cavalier way" in which she was being treated. She knew why, she said. It was because she was a woman, and the four-person team consisting of herself, two female graduate students, and a male technician, Luke—whom she had brought along only because he was able to open the big claw grabs—had been led by a woman. "No way would Washington pull a stunt like this," she declared.

"It's no stunt, Dr. Shalit," Tate replied evenly. "Quite frankly, I'm as upset about it as you are."

"Oh—" The wind, as Scotty observed later, had gone right out of her sails, when the captain agreed with her for once.

"You must realize, Captain," Dr. Shalit said, "if it's a bona fide case of a ship in distress I would have no objection, none at all. But if I understand your instructions correctly, they're not sure."

"That's how I understand it," Tate replied. "I've requested we be recalled as soon as they ascertain—"

"Quite!" Shalit agreed. "My first reaction, however, is that knowing the government—" She rolled her eyes. "—it's probably to rescue some fool trying to set a paddling-the-Pacific-in-a-canoe record or something."

Tate smiled. "Well, at least the weather is pleasant."

"So far," Scotty interjected, as ready to spread doom where optimism threatened as he was to spread bonhomie when others were pessimistic, "forecast is for a Force Ten."

"Then," Tate said, "we'd better increase speed."

Aboard the much larger bridge of the *Southern Star*, the computerized readout incorporating five extra knots told Mendev that his ship was consuming fuel at too high a rate, an exponential, rather than arithmetic, increase from 19,500 gallons per hour to 20,000 gallons per hour. The increased speed was hardly noticed, however, by most passengers. George Lynch, who, despite his addle-brained, booze-induced confusion about the precise location of bars, cinemas, casinos, and other facilities aboard the *Star*, was aware of the change. In fact, the increased slipstream, he told Martha, made him thirstier than usual. "More salt in the air," he explained as they took their stroll around the sundeck, prior to the first sitting for dinner. Here, the breeze played havoc with Martha's hair, the stars a riot of twinkling silver in the velvety blackness above them.

"We keep going at this rate," George predicted, "and we'll be in Fiji a day earlier."

"They know what they're doing," Martha said, dismissing George's hypothesis. "Just relax, why don't you?"

Below them on the port side, down on the flying bridge, Mendev was hunched over the big swivel-mounted binoculars.

"Well, what's he looking for?" George said.

"Whales," Martha replied. Sometimes George just wouldn't shut up. Always sticking his nose into other people's business.

Mendev was moving back from the flying bridge into the bridge proper.

"How ya doin'?" George called down.

"For God's sake, George!" Martha said. "Don't make a spectacle of yourself."

"Just saying howdy."

"Ships' captains don't say *howdy*."

"Sure they do. That Captain Val, he's—"

"Valery," Martha corrected.

"Yeah, well, he looks like a real nice guy. Always friendly."

Getting food was tougher than either Frank or Healy had anticipated. What they hadn't counted on was the elaborate nightly parade of food before the assembled passengers in the vast and elegantly decorated grand salon. The mouth-watering smells and appearance of everything on the long, glittering silver trays tormented the two men's taste buds as they watched the seemingly endless line of waiters, turned out in immaculate brass-buttoned white coat and blue trouser uniforms, heads erect as if parading before royalty, gazing straight ahead, oblivious to everything other than putting on a good show.

As the food parade made its circuit around the vast salon, a bass baritone in traditional costume began a stirring song, a celebration of joyful life. Frank and Healy peered in from the darkness like two orphans, invisible to the horde of more than two hundred admiring diners attired in everything from casual semitropical attire and jeans to formal dinner suits, appetites piqued by liberal servings of predinner cocktails.

Though thankful for the cover of night, Frank and Healy began to doubt they would ever be able to penetrate the closely supervised food train that was catering so meticulously to the whims of the passengers, several of whom, like George Lynch, were already well tanked by the time the main course dinner arrived. George began an impromptu assist to the bass baritone, his unsolicited effort entertaining some of the passengers, annoying others, and embarrassing Martha.

For all his years at sea on work ships such as the *Petrel*, and all his promises to Gloria that "sometime" he would take her on a holiday cruise, Frank had never been on a cruise ship before. But now he stumbled upon the trick, as did Healy, to getting free food. After watching the first sitting, composed mainly of the relatively younger, mid-fiftyish contingent, they observed frantic activity among waiters rushing to clear the tables for the *second* sitting, which consisted of the older and generally more formally attired passengers. Following several of the uniformed crew down toward the kitchens, awaiting the opportunity to plunder one of the trays, the two men nevertheless remained vigilant for Orloff, who, Healy warned, "must be asleep" if he hadn't yet discovered them gone. On the other hand, as Frank pointed out, the crowd of people streaming out of their cabins for mealtime would make it much more difficult for the Russian to use his agents as effectively as he otherwise might have.

"What happens *after*?" Healy asked as they dropped back so as not to get too close to a silver salver barely ten feet ahead of them, bearing the substantial remains of an Alaskan red king salmon. Healy's earlier optimism, Frank noticed, seemed to desert him in inverse proportion to his hunger.

"After," Frank said, "Orloff'll have two hundred agents."

"Bloody hell!" Healy said, and quickly looked around, hoping no one heard him. "You mean the crew?"

"Yes," Frank answered. "A big bonus for the guy who makes us."

"*Idite proch!*"—Out of the way!—a waiter yelled brusquely, his brass buttons shining like spots of gold as he turned sideways in the corridor. Without breaking his stride, he sailed majestically between the two of them toward the main galley. Ahead, the remains of the Alaskan salmon stopped in line with other trays waiting their turn to be put on the dumbwaiter and taken down to the busboys on the deck below. A steward who had been unloading dirty cutlery and dishes from his tray almost collided with an outcoming waiter from the kitchen who was holding a silver salver high above his head as he adroitly negotiated the swing doors, emerging with a jellied ham paté. The paté was quivering in the sea swell that Frank noticed had grown more pronounced in the last half hour.

"Right," Frank advised Healy as the waiters flashed by on their return journey to the dining room. The tall Englishman was astounded at the brazen speed with which Frank approached a tray laden with leftovers in the dumbwaiter and snatched the starched linen cloth out from under the leftovers without disturbing them, flicked the cloth free of crumbs and placed it on an empty tray nearby. All in a matter of seconds. "Follow me," Frank ordered, quickly infiltrating the line of impatient waiters rushing into the kitchen. A harassed sous chef, yelling something at them in Russian, which Frank assumed was a table number, pushed two trays at them, each loaded with Alaskan king crab, broccoli, and baked potato. Without a word Frank turned back toward the grand salon, Healy following. Slowing, Frank glanced behind him, let several waiters pass, then turned right, Healy still in tow. They passed the library and casino, took an outer door onto the deck and ducked behind a lifeboat, where they couldn't be observed by strolling passengers. Neither of them spoke for five minutes as they devoured all but the broccoli, which Healy tossed overboard, together with napkins and trays. The linen shone for a moment on a wave top in the undulating light cast by the portholes below them before it was whipped into the darkness astern of the huge ship.

For ten minutes or so Frank felt no effect from the meal other than the rushed satiation of his hunger. Then the hastily downed food started to work its magic and he told Healy he felt like a new man, which, Healy replied, was just as well, because he "sure as hell" wasn't going to risk going back for dessert.

"Listen," Healy said, keeping his voice low as they resumed walking around the deck in the apron of darkness beyond the deck lights. "This should be a good time to have a go at the radio room. End of the four-to-eight watch guys changing shift. What do you think?"

"Let's go."

They approached the dimly lit CREW ONLY BEYOND HERE sign on the staircase leading up to the bridge. Ahead on the bridge's port wing they could see an officer's cap silhouetted against a cloud-shrouded moon. It was Valery, having emerged from the wheelhouse for a breath of fresh air.

Frank heard the click of the switchblade Healy had taken from the Russian he'd tackled in the cell. "No," he whispered, gripping the Englishman's wrist. "Wait till he goes back into the wheelhouse," adding, "Open your hand." In the wash of moonlight, Frank wrote down Brownlee's number on Healy's hand.

Then the two of them started up the steep stairs toward the bridge on the port, radio room, side. But hearing the sound of a sliding door, they quickly backed down the stairs, slipping in behind the nearest lifeboat. Valery appeared again on the bridge's wing.

"Shit!" Healy spat out angrily.

After five more minutes, when the traffic of the watch change had ended, Frank decided it was time. As he moved out from the shadow of the lifeboat toward the staircase on the lee side of the bridge, every nerve taut, he felt the soft breeze of the trade winds, and the ship gently undulating over one of the long Pacific swells. He kept one eye on the portside lookout, who, as duty demanded, was gazing westward into the night. He knew, as did Healy, that their only chance of success lay in being able to pass quickly through the now open portside door before either the lookout heard them or someone walking out from the bridge saw them approaching the top of the steep gangway. The lookout turned his attention due south. Frank froze, he and Healy crouching. Frank could hear Healy breathing tensely behind him, but luckily, the lookout did not turn around to look back at the superstructure of the ship, instead resuming his westward gaze across the vast expanse of dark ocean.

A few steps from the top Frank glimpsed pinpoints of red and green lights blinking on the segmented arc formed by the control panels. He turned and whispered to Healy, "I forgot to tell you, whichever of us gets through—"

The lookout saw him.

It all happened so quickly that for Frank it took on the surrealism of nightmare. Seizing the moment, he'd darted ahead of Healy into the darkness of the bridge, looking for the glow he knew would mark the chart room and the radio room behind it, when suddenly the bridge lit up. Intensely bright light momentarily blinded him. He saw Orloff step out from the chartroom, and Valery, in the center of the control panel, looking distraught, but Frank knew intuitively Valery wasn't going to help him.

"Grab him!" Healy yelled.

Orloff and the radioman stepped forward, and Frank realized Healy was yelling at Orloff, *not* at him.

Jesus! He'd just given Healy Brownlee's number, and— Healy grabbed him from behind. Ahead, the starboard door opened and a steward stepped in bearing a tray of steaming mugs, squinting like a hare caught in a headlight's beam. Frank had one foot on the console and was over it before Orloff could lay a finger on him. As the radioman darted around the far end of the console to grab at him, Frank reached the starboard door. Healy's knife swished past him, into the door frame, a second knife slashing his back. The steward fought for control of his tray, and losing it, a clattering avalanche of falling cups, hot steaming coffee, hot chocolate, and tea rained down on Healy, who slipped on the liquid-slicked decking, crashing into the door's edge, his hands splayed like a flying opossum. Thrown back, his head struck the steel deck.

Frank snatched the knife and ran for his life, slithering down the starboard stairway's rails to the salon deck. Startling a group of strolling passengers, he exploded through them, cutting through an open passage to the port side of the salon deck, through one of the many doors, down to the restaurant deck, then the information deck, lights flashing by him like tracer, an elderly couple separating in fright, saying, "I'll complain to the . . ." down to the main deck where most of the passengers' cabins were. Any open door would do.

* * *

"Are you all right?" the felled drink steward asked Healy, trying to help the Englishman up off the slippery deck.

Healy smacked the man's arm away. "No, I am not all right!" Next, Healy's venom was aimed at Valery. "What the hell were you standing there for like a bloody mummy?"

"Never mind," Orloff said impatiently. "Did you get it from him?"

Healy got up, his steward's uniform stained with hot chocolate and coffee. "Yes," he answered angrily. "I did. But I spend all this bloody time in that shithouse down there faking everything I could, and then stuffing myself with crab—which, I might add, I'm not fond of—and then you lot fuck everything up." He was glaring back at Valery now. "*You* could have stopped him!"

Orloff ignored Healy's outburst. It wasn't clear that Valery could have stopped the American even if he'd wanted to. In any case, Orloff wasn't overly concerned.

"Can we turn the lights out?" Valery asked. "It's difficult to see the controls."

"Yes, yes," Orloff agreed.

"Turn the lights off!" Healy shouted. "Is that all you're going to do? That Hall's one tough American bastard, believe me. You let him run loose and God knows what will happen."

"Calm yourself, Mr. Healy," Orloff said. "You've done well. Exceptionally well. Now that we've got the contact's name, we can send Washington anything we like. Give them the wrong coordinates. They'd be hundreds of miles off course. Never catch up to us."

"Oh, that's brilliant, that is, Colonel," Healy said, his tone bitterly sardonic. "You send them a screwy location and it doesn't mesh with the satellite picture, so they'll know he's in trouble."

"You might be interested to know," Orloff responded, "that the weather report Captain Valery has given me forecasts heavy cloud over the entire area. Bad weather from here to Fiji."

"So?" Healy said.

"The cameras aboard the satellite will be blocked by—"

"Blocked, my arse!" Healy said, his accent now even more marked than usual. "Jesus Christ! What do they teach you in Moscow? New infrared will cut right through that cloud cover." Healy realized, however, that he'd overplayed the point, knowing full well that if the weather were bad enough, certain sea and atmospheric conditions in the ionosphere were in fact capable of blanketing satellite "real-time" transmissions.

"Well," he said, "I still wouldn't risk sending them the wrong location, because if conditions clear and they *do* get photo confirmation of where we are and it doesn't jibe with our transmission, they'll know we're feeding them garbage for a reason and want to find out why."

"It might interest you to know," Orloff replied, "that we're not all as—" He paused, searching for the English word. "—that we're not all as *inept* as you so rudely suggest. We have, as you call it, a 'fallback' strategy."

"And what's that?" Healy demanded, just as rudely as before, thinking the Russian was bluffing.

For the first time Valery took an interest in the exchange. He detested both Orloff and Healy—they were two of a kind—but enjoyed seeing Orloff being put on the spot by his English spy. Valery also found the Englishman's accent different from most he had heard. Burgess, MacLean, and Philby—that whole nest, he'd been told—all had upper class accents. Healy's seemed more visceral—working class.

"We can play it," Orloff answered, "how do you say— 'straight.' "

"What the hell are you talking about?" Healy demanded.

But Healy's temper, despite his tone, was subsiding, and though not ready to admit it, he saw Orloff's point clearly enough. Rather than sending a false message, Orloff was going to give the *Petrel*, via Brownlee, the *Southern Star*'s *correct* position. He had to admit the Russian was damned quick on his feet, changing strategy.

"Draw them to us?" Healy posited. "A trap?"

"Da!" Orloff said, with his Slavic shrug. "Tomorrow night

or the evening after. Write out the message Hall told you he wanted to send, and give it to the radio operator here."

Valery suddenly realized just how far ahead Orloff had planned his options, understanding for the first time the true reason for Orloff ordering them earlier to increase speed. This way they could slow, even stop, to deal with the *Petrel* and still maintain their schedule. If the colonel wasn't anything else, Valery had to concede, he was more cunning than most FSB heads of station.

"How will you stop her?" Valery asked.

"Oh," Orloff answered, dismissing the question with a wave of his hand. "Any number of ways, now that we're well into international waters. You remember the *Stockholm*? That's a possibility."

A cold shiver ran down Valery's back. It was the *Stockholm* that had collided with the *Andrea Doria*, sending her straight to the bottom.

"And that," Orloff continued, "was a *big* accident. The *Southern Star* accidentally colliding with a small oceanographic vessel—a crew of what, twenty, thirty, at the most—will hardly rate the evening news anywhere."

"What about our reputation?" Valery challenged. "The cruise line, the reputation we have painstakingly built up as—"

"Captain," Healy cut in, his tone that of realpolitik, "we don't give a shit about your cruise line. The Rone is worth more than all the cruise lines, East and West, put together. So just do as you're told."

"Unlike you," Valery said, turning angrily toward the Englishman before he could stop himself, "I do not measure the worth of everything in dollars. I am not a paid traitor who sells out his—"

"Shut up!" Orloff ordered. "He's quite correct. The computer's worth—and not just in dollars, Captain—cannot even be measured against your precious ship. Moscow has ordered us to get it by any means, and that is what I intend to do. If ramming the *Petrel* is not possible, I have several other measures in mind." He turned to Healy. The Englishman was now more discernible, the colonel's eyes having readjusted to the bridge's darkness from the bright light of a few minutes before. "Who is his contact?"

"A Brownlee. Here's the number." He held out his hand.

Orloff laughed heartily, the first time Valery had seen him do so. "I used to do this at school. Write notes on my hand."

"Yeah," Healy cut in, "well, before we all die laughing, we'd better waste Hall."

Valery didn't understand the use of "waste" for a moment. When he did, his alarm was directed at Orloff. "But why? Now that you've got—"

"Don't worry, Captain," Orloff said. "We'll spill as little blood on your precious ship as possible."

"But now that you have the contact name, this Brownlee," Valery pressed, "why not let Hall—"

"Because, you dunce," Healy said, "he's as cunning as a shithouse rat and he'll try to stop this ship. Can't you get that through your thick head? The bastard knows ships—inside bloody out—as well as you do. Better probably. He's an oceanographer." Healy looked over at Orloff. "And you said he's an ex-commando?"

"SEAL," Orloff said.

"Then he'll try to think of a way to sabotage us."

Mendev, in his bathrobe and looking the worse for wear, now appeared on the bridge, having been woken by the ruckus, and his question was how Orloff was going to catch Hall amid all the passengers. "We're carrying over four hundred people aboard."

"With strategy," Orloff replied. "We'll catch him by doing precisely what he has done ever since he left Washington State and evaded our Swiss friends' freelancers. We will do the unexpected."

Orloff began writing out the message for the radio officer to send Brownlee.

"All right," Healy said. "But what are you going to do about that Treasury woman?"

"Well," Orloff responded, "we can't have her nosing about."

"Do you think Hall recognized her when I showed him the photograph?" Orloff asked.

"No," Healy said, "he didn't."

"Ah, then we needn't have shown it to him," Orloff said. "Still, it's better to be sure." He paused. "But then who sent her?"

"Probably this Brownlee in Washington, D.C.," Healy said.

Orloff nodded thoughtfully, then handed Healy a key to one of the ship's penthouse suites, with its own balcony, on the restaurant deck. "Number 402," Orloff told him. "On the port side. You've done well, Mr. Healy. Clean up and rest. I'll see you in the morning. If you want anything in particular, Captain Valery will look after it—won't you, Captain?" It was clearly an order, not a request.

"Where are you going?" Healy asked as Orloff made his way to the portside door.

Orloff smiled. "To catch Mr. Hall."

The Englishman appreciated it. It was time Orloff and his people did their share. He was tired out; a bit of R and R was in order.

"By the way, Mr. Healy. Even though they will get considerable bonuses, some of my men, particularly in the laundry, complained that you were overly rough."

"You wanted me to be convincing," Healy said. "That's what I gave you."

"Even so, they said you . . . seemed to enjoy it a lot."

"Earning my pay," Healy said unapologetically.

Orloff shrugged and left the bridge. Healy, his face catching the amber reflection of the radar sweep, was unbuttoning the stained jacket when Valery, who by now utterly despised him, asked, "And when you, as a traitor, have given them everything they want, do you think they will leave *you* alone?"

"They?" Healy asked.

"KGB, FSB," Valery explained, "whatever they call themselves nowadays."

"For a Russian—" Healy began.

"Estonian," Valery corrected him.

"All right. For an *Estonian* you know bugger all about your own mob."

"What do you mean?"

"I mean, sweetheart, that one thing FSB's Moscow Center does is bring back its own people. You worry about the cruise line's reputation. Well FSB's got *their* reputation to think of too, and if word gets around that they pay an agent then bump him off—Moscow Center knows it's zippo for recruiting any more foreign agents. No more goodies from the West. Besides," Healy added, grinning, "you don't give away the whole game, do you?"

By this Valery understood the Englishman to mean that if an agent, like him, was smart, he wouldn't tell Moscow everything about the Western secrets he was selling until his new identity, most probably Swiss, along with a Swiss bank account, had been arranged to his satisfaction. In fact, he was correct in this assumption.

"It was easy, then," Valery said, his tone more accusatory than questioning, "for you to betray the United States, your adopted country."

"Oh, spare me the sermon, mate. I notice you're not exactly chummy with the Russians, but you get paid, I presume."

Valery flushed with embarrassment.

"Yeah, I thought so," Healy said. "Well, I'll tell you something else, *Staff Captain*. Right now I wouldn't mind some champagne and one of those tarts the colonel has stashed aboard for 'extracurricular activities.' " He smiled. "If you know what I mean."

It was the most unsavory thing Healy could have asked Valery to do, and Valery knew the Englishman had done it out of pure spite, in retaliation for his calling him a traitor, which you couldn't be if you didn't belong in the first place, Healy hating Americans as much as his own people. Money was the only citizenship he wanted, or trusted. Leaving the bridge, he told Valery, "Blond or brunette, I'm not fussy. But big tits."

The radio officer laughed at Healy's remark and went into

the radio room to send the message to Brownlee, a message that Orloff had no doubt Brownlee would in turn send to the *Petrel* and the trawler shadowing the *Star*.

Valery followed the radio operator into the transmitting room and, indicating the starboard door of the bridge where Healy had just exited, made a dismissive gesture as if wishing some foul odor away. "You'd better call up one of Orloff's whores for the pig."

"Yes, sir. One with big—"

"Shut your mouth!"

CHAPTER TWENTY-NINE

THERE WAS A raging argument at the White House as to whether the message Brownlee had received, GIFT SENT TO MRS. BURKHANOV and signed FRANK was genuine.

"I think it is," Donna Fargo argued.

"I don't," Lawson said, nervously adjusting his bow tie. "It's signed 'Frank,' not Frank with an e, as Hall and Mr. Brownlee agreed."

"I know that, Lawson," Donna replied, "but he was probably pressed for time and simply forgot to add the e."

"I think Donna has a point," Brownlee concluded.

"The only trouble I have," Donna said, "is that if it's genuine, it means the computer was transferred to *Burkhanov* under cover of darkness. If so, I must admit I don't understand how they could have done that without these two men of Freeman's on the—" She glanced down at her notes. "—on the Coast Guard's *Tuna Ghost* seeing it."

"Oh, that's easy," Brownlee said, in the know-it-all tone he adopted after having sought expert advice. "Chief of Naval Ops said the *Tuna Ghost*'s radar could easily miss any such transfer between the *Star* and the *Burkhanov* at night, given the size of the Pacific swells. He said the *Tuna Ghost*'s radar would lose the transfer launch or whatever they used in the clutter."

"Clutter?" Donna pressed him.

"Well—something to do with big waves, signals and stuff." His tone suddenly became aggressive. "Point is, if we agree the signal is genuine, I think we should tell the *Tuna Ghost* to board the *Burkhanov*."

"Fine," Donna responded, "but how about Frank Hall?"

Brownlee had already thought that one through, but knew Donna wouldn't like it. "I've talked with the President. The bottom line is, we *have* to get the Rone. That's priority one. I mean, we can't do anything else until we've found it." Before Donna could object, he quickly added, "I mean, we can't stop or storm the *Southern Star* looking for Frank without any evidence of wrongdoing. The President certainly doesn't want another *Ernst Mann* fiasco. So no computer, no—"

"So he's on his own?" Donna snapped.

"He knew that going in."

"You bastard!"

"Hey, I didn't say we were pulling the *Petrel* out. We can keep her on the *Star*'s trail. That way we cover both bases, right?"

"The *Petrel*'s hours away," Donna said, turning on the hapless Lawson. "Isn't she?"

"Ah, yes. I believe so."

"Believe so or know so?"

"Yes, she's hours away."

"And," Donna said, still fuming at Brownlee, "the *Petrel* can't do anything without evidence. *Right?*"

"Like I said, Donna, he knew that going in."

As Tate sat in the chart room, looking up the marine registry, he braced against the Pacific swells which, while noticeable enough on his oceanographic ship of only 550 tons, he knew would be barely perceptible to those aboard the much bigger 20,000-ton Russian vessel next to which the *Petrel* would look like a rowboat. From the computer's register he noted that the *Southern Star*'s most telling feature was an enclosed area and a double stack that swept back toward a kidney-shaped pool on the sundeck. Tate, always an avid student of other ships, let the remaining groups of five digits that made up an incoming message chatter away as Scotty Redfern entered the bridge to take over the eight-to-midnight watch.

The second officer, whom Redfern was relieving, noisily slid open the bridge's portside door, and Redfern grimaced, anticipating a bang as the door closed.

Bang!

"Jesus Christ!" Redfern said. "If I've told that laddie once I've told 'im a hundred times not to—"

"Scotty!"

Redfern spun around, for Tate was a man who seldom shouted, either in alarm or provocation. "What is it?"

"Washington says Frank Hall might be aboard!"

"Well, wouldn't that rip your troosers?" Redfern proclaimed, both men struck by the fact that if Washington had put Frank Hall aboard, there must be, as Redfern said, "a hell of a lot more to this than meets the eye. He added, "So what have the Roosians got aboard that's so valuable?"

"Beats me. Ours not to reason why . . ."

Ronnie Shear, bracing himself in the wheelhouse of the undercover Coast Guard trawler *Tuna Ghost*, couldn't see that well through the binoculars with his bunged-up eye, but it seemed to him that there was another, albeit smaller, trawler about five miles astern. Normally, given the number of trawlers working the rich fishing grounds off the West Coast, this wouldn't have occasioned comment, but he was remembering Freeman's warning about possible militia countermeasures—about the fact that if the Rone wasn't delivered to its potential purchasers, the militia would lose enough money to field an army.

"What d'you think?" Ronnie asked Art Wright, who, despite being given the first eight hours off as a rest period following the fatigue of the tunnel fiasco and the futile search of the *Ernst Mann*, had found it difficult to sleep. Given the worsening state of the sea, he had come topside for a breath of fresh air. He took the binoculars from Ronnie, his body unsteady, not yet having found his sea legs. "Probably just another trawler out fishing."

"Don't see any nets out," the *Tuna Ghost*'s Coast Guard skipper cut in. In his grubby fisherman's garb, like that of his half-dozen crew, he matched the *Tuna Ghost*'s deliberately ill-kempt appearance. "Still," he added equivocally, "that doesn't mean anything. Nets don't go out till there's something to fish. And we haven't got nets out."

Ronnie had shifted his attention to the cruise liner a few miles ahead. "The *Star* looks like she's increasing speed."

"Ah," the *Tuna Ghost*'s captain assured him, "we could catch her in no time. Old *Ghost* here might look a piece of junk, but we've got a brand new GM two-hundred-horsepower diesel down below. We could take that Russian tub anytime."

"Captain!" It was one of the *Ghost*'s crewmen, stationed by the stern's net drum. "Mr. Shear's right. That other trawler's tailing us."

The *Ghost*'s captain wasn't convinced. Everybody on board, including Shear and Wright, was understandably eager to make up for coming up empty-handed on the *Ernst Mann*. The Coast Guard crew was still convinced it was a huge cache of drugs that Freeman's commandos had been after. Meanwhile, Ronnie Shear was discovering that Freeman's suggestion that the *Tuna Ghost* not draw attention to itself, by acting like any of the other trawlers that plied these waters, was easier said than done. The fact was, by now, the *Tuna Ghost*, following the *Star*, and whoever might be following the *Tuna Ghost*, were all well beyond the continental shelf zone where trawlers of any ilk were few and far between.

* * *

Aboard the *Push 'n' Shove*, Brenda Fowler said she'd "made" the *Tuna Ghost*, one of the 130-foot-long "Clipper" class boats, the moment it broke out of the fog bank. *"Tuna Ghost!"* She laughed derisively. "Those dumb fuckers. They're like the highway patrol. They buy an old, beat-up van, stick a souped up V-8 in it for hot pursuit, then think everyone in the county ain't gonna catch on after a week or two. Shit, most o' the guys in La Push already know it's a Coast Guard ship."

"You don't mind going toe-to-toe with her?" Neilson asked.

"You kidding? Those Coast Guard bastards ran my daddy onto the rocks. He was haulin' cigarettes up to Canada. Tax free. You'd'a thought he was runnin' heroin!"

"She's a game one, eh?" Brock commented to McBride.

"Talk's cheap," the militia leader said. "How d'you think Cawley'll do?"

"I'll do fine." Cawley was right behind them. "Don't worry about me, Major."

"I meant," McBride said, "were you seasick?"

"No. You meant can you trust me when *Push 'n' Shove* closes in on the *Ghost*. You boys think I'm a soft apple grower."

"I didn't—" McBride began.

"No, no," Cawley said. "I was. But that bullet changed everything. When you read it in the newspapers, it doesn't sound like much—a rubber bullet. But if it hits you in the head, it can kill you." He paused, grabbing the trawler's gunwales for support against the rising sea. "Well, I don't mind telling you I thought I was going to die. Bunch of fascists shooting at me and those youngsters just 'cause we'd come to town and didn't agree with the World Trade Organization." Now he turned away, bending down to check a box of Coke bottles, all of which he'd filled almost to the top with gasoline and soaked rags stuffed into their necks. "I'm not a fool!"

Brock followed McBride up forward, the *Push 'n' Shove* taking spray over the bow.

"When do you want to do it?" Brock asked him.

"Now, while it's clear. Sea's picking up. Forecast is for gales from the west."

CHAPTER THIRTY

FRANK, HIDING BEHIND one of the big sixty-person lifeboats on the starboard side, tore off his crewman's jacket, saw its back was slashed, and was surprised to discover that what he had thought was perspiration was in fact blood. One thing was certain: he had to change—a man with blue trousers and white jacket, its back bloodied, was hard to miss. Yet he couldn't move far with Orloff's goons prowling around. His only hope lay with the passengers. But what chance, he asked himself, did a wounded crewman have of convincing a passenger to help him? None. Unless . . .

There was only one way. He didn't like the idea—in fact he hated it—but he was now in what an old college prof of his used to call "Hobbes country," a state of war where the life of a man was "poor, solitary, nasty, brutish, and short."

He moved farther down the deck, using the line of lifeboats as a blind. He heard raised voices above him on the upper deck and saw the beams of flashlights slicing the salty air. Right now Orloff had his FSB men plus perhaps a few off-duty seamen to aid in the search of the big ship, but soon, in another hour or two when the second sitting in the dining hall was over and the pressure reduced on the kitchens, Orloff would be able to call on the ship's "hotel" manager's staff. Everyone except the engineer, bar attendants, and the bridge watch would no doubt be conscripted to search for him. In his favor, Frank knew that on such a large vessel there were nooks and crannies that even a lot of the crew probably weren't aware of. But despite this he knew time was against him.

He was grateful the eastward-blowing trade winds had stiffened considerably since sunset—these would reduce the ship's speed, albeit slightly—and in the last hour or two a string of anvil-shaped storm clouds had begun assembling in battle order along the horizon, threatening a storm. But against this he knew that the full moon, at least for a while, would afford the searchers more light.

The moonlight, the salty smell of the sea air, and the roll of the ship momentarily evoked memories of his many oceanographic trips off the Oregon coast with Gloria. Or had he thought of her because of the danger he was in, of what he was about to risk, when only a few days before he had been with her? Then, just as quickly, the realization of the danger he was in pushed her out of his mind.

Taking advantage of the thick darkness as the moon slid into cumulus, he made his way from the lifeboats to a spot behind the tall hulk of a ventilator shaft that stood six feet above the deck, near the huge, two-hundred-foot-long dining salon. He felt like a gigolo looking for his mark, someone who—to be blunt—he could *use* to help him, at least until he could find the Treasury agent's whereabouts on the ship.

The kind of woman he was looking for would be in her late thirties, possibly early forties, by herself, and most likely laughing a lot, particularly if a man was holding court at the table. If you kept watching her, she'd appear now and then to be staring off into the distance, into nothingness, into dreams of what could have been, but overall there would be a forced gaiety from her, lest anyone notice her loneliness. She would be thanking the waiters a lot, looking around at them, but was the kind of woman who, if you got close to her and made the slightest suggestion of how "attractive" she was, would be on guard, rebuffing any overt advances with the haughtiness of exiled royalty. In the long run, however, she would be the most reliable mark, the most likely, because of her loneliness.

But there wouldn't be time to dance, literally or figuratively. If she didn't come willingly, then, God help him, he'd do it the hard way and flash the knife that friend Healy had tried to kill him with.

Ten minutes later he saw her and felt a surge of excitement. Red hair, strapless black dress, nice figure, but nothing sensational. Her shoulders and hair looked the same as the Treasury agent's he'd seen in the photograph Orloff had shoved in his face. She was being silly, the rest of the passengers at the table kidding her as she played eeny-meeny with two desserts. As she turned to face the waiter full on, Frank could see it wasn't the Treasury agent after all.

"Bellowing out like that! At dinner!" Martha Lynch charged reproachfully, George getting an earful as he and Martha began their after-dinner stroll around the promenade deck.

"It was just a joke, Martha . . . just fooling."

"A joke! Embarrassing me like that." There was a pause as they reached the bow end of the restaurant deck and Martha bent her head in the sudden gust of wind, one arm shooting up to hold her hair in place. George took the corner unsteadily, bracing himself against the rail.

"Wouldn't be so bad," Martha continued, "if you had a voice."

"Well, Martha, I was in the choir at—"

"Where? Castroville. Some rinky dink town in California." George hiccuped. "Artichoke capital of the world!"

"Oh, it's no good talking to you. I'm going to bed."

"I'll join you."

"You certainly will not! In that condition?"

"You make it sound like I'm pregnant," George countered happily.

"You're *smashed*, that's what you are. You go have a cup of coffee. Sober up. And keep away from the edge. You'll fall off!"

"Ah, c'mon, Martha. Let's have a little fun." He slipped his arm around her waist.

She waved off his breath. "Not tonight. You're grounded."

"Tomorrow, my little cooing turtle—"

"Maybe," she cut in. "If you don't do W.C. Fields."

"It's a deal."

They passed a large ventilator and turned left through one of the big teak doors into the waiting area near the elevators, which were situated in the grand lobby outside the dining room. By the time George and Martha reached the main deck, two flights below, George was feeling thirsty again. "I think I'll go up for a coffee."

"You don't have to go up," Martha said. "There's a coffee shop down here—at the back."

"The *back*!" George exclaimed in mock horror. "You mean the *stern*?"

"Whatever."

When George reached the stern coffee shop, so dimly lit that he had difficulty making out the waiter behind the black leather panel counter, he made a wondrous discovery: you could order liqueurs along with your coffee.

"Sorry," the attendant told him, "no credit cards in the bar."

"Not even American Express?" George joked, looking around at the few patrons left in the bar, now that the second and most hectic dinner hour was under way.

"Always leave home without it," the barman said.

George and the sprinkling of guests applauded the lame joke, and George signed another traveler's check, entering "General Expenses—Martha" on his record slip, dating it the day before. After the fourth Tia Maria he turned to the other customers, a couple smiling politely from a corner booth, another couple at the counter on high chairs, and a tall Fijian who looked to him like one of the singers they were going to feature later and who was contemplatively spooning the foam out of his cappuccino. There was soft jazzy music in the background, and when George finally got up unsteadily to do what he called the "circuit" and left the coffee bar, he found, once he was on deck again, that the stern pool, a "drunk's net" across it, was even more deserted than the coffee shop.

He made his way to the starboard side, looking down at the ship's wake, and it reminded him of the time as a very young man when, after lying about his age, he had joined the Navy and been shipped out to Guam. It brought back all the memories of youth, of hard times and good times, but above all the hope of years stretching out before you unending. He retreated from the strong blow of the wind and lowered himself awkwardly into a canvas deck chair by the pool on the leeward side. It was a thing that always surprised him on any ship, let alone a big liner like this: how a few steps one way or the other could make all the difference between you enjoying the cruise, having your hair blown wildly, and getting a bad case of windburn. Now that he was in the lee of the ship, the breeze was just that, a featherlike zephyr ruffling the turquoise skin of the pool. He lay back and gazed up at the stars. Martha wasn't a bad old sort really. Damn loyal. But some of those young things he'd seen earlier that day—my oh my.

The redhead—about thirty-five, Frank guessed—was leaving the dining salon with a couple, but at the elevators, though he could see them asking her to go on with them down the passageway toward the disco, she shook her head and waved goodbye. She pressed the second elevator's button and waited. She was alone, but now Frank could hear passengers approaching from behind him, laughing and shouting above the increasing breeze as they moved from the windy starboard to the port side.

It was now or never. He saw the elevator stop and open in front of her, a group of boisterous teenagers erupting from it, almost knocking her over. She glared angrily at them as they buffeted her, running down the corridor toward the pulsating disco. Frank moved quickly from the deck to the elevator just as the door was closing. She glimpsed him coming and pushed the button to open the door.

"Thank you," he said. The door closed and he turned to face her. "Now listen to me." He pulled out the knife. "If you make a sound I'll kill you." He felt sick the minute he said it. He pressed the release button on the switchblade and its bright sheen flashed in the elevator's light. Her mouth was wide open, her hands in front of her face, trying to stop herself from screaming. A whisper came out, unheard—her hazel eyes unblinking in sheer terror.

"Your handbag," he said, holding out his free hand. "Quickly!"

He opened it and saw the cabin card, easily distinguishable, a green and white wave pattern overlaid with a miniaturized deck plan of the ship. He glanced at the floor number she'd pushed: the sport deck, which meant she was in one of the cheaper cabins, a deck above the waterline. "What number?" he demanded.

"It's 302," she said, her voice raspy, dry with fear. He thought for a second. Her room would be midships.

He could smell her perfume, a rich, deep rose scent filling the air. As he looked more closely at her, he saw hers was a mudpack beauty, manufactured, her hair carefully coiffed, makeup hiding imperfections so well it was difficult to know what she'd look like in the morning.

"Walk ahead of me when we leave the elevator," he instructed her. "No hysterics. Just calm and easy. Understand?"

The knife conveyed no other alternative. He hated it. She tried to speak: still nothing came out. She saw blood dripping from him onto the elevator's gold-speckled carpet. She was terrified.

"You all right?" he asked stupidly, afraid she might faint on him. That would have been her best move, but she was too scared to think. It was all she could do to just nod. When he returned her purse, she took it hesitantly then held it close to her, one hand still on her throat. The elevator slowed.

"Put your hand down," he told her.

As they got out, a group of late diners, smelling of garlic and alcohol and chatting pleasantly, crammed past them into the elevator. Frank, careful to keep his bloodied back hidden, turned away.

The elevator doors slid closed behind them, and Frank directed the woman down the passageway, sidling along the corridor, his back to the wall lest the wound start bleeding badly again.

"Not so fast," he told her. "Slow down."

In thirty seconds they were outside 302. Her hands were shaking so much he had to open the door himself. Once inside, he told her to sit on the bed, and after he'd glanced back to check that there were no telltale bloodstains on the carpet outside, he slid the dead bolt beneath the lock into position and inserted the chain.

"I'll—I'll do anything . . ." she began. "But please don't—"

"I don't want you to do anything," Frank said, pocketing the knife. "I only want you to listen, then maybe you can help me."

"Sure," she said, "anything, I'll . . ." She was gabbling.

"Be quiet!"

"Yes."

"This a single or a double?"

"It's . . . it's . . . a double," she said.

He looked around quickly after noting the closet pull-out sofa bed just beyond the vanity. "No it isn't. Go in the bathroom," he ordered.

"Oh . . ." she began, "oh my God—"

"Don't worry," he told her.

"*Worry?* I'm petrified."

This was shitty work for a SEAL, for anyone, but he had no choice—other than give himself up.

CHAPTER THIRTY-ONE

ORLOFF'S MEN HAD combed the deck areas but found no one except an elderly couple by the railing in the lee of a forward lifeboat, invigorated by the night air and whispering sweet nothings. The FSB colonel was now in a dilemma. He asked, or rather, ordered, Valery and Mendev to meet him in the radio room while the ship's first officer took the two remaining hours in the eight-to-midnight watch. There, Orloff pressed upon them the urgency of finding the American, his concern exacerbated by calls from the purser and radio officer warning him that several passengers requesting to send radiograms and/or faxes had to be stalled by polite explanations about "atmospherics."

Mendev, stern, bullish-looking in his summer whites, stood glumly in front of Orloff. The captain's noncommittal silence cloaked a determination not to do anything that would even remotely impede what he hoped would be his promotion to commander of the *Gorbachev*.

"Well," the colonel turned to Valery, "have *you* anything to suggest?"

The Estonian shrugged. "We can't go barging into cabins. It would create an uproar, a very bad—" He was about to say it would be a very bad image for the ship but knew that Orloff cared nothing about this. At the same time, Valery knew his own career and possible recommendation for *him* to be promoted to bridge captain of the *Gorbachev* hung in the balance. His ineffectual attempt to stop the American on the bridge would already be a mark against him in Orloff's book.

"Perhaps he will try the woman?" he suggested to Orloff, referring to the American Treasury agent aboard.

Orloff's agitation now became outright scorn as he stopped pacing across the sparsely decorated but large, functionally furnished suite. "Oh yes," he said, "very good, Captain. It's easy to see you've no intelligence training at all." Orloff knew this wasn't true, as every merchant marine officer automatically underwent *trenirovka ob inostrannykh portakh*—the foreign ports training course—given by the FSB and the old KGB's First Directorate. In short, they had received standard instruction on how and what to look for in foreign ports, taking particular notice, with the aid of handheld GPS—global positioning satellite—units, of the precise routes the port's pilot took in entering the harbor, confirming changes in sandbar locations, et cetera, for the use of Soviet submarines in time of war.

Valery was embarrassed by his suggestion that the American would seek to ally himself as quickly as possible with the U.S. Treasury agent, but then Orloff abruptly reversed his thinking.

"Of course, Hall knows that his approaching the Treasury agent is the last thing we would expect him to do because it is so obvious."

"Therefore he'll do it?" Valery added. Orloff pulled out a small green spiral-bound notebook, flicking the pages open and then picking up the telephone. For a moment Valery thought he was dialing the Treasury agent's cabin, then realized by the colonel's tone that he was calling the head purser's office, closed to passengers at this time of night but not to staff catching up on the paperwork.

"Choamsky!" Orloff ordered. "Four men. Main deck elevators. Now! A spill!"

"Spill?" Valery asked as Orloff told Valery and Mendev to return to the bridge, that further instructions would follow. Mendev shrugged as if he didn't know what was going on and moved off, but Valery could tell he knew, and on his way forward to the wheelhouse Valery knew too. "My God," he said to Mendev. "They're going to—"

"Keep out of it," Mendev cautioned him.

The moon had been swallowed by cloud, and in the darkness Valery felt the *Southern Star* rise and crash into an oncoming swell, Mendev taking a firm grip of the rail.

Walking out on the starboard wing of *Tuna Ghost*'s bridge, Art Wright looked around to make sure none of the Coast Guard crew were nearby before he asked Ronnie Shear, "D'you think the Rone's on the *Burkhanov*?"

"I don't know, Art, but we're gonna have to board her. That's our orders. You don't have to whisper, by the way. General Freeman says the White House has authorized me to let the crew know what we're after, because this is our last chance. We're well beyond our territorial limit."

"Man, I don't want egg on my face again," Wright said. "That damned *Ernst Mann* bullshit was downright embarrassing."

"Mr. Shear!" It was the *Tuna Ghost*'s captain. "We've got another blip ahead of us—in addition to the *Southern Star*."

"You think it's the *Burkhanov*?"

"Not sure. She's just come onto the radar screen. If it *is* the *Burkhanov*, she's either slowed down to a near stop, possibly waiting for the *Star* to catch up with her, or she's turned around and heading back to the *Star*. We can't tell whether she's coming or going just from the radar blip."

"What would be the sense in her coming back?"

"Don't ask me."

"Can we reach her before the *Star* does?"

"I think so. If we pull all the stops out."

"Let's do it."

Within seconds Ronnie Shear and Art Wright could feel the vibrations in their feet as the big General Motors diesels thrust the *Tuna Ghost*'s bow higher into the incoming swells, the pulsating engines racing to reach the *Burkhanov* first.

Frank looked quickly about the redhead's bathroom: cosmetics, toothpaste, brush, a "lady" safety razor on the sink, knee-high stockings drying over the shower curtain rod, and pink panties on the doorknob. He opened the small mirrored cabinet above the sink: Midol, Playtex tampons, and a bottle of light green pills—Ativan tranquilizers, five milligrams, sublingual. "Take as needed." His eyes met hers and she looked at the floor.

"Sorry," he apologized, "but I have to check."

"For what?" she asked, her embarrassment making her brave. "Guns?"

"Listen, I want you to wet a towel, clean my back off. You have anything I can bandage it with?"

"You won't die from that," she said, her face still beet red from when he had seen the Ativan, trying now to show she was no nut case, the pills were just for her nerves. A lot of people took them. She was a computer operator in a brokerage firm. High pressure and the stress of nanosecond trading on the Net had gotten to her, that's all. It had gotten to a lot of people.

"I'm not worried about dying," Frank responded. "I just don't want to be dripping blood all over your suite. Right?"

She was looking straight at him now, angrily, no more staring away at the floor, her breasts rising and falling, a deep white cleavage in the black dress.

"Look!" Frank said. "We can do this the easy way or the hard way."

"Have I any choice?"

"Yes," he said. "Pretty soon some guys are going to be knocking on doors. And if they find me in here, you're not going to finish the cruise. They won't risk any leaks. Got it?"

"I'll tell them you forced me."

"They won't care."

She thought about it for a few seconds and then reached for one of the fresh towels on the rack above the toilet. "What did you do?" she asked, turning on the basin faucet.

He thought of the elevator repeatedly bumping against the dead arm of the man who'd held Gloria hostage, and the other creep, who got away. He pushed aside the black spandex pants and the *Southern Star* T-shirt and sat down on the toilet. "I killed a man."

There was silence, and he could see steam rising from the basin. "Go easy on the hot water," he said.

"What did he do to you?" she asked.

"He tried to kill *me*."

"Why?"

"It's a long story. It'd take all night." He paused. "The Russians are trying to steal some very high tech stuff from us." The warm towel felt great on his back—until it touched the wound. He winced, something Aussie Lewis would have ribbed him about.

"Relax," she said, pressing on it lightly.

"Have to stop this damn bleeding. You have any bandages?"

"I can make some. Tear up a sheet."

Frank thought for a second. "No, they'll be looking for that kind of thing. Damn Russians'll know if someone uses too much toilet paper in the next forty-eight hours."

"I could use something of mine—a T-shirt."

He turned to look up at her. As their eyes met, he smiled. It felt as if he hadn't done that for a long time. "You would?"

"Yes," she said, her gaze locked on his.

"Well," he said slowly, still smiling, "so long as there's nothing rude written on it. I like my bandages clean."

"Brand new," she assured him. "Never been used before." She paused. "Ever." Something had changed; he saw it in her eyes. Was she beginning to like it, the edge of danger? Trusting him. Or was it all a con?

"If I give you a message, will you take it to the radio room for me?"

As he spoke he noticed a bulky black sweater on a hanger in the closet. It looked like a man's, too big for her. Or maybe big and sloppy was in fashion again. Crazily, he thought of an old New York pizza TV commercial with Donald Trump announcing, "Go big or go home!" Was he becoming delirious? Maybe it was the loss of blood and the fatigue.

"Yes," she answered, "I'll take it up but I don't know where the office is."

"Radio room," he corrected. "It'll be aft of the bridge. But never mind, you can give it to the purser." He indicated the small writing desk behind her. "Can you get me a sheet of paper?"

She brought him the fake leather folder from the desk with *Southern Star* stationery, including several blank radiogram sheets tucked into the side pocket, together with embossed envelopes. He noted the ship's logo had been printed off center. Every now and then the Russians slipped up. Maybe they would again, but thanks to Healy, the bridge would now know about Brownlee. Frank knew that any message, however innocent he might make it sound, would have to go to someone else, someone who could grasp the problem quickly and notify Washington. He needed to let them know that he was sure the Rone must be aboard and that therefore boarding the ship would no longer be an international incident that would blow apart the delicate U.S.-Russia-China arms limitation treaty negotiations in Geneva.

"Can you act?" he asked her, half jokingly.

"All my life," she said, and in her sad hazel eyes he saw the flicker of humiliation. There was an awkward silence.

"What's your name?"

"Angela."

He nodded, then, using the leather folder like a clipboard, he wrote the message as she turned and took out a pair of scissors from her sewing kit. They were small, but she knew they were razor sharp.

Not bothering to shower, Healy had stripped to his boxer undershorts. He believed women, especially whores, secretly liked a man's natural sweaty odor; they just wouldn't admit to it. He grabbed a handful of ice from the drink tray, plonked it into the crystal glass, splashed in a generous helping of Johnnie Walker Black Label, and sat waiting for one of Orloff's FSB tarts. Soon he heard a knock on the door and opened it. Jesus Christ! There'd been a mistake, either that or Orloff's minions had misunderstood his curt instructions on the kind of woman he'd required. Or perhaps this was his Russian friends' idea of a joke. A peroxide blonde, she had big breasts to be sure—they were bulging out of the green satin dress—but she was big everywhere. Enormous. Repulsive, he thought, unless you had a fetish for fat. The fact that her hair was done in a tight bun only emphasized her bulk. She was smiling accommodatingly.

"My name is Tatyana," she said in a soft, demure voice that belied her size. "You would like some company?"

"Yeah, but not with you. I told your boss I wanted someone with a good figure."

She stiffened but held the smile. "I am the only one available."

"You're joking." He looked her up and down like a horse trader, not at all happy with what he saw but needing a mount. "You sure you're the only one available?"

"Yes."

"All right," he said reluctantly, as if doing her a favor. "A blow job, but careful with the teeth—ship's rolling."

"I know my job."

"Yeah," he said, closing the door. "I'll bet you do."

Then she hesitated. "I need some drink."

He pointed to the tray. "Help yourself."

George Lynch, fortified by Kahlúa liqueur, was all but oblivious to the roll of the big swells as the *Southern Star* entered rougher water, the pile of deck chairs from which he'd extracted the one he was sitting on by the pool emitting protesting squeaks as the ship yawed in a big cross swell. The bright turquoise pool lights suddenly went out. The black kidney shape was now only dimly outlined, and beyond that a trellis of roses, the latter—real or imitation? he wondered—looking like dark spots against a silvery cloud as the moon momentarily slipped through another offense of cumulus. George thought he saw movement near the stern then heard a muffled voice, then a cry, like a baby bird falling from its nest, and smelled a whiff of perfume. He tried to get up but the canvas deck chairs on the *Southern Star* were low-slung affairs, not made for anyone over fifty, or at least for anyone who wanted to get out of them quickly. When he finally did make it, the ship's roll seemed more pronounced, but he wasn't sure since he was still a little dizzy from all the Kahlúa. As he walked down past the pool, he made out the dim outline of four or five men. One of them, more visible in the fleeting moonlight, was wearing an officer's short white dinner jacket, complete with bow tie. He looked like one of the pursers who a day earlier had cashed several of his traveler's checks. The man heard George, and turned abruptly. "Good evening."

"Howdy. You fellas doin' some night fishin'?" George was guffawing at his own buffoonery, the officer translating to his crewmen in Russian. A few of them, clustered by the stern's emergency hydraulic arm and boom, laughed politely.

"Not this night," the officer answered. "Too windy for the lines. Yes?"

"Aw, I fish in worse than this." The group of seamen was disbanding. The moon disappeared altogether now, and one of them, smelling strongly of nicotine, bumped into George.

"What's wrong with the lights?" George asked. "Blown a fuse?"

"Yes, Mister . . . ?" the one in the officer's cap began.

"Lynch," George said, putting out his hand, gripping the rail with the other. "George Lynch."

The officer shook his hand. "My name is Orloff."

"Howdy."

"Are you enjoying your cruise, Mr. Lynch?"

"Yes, sir, I sure am. Only one complaint."

"Oh?" the officer said in a tone of immediate concern.

"Oh hell, ain't that bad," George went on. "But they just told me back there I can't buy drinks on my credit card."

"Ah," the officer said, clearly relieved, his face still hidden in the darkness. "I am afraid this is company policy, Mr. Lynch. In the past we have had many . . ."

"Fly-by-nighters," George suggested.

But the officer didn't seem to understand this phrase, and asked, "You were at the coffee shop?"

"Yes."

"But I am confused," Orloff said. "The coffee shop must now be closed."

"Maybe," George responded jovially, indicating the pile of deck chairs. "I've been 'sunbathing' out here." He laughed. Orloff joined in the joke, inviting George to his cabin for a nightcap. "To compensate you," Orloff continued good-naturedly, "for our credit card policy."

"Why, that's mighty nice of you. But the missus'll be expecting me."

"Just a quick one, Mr. Lynch," Orloff said encouragingly, affecting a degree of difficulty with English, "how do you say—one for the road?" The moon was sliding out of the cloud.

"Well," George said, "I wouldn't mind, but—hello, what's this?"

Orloff saw the inebriated passenger bending down in the moonlight, picking up something from the deck. It was a woman's shoe.

"Ah," George said. "Cinderella!"

Orloff said nothing.

"Fairy story," George explained. "Round midnight . . . carriage turns into a pumpkin."

Lynch's comment made no sense whatever to Orloff but he put his hand out for the shoe, telling the American, "You would not believe what lost things we have aboard the ship."

"You mean lost property," George corrected in good humor.

"Yes, of course. *Property.* Do you know, some passengers lose their teeth?"

"Dentures?" George said.

"What—oh, yes. Dentures."

"That's nothing," George said on their way to Orloff's cabin. "When I was in the Army I remember this time we had a fella wore a toupee—"

"A too pay?" Orloff asked.

"You know," George said, grabbing a clump of his own hair, almost stumbling into the increasing roll of the ship. "Fake hair."

"Ah, you mean a *parik*—wig?"

"Yeah, only a little bitty wig."

"Yes, I understand."

Later Orloff would have two of his men deliver George back to his cabin, and hopefully by the time morning broke, the American would be so drunk from double vodkas he'd have trouble remembering the name of the ship, let alone recalling where he'd been or exactly what had happened at the ship's stern.

"Can you read it?" Frank asked.

Angela had cut the last strip of one of her T-shirts she was using for bandages, and as she leaned over to read the message he'd written, Frank felt awash in her perfume, her long auburn hair brushing his cheek, her moist, coral red lips moving sensuously as she read back the radiogram, then paused. Either she was unable to make out his handwriting, he thought, or wanted the moment to last.

He had addressed the message to Donna Fargo, putting the unlisted Western White House number to the right of the name:

If you wish to acquire Chevron stocks you must make offer before Star arrives in Suva. Reply immediately. Franke.

"You'll have to sign it. Don't use your real name," he told Angela, realizing he didn't yet know her last name.

"You mind telling me what it means?" she asked.

"It means if this ship isn't boarded before we get inside Fiji's twelve-mile protected zone, Moscow'll get the biggest present it's had since Philby and Walker."

"Who were they?"

"Spies. Philby was a Brit." Like Healy, he thought. "Walker was U.S. Navy. Gave Russians the kitchen sink and then some." How could anyone, he wondered, not know who either Philby or Walker was? Or was it a pompous presumption on his part by someone who, because of his long Navy SEAL and civilian salvage experience, had been acutely aware of

Philby's treachery and Walker's gift to the Russians of America's most top secret submarine technology, including its codes?

"Do I take it up now?" she asked.

"Yes, but if they're taking other messages at the same time, don't press. I don't want it—or you—to stand out in any way."

Angela nodded, and before he could stop her, signed it Kathleen Shaw. The K was written with an elaborate flourish. Gloria had told him once that such handwriting denoted a passionate nature. It seemed odd for someone who seemed overtly restrained. Repressed passion perhaps?

"No," he said, "you'd better write the message, in case they compare my writing to something of yours."

"Are they that paranoid?"

"They're that careful," he said.

He pulled out the radiogram form below the one he had written on, and seeing a light trace of the message in his own hand, tore it up and put it in the toilet. It took three flushes for the paper to completely disappear, the cistern making a choking noise. Angela could see blood had seeped through the bandages she'd made from the T-shirt.

"Where are you going now?" she asked him.

"Somewhere to rest awhile," he said disingenuously, looking straight at her. Her eyes were beautiful in the sense of vulnerability they conveyed. "I need to lie low till morning at least," he added.

"But won't they be looking for you all over?"

"Yes."

"You can stay here," she said, adding, "I won't bother you. I mean, I believe you."

He looked at her long and hard. "Thanks," he said quietly. Was she acting? He'd forced her into her cabin at knife point and now she was going to help him? Unless her behavior was an example of the Stockholm syndrome, in which hostages, like those taken in the famous Stockholm Incident of 1972, identify with the plight of the captor against a hostile world and decide to help him. He had to admit it was a definite possibility for a desperately lonely woman. Or, his earlier suspicion returning, *was* it a con?

She walked to the door then turned. "You can trust me."

"I know," he said, unsure that he could. She hesitated before opening the door. "What's wrong?" he asked.

"I'm very nervous," she said. "I've—I've never done this sort of thing. . . ."

He walked over to her and, placing his hands gently on her shoulders, said, "You'll be just—"

She turned. "Hold me."

He could feel the folded switchblade pressing hard against her. "You don't have to do it, Angela. I'll under—"

"I want to."

He didn't know what to think. The only thing he was sure of was that he desperately needed sleep, his thinking fuzzy with fatigue.

She left.

He felt cold, and borrowed one of the bulky black sweaters.

CHAPTER THIRTY-TWO

TUNA GHOST'S BOW was enveloped in spray which, whenever the moon slipped through clouds, suddenly became luminescent and then just as suddenly disappeared as the line of what the Coast Guard captain called "L Threes"—anvil-shaped thunderheads—gathered in a formidable line to the west. Whereas the *Southern Star* was alternately visible to the eye because of her pinpoints of light, the *Burkhanov* was invisible to the naked eye, appearing on *Tuna Ghost*'s radar only as the clipper crashed into the big swells. Aft, the two-man gun

crew beneath the superstructure designed to look like the live
bait tank of a tuna clipper, but that covered the eighty-four-
pound M-2 .50 caliber Browning heavy machine gun, were
having a rough time of it. Their condition was exacerbated by
the absence of any porthole or aperture other than the warm
air intake hose from the ship's engine room. For them, unlike
some of the other ten-man crew, the *Tuna Ghost*'s arrival
abeam of the *Burkhanov* couldn't come soon enough. It
would be an opportunity for them to get a blast of fresh air
and a chance to fix their eyes, and hence their sense of balance, on a horizon, however dim in the transient moonlight.

"How far, Skipper?" one of them asked on the intercom to
the wheelhouse.

"Three miles. Not long now. Everything operational?"

"We're ready." As if to reassure himself, the feeder checked
the belt of the armor-piercing incendiary and tracer combination .50 caliber ammunition. If the gun wasn't checked fre-
quently enough, the aluminum belt and its rounds could be
encrusted with fine particles of salt that could jam the weapon.

"It'll be fine," the gunner said. "You worry too much."

For once, militiaman Cawley wasn't worried. He was keen
to prove himself aboard *Push 'n' Shove* after having over-
heard Major McBride questioning his mettle. He'd made a
decision, as he knew his fellow militiamen had at Wills Creek,
that there was no going back, and he was determined to give a
good account of himself once they closed on the *Tuna Ghost*,
which, just over a mile ahead of them and only intermittently
visible on their radar, was obviously increasing speed to
reach the *Southern Star*.

"Can you catch her?" McBride asked Brenda Fowler.

For the first time there was an edge of doubt to her voice.
"Should be able to. Swells are getting bigger."

"Can you do it or not?"

"Yes, but not as soon as I thought. We'll overtake her, but it
might be half an hour before we draw level with her."

McBride left the wheelhouse, banging the door closed.

Even in the darkness Neilson could sense his commander's irascibility. "What's up?" he asked McBride.

"Meryl Streep has doubts."

"We're not gonna catch the *Tuna Ghost*?"

"Yes, but it's going to take longer than she thought."

"Weather's getting worse. Maybe that's what—"

"I don't care what it is," McBride said, a billowing cloud of spray breaking over the *Push 'n' Shove*'s wheelhouse and drenching everything, including the winch drum astern.

"Well," Neilson said, trying to inject a note of optimism, "we don't need to be right up against her if we use the disposables. Their range is what? Three hundred yards?" He meant the A-T4s, the disposable antitank rocket launchers that could destroy a fully armored tank, let alone smash through the side of a trawler.

"Don't be damn silly!" McBride told him. "In a sea like this, three hundred yards is too risky. One second you're on top of a wave, the next minute—could overshoot it easily. We have to get in close. And if *Meryl* can't get us in close, we're screwed."

"She'll get us—" Neilson began, ducking to avoid the full downpour of a breaking wave.

"She'd better," McBride said, "or else I'll put her tits in a wringer."

Frank awoke to the sound of a key in the lock and rolled over to the off side, beside the door, knife in hand.

When Angela came in, she was flushed with victory. "No problem," she said. "Easy as that!" She snapped her fingers. She looked as if she'd been drinking, but she hadn't, Frank knew; it was the elation of an amateur. She'd done it.

"What did they say?" he asked.

"Nothing. Super polite."

"Did they send it right away?"

"Well, yes. I meant the clerk—whoever he is—took it from me. Gave me a receipt." She waved the yellow slip at him as one would a winning lottery ticket.

"Doesn't mean they've sent it," Frank said.

She looked crestfallen. "Oh—"

Frank gripped her wrist, steadying the receipt, staring down at it in disbelief—the shock so sudden he could feel the blood surging through his temples.

"Jesus! You put the room number on it! You put your goddamn room number down!"

"Yes."

"Listen," he said, his voice racing. He couldn't undo her error, only react to it—fast. "Those people at the table with you. In the dining room. Know any of them?"

"Not that well, I—"

"Doesn't matter. You go to one of them. Fake a—I don't know, illness, nervous breakdown, anything. No, that won't work, they'd call the ship's doctor. The important thing is, stay with your friends till we get to Suva."

"But that's not till—"

Frank strode into the bathroom and snatched the Ativan. "Stay with your friends," he commanded, thrusting the vial at her, "or you won't be needing these."

"What do you mean?"

"I mean you'll be dead. C'mon." He walked quickly to the door, paused, and opened it slowly. He glanced down the corridor. It was as much his fault, he knew. He should have told her about the room number, an oversight in the rush of the moment, goddammit, but one that could get both of them killed. The passageway looked much longer than he remembered. And more dangerous.

"Where are we going?" she said frantically.

"To the disco club. Ring one of your table friends from there. Anywhere but here. You know their names?"

"Yes, but why the—"

"Whatever you do, don't be alone. Wait for them to come pick you up. And if anything goes awry and you're separated—" He remembered her gym attire. "—meet me down below on the sport deck."

"What do you mean, *awry*?" she asked nervously.

"If something goes wrong."

It was well after midnight as they walked quickly down the hallway, but Frank knew the disco would go on for a few hours yet.

"You think they didn't send the message?" she asked.

"I'm not sure of anything right now. Maybe the purser you gave it to hasn't sent it up to the radio room yet, otherwise they'd already be here. Point is, they'll check out the cabin of everyone who's given the purser a message, and if they find anything incriminating—"

A noisy bevy of young revelers was approaching, their rapid-fire conversation pierced by shrieks of laughter.

"They won't find anything," she proffered.

"Listen, Orloff's a pro. The bloodied towels'll be the first thing they'll see."

A crewman came around the corner, one of General Chang's "laundrymen," and instantly recognized Frank. Frank dropped him with a SEAL blow to the throat. Angela gasped as the figure crumpled, and Frank kept steering her fast toward the disco. She could see that despite her ad hoc bandages, beneath the bulky black sweater he was wearing blood was seeping through. Two more crewmen were coming toward them, and he pulled her to him, kissing her hard.

"I'll stay with you," she insisted.

"No you won't," he said gently, pushing her away and ahead of him into the gut-punching noise and marijuana-laced phantasmagoria of the disco's dim entrance, where they had to shout to hear one another. Frank was frantically re-calling the fracas on the bridge and the only man who hadn't joined in the attack against him—the Russian staff captain.

"Join your friends," Frank told her, the disco's drummer giving Angela the eye. "But if you're questioned by any of the officers or crew, call the staff captain, Valery." He repeated Valery's name. "Complain that while you were out, strolling on deck, someone broke into your cabin."

"Where are you going?"

"Remember—stay with someone!" he said, and was gone.

"Hello, dearie!" It was a middle-aged Lothario, open-necked Hawaiian shirt, hairy chest and gold chain, oozing out from the disco crowd beneath the frenetic flashing of purple and crimson strobe lights. His breath reeked of booze and cigarettes.

"Get lost!" Angela told him.

"Ooooh, I like 'em tough."

"Listen, beer-belly, if you don't get out of my way, my boyfriend'll pulverize you."

"Just wanna buy you a drink!"

He was so drunk he could barely stand, especially now that the ship was rolling even more.

Despite the intermittent strobe show, it was so dark she couldn't make out his face. At least it was good cover.

"All right, lover," she said, so confused, angry, and alone she didn't care. "Champagne."

He performed an obscenely inept attempt at a twist. "Ooooh, champagne's comin' up, baby. Yeah!"

"In a bucket," she said, looking about for anyone she might recognize from the dining room, but no one noticed her, or so she thought, and the beat kept on.

The banging at the door sounded like someone was trying to knock it down. Healy, groggy-eyed, lifted his head and looked down at Tatyana, her head still between his legs where, plied with Johnnie Walker Black Label, she'd been doing what he'd told her to do, and afterward, had fallen asleep. She was snoring now, in a strange, gurgling way— like a sinkhole. "Hey, you!" He pulled her off and she slithered from the bed, clutching the gold-colored spread and a tangle of sheets. She awoke then, protesting with a stream of Russian, one hand grasping the edge of the bed.

"Shut your face!" Healy told her, kicking her arm as he reached beneath his pillow and pulled out a Makarov 9mm. "Who is it?"

"Assistant purser. Open the door."

"Who?" He'd heard but wanted to verify the voice. When he heard it again, he knew it was Orloff, and as he opened the door he saw from the Swiss clock on the cabin wall that it was nearly one A.M.

Orloff looked harried. "Your phone was off the hook," he snapped. "What were you doing?"

"Playing chess," Healy countered dryly, pointing the gun toward the tart who was struggling to her feet, clutching a sheet with one hand, brushing a tangle of hair back with the other and fleeing to the bathroom. "Bitch doesn't know a rook from a pawn."

Orloff caught a whiff of the stuffy mixture of whiskey, stale smoke, and a fishy smell. "A microcosm," he said, looking around, "of the West."

"Hey," Healy said, grabbing his clothes, "spare me the purity of the party bullshit. What d'you want?"

"I told you never to take the phone off the hook."

"Yeah, well, I've got this thing about being interrupted during sex."

"I have this thing about saboteurs being on the loose."

Orloff was watching Tatyana snatching an errant tail of the sheet from the bathroom doorway so she could close it, and was amused by her sudden need for propriety.

For a second Healy stopped stuffing his China silk shirt in and looked over accusingly at him. "For chrissake, you mean you haven't caught Hall yet?"

"There are over six hundred people aboard this ship, including crew, Mr. Healy. He's a fox, this one."

"Well," Healy said, the sarcasm dripping in his voice, "I did have something to say on that score, didn't I?" Before Orloff could counter him, Healy went on, "Have you found the Treasury bitch?"

"Yes."

"Well?"

"No problem," Orloff said. "She fell overboard."

"All right then, that means he must be holed up with someone else and he could've got a message out."

"Her name's Angela Chabot," Orloff informed him, explaining about the message "Franke" had tried to send. "We think Hall chose her at random. He was careful, though. She's single, unattached."

"I told you, didn't I?" Healy said, pulling on his shoes. "He's as cunning as a shithouse rat. Any point in squeezing her?"

"I don't think so. She was merely a courier."

"Did he get it off with her?"

Orloff pretended he didn't understand the colloquialism.

"Fuck her?" Healy said.

"I didn't concern myself with that," Orloff said caustically.

"Well, maybe you should."

"Why?"

"Use her as leverage—if he has a thing for her?"

Orloff was silent, and suddenly Healy stopped tying his shoes, looking over at the Russian. "Jesus Christ! You haven't got her?"

"Not yet."

Healy was alarmed. "Listen, Colonel, I don't want to cramp your style but you'd better cap this wildcat pretty soon, before we get to Suva."

Orloff's tone was unconsciously revealing his anxiety, his lower denture sliding into an underbite, clenching hard on the molars. "I'm aware of that, Mr. Healy. That's why I require you. I expect you to help us," he insisted, explaining his demand by pointing out, "Apart from Valery and the two or three men on the bridge at the time, you and I are the only ones who can identify him."

"What's wrong with your photo department? Your ship's newspaper? You've got the son of a bitch on video. Can't you make prints?"

"And do what?" Orloff retorted.

"I don't know," Healy answered aggressively. "Put him in the ship's paper or something, winner of your daily lottery draw. Make it into a lark—a hundred bucks for the first person to find the winner."

Orloff was frowning. "A *lark*?"

"A joke," Healy explained. "You know, make a game of it."

"I've contacted Moscow," Orloff announced woodenly. He

could see Healy was as worried as he was, that it was not only his own career in the FSB at stake or those of General Kornon, General Chang, and the Swiss industrialist, Reinhard Klaus, but Healy's as well. Everyone's stake in the theft of the American's Rone was at risk. Everyone was in danger.

"What did Moscow say?" Healy asked.

"They have a plan."

"Who's they?"

"Does it matter?"

"I want to know if it's top level. I've done my bit—I don't want any second stringer screwing around with my future."

"It is not a second stringer, I can assure you of that."

"That still doesn't tell me who it is."

"General Kornon is in overall charge, Chinese General Chang assisting." Tatyana emerged from the bathroom. With her mousy blond hair combed out now to shoulder length, ruby lips, and redolent with cheap perfume, she strode past the two men with a haughty air of superiority. Pausing at the door, she addressed Orloff in such a vituperative tone that Healy raised his eyebrows in surprise. She slammed the door shut after her.

"What did she say?" Healy asked.

"She says she was humiliated by you," Orloff explained. "That she only did it for the Motherland."

"Oh dear," Healy said, "and here I was thinking it was all for love. Actually," Healy went on, "she wasn't half bad. Knows how to use her tongue." Looking in the mirror, he began combing his hair. "How did you do the Treasury bird, then?"

"I told you, she fell. There was no problem," Orloff answered, with obvious irritation.

" 'No problem' can mean any damn thing with you lot." Healy flicked the comb to make a wave from his midline to the right. "Did she scream?"

"Perhaps, but the sound of the prop down there—"

"Did she scream?" Healy demanded, staring at him.

It struck Orloff, hardly a squeamish man, as an odd question at best—perverse at worst. He answered nevertheless. "Yes, she screamed."

Healy smiled. "So, what are you going to do about Hall?"

"That ship, the *Petrel*," Orloff said by way of a counter-shock in the ongoing game of oneupmanship between the two men, "is on our radar. Fifty miles away."

"So?" Healy asked, continuing to comb, refusing to concede any sense of alarm. "They can't board us. Pissy little ship like that."

Despite the bravura of the Englishman's reply, however, Orloff could tell that this man who, as Hall now knew, had stolen the Rone's secrets was obviously more concerned about the proximity of the American ship than he was willing to let on, and the colonel enjoyed it. Orloff was prepared to die for Mother Russia, and he detested America, which, he believed, reveled in Russia's post–cold war disarray, but he had no affection for men like Healy, Ames, Walker, Philby, Burgess, and the rest who had sold out their own country. Still, he knew he must put personal prejudices aside and obey Kornon's coded directive from Moscow to demonstrate *gibkost*—flexibility—the ability to adapt to the changing circumstances.

There was a knock on the door and a thin, anemic-looking woman with carefully coiffed jet-black hair and a strangely expressionless face entered the cabin. She was carrying a navy-blue tote bag, and without so much as a glance at Healy, pulled out the chair from the dresser recess and opened up the bag, taking out small thumb-sized triangles of cream-colored foam rubber sponges, blush brushes, and small powder pads. Healy now recognized her as the same woman who had made him up with the bruises required to convince Hall in the cell that his English cellmate had also been roughed up.

"What's she doing?" Healy asked.

"Your face, of course," Orloff answered.

"What's wrong with my face?"

The woman was laying out several kinds of sunglasses, a variety of silver-dollar-sized blush tins, and a clean napkin atop the dresser before the mirror, her grin telling Healy that she understood enough English to get the gist of his puzzlement. Orloff, however, was his usual serious self, surprised only by the Englishman's apparent naiveté.

"Do you want to be recognized by Hall?" he asked Healy. "He'll be on the lookout for you now."

"All right!" Healy said grumpily. "What do I have to do?"

Orloff spread his arms like a babushka, all-encompassing, comforting, understanding. "Do? Nothing, just sit. Natasha here does all the makeup for our entertainers aboard. She's a graduate of—"

"Yeah, well never mind about all that. Just get on with it."

A few moments later a younger, plump woman in a severe gray suit that reminded Healy of cold war East German border officials brought in several ties and cravats draped over her arm. Natasha meanwhile began with the hair dye.

As the transformation took place, a smile replaced Healy's early intransigence. He was enjoying his metamorphosis from a brown-haired, blue-eyed, forty-year-old scientist to an imperiously mustachioed aristocrat with jet-black hair that made his eyes more piercing, more dangerous-looking. "A cravat," he told the stern-faced assistant. "No tie."

Orloff looked at the two women, commenting dryly in his native tongue that it was no wonder Dr. Healy had made his way up so far from the bottom of the capitalist bin; he was so quick to adapt. A chameleon. Orloff turned to Healy, switching back to English as he indicated the Englishman's reflection in the mirror, and held up a pair of sunglasses for Healy to try on.

"Will this stay on?" Healy asked, tapping the mustache Natasha had affixed.

Orloff translated the question for Natasha, whose expressionless face now ballooned like a French chef being insulted in her own kitchen.

"Of course," Orloff answered for her. "She says the strongest trade wind will not blow it off."

"What if I go down on a bird?"

Natasha looked at Orloff, waiting for the translation. It was nothing, Orloff told her. Natasha studied Healy's face, nodded with satisfaction, and began repacking her paraphernalia.

As the Englishman rose and took the Makarov from the dresser table, checking the clip, the cold war woman offered him a blue blazer. He ignored her and instead turned to Orloff. "I've been thinking, Colonel. That redhead. The one who brought the message to the purser. Angela whatever—"

"Yes?"

"What room's she in?"

"It's 302, but I told you she's not there now."

Healy was palming his temples, smoothing down his hair. "You really think she ought to be left free to gab? To talk?"

Orloff shrugged. "Perhaps not. But if she doesn't know anything about the Rone—"

"Yeah," Healy cut in, slipping on the blue blazer, checking his arm length against the sleeves. "But we don't know that, do we?"

"No," Orloff admitted.

"I'll do her," Healy said, studying himself in the mirror, his eyes hidden by the shades. "For free."

"Discreetly," Orloff said somewhat officiously, moving toward the door.

"Well, I'll tell you what, Dick," Healy said, looking over hard at the Russian. "I won't leave her fucking shoes on deck."

Orloff stopped, taken by surprise.

"Close your mouth, Colonel. You'll catch a fly."

"How did you know—about the shoe?"

Healy passed him in the doorway and said nothing as they walked toward the elevator, Healy waiting—for effect—until the elevator door opened. It was empty. "Because, Dick, this is the heavyweight division. I'm not some fucking technician you've hired off the street. I keep an eye on things—keep myself informed."

"Which one of my men told you? I will—"

"Don't blow a fuse, comrade. I didn't say it was one of your men."

"Who was it?" Orloff persisted.

Healy patted him on the back. "Curiosity, Dick, killed the cat."

"My name is not 'Dick,' " Orloff protested as the elevator descended to the sport deck. "Please do not call me this."

"No sweat. Colonel."

The elevator came to a gentle stop at the sport deck level.

"Racquetball?" Healy joshed. "Squash? Tennis?"

"Do you think in the next seventy-two hours—" Orloff glanced at his watch. "—in the next sixty hours, I should say, that your accent can match the cravat?"

It stung, but Healy tried hard to keep his temper. "What's wrong with my proletarian accent, comrade? B'sides, these dumb American tourists don't know a cockney from a count."

"Still, I wonder if you can blend in before someone recognizes you—for what you really are? Whether you can—" Orloff hesitated, searching for the right English phrase. "—carry it off?"

Healy flicked up a corner of the cravat and stared back at Orloff. "Just watch me, Dick!"

CHAPTER THIRTY-THREE

HER BOW PLUNGING into yet another heavy swell, the *Tuna Ghost* was less than a quarter mile aft of the *Burkhanov*, the latter still four miles southwest of the *Star*, when Ronnie Shear, the pain in his injured eye abating because of the cold spray, told the Coast Guard captain to radio the Russian container ship to heave to. The message wasn't getting through, however, the 156.7 megahertz channel nothing but fierce static.

"Atmospherics?" Shear asked, able to hear the surge of interference from the starboard wing. The *Tuna Ghost*'s radio operator either didn't hear him over the sea's roar or was busy trying other frequencies. "Son of a—" He whipped off his earphones as if he'd been stung. "That's not atmospherics, Captain. The bastards are jamming us. They're hitting us with an amplitude you wouldn't believe. Nearly blew my ears off!"

"Not again!" said Art Wright, grinning as the *Tuna Ghost* took another blow from a cross wave that rattled the wheelhouse.

"What d'you mean?" Ronnie asked him.

"Well, it's not quite the same," Wright answered, "but the *Ernst Mann* pulled the same kind of crap on us. Said they couldn't get us on the radio. The *Hornet* skipper had to use a bullhorn."

"I can do that too," the *Tuna Ghost*'s captain put in. "And if the bastards still don't hear me, I'll fire a burst across their bows. That ought to get somebody's attention." With that, he turned to the *Ghost*'s bosun. "All right, Johnny, get the lid off that damn bait tank."

"Boys'll enjoy the fresh air," the bosun said.

"Yeah. And young Shear's been waiting to fire that Browning since he qualified." As the *Ghost*'s captain took the battery-powered bullhorn from its cradle, the bosun switched on the deck lights and three other men, bracing themselves against the impact of the waves, made their way astern and began sliding the wooden hatch off the concealed machine gun.

"Time to strike the colors!" Wright said.

"Hit 'em with our lamp!" the captain instructed his first mate, and within seconds the halogen beam reached out over the gray, rolling walls of water, finding nothing at first but occasional whitecaps, then settling on the *Burkhanov*'s port side. Expecting to see a towering wall of steel in front of him, Ronnie Shear was surprised by how low the ship was in the water, weighed down by the mountain of containers, some newly painted but the majority of which were scarred by rust and the handling of the gantries. But then he and everyone in the wheelhouse was more surprised by the apparent collapse

dead ahead of them of the seaward side of a container amidships. It was as if some terrified, prehistoric animal, struck
dumb by the halogen's spotlight, was no longer able to support its own weight, the side simply falling outward like a
truck's tailboard. But surprise turned to horror as Ronnie
Shear, on the *Ghost*'s starboard wing, screamed, "Cut the
light! Cut the—" It was too late, the long, thick dart having
already shot from its mount in the container.

"Hard left, hard left!" shouted the *Ghost*'s captain, but
there was no chance, the homing torpedo not needing its
sonar-equipped guidance head. This was point-blank range,
and the *Ghost* exploded two seconds later in a curling orange-
black ball of fire that was as devastating as it was short-lived.
The *Ghost*'s crew, Art Wright, and Ronnie Shear were incin-
erated before the white-hot debris sizzled and sank into the
sea, unheard and unseen by anyone in the ear-dunning sound
of sea and wind, except by those aboard the blackened-out
Burkhanov.

Apart from the momentary flash of the explosion, a mere
pinpoint of light on the horizon, the only confirmation that
Orloff had of the *Tuna Ghost*'s demise was a faint rumble like
distant thunder. But it was enough.

Aboard *Push 'n' Shove*, however, the torpedo's hit was
seen from less than a mile away, and Neilson swore he felt a
heat wash pass over their boat. The explosion briefly illuminated the trolling poles that were acutely angled high behind
the wheelhouse like lances disappearing into the night. Brock
and Cawley were nothing less than open-mouthed at the force
of the explosion that had simultaneously ripped open and
scattered the remnants of their intended prey in the sea
around them.

"Mother of God!" Gunner Brock, having felt but not seen
the detonation, scrambled on deck, only to see the rain of
fiery debris that was quickly extinguished amid choppy waves
but that gave off enough light for him to catch the smile of
satisfaction on McBride's face.

Cawley, on the other hand, was clearly shaken, and turning to McBride, he asked, "You think there are any survivors, Major?"

"No."

Brenda Fowler, still at the helm, was about to send her wheelhouse lookout to confirm with McBride that they should turn back to La Push when a radio message, a courtesy "ships-in-the-area" advisory, came in from the *Southern Star*, reporting that the *Star*'s Doppler radar showed a "possible squall approaching" from the north.

"We're not going back to La Push," McBride told the lookout messenger. "Tell Meryl—tell Captain Fowler we'll be following the *Star* for a while."

"What's up?" Brock asked.

"Possible squall," the militia leader replied, showing Brock the message and explaining that it meant the *Southern Star*'s radar had picked up another vessel approaching from the north. Behind them, above the sea's growing fury, they could hear Cawley vomiting.

Frank, now fitted out with a finely veined beige corduroy jacket he had lifted from the disco's cloak room to replace the sweater he'd been wearing, a cap that added years to his appearance, and a pair of tan wing-tipped Oxfords swiped from the dozens of pairs of shoes placed outside the cabins for valet service, looked like any other elderly tourist. It helped that he had a slight limp, a result of having pulled a muscle during his escape from the *Star*'s bridge. At least he'd thought it was simply a muscle pull, but now and then, without warning, the leg would give way.

In the ship's mall, all but deserted at this time of morning, the boutiques were closed. The only shop open was a small drugstore carrying odds and ends, from greeting cards and magazines to a rack of assorted rubber-tipped walking sticks beneath a swivel display of the latest mirrored sunglasses. Frank pulled one of the walking sticks out, a gnarled, "genuine Irish" shillelagh "made in Tokyo." The natural notches on it looked as machine-turned as the rest of it, but at least it was sturdy and would take his full weight. The only problem was, he had no money. As he heard someone coming out from the back of the shop, he walked toward the counter, leaning heavily on the stick as if he'd owned it all his life.

"May I help you?" asked the pharmacist, a woman in her early forties with high-browed Slavic features.

"You have Tylenol 3?" he asked in a southern drawl.

She smiled apologetically. "Tylenol 3 can only be bought under prescription." Her English was perfect. "Are you in discomfort?"

"No," Frank replied, "I'm in pain."

"We can give you 222's or Tylenol 1," she proffered.

Frank, shifting to crotchety mode, irritably waved her suggestion aside and walked away, faking a slight tremble in his arm. "Two twenty-twos got too much caffeine in 'em," he said without looking back. "Give me the jitters. I want the number 3s."

"You could see our doctor, sir. Would you like me—"

"No, no," Frank replied grumpily, mumbling about doctors and "damn voodoo." By the time the conversation was over, he knew she didn't even suspect that he'd stolen the walking stick. It was no great feat in itself, merely one of the dozens of deceptions necessary for him to survive, but, like all the others, it took energy that he knew he should husband for what might yet come. In any event, the stick made him look older and enabled his left leg to take his weight.

Heading down from the mezzanine cinema, he saw four crewmen, about seventy feet in front of him, the maroon-carpeted passageway looking like a tunnel. They kept on coming, then split into two pairs, one disappearing off to his left to search the passageway on the starboard side, the other two coming straight at him down the portside passageway. Bent over so his face couldn't be seen, his cough-racked body adding to his aged appearance, Frank stopped, grasping the rail that ran interspersed along the front of the inside cabins for the full length of the ship.

The two crewmen walking toward him, like so many others, had been hastily conscripted by Orloff against the

Star's "hotel" manager's objections, but volunteers had not been wanting once the colonel offered a substantial bonus— in U.S. dollars—for whichever two-man team managed to flush out Hall. One crewman, an engine room oiler, had asked the colonel what to do if the American resisted them.

"Kill him!" Orloff instructed. "He is a threat, comrades, not only to this ship, but to every one of your loved ones." Orloff needn't have bothered with his explanation. For most of the crewmen the bonus, more than twice what any of them could earn in a year, was inducement enough.

The two men coming down the port side were now only feet away. "Excusing me," one said, and Frank smelled cooking oil, a kitchen hand wanting to make a name for himself. "Can we be of assistance?"

Frank didn't answer.

"I think maybe you should come to hospital. *Da*?" In a flash, as their eyes met, Frank knew the Russian had made him.

"*Da*," said the second man, moving in, the end of a long rubber flashlight protruding from his jacket pocket.

"*Nyet!*" Frank said, catching the man closest to him in the groin with his knee. The second man, stunned by the stick, crashed against the opposite handrail. Frank brought the walking stick down hard. There was a crack of bone, a scream, and doors were opening.

Frank ran down the corridor, the two crewmen writhing in the hallway that was quickly receding behind him as he headed toward an outside door. The last thing he heard was a surge of static from what sounded like a walkie-talkie.

He felt a blast of cold, salty air, glimpsed a sprawl of stars off to the west, the east a solid wall of black cumulus rimmed by moonglow. Now, dancing in front of the stars, there were two or three flashlights, a search party crossing the apron of decking beneath the bow, turning toward him. From the stern behind him he could hear more voices, a lifeboat cover suddenly illuminated by a searcher's light, and the sound of the lifeboat's lashings being retied. From the information deck, taking two steps at a time, he reached the restaurant floor's outer deck. More lights, the moon, dammit, breaking from cloud, flooding the superstructure, aiding the searchers. Somehow he had to buy more time, run interference until the *Petrel* could reach—

He heard more voices and, quickly opening a door to reenter the restaurant deck, made his way into one of the men's washrooms. Passengers used to complain in the old days about the coarse quality of the Soviet "dunny" paper, as Aussie Lewis used to refer to toilet rolls, but now, as Frank discovered, it was all "Purex—Soft as a Baby's Bottom." Perfect for his purpose.

In seven minutes flat he'd torn up enough toilet paper to jam each stall's U-pipe solid, except for one in use by someone being seasick. Then he pushed all the flush buttons and repeated the procedure in three more washrooms—his idea being not simply to have each toilet bowl overflow, but to block it so thoroughly that it'd be a quarter- or half-hour job with plunger and hooks to free each pipe. The flood itself would take hours to mop up, and the mess . . .

Going out past the elevators, approaching the central circular stairwell leading down from the restaurant to the information deck, he saw three crewmen, their heads bobbing as they began climbing the stairs in his direction. The elevator behind him opened and a ship's officer saw him, pressed the Down button and stepped back inside before Frank could reach him. Frank saw that the man hadn't been armed—either that or, more likely, he was under strict orders from Orloff not to fire anywhere in the passenger area or where a shot might be heard, for fear of the melee of hysterical complaints—which would only further help the American.

Frank limped heavily toward the staircase. Two of the three ascending crewmen looked up, the third man huffing and puffing behind them. Two swipes with the walking stick knocked one man down and sent the other leaping over the stairwell to escape, hitting the information deck with a thump. Up and running Frank jumped over the man he'd felled with his shillelagh and pursued the remaining man toward the door leading to the deck, until his leg gave way and he crashed to the floor. Through the door's glass partition he could see one of the search parties about to enter the restaurant deck. There were just too many of them. It was getting worse by the second. His leg was throbbing red-hot down his sciatic nerve but he kept running, back down the hallway, dragging the walking stick along the cabin doors as he went, bringing irate passengers in a variety of sleepwear out into the corridor to better confuse his pursuers.

He heard voices behind, closing, and stepped around the corner of the first cross aisle—waiting. He brought the stick around hard, as if for a home run, the impact doubling one man, who tripped another, but he missed the other two and saw a glint of steel. Frank jabbed the stick at the man holding the knife. The two circled him, Frank's eyes flicking now from the knife to the other man, who was sidling up along the wall. Frank got him with the stick, the man crumpling, Frank swinging back at the blade. The man pitched forward, clutching his knee, but the knife was in Frank's left shoulder. He pulled it out and the blood spurted. Frank raised the stick again but the crewman who'd used the knife was scurrying away, the crewman against the wall up, making a dive for the American. The Russian was brave but no match for the shillelagh, and decided on retreat. Too late. The shillelagh felled him. Frank paused, catching his breath, and folded the switchblade, pocketing it and dragging the unconscious crewman around the corner into the cross aisle. Leaning back against the wooden rail, he took off the corduroy jacket he'd stolen from the disco, its left arm and shoulder soaked and smelling vaguely metallic from the blood, and pulled on the crewman's white steward's jacket.

"What's going on?" came a sleepy inquiry from down the main passageway.

"Fire!" Frank yelled with all the urgency he could muster, emerging now from the cross aisle in the steward's white coat, looking the worse for wear, still carrying the stick and affecting a Russian accent. "We must abandon ship already. Hurry please. *Da.* All passengers to lifeboats."

Farther down the corridor, using the switchblade, he sliced

through the passageway's speaker wires, saw the fire alarm box and smashed its gleaming face with the shillelagh's grip. The ringing was so loud it momentarily alarmed even him. Doors were now flying open, the full range of night attire visible, from old men in pajamas and half-naked young women in transparent nylon to matrons in curlers, all protesting vigorously at their rude awakening until their irritation suddenly turned to fright as Frank kept yelling, "Fire! Your lifeboats please!"

"What—where—"

"Fire in engine room," Frank explained, "all passengers on deck please," the blood seeping through his crewman's jacket adding credence to his already convincing tone.

In the commotion he was causing, Frank received an unexpected assist, for while he'd banked on the toilets overflowing, diverting some of the crews as emergency cleanup squads, the water was now a minor flood sloshing from side to side across the carpeted corridor, convincing many of the passengers that the ship was actually sinking.

"Oh God, Henry, Henry!" he heard a woman scream. "We're sinking!"

Within five minutes over two hundred people, including a few red-faced crew members hastily hitching their trousers, were exiting passenger cabins, filling then jamming the passageways of the information deck, this panic-stricken swarm quickly swollen by the panic-stricken surge of passengers coming up from the main and sport deck below, clogging passageways and stairwells between the decks. The carefully practiced lifeboat drill of only twenty-four hours ago was completely ignored, everyone fighting to be first up and out onto one of the twelve big lifeboats on the salon deck. Some passengers broke out in eddies from the frantic, babbling stream to stand by the oil-drum-sized Beaufort canisters designed to unfold upon hitting the sea, inflating into igloo-shaped covered rafts that held emergency rations, drinking water, and other survival aids.

"Fire! Engine room—hurry!" Frank kept yelling. "Boat stations. Please stay calm! Everybody calm!"

"Calm your goddamned self!" bellowed an irate banker. "We need some order here—"

"Fire! Fire!"

No one could remember who'd started the alarm. There were as many versions as passengers, some saying it wasn't a bloodied crewman at all but one of the passengers, a man with a cap, a drunk, one of the officers . . . But no one could stem the rushing tide of the passengers. On deck, fist-fights broke out, one elderly and hysterical lady losing her spectacles in the crush and misreading her lifeboat number—mistaking a continental 7 for a 9, beating a younger woman who was trying desperately to make her way to the next boat, while others ran around, yelling and screaming, confused as to which was their boat.

Working his way through the crowd, Frank, in a confessional tone, as if too ashamed to say it aloud but feeling it his duty to inform them, intimated to as many passengers as he could that it was like "the *Titanic*"—not enough lifeboats to go around. The effect, his mere mention of *Titanic*, was electric. Panic now spread to some of the crew members. On the promenade deck there was pandemonium, some people shoving one another so violently they were knocked down, barely escaping from being trampled underfoot by scuttling beneath the lifeboats to the scuppers, only inches away from sliding overboard in the increasing sea. It was too bad, Frank knew, but by unwittingly helping him, the 450 passengers could end up saving many times their number if he could either delay the ship or keep Orloff and the crew away from him until the *Petrel* arrived, giving him at least a fighting chance at stopping the big American defense computer from reaching Russian and/or Chinese hands.

Captain Mendev had quickly rushed to the public address system, pleading then ordering people to calm down, stating there was no fire, that the ship was not sinking, but with Frank having sliced the PA circuit to more speakers, Mendev was talking to no one but himself on most decks, and on others, where the PA was working, his voice couldn't be heard above the general pandemonium. Livid, he swung on Valery.

"Now," Mendev said, "even you can see this madman must be stopped or we are both ruined."

Valery simply nodded. This time Mendev was right. You couldn't tolerate chaos of this magnitude aboard a ship. Apart from the millions of rubles of damage that were being heaped upon the ship's interior by the flooded toilets and the general melee, if the American was not caught, done away with, "this business," as Mendev angrily called it, would ruin both their careers beyond any possible repair. Then water damage reports started coming in, of passengers sloshing through the toilets' runover, many crewmen creating an exaggerated sense of the damage, which was exacerbated by the ship's increasing roll.

"They say it's like the *Titanic*," someone said.

"An iceberg!" someone else screamed. "We've hit an iceberg—"

"Shut up, Edith, goddamn it! We're on the goddamn equator!"

Amid the bedlam and perfumed sour smells of close-pressed humanity, a tall, impeccably dressed Englishman with willow green cravat was moving slowly but deliberately, with exemplary control, his head above most of the crowd, his dark eyes taking in everything and everyone imperturbably. "Do quiet down," he told an elderly lady from New York, calming her hysteria as she sobbed uncontrollably, jammed hard against a bulkhead by the crowd. "That's a good chap," he told another American, possibly her husband, whose silk robe, Healy noticed, was inside out. "Do look after her. It's a false alarm, you know."

"Are you sure of that?"

"Absolutely, old man."

"They won't let me out," screamed another passenger. "They won't—"

Awed, the man in the robe saw Healy continue to calmly push his way through the crowd, with the magisterial authority of a Moses parting the Red Sea, not looking *at* the crowd so much as *through* it, as if searching for someone in particular.

On the main deck immediately below the information deck, Frank had intended to repeat his fire alarm and toilet-plugging performance, but found it wasn't necessary. He was gratified by how fast the diversionary panic he'd created had spread throughout the entire ship, though he did glimpse one couple, the man—it was George Lynch—looking surprisingly unconcerned, he and his wife among the last to vacate their cabins, half of whose doors had been left open in the hurried mass exodus.

"Huh," Lynch said to his wife, Martha, "in the next *Fielding's Guide to World Cruises*, this tub won't get a single goddamn star."

Even so, with things having gone *awry*, as he'd warned Angela they might, Frank was hardly in a mood to celebrate the success of his diversionary tactic as he fought against the current of frightened passengers he'd created, making for an exit between the decks where he could descend to the sport deck to see if Angela was outside the gym. Given the stampede to the lifeboats, he never doubted it would be empty of even the most ardent body builders.

He was right. He saw Angela, worried, pacing but waiting for him, the gym deserted, several step machines still going, mute testimony to the success and speed of the panic he'd induced. Perhaps they had *all* seen *Titanic*. He allowed himself a smile.

"What's so damn funny?" A different Angela now: her face florid, hair mussed, stockings sodden, a piece of toilet paper, obviously unseen by her, clinging to one of her legs like a second skin.

"Nothing," Frank said. "You had a rough time?"

"Between being mauled by a drunken slob and having to fight my way to an exit, yes!"

He paused. "Sorry I got you into this."

"So am I."

"Let's get away from here."

"I'd like to. Up to my cabin."

"No way."

"Why not?"

"Because they could be looking for us up there."

"For *us*?" she charged. "You mean, for *you*."

"Maybe for you too." He'd said it before he could stop himself and he knew it sounded damn petty. It was. "I mean," he added hastily, "because you were seen with me on the way to the disco." He was tempted to add, And because you were dumb enough to put your room number on the message I gave you, but he knew she wasn't dumb. She was innocent, and he'd gotten her into this mess.

"C'mon," he said, his tone conciliatory, taking her hand.

"Where to?" she demanded.

"Down."

He tried lightening her black mood by telling her that the chaos he'd caused would cost Mendev or Valery free drinks until Suva just to calm the passengers down, and that he doubted anyone would be in the mood for the traditional King Neptune caper scheduled for mid-morning.

It wouldn't be Captain Mendev or even Valery who would respond with a brilliant counterstroke to his diversionary tactic, however, but General Kornon, whose senior POD agent aboard the *Southern Star* was sending an innocuous-sounding message to the Hotel Kosmos in Moscow, ostensibly to a relative but in fact reporting the present debacle. It was a message to which General Kornon, with visions of his old American nemesis and of another exile in Ulan Ude rising before him, immediately responded.

Within seconds of receiving the *Southern Star*'s message of the chaos, and the approaching radar blip that Mendev surmised was the American vessel, *Petrel,* General Kornon in Moscow was on the scrambler, first to General Chang and the Guo An Bu intelligence service in Beijing. Then he called his POD/FSB liaison officer, Ustenko, in Moscow.

In his darkened apartment, heavy with the odor of cold cabbage soup, Colonel Ustenko peered myopically at his alarm clock, the green luminescent hands pointing to four.

Momentarily he thought it was four A.M., then recalled he'd slept in most of the day, exhausted by a long early morning phone conference with Reinhard Klaus in Zurich, assuring the Swiss financier that, despite "some initial delay," all was proceeding as planned.

"What's the matter with you, Ustenko?" Kornon demanded, his gruff tone a measure of his anxiety over the message from the *Star* that the American, Hall, was running amok.

"I'm sorry, General," Ustenko answered. "I was up most of the—"

"Yes," Kornon cut in. "Carousing, no doubt." He didn't press the matter further, Ustenko noticed—either because the general had a pang of guilt about his own dalliance with the voluptuous Vanya from Tass's sports desk or because his call was a matter of dire urgency that didn't permit extraneous discussion. In fact it was both.

"Ustenko, I want you to contact FSB's Director Bykov immediately. Have him contact the *Southern Star*'s captain and—"

"Which one?" Ustenko asked. There was a moment of confusion before Ustenko clarified his question. "Tell Mendev or Valery?"

"Mendev, of course. That Estonian fairy is purely decoration for the passengers. Tell Mendev that Beijing, upon my insistence, has agreed to *assist* the *Southern Star* by dispatching one of their trawlers out of Suva, under General Chang's command. Orloff," Kornon explained to Ustenko, "suspects the American oceanographic vessel *Petrel* is dogging him."

"What's wrong with this Valery?" Ustenko asked.

"Oh," Kornon said scornfully, "*he* won't get his hands dirty."

"He may have to," Ustenko said.

CHAPTER THIRTY-FOUR

MENDEV, CONSCIOUS OF the fact that, apart from assuring his passengers' safety, the first rule for a captain of a cruise ship of any line was never to alarm them, sought to limit the damage the American had already done. Accordingly, he hatched a plan extemporaneously which, he told Orloff, would at once placate the passengers and assist him, his crew, and of course Orloff in finding Hall.

The plan, which even Valery, who was feeling decidedly left out of things, admitted was ingenious, was borrowed from Healy's earlier suggestion. Mendev would announce a "double-win" *Southern Star* lottery contest. The American passenger, Frank Hall, of Astoria, Oregon—his photo, like his address, taken from his Oregon driver's license—would be declared the first winner of the "double," a Xerox copy of his photo posted throughout the ship. The runner-up would be whoever was first to locate the "lucky Mr. Hall," the prize a full refund of the cost of their trip.

"That's bound to get them looking," Mendev said, clearly pleased with himself.

"Undoubtedly," Orloff responded, his tone dismissive. "And when they see Hall, they'll approach him smiling with dollar signs in their eyes. A perfect opportunity for him to recruit whoever approaches to help him—as he did with the woman in 302."

There was silence on the bridge.

"Better," Orloff insisted, "that you show his picture with a description of him as the violent and mentally deranged passenger who carried out this act of vandalism, of terrifying everyone, especially the children, and to advise anyone who sees him to on no account approach him but to immediately report his whereabouts to any member of the crew. That way," Orloff added, "no passenger will dare approach him." He then left the bridge, returning a minute later from his cabin aft of the radio room to hand Hall's wallet to Mendev, noting with wry satisfaction that Hall's driver's license photo, like those of most licenses, already made its owner look like a wanted criminal. "Have the purser enlarge it on our color copier and run off several hundred copies. Send some down to me as soon as they're ready. We'll distribute them among the passengers. Their blood is up, I can tell you."

"I know *that*," Mendev said, adding, "Do you want a picture of the woman too?"

Orloff thought about it for a second as he checked the slide on his Beretta 9mm Parabellum, then shook his head. "No."

"Why not?" Mendev asked, surprised by Orloff's answer. "She might be with him. You know how the Americans are— always running back to save cunt."

Valery winced at Mendev's vulgarity.

"Yes," Orloff said. "She probably is with him."

"Well, then?" Mendev pressed.

Orloff was, if nothing else, a quick thinker, something of which everyone on the bridge was now well aware. His shrewdness was evidenced by his quick dismissal of Mendev's "lottery" scheme, which now appeared amateurish next to Orloff's "mentally deranged passenger" strategy. "No," Orloff repeated, palming the magazine of fifteen cartridges into the ambidextrous pistol, then slipping it into the NATO shoulder holster he'd purloined during the mess in Kosovo. "If we distribute a photo of her, it'll tell her for certain that we know about her."

"But if the passengers are encouraged to look for her as well," Mendev objected, "it could cut our search time by—"

"No photo of her!" Orloff snapped. "No mention of her. Understand?"

"All right," Mendev agreed. "But I don't understand—"

"I do."

* * *

Upon seeing the photo of the "mentally deranged" vandal, wherever he was, who had roused everybody in a panic in the middle of the night, one outraged American tourist opined that "they should shoot the son of a bitch!" It was a sentiment shared by many of his fellow passengers.

"Don't worry," chimed in another, waiting impatiently outside his cabin as harried crew members sponge-mopped up what they could from the sodden corridor carpet. "If the Russkies get him, they'll take care of him. One thing about these Ivans is they know how to take care of troublemakers."

There were grunts of agreement, then a fiery outburst from one of two crewmen mopping one of the flooded cabins nearby. It was all in Russian but the passengers understood well enough. He was clearly exhausted, telling his comrades they'd done enough, stamping on the carpet, water oozing out of it, demonstrating that the sponge mops were clearly inadequate.

Orloff and four crewmen came sloshing through, telling the passengers of flooded cabins on the information deck and the main deck immediately below that while the toilet-produced flood was being mopped up, the ship's stern decks and cabins would be closed due to cleanup machinery. He also explained that the cruise line would be financially liable for any injuries incurred should an elderly passenger trip over one of the myriad snaking hoses, pumps, et cetera. To those relatively few passengers in the aft cabins on the four decks above the information deck level, Orloff gave assurances that protective vinyl blackout sheeting would be placed aft to protect them during the night from the harsh glare of the work lights the crew would need, and he promised the noise level would be kept to a minimum.

"And all because some yahoo is permitted to run amok," George Lynch opined in an accusatory tone.

"I'm sorry," Orloff responded with such obvious sincerity that George Lynch couldn't help but feel sorry for the Russians.

From his preretirement days as an insurance salesman, George knew how tough it was dealing day in and day out with the public. "Ah, never mind, bud," George assured Orloff. "We'll be just fine up forward in the restaurant." George winked. "I assume the bar'll be open?"

"Of course, Mr. Lynch. Free drinks till dawn."

"Attaboy!" With that, Lynch happily led the way forward.

Orloff couldn't have been happier, the alcoholic Lynch having played right into his hands. Mendev meanwhile was busy readying Orloff's handpicked members of the crew, twenty in all, to implement Kornon's counterstroke against Hall. Typically, Valery, on Orloff's "suggestion" to Mendev, had been excluded from the plan, Orloff unwilling to trust the tall Estonian. But by virtue of his rank and out of simple curiosity, Valery confronted Mendev. "May I ask what is going on?"

Pretending not to have heard him, Mendev grabbed the ship's megaphone. He left the bridge, and walked quickly astern, where he looked down at the main deck's stern area, a tapered space about the size of a tennis court. "I want those portside blackouts reefed in tight!" he instructed the crewmen. Rigging working lights, cables, pumps, hoses, and positioning the stern boom—the latter normally used for dockside loading in poorly equipped Third World ports—the stern party's activity was so frenzied that Valery was concerned Orloff might have sanctioned "triple overtime," an economic measure so rash on Russia's cruise ships that it required special permission from Moscow. Perhaps Orloff had radioed for such permission. Besides, the Estonian thought, what would he, Valery, know about it? He was only a *staff* captain.

With the ear-thudding noise of the four massive diesels pounding below them as they descended a "Crew Only" steel-grill staircase, Frank paused while Angela removed her high heels and felt the increased speed of the big ship as it struck the heavy Pacific swells harder, its yaw increasing despite its state-of-the-art Sperry fin stabilizers.

"What the hell are they doing up there?" Frank asked, referring to the sudden surge of speed when, for the comfort of the passengers during the mop-up, he'd assumed the ship would have slowed down and headed into the wind for a spell, to give the crew steadier conditions to work the pumps. Angela, however, took his question as being directed at her.

"An officer told us they'd have to pump out a lot of the cabins that were flooded. So they're rigging up all kinds of machinery, blackout curtains, hoses, and—"

"No," Frank cut in, "I mean why are they speeding up?"

She shrugged and had to raise her voice over the gut-punching noise of the engines. "Guess they want to get us to Suva to dry us all out and—"

Frank suddenly stopped on the grate stairway, causing her to bump into him.

"Blackout curtains?"

"What—oh, yes."

"What for?"

She shrugged. "I don't know. Something about protecting the passenger cabins at the back of the ship from the light."

"Aft," he corrected her, out of habit, as a teacher might correct a student's grammar.

"Aft?" she said.

"It's aft, not back of the ship."

"The *blunt* end!" she countered. He paid her no heed, still puzzled by her mention of the Russians' use of blackout curtains. "All you have to do to shut out the light," he said, "is close the porthole covers."

"You mean the *windows*."

He looked at her quizzically. She gave him an ersatz smile, explaining, "Stern suites are deluxe twins with full ocean view. I know, I couldn't afford one. They don't have portholes, they have full-length *windows*!"

"Touché! So why don't the stern deluxe ocean views that haven't been flooded simply close their bloody windows?" The moment he'd said it—used the word "bloody"—he realized he'd also been worrying about the whereabouts of the turncoat Englishman who would no doubt be looking for him, along with the Chinese and Russians. But for now his thoughts turned back to Angela's mention of the blackout blinds. He was convinced something wasn't kosher, that the blackout blinds were in fact a blind, but not to protect the passengers from the glare of the ship's bright stern lights.

Frank turned around, shouting above the noise of the engines, two decks below. "C'mon," he said. "We're going topside."

"Why?" Angela's exasperated question was swallowed by the thunder of the big combined diesel and gas exhaust turbine engines gearing up. "I thought you said they'll be looking for us up there!"

"Yes," and he took her hand again, but this time she felt it was more to hurry her than to protect her.

The "trawler," S-31, though nominally under General Chang's control, was under the immediate command of its master, Captain Li. Nor was the S-31—a ship out of Suva—a trawler. She was a Mirnyy class Whalekiller of 825 tons, a converted U.S. mine sweeper at one time purchased by the Russians, then resold to the Chinese, who, in order to circumvent the moratorium on killing whales, claimed it was an ocean survey ship. In fact, as Kornon well knew, the Whalekiller was still hunting whales, albeit clandestinely, for the insatiable Asian markets. Even the whalebone was sold, if not for fertilizer then for scrimshaw, the ancient carved bone rings and trinkets still eagerly sought by tourists and collectors from Shanghai to Honolulu's International Marketplace. And when it wasn't hunting down whales, the trawler served as an AGI—an intelligence-gathering spy ship—bristling with aerials and satellite dishes which were explained away as "navigational aides."

There had been other "trawlers" available, but the Whalekiller, despite its 208-foot length and thirty-one-foot beam, was the fastest in the fleet, its 3,100-horsepower diesel capable of driving it to a top speed of eighteen knots—almost twice that of the American vessel, *Petrel,* reportedly shadowing the *Southern Star*, and over one and a half times the American ship's weight.

By now Wu Ling, in the manner of so many who are forced by circumstances beyond their control, had begun to adapt. It was either that or watch Chang—so servile in the presence of the Swiss banker and his superiors but so ruthless in his own domain—destroy her family. And, though she would never admit it to her family, with her acceptance of her fate as Chang's concubine came a growing appreciation of the advantages it bestowed. As Chang had promised, she now wore the finest Suzhou silk, from her underwear to the tight, split-thigh *qi paos*. And with the whiff of wealth she inhaled came a new confidence, so much so that she dared from time to time to ask Chang where they were going and why, as she did now on the bridge of the Whalekiller.

"We are going to protect our investment," he told her.

"The supercomputer?"

He took up the pair of binoculars from the hook by the compass's gimbals mounting. They could see the radar blip that was the *Southern Star*, and soon her lights should be visible. "Go to the cabin," he told her. "I'll be down shortly." She did as she was told. Whenever he was anxious, he sought release. She wasn't in the mood, but that didn't matter to Chang. His anxiety about the whole project, the fact that from now on much of the success of the operation would depend on him, together with his desire to show the arrogant Klaus that he could deliver, combined to inject his libido with what his Guo An Bu agents aboard called a case of "must"— a need, as the normally humorless Guo An Bu agents joked, to show that he was literally "on top of things!"

"You see the *Southern Star*'s lights?" Chang asked the Whalekiller's captain.

"No," replied Li, a taciturn man not unlike, as he understood from the Guo An Bu's printout, his opposite number on the American vessel *Petrel*. The *Southern Star* had reported that the *Petrel* was now approaching her from the opposite direction of the Whalekiller, steaming due west toward the cruise ship. Chang quickly replaced the binoculars. "I'll be in my cabin."

"Lots of 'Bamboo in the Wind' aboard *that* cruise ship,"

proffered the Whalekiller's junior officer of the watch. There was stifled laughter from one of the lookouts.

"Keep your eyes out for the *Southern Star* and the enemy ship," Li said shortly.

"Yes, sir. I think we should be seeing them soon."

Li said nothing, hands behind his back, legs braced from long years of practice against the Whalekiller's roll, his almond-shaped eyes fixed on the radar, the dot that was *Southern Star* working its way in from the periphery of the amber screen.

All the White House would tell Gloria Bernardi—indeed *could* tell her via her two Secret Service minders—was that her fiancé was out of the United States, his exact whereabouts unknown "at this point in time."

Of all bureaucratic jargon, the phrase "this point in time" infuriated Gloria the most. It was merely a euphemism for "now." "You mean," she lambasted her minders, "that *right now* you don't know where the heck he is or what he's doing?" Even in her worst moments she had a habit of using "heck" instead of an outright profanity. It was a trait in her so unlike most others Frank knew—especially unlike Aussie Lewis, whose Australian-born profanity was legendary—that it both amused and endeared her to him.

Andrew and Shirley couldn't help her much. They didn't know where Frank Hall was either, and all that presidential adviser Brownlee, via presidential assistant Donna Fargo, would tell them was that Miss Bernardi would be informed of any new developments the moment the White House knew something definite.

"I could live with bad news better than this," Gloria blurted out.

Andrew, despite Brownlee's instructions to add nothing to his official communiqués from the White House, added sympathetically, "I know. Uncertainty's corrosive—much worse than knowing."

Gloria looked at him, his eyes hidden by the de rigueur shades. She was touched by his empathy.

"Thank you."

CHAPTER THIRTY-FIVE

EVEN BEFORE REACHING the main deck level, Frank and Angela could hear the distinctive putt-putting sound of pumps above the deeper heartbeat of the ship's engines, which became fainter the higher they climbed the staircase. Approaching the stern's starboard exit door that led out onto the deck itself, Angela paused to catch her breath. Frank, despite the danger they were in, was momentarily distracted by the sensual rise and fall of her breasts. Admonishing himself for the lapse in concentration, he peered through the door's glass panel to make sure the margin of deck, about ten feet in width, which ran all around the ship was deserted. The only thing visible was a blue blackout curtain, weighted down by a series of gray sandbags that resembled a segmented snake stretched across the deck. "What's behind the green door?" he asked in an attempt to release the tension.

"What?" Her voice was strained, her breathing more labored, despite the rest.

"Wait here," he told her.

"I'd feel safer with you."

"No. If anything happens to me while I'm on reccy—" He had unconsciously slipped into his old SEAL vernacular. "—better you're not with me."

"So what'll I do if you don't come back?"

What could he tell her? Try to hide till the ship reached Suva? Throw herself on their mercy? Maybe she'd been right and they weren't looking for her after all? And maybe water wasn't wet. He had no answer other than a feeble "I'll be back in a minute," and was gone, his shadow becoming elongated as he approached the huge blue vinyl drop cloths that the stern work lights had turned pale blue, but through which only more vague shadows could be seen. Frank withdrew the moment he saw his shadow cast on the curtain, afraid it would be spotted on the other side. He returned to the starboard exit door where he'd left Angela. She was gone. Jesus!

"I'm up here!" She'd moved up half a dozen stairs toward the restaurant deck and was sitting down, resting.

Frank swallowed with relief. "I have to try the corridor again," he told her. He looked through the door's glass panel, but because of the acute angle she was coming from, he couldn't see the elderly woman approaching along his side of the corridor. He almost struck her with the door.

"Oops!" he said.

She glared at him for what seemed to him an eternity. Did she recognize him or was she merely annoyed?

"Pardon me, ma'am."

"You should look where you're going, young man!"

"You're quite right." *Grouchy old bitch.*

He walked briskly, but not too hurriedly, back toward the stern, where he could hear the two-stroke pump engines growing louder. Glancing behind only once to reassure himself that apart from the old woman the long corridor was deserted, he crossed to the other side of the corridor, where his shadow on the drop sheet would be minimal. He passed more open-doored cabins from whose flooded interiors corrugated hoses ran out into the corridor. His old SEAL training told him that as a right-hander it would be easier for him to pull, or rather inch, the weighted curtain away from the bulkhead on the starboard side than on the port in order to see what was going on. He heard voices then, two men talking only a few feet away on the other side of the vinyl sheeting that curtained off the corridor from the stern and beneath which carefully taped-down, six-inch-diameter hoses passed out onto the deck.

Whoever he'd heard talking on the other side seemed about to pull the sheeting aside and come through.

Frank dove into the nearest of the vacated cabins, turned

right into the bathroom, and stepped smartly into the shower recess. Carefully, noiselessly, he drew the shower curtain shut and took the switchblade from his pocket—the blade, he noticed uncomfortably, still stained with his blood.

Gloria hadn't eaten all day, her stomach contracted by anxiety about Frank, and she was furious at the Secret Service for its refusal to answer questions.

"Are you robots?" she asked Andrew and Shirley angrily, and was immediately angry at herself. Hadn't Andrew genuinely sympathized with her plight?

But it wasn't sympathy she wanted, it was hard information. Where was Frank, and was he in danger, and if so, what were the Secret Service, or whoever the heck was in charge of this covert business, doing about it?

Andrew reminded her once again that neither he nor Shirley had been told anything other than to guard her. Gloria turned to Shirley. "Can't you press for more details?"

Shirley didn't reply. She was looking out through the window for anything unusual. "That red Toyota pickup," she said. "Is that normally parked here?"

"What?" Gloria said. "Oh, I don't know," and turning to Andrew, "Can't you tell them—" Suddenly she was crying, mad at herself for doing so in front of the agents. Shirley glanced at her, then resumed surveillance of the Toyota.

"I have told them," Andrew assured Gloria, looking over at Shirley as if he could use some help. None came. He was about to put his hand on Gloria's shoulder to comfort her but restrained himself. It was absolutely verboten to touch these days unless you were arresting someone. "Next time I call—" he began.

"Call BCI," Shirley cut in, surprising both of them. "That Toyota's been there all day. Looks fishy."

The Bureau of Criminal Investigation yielded nothing. The owner of the Toyota had no rap sheet, not even a speeding or parking ticket, though if the pickup remained there for another hour, beyond the three P.M. zone limit, he'd get one.

* * *

The voices Frank had heard behind the vinyl drop cloth grew fainter and were soon swallowed up by the incessant thumping of the pumps. He folded the knife, left the shower recess and went back out into the corridor. Already he could detect the foul odor of soaked carpets drying, a steady current of artificially warmed air, inexplicably shot through with a stinking rotten meat smell, pumped in through the hosing that snaked in from the stern through the carefully cut holes in the vinyl sheeting. In order not to cast a tall shadow on the curtain by standing up, as he had previously—which might have been the reason for the two men's approach—Frank now lay down on the wet carpet. The toilet-flood water stinging his arm wound, he glanced back at the corridor now and then, while carefully peeling away a strip of masking tape that had been used to seal the hose holes at the bottom of the sheet.

Peering through the small opening he'd made, he at first saw only what seemed to be a confusion of pumps and hoses, and crewmen walking briskly about, bracing themselves against the roll of the ship. Then he spied a group of men at the stern rail, just beyond the whale-oil-drum-sized Beaufort life raft container. Their attention was directed out, seaward, not at the ship's superstructure where all the blow-drying was under way. He saw a purplish flash—probably an oxyacetylene torch—and now, in addition to the whine of heavy-duty fans and the frenzied putt-putting of the assorted pumps, he heard the deeper thump of a winch being engaged. He guessed it was one of those normally used to lower the heavy all-enclosed lifeboats, and saw a boom and block through which a cable was being threaded and lowered, and nearby, on the deck, a huge metal trunk about half the height of a merchant ship's container. On the deck, chains and cables were attached to several of the large, orange, metallic-skinned ball-shaped buoys of the type he and many other marine salvage companies and ships used.

"What the . . . ?" he whispered to himself, and felt a touch on his back. His head jerked around.

It was Angela.

"Jesus Christ!" he hissed. "You frightened the—get back—you'll cast a shadow!"

"It's creepy down there!" she hissed back, indicating the deserted stairwell. "All you can hear—" she began, stopped, and said simply, "I don't want to be alone."

"Well," he assured her in a hoarse whisper, "you won't be much longer. You can come with me."

"Where?"

"Engine room, then overboard."

She stared wide-eyed at him in fright. "Over—"

"C'mon," he said, crawling back in what in his SEAL days he used to call a "lizard exfil"—for exfiltrate.

"You're crazy," she said. "I'm not going anywhere but—"

"Suit yourself," he said impatiently, an uncharacteristic brutality in his voice. "If you stay aboard, they'll find you eventually. You stand a much better chance with me."

"Of what, *drowning*?"

"No way," he said, taking her by the hand, wincing with the pain of his wound, which had started bleeding again after he'd had his weight on it, lying down stretched out on the corridor carpet. "Look, I haven't time to explain everything, but you'll be safer with me. The Russian-Chinese Mafia on this ship are out for blood. And," he added, "you won't have to swim more than a few strokes. Promise."

She looked as if she was shading her eyes, but she was rubbing her forehead as if trying to contain her confusion and fright. She'd begun a cruise that had turned into a nightmare.

"C'mon!" he commanded her. "We haven't got all day."

"I don't know," she began, but the shadow of someone who'd heard her on the other side of the vinyl was approaching the curtain. Frank made up her mind for her. He snatched her hand and pulled her back along the corridor to the crew's stairwell between decks. With Angela following, half willingly, half dragged, they went back down past the service deck and below the still deserted sport deck to the engine room.

The cavernous, ear-dunning world of the engine room,

where the four big cream-colored diesels drove giant pistons in relentless slavery, alarmed Angela, as it did most people who'd never witnessed this thundering netherworld that made the lounge lizard life above possible. The hot gust of diesel fumes, though faint by old standards, initially overwhelmed her. She stopped and gasped for air, only to swallow more of the foul petroleum odors that ships' engineers the world over take in like mother's milk, but which for normal mortals often causes instant nausea and headache, followed by a gush of saliva that begs to be spit out.

"You okay?" Frank asked her. "You look—"

"I feel sick."

"You want to wait back in the stairwell?"

"Yes."

"But don't wander," he ordered. With that, he slid down a set of stair rails with the expertise of long experience at sea, his feet barely touching the stairs, his weight borne almost entirely by his arms, for which he immediately paid a price, as his wound opened again and bled.

Like most computer-run engine rooms, the *Southern Star*'s was staffed by only a few operators who, in obeyance to modern safety regulations, were wearing bulbous lime-green ear protectors. These could be easily seen against the pastel-colored engines, and prevented the operators from hearing Frank enter their domain.

Crouching low, he worked his way along the T-shaped catwalk between the first pair of engines, his body involuntarily trembling from the vibration, despite the diesels' rubberized mountings. Easing the fire ax from its bracket, he proceeded toward the fuel injector pipes. Suddenly, a pair of green overalls was in front of him, the Russian oiler's jaw dropping in surprise. The man shouted before Frank hit him in the stomach with the ax's handle, then brought it up under his chin. There was a barely audible crack, and then the oiler lay out cold on the catwalk. Frank looked about and saw only one other man, about twenty yards away, leaning over a computer terminal by the ship's telegraph, one leg propped on the rim of a sand bucket into which he tossed a cigarette butt before returning his attention to the computer screen, tapping the keys. Turning left at the end of the catwalk, Frank approached the fuel injectors. He lifted the ax, ignoring the needle-hot stab of pain from his wound, and brought it down with all his strength—hot diesel fuel spurting everywhere. Quickly he moved to the second injector and did the same. As he quickly approached the third pipe, he saw the operator from the computer running toward him. Frank reached and split open the third injector as the man reached him, brandishing a huge monkey wrench. It was a standoff until Frank, fearing the Russian might have hit a bridge alarm, though he couldn't hear any, threw the ax. The man ducked as Frank ran back along the catwalk. He heard the Russian yelling and then a clatter, as the Russian threw the wrench at him and missed.

Frank yanked open the door to the stairwell, yelling at Angela, "We're outta here!"

She ran up the stairs, almost slipping on the metal deck in her panty hose, clutching her shoes in one hand, hauling herself up by the rail with the other, until they reached the starboard side of the service deck. There were no carpets on these work decks to muffle sound, and Frank heard someone approaching around the mid-corridor corner. The noise was coming from beyond a set of swing doors. Glimpsing a food trolley laden with cartons of everything from champagne to frozen beef, the unoiled screech of one of its wheels echoing shrilly from hard steel floor to bulkheads, Frank quickly pulled Angela after him into an alcove. Its shelves were piled high with toilet paper and paper towels, and both of them tried to quiet their breathing in the cramped space.

The trolley, pushed by a slim Chinese man humming to himself, passed them and was pushed through the second set of swing doors. They emerged then, and ran farther down the depressingly yellow-bulb-lit corridor. What a different world it was down here from the fantasy of the upper decks, Frank reflected, not for the first time. When they reached one of the starboard side's forward loading bays, he began turning its unlocking wheel counterclockwise.

"Unstrap that Beaufort!" he called out to Angela, indicating one of the oil-drum-sized containers cradled against the bulkhead while he continued to spin the wheel that would open the loading bay door. He guessed that the door was no more than four to six feet above the water. In her panic, forgetting the "abandon ship" drill, Angela fumbled with the V-shaped canvas strap on the Beaufort, working against instead of with its snap-free mechanism. "Here," Frank said, and took over, unsnapping it, rolling the drum out of its cradle up toward the loading bay door that wasn't yet open. "Stand against the drum," he told her. "Keep it from moving until I get the door."

When he opened the door, the red caged light above it flashed and an alarm bell rang. "Shit!"

He rolled the Beaufort drum to the door, the ship's foamy slipstream, bloodred in the alarm light's glow, racing past. The ship had been slowed by his sabotage of the fuel lines, but its forward momentum was not yet arrested. He glanced about for life vests, saw one on a hook by the cradle, thrust it over Angela's head and pulled the ties. "Jump!"

"What—" He pushed her out and leaped after her. He saw the phosphorescence boiling around her as she thrashed in panic, her sodden clothes weighing her down, and felt himself slammed into her by the ship-created current, his nose numbed by the impact. He heard her gasping for breath and grabbed her hair. "Calm down! For chrissake, I've got you. You're all right!"

She was still spluttering when he saw the Beaufort raft unfolding like some big, orange chrysanthemum beyond the penumbra of the ship's lights. Floating on his back, placing his weakened left arm about her chest, he frog-kicked his way toward the raft. "Relax!" he implored her. "You'll be all right."

She said something but immediately began retching, having swallowed saltwater. Soon the illuminated island that was the *Southern Star* disappeared into the heaving darkness.

On the ship's bridge, yelling above the crash of a huge

wave, Orloff was ordering the radio officer to alert Chang's Whalekiller that a Beaufort raft was missing from the *Southern Star*.

CHAPTER THIRTY-SIX

NOW THERE WAS no doubt in the White House that the seven-man standby force at Boeing Field, originally suggested by Donna Fargo, should be unleashed to reinforce the *Petrel*, which was closing on the *Southern Star* and *Burkhanov* but whose oceanographic crew lacked the requisite military know-how. Despite the smothering noise of the approaching storm, the fact that sound travels underwater at four times its speed in air had allowed the seabed microphones of the SOSUS network to pick up the noise of *Tuna Ghost* exploding. Though what caused the explosion was still a matter of conjecture, it was decided that in light of the message received about the transfer of the "gift" to the *Burkhanov*, and the proximity of the Russian container ship to the *Tuna Ghost* before she sank, something drastic had to be done. Brownlee grabbed the list of the seven-man commando team that Freeman had on standby. It would be led by Medal of Honor winner Brentwood and include Choir Williams, Aussie Lewis, Salvini, and Joe White, plus an ex-Delta man and a former Green Beret commando, selected by Freeman to replace Art Wright and Ronnie Shear.

"I think that the team Freeman has assembled—" Brownlee saw the President turn on him at the mention of Freeman's name and quickly corrected himself. "I mean, I think the commandos should hit the *Burkhanov*. This is our last chance. Once they get to Suva—"

"I agree," the President said, "but let's play it close to the chest vest with those civilians aboard the *Petrel*. Tell the *Petrel* captain only as much as he needs to know."

"Yes, sir," Brownlee said.

"What about Frank Hall?" Donna asked, hoping the President might be more receptive to her concern than Brownlee had been earlier, with his curt "he knew that going in" response.

"A container ship is one thing," the President answered. "A cruise ship is quite another. We can't have our military people running loose on the deck amid—how many passengers is it?"

"Over four hundred," Brownlee answered.

"But there's a storm predicted, Mr. President," Donna pressed. "More of the passengers'll probably be inside and—"

"No," the President said emphatically. "Brownlee's correct. Hard as it sounds, the computer's what we're after. We have to focus on that."

"He's all alone, Mr. President," Donna said.

"Yes, I know. You don't have to remind me. But—well, he knew that going in."

Donna glared at Brownlee.

"Send the team to the *Burkhanov*," the President ordered.

High above the sea, west of Boeing Field, Sal Salvini shouted over the roar of the Hercules's four turboprops, "Would've thought they might have given us an unmarked aircraft, seeing that everything's so hush-hush."

Aussie Lewis shifted his weight against the cargo net. "We're at twenty thousand feet, Sal. Who's gonna bloody see us from down there? They can't even hear us at this height."

Sal shrugged, conceding the point. Was he getting that rusty? Aussie tried to give Sal a good-natured, reassuring thump on the shoulder but found it difficult to move. His medium-built frame was laden, like that of his eight comrades, with over seventy pounds of gear. In addition to his oxygen mask and specially designed Kevlar helmet, necessary for a HALO—high altitude, low opening—combat jump, his equipment included a wet suit; two steerable chutes; a rucksack with medical kit; a survival GPS unit; ammo; grenades; a bubble-less, noiseless rebreather underwater unit; mini radio; night vision goggles; PRC ultra-high-frequency survival rescue radio; Arpac shoulder-fired missile; and a retractable-stock Heckler & Koch submachine gun. The latter, like his Glock 9mm pistol and the weapons of all six other members of the team, had been sanitized, its serial number removed. The Glock, equipped with a Trijicon night sight, was not standard issue, but because of their SEAL and ALERT training, they were permitted, indeed encouraged, to carry their weapons of choice. Aussie Lewis favored the metal polymer Glock for its relatively small number of parts and the fact that its manufac-turers had modified the firing pin for underwater use, pri-marily with the SEALs in mind. Plus, it had a big capacity seventeen-round magazine.

Salvini's weapon of choice was a Chinese AK-47. Admit-tedly not as accurate as Aussie's HK-MP-5 or as room-clearing capable as David Brentwood's Mossberg shotgun, the AK-47 had nevertheless saved his life in 'Nam during a raid in the infamous Rung Sat Special Zone. For one vital moment a Viet Cong in the thick growth beneath the jungle canopy, hearing the telltale stutter of an AK-47, assumed it was a fellow VC firing nearby and hesitated, allowing Salvini to get him with a full burst.

The four remaining men—the Green Beret commando, the ex-Delta man, Choir Williams, and Joe White, who was still in a rage over the loss of Art Wright aboard the *Tuna Ghost*—chose to arm themselves, as Aussie had, with a Heckler & Koch 9mm submachine gun and a Beretta 9mm pistol as backup.

In front of the seven-man team on the Hercules's load roll-ers, a sanitized twenty-four-foot-long SEAL beeper-equipped, rigid inflatable boat sat ready on its pallet, but because its chute, unlike the steerables issued to Freeman's team, could not be controlled during descent, there was the risk that the RIB might "land" miles from the commandos' own drop zone.

It was so difficult for the seven commandos to move, with all their gear, that it was up to the C-130's loadmaster and three air crew to ease the boat through the dim light of the plane's interior toward the Hercules's rear.

The ramp yawned open into an infinity of blackness. The red standby bulb went green. The loadmaster and his three Air Force crewmen, collars flapping furiously, wind whistling over their helmets, gave a concerted push on the pallet, then left it to the rollers. The weight of the big, rigid inflatable and its tightly stowed gear, including Mercury outboards, extra oxygen tanks, limpet mines, ammunition, and satchel charges, dropped out of the Hercules, producing a deafening clatter. Allied with the trailing of the giant cargo chute's straps, it created a sense of everything coming loose, a cacophony of noise replaced just as suddenly by the steady thunder of the four Allison engines. It was hoped the boat was now deployed beneath the hundred-foot-wide canopy. The ramp closed and the Hercules's pilot made pattern, "driving in circles," waiting for the RIB to "land" on the ocean's surface, where its beeper, changing tone upon impact, would give him the grid of sky into which he should drop Brentwood's seven-man commando team.

"Better them than me!" the co-pilot intoned through his chin mike. "Weather report says we're gonna have a Force Eight—possibly Ten." It meant high winds on the open sea—twenty-eight knots plus.

"They'll be down before that," the pilot assured him.

"Sure, but they'll be smack in the middle of it later."

"Hey," the pilot said, "life's tough. That's what they get for volunteering. Besides—"

"That's funny," the co-pilot cut in. "The beeper signal on that RIB. It's fading."

"Well, it doesn't have that much range, otherwise the *Southern Star* would pick it up. So long as we can still hear—"

"Shit! It's gone!"

In the stygian darkness 5.7 miles below them, Captain Tate's radar operator also heard the beeper cease transmission.

Nevertheless, having been tracking it, the *Petrel* was in the projected grid, an area of twenty-five square miles of ocean into which the RIB should be descending. And Tate had already rung down to the chief engineer to give him full speed ahead and had posted extra lookouts, including a man aloft in the research vessel's crow's nest, another man stationed at the bow, one by the stern winch's A-frame, plus two more amidships on either side of the vessel. Having committed a third of his ship's complement of five officers and ten crew, Tate had to call on Dr. Shalit and her three assistants to stand as lookouts on the flying, or fair-weather, bridge immediately above the main wheelhouse, in order to permit his "off" watch to sleep.

"Precisely what are we looking for?" Dr. Shalit asked Tate and Redfern after plodding up to the wheelhouse, her tone sharp to the point of insult. She had earlier acquiesced in going to the aid of a ship in "possible distress," as Tate had put it to her, but her suspicion was aroused by the lack of any further information.

"We're looking for an inflatable," Tate informed her. "A twenty-four-foot-long rubber boat."

"Which should have been released on touchdown," First Mate Redfern put in.

"What's going on?" Dr. Shalit demanded.

Rather than waste time either arguing with her or admitting that he too was in the dark about the exact nature of the mission—knowing only that he was to pick up the raft and the seven "operatives," as Brownlee's message had referred to them—Tate ignored Shalit's question, telling her instead, "It'll be difficult to spot. No profile to speak of."

"Lights surely!" Shalit said.

"Ah, no," Redfern replied, the *Petrel*'s big Zeiss binoculars in hand. "I shouldn't think so, Doctor."

"Why not?"

"Ah, possibly the batteries," the Scot responded. "Think they've had the lolly."

"The *lolly*? Whatever are you talking about?"

"Dead," Redfern said, suspecting there wouldn't be any lights on the RIB, lest the *Southern Star* spot them.

"Well, I assume there are people aboard!" Shalit asserted.

"No one at the moment."

"No one?" Shalit glanced inquiringly at her technician, who was just entering the bridge, then back at Tate. "This is all very odd, I must say."

"Aye," Redfern concurred. "But we should pick up their beepers soon."

"Beepers?" Shalit echoed. "I wasn't told anything about *beepers*."

"Anything yet?" Tate asked his radio operator, who was listening intently in his cubicle aft of the bridge's map room.

"Not yet, Captain," the radioman replied. "I suspect they'll be jumping about now."

"Who's jumping?" Shalit demanded, now utterly confused. Bracing herself as the *Petrel* rode a heavy swell, she grasped the compass's mounting, her bosom pinning her technician against the bulkhead. "Get out of my way, Harris!" She turned on Tate. "I want to know who's on this rubber thing and for what reason. I'm not about to be treated like some—"

"They're jumping!" the radioman cut in.

Dr. Shalit looked from him to Redfern to Tate but got no response, the bridge crew galvanized by the news.

As leader of the seven-man HALO jump, Brentwood was first out over the ocean grid. He dove into the face-numbing cold, the wind screaming in his ears, the adrenaline rushing through his veins as Aussie, Salvini, Choir, Joe White, the ex-Delta man, and the Green Beret, not far behind, plunged seaward at over two hundred feet per second.

After two minutes, at approximately 2,500, glancing through their night vision goggles at their respective Hitefinder free-fall timers, they would deploy their steerable chutes, hopefully having already spotted the white, warm smudge through the infrared goggles that would be the *Petrel*, pitching and yawing against the cold, green background of the sea. Fifteen to twenty miles westward, rows of white dots and a white blur would be the *Southern Star*'s portholes and the trembling heat exhaust coming from the stack.

On the bridge of the Whalekiller, Captain Li rang Chang's cabin. He interrupted the general who, looking like a landed fish gasping for air, was approaching an ecstatic high. Wu Ling, by now having learned to enjoy her power over him, prolonged the tumescence of his "Bamboo in the Wind," leaving her tongue-teased victim and commander of all Guo An Bu agents aboard the Whalekiller prostrate with expectation. "Now," he pleaded. "Now!"

"General," came the invasive crackle of Li's voice. "Our electronics warfare officer has picked up a beep."

Chang gestured frantically to Wu Ling to finish up. Instead, she raised her head and demurely handed him the phone. "General?" The captain was insistent.

"Yes, yes, I heard," Chang said hoarsely. "I'll be there in a second." Chang swung his legs off what used to be the harpoon gunner's "soft class" mattress, grabbing his trousers. "I could have your brother shot!" he shouted at Wu Ling. "You aren't the only whore in Shanghai, you know."

"I know," she said, her tone coy. He could smell her perfume washing over him. Pulling on his army jacket, its rainbow campaign medals catching the cabin's light, his fingers still shaking from his anticipatory release, he clumsily buttoned up. Next, snatching his cap from its peg, he snapped the fingers of his free hand at her. "Just like that I could have him shot!" A swell came and knocked him off balance. Wu Ling did not dare laugh, however. It was a delicate balance, her power over him, his power over her, and right now she knew that, like most men denied sexual release at the last moment, his anger would take time to subside. Meanwhile he'd be only too happy to shoot anyone who got in his way.

"What is all this about a beeper?" he barked upon entering Li's blacked-out bridge.

"Good morning," Li said heartily. "We're receiving an interesting signal." He seemed excited.

Chang grunted. "Is it that spy ship, *Petrel*?"

"No. We've already got *her* on radar, but this signal isn't coming from her direction at all. It's much closer to us." Using his chart room's Gerber rule, he drew in lines between the positions of the American *Petrel*, his own Whalekiller, and the Russian *Southern Star*. The result was a triangle, showing *Southern Star* at the apex of the triangle, at a position ten miles to the north of Li, and the *Burkhanov* a few miles west of the *Star*. Twenty miles east of the midpoint between Li and the Russian cruise ship lay the American *Petrel*. "But the beeper signal we're hearing," Li explained to Chang with a smile, "is coming from here." The point of his dividers was resting on a small circle, marking the position from which the *Southern Star* had transmitted her signal to the Whalekiller an hour ago.

"Oh," the general said, and then the full import of Li's comment struck him with the force of a physical blow. So that's why Li had given him such a vigorous "Good morning."

"It's Hall!" Chang declared. "We've got the bastard!"

"Looks like it," Li agreed. "He must be on the *Star*'s missing raft."

"I will personally shoot him!" Chang promised, his hand tapping his holstered Walther .32.

"And the girl?" Li inquired in a mischievous tone his helmsman had not heard before.

"We'll see," Chang responded jocularly, his smile illuminated by the amber sweep of the radar's arm, the luminescent blip that was the *Petrel* just over eleven miles to the northeast.

"Are we at full speed?" he inquired.

"Maximum," Li assured him. "Eighteen knots. At least five knots faster than the *Petrel*, according to the ship's register."

"How long till we reach Hall?"

Li glanced at the chart. It was a distance of about twelve miles to the beeper. "Sea's rising," Li responded, "but there's no doubt we'll beat *Petrel* to him, even if *they've* picked up his signal."

"Reduce your speed to half," Chang said.

"I—I don't understand," Li began. "I thought—"

"Do as I say!" Chang commanded sharply, buoyed up by the realization that, having been put in charge of the next-to-last leg of the mission to secure the Rone, he would be in a far better position than Kornon and Herr Klaus had anticipated to shepherd the Rone on its final leg. Then everyone in Beijing, Moscow, and Zurich involved in the heist would know that it was the Chinese general who had *delivered*.

CHAPTER THIRTY-SEVEN

FRANK HAD HAULED himself aboard the Beaufort raft first. He knew from his salvage work and Special Ops days that any potential rescuer has a much better chance of hauling an exhausted and, in Angela's case, panic-stricken victim aboard by getting himself aboard first.

No sooner had Angela flopped into the heaving, six-foot-diameter igloo that was the interior of the plastic-domed Beaufort raft than she began to be violently ill, the sour stench of her vomit obliterating the smell of the sea. Frank had ignored her, immediately grabbing the raft's emergency locator beacon from its gunwale sleeve and activating its beeper.

Later—a minute or an hour, Angela had no idea—she heard him cursing in frustration as he failed to make any headway with the raft's compact fiberglass oars in his attempt to turn the small craft amid the increasingly powerful swells. He was aiming at the cluster of three huge, dark orbs that were the buoys he'd seen attached to the trunk as it was lowered from the *Southern Star*'s stern. He had anticipated that, though swept astern in the wake, like the cluster of three buoys, his and Angela's raft would bypass the buoys. He'd hoped to lash the raft to the buoys and await rescue by the *Petrel* or, if the gods were with them, by any other ship en route to or from Suva. But the outer V of the *Star*'s wake was taking the raft farther away. Quickly, he lashed the end of the raft's coil of quarter-inch rope about his waist.

"What are you doing?" Angela cried.

"I'll be back," he said. He hoped. Diving into the sea, he struck out abeam of the raft, into the widening wake.

It felt as if his body had suddenly been hit by the effluent of a storm drain, the fiercely bubbling stream generated by the cruise ship's propeller sucking him in, driving him toward the three giant buoys with alarming speed. He tried to slow himself, attempting a backstroke, but it was a fruitless effort. His arms and legs flailed ineffectually against the ship-created current, the giant orbs of the buoys racing madly at him, rising and falling out of sync on the swells.

He smashed into one of the chains anchoring the buoys, his head striking a U-bolt and his body going limp.

Aussie Lewis, fifteen miles to the east, pulled his rip cord, heard the snap of the canopy opening, and felt his body jerked upward. Then he hit the water, tugging hard on both Mae Wests, two being necessary to keep his gear-weighted body afloat. The hiss of the CO_2 cartridges inflating the life vests was all but drowned by the overriding noise of a wind-whipped sea that, sloshing against his HALO helmet, was growing more turbulent by the minute. But he had seen the pinpricks of the *Petrel*'s running lights through his night vision goggles only a mile or so behind him. He was reasonably sure of a fast pickup. Having failed to spot the RIB that the Herc's crew had dropped, Aussie was confident that the *Petrel* had already snagged it.

Instead, what the *Petrel*'s first mate, Redfern, had seen through his binoculars was now confirmed by several of

Petrel's crew busy with long-handled grappling pikes. It was the remains of the RIB. Its chute having tangled, the RIB had plummeted seaward like a brick, the impact so massive that the wooden pallet intended to stabilize the boat during normal descent exploded, imploding the rigid inflatable with hundreds of wooden shards with the force of tornado-driven two-by-fours. The result was a dark flotsam of debris now undulating on the swells over such a wide area that it created the impression that something many times its size had been sunk.

Joe White, exiting the Hercules, had dived from the thirty-thousand-foot exit altitude to three thousand feet, his comrade, the ex-Delta man, following without incident until, at less than five hundred feet from chute deployment level, White collided with a flock of glaucous-winged gulls. The Delta commando coming down behind him estimated that the gulls, no doubt attracted by the phosphorescence of the *Petrel's* wake and gliding in its stack's warm air currents, were probably traveling at no more than twenty miles an hour. But this meant the combined speed of the impact was in excess of 150 miles per hour. White's body went limp, tumbling in a "falling leaf" spin. His chutes remained undeployed; his heavy, gear-laden body hit the water with the force of an unexploded bomb, and with the life vests not inflated, he sank immediately from view. The Delta man, his chutes deployed, vests inflated, tried to reach the spot marked by the dead gulls but, weighted down, all he could do was rail against fate and strike the water impotently in his anger as he waited, his pinpoint saltwater-activated vest light coming on, the *Petrel* taking just over eleven minutes to haul him aboard. Choir, like Brentwood, Salvini, Aussie, and the former Green Beret, was also down by now and waiting, thoroughly depressed by the fact that the RIB was gone and a teammate dead. Two strikes against them before they'd started.

Regaining consciousness and fighting the waves of nausea passing through him after being swept into one of the buoy's heavy chains, Frank quickly slipped the loop of thin but strong nylon rope up from beneath his shoulders. Using a bowline knot, he tied it about one of the buoy's anchor lines. Then, using the rope in the same way he'd use a "feel" line through a minefield at night, he began pulling himself back toward the life raft, the latter invisible, the moon screened by rapidly building cumulonimbus. He was forced to pause, however, only a few yards out from the buoys, momentarily overwhelmed by the stench of rotten meat, a whiff of which he'd first noticed while peering through the slit in the vinyl sheet astern of the *Southern Star*. Though he'd once prided himself as having, like other SEALs and other ex–Special Forces types, an "iron gut," supposedly impervious to the mangrove rot and other dead things of the Mekong Delta, Frank now found himself throwing up, inadvertently swallowing seawater, which made him curse and throw up even more. Adding to his physical distress, there was an unmistakable sixth sense of unseen danger all about him, the kind of intuitive feeling he'd honed wading chest deep in the Mekong Delta's swamps, alert for ambush and water snakes.

Muffled by sea noise and high winds, Angela's hysteria wasn't audible to Frank until he was just feet from the heaving raft that was visible one moment as a small, dull, tent-shaped orange glow—Angela must have located the emergency flashlight—and gone the next in the deep troughs between the waves. When he finally reached the craft, he grasped a loop of the rope scalloped about it and pulled himself around to the hatch opening. Angela was screaming at him, "Where've you been? Where've you—"

"Calm down," he said. "I—" He felt her hand slap hard against the side of his face, and then for several seconds felt nothing, the sting of the blow delayed by the cold of the seawater. It was a tropical ocean, but he knew that exposure to the sea in such stormy conditions could easily result in hypothermia.

"You bastard!" she shouted.

He shoved her aside. "Get a grip on yourself," he said roughly, snatching the flashlight from her.

"Did you see them?" she shrieked.

Still catching his breath, the raft pitching violently, he felt in the space beneath the rubber gunwale for the Beaufort's parachute rocket, smoke float, hand flare, and foil-covered Gravol packs, in that order.

"They're all 'round the boat!" Angela told him, her voice quavering.

"Who?" he said, popping one of the pills out of its foil cocoon. Not waiting for an answer, he gave it to her. "Take this—you'll feel better."

"Sharks!" she shouted. "All around the boat!"

"Raft," he said petulantly. She was obviously hallucinating. Sheer unadulterated fright. He hadn't seen any sharks.

"Can't you smell them?" she shouted.

"You can't smell sharks!" he shouted back, but then recalled his own sense of danger in the water, the gut-turning stink of rotting meat not far from the buoys. But if there'd been sharks, why hadn't they attacked him? He realized then that his temporary unconsciousness after hitting the U-bolt might have saved him from attack. Stunned, his body had been immobilized, while the predators, if there were any around, had ripped into the meat that Orloff and his FSB lackeys had dumped overboard to attract the man-eaters as a disincentive to anyone interested in snooping around the buoys in the shipping lane.

But now, having secured the raft to a fixed position—the anchored buoys—his hope of rescue before the seas got too rough and capsized the raft soared. Holding the stick flare outside the hatch, he pulled its pin, waiting for the two to three minute delay. "Sharks won't harm you," he told Angela. "You're safe in the raft."

It was a lie. If the muck the Russians had ditched overboard was in the vicinity of the raft, they were in trouble. No matter what all the shark professors said, in Frank's experience a shark in frenzied attack didn't seem to see its target once it got in close. It was like watching Gloria's cat whenever she'd dropped a treat right before the cat's nose. Its senses of smell and sight seemed suddenly to desert it. In the

shark's case, this meant that after initially being lured by
blood in the water, the predator would just blindly rip and tear
at whatever it bumped up against, including the raft.

The flare shot out of its tube in a shower of sparks,
streaking high into the pitch-black sky, burning like a tiny sun
as it descended beneath its chute.

Racing against the approaching Force Eight to retrieve the
remaining three commandos, Captain Tate launched the *Petrel*'s own smaller Zodiac through the research ship's stern
A-frame.

He'd been told by the ex-Delta man that Joe White was
dead. With Aussie Lewis, Choir Williams, Salvini, and the
Green Beret remaining to be picked up, Tate radioed his
bosun aboard *Petrel*'s Zodiac the position from which the
parachute flare and the emergency locator signal he was now
receiving had originated. The bosun, busy punching the coordinates into his handheld but lanyard-secured GPS, yelled
out to one of the three crewmen with him to take over retrieval of the four remaining commandos by means of a
"snatch." The snatch, a rubber loop held abeam of the Zodiac,
could be effectively snagged by the arm of a swimmer, who
would then be hauled smoothly aboard the Zodiac still under
way. Then, with the six commandos aboard, the Zodiac could
proceed to the location of the signal transmit.

Aussie's right arm caught the loop, locking onto it. But
with all his gear, plus the two fully inflated Mae West vests
the weight of his gear necessitated, the Zodiac's outboard operator was forced to idle the Mercury. He put the Zodiac's
bow into the wind to minimize roll, while the two other
crewmen aboard the Zodiac grunted and strained, dragging
Lewis up over the gunwale.

"Welcome aboard!" the bosun shouted.

Aussie, in an extraordinary exchange, given the darkness,
foul weather, and urgency of the mission, saluted the bosun
nonchalantly with a tap of his finger on his HALO helmet,
yelling loudly against the howling Force Eight, "What happens when you give a lawyer Viagra?"

'What?" the bosun obliged.

"He grows taller!"

Sulking in her chief scientist's cabin, pointedly ignoring the ship's company, who were on deck, Dr. Shalit was composing a letter of complaint to the National Oceanographic and Atmospheric Administration, deploring the "high-handed . . . secrecy obsessed . . . waste of U.S. taxpayers' money." What she meant was she couldn't stand not being told precisely what was going on. Her fury at being excluded only increased as Tate, via cabin intercom, now advised her that it might be best "if all oceanographic personnel remain below until further notice."

"Why?"

"There may be a lot of activity on deck, Doctor."

"Doing what?" she said tartly, adding before he could answer, "I assume it won't be oceanographic work, for which this ship was built."

"I'm afraid I can't say."

"Or won't!" she charged.

"Dr. Shalit," he responded with exemplary restraint, "I'm under orders, which means *everyone* on the *Petrel* is under orders. All I can tell you is we have six heavily armed men aboard, and they don't look like they'll be taking water samples."

Forward in the *Petrel*'s starboard wet lab, Brentwood, Lewis, Salvini, Choir, the Delta man, and the Green Beret were busy unpacking their weapons from transparent watertight sheaths and checking gear from throat mikes and radios to the slides on their backup pistols. Each man slipped a condom over the end of his submachine gun, in Brentwood's case, over the barrel of his twelve-gauge shotgun, and brainstormed the approaching mission.

Secret Service agent Andrew put down the phone in Gloria Bernardi's apartment and hesitated before he spoke, Gloria interpreting this as an augury of bad news.

"What is it?" she pressed, heart racing. "What's happened?"

"I've asked the White House for more information," Andrew replied apologetically, "but all they'll tell me is that he's on a highly classified job for Uncle Sam."

"My God, I know that, Andrew," Gloria said archly, immediately regretting her tone.

"They're terrified of a leak," Shirley said, still watching the street. Though she was reasonably sure that the man Gloria had called Larry, the Gauloise smoker, from the cigarette butts found in the California Hotel room, would be out of play now that Gloria's boyfriend was involved, she still wondered what the hit man had been hired to prevent him from doing.

Gloria, her nerves at breaking point, went into the bathroom, closed the door, and flushed as if she had business there. She couldn't shake the feeling that Frank was in mortal danger. Was it psychic? She doubted it. It was the fear, ever since he'd left her, that something terrible would happen. Salvage work, he'd often told her, wasn't like it's portrayed in the movies—there's not always a happy ending.

She heard a knock on the door, oblivious to the fact it had been fifteen minutes since she'd left the two agents.

"You okay in there?" It was Shirley's voice.

"Yes."

CHAPTER THIRTY-EIGHT

THE FORCE OF the shark's attack on the apogee of a swell upturned the raft. Frank and Angela were tossed about like corks, trapped in the sea-invaded canopy. Reaching out with his right hand, Frank felt her struggling, his other hand quickly feeling about the watery blackness for the canopy's opening. Though it seemed infinitely longer, he found it after only a few seconds and pushed her out as another Force Eight wave struck, pushing the waterlogged raft, with him still in it, into a deep trough.

By the time he got out and surfaced, the raft was collapsing all about him, air escaping from the gash, where the shark had ripped and torn.

Angela had vanished. All Frank felt about him was flotsam from the sinking craft. Futilely he called her name again and again. In a race against the deflating raft, he hauled himself through the raging sea by means of the nylon rope connecting the sinking raft to the giant buoys. By the time he reached the buoys, clinging to their anchoring cables, he was praying for Angela. He was filled with a terrible guilt, knowing, as had happened once to a colleague on a mission off 'Nam, that every second the predators spent devouring her bought him more time.

Aboard Li's Whalekiller, General Chang, both hands on the radar console's roll bar, watched the luminescent amber dot that was the *Petrel*, also heading for the location of the emergency beacon. Li had remained puzzled by the general's insistence on half speed. Then he realized that the canny PLA commander would no doubt save the Whalekiller a lot of work, though it was the bigger vessel, if he let the *Petrel* do all the hard winching necessary to raise the giant buoys. Li had come to realize that the PLA commander was a lot smarter than anyone had given him credit for, and wasn't, appearances to the contrary, entirely preoccupied by his concubine's bedroom antics.

Ironically, it was the light of the moon that made it more difficult for First Mate Redfern to discern anything definite. When the clouds briefly parted, the glint of the moonlight reflecting in his binoculars frustrated his scouting efforts. Even so, the huge buoys were intermittently visible, appearing and disappearing on the vast heaving and wind-whipped surface as the Force Eight waves metamorphosed into the white horses of a Force Ten.

Aboard Li's Whalekiller, the radar image of the *Petrel*, like the Whalekiller's image on *Petrel*'s radar, also became intermittent due to the sea clutter produced by the waves segmenting both the transmit and bounce-back reception of radar pulses between the two ships.

Neither *Petrel*'s Tate nor First Mate Redfern was able to make out the marking of the other ship now six miles to the southwest of them. Redfern assumed it was trying as valiantly as the *Petrel* to reach the location of the emergency beacon and flare, both of which the other vessel's captain must also be aware.

Despite the moonlight, however long it would last, Redfern caught only glimpses of the Whalekiller. The *Southern Star* was by now much farther west, lost in the sea clutter. And nearer, in the vicinity of the *Petrel*, Redfern saw something that looked like it could be a floating log, and so he advised Brentwood's six-man team on the Zodiac about it, lest the raft inadvertently strike it on its return to the *Petrel*.

It began to rain. Though not yet heavy, it was enough to spatter the bridge glass, and obliged Redfern to switch on the spin wheel directly in front of the helmsman. It spun the water off, but with the glass dirtied by stack smoke, as when the *Petrel* had earlier been headed downwind, the spin glass wasn't as clear as it might have been. It was Tate's bow lookout who spotted the momentary blur of a reddish-orange float flare burning in the smudge of rain. He called the bridge and gave the bearing: one niner seven.

One of Li's lookouts, high above the Whalekiller's well deck midway between the bridge and harpoon mount, had seen the float flare first, however, and though careful not to increase speed above nine knots, Li had already corrected his course toward the three huge buoys.

George Lynch couldn't sleep. It wasn't just Martha snoring in the other twin bed, but a combination of the noise of the

Star's pumps, the ship rolling, and Martha's refusal to allow
him to spend the early hours of the morning taking advantage
of Orloff's open bar.

"We're on vacation, for God's sake!" he'd told her, but
she'd taken no notice, and he knew they'd entered the marital
silent zone against which there was no known defense.

Had it not been for this enforced sobriety, George might not
have remembered the ladies' shoe he'd seen on the stern deck.
Whether it was the nerve-wracking din of the pumps or the
edginess that always accompanied his dry-outs—probably
both—he found it impossible to relax. In the darkness of his
cabin, what had merely been a passing recollection of his
drunken encounter with Orloff at the stern became an idée
fixe. What hadn't seemed odd in his alcoholic haze now
seemed downright strange: a bunch of crewmen and an officer astern, and a woman's shoe. And Orloff's extraordinary
friendliness, taking him to his cabin for a nightcap, or rather,
nightcaps. George couldn't even remember what they'd been
drinking. Jesus, he'd smelled a woman's perfume but there
was no woman there, only her shoe!

He called softly across to his wife's bed. She didn't reply.
Firespill, the book she'd been reading, lay limp in her hands,
her eyes closed and her chain-attached reading glasses, which
he hated, still on. "Martha!" He had to tell someone. He got
out of his bed, crossed to hers, but couldn't bring himself
to wake her. Instead, as he did almost every night—at least
every night he was sober—he gently took the book from her
hands, then began the delicate business of removing her
glasses, the damn chain invariably catching in her hair. The
ship rolled hard to port, shuddering against the gale's assault,
and he almost fell on top of her. She murmured and turned
closer to the bulkhead.

It's like the *Titanic*, George thought, remembering how the
girl almost jumped. Only this one *did* jump. All they had left
was her shoe.

George was busting to tell someone. But then maybe he
was mistaken. Maybe they had pulled her in—kept it all

hush-hush for her sake and theirs? He'd ask Orloff. Have to wait till morning, dammit! No, wait a minute. Orloff had been on the midnight-to-four watch, having come down to calm the passengers during the great flood. He'd still be up probably, and bored too. Maybe they could have a drink? George looked across at Martha, still snoring. That woman would sleep through a tornado, he thought. Trying not to make any noise, fighting the roll, he pulled on his trousers and buttoned up a loud South Sea sport shirt. All the while, he found it difficult to maintain his balance, the big ship not only rolling but pitching high, the seas spattering even the higher decks' portholes with spray.

He didn't have far to go to find Orloff in the forward restaurant bar. He was chatting amiably with a handful of hard drinkers who, unlike George, hadn't succumbed to wifely dictates or any other restraint such as seasickness.

"Ah, Mr. Lynch!" Orloff said. "Come to join us?"

The Russian, George sensed, was pleased to see him, as if tired of the boozy babble around him.

"You are looking for liquid refreshment?" he asked George.

"If you guys haven't drunk the ship dry."

"Not yet!" one of the drinkers replied loudly. He was a hefty man, his florid face in striking contrast to the starched white table linen that was stained with wine and the crumbled remains of pretzels and peanuts.

"What will you have, Mr. Lynch?" Orloff inquired.

"George," Lynch insisted.

"All right, *George*."

"Got any bourbon?"

"Mr. Jack Daniel's," Orloff announced.

"On the rocks," George told him.

The colonel was pouring the drink, the florid man telling the clump of four other drinkers a joke, when George said, "Mr. Orloff."

"Sergei, please," the Russian said, balancing himself against the roll while handing George the drink.

"I know about the shoe," he said, winking at Orloff.

Orloff's body overcompensated, caught out by the pitch of the ship. He spilled the drink. "Shoe?"

"Yeah," George said, taking the drink, "that red shoe."

Orloff strained to hear over the sudden laughter of the other drinkers and the whistling of the gale. He gestured George away from the raucous drunks toward the swing doors that led to the kitchen. "Can't hear you," he told George.

"What?"

"Can't hear you." Before George could repeat himself, Orloff countered, "I feel like a—" He hesitated. "How do you Americans say—a bite?"

"What? Oh, yeah. No thanks, I'm not hungry."

"I am," Orloff said. "Join me while I make a whopper!"

George laughed. "A whopper's a hamburger," he explained. "Burger King."

"Ah, yes," Orloff said. "I'm getting it confused." He opened the swing door for George. "What were you saying about a shoe? You lost a shoe?"

"No, no," George began. The doors leading into the kitchen, aided by a particularly hard roll, swung wildly.

When David Brentwood, aboard *Petrel*'s Zodiac, saw the winking light that was the orange float flare bumping amid the giant buoys' anchor cables, he also glimpsed in his flashlight beam what he thought was a human shape. He told himself it wasn't, knowing that seeing what one wants to see was a delusion that affected Special Forces personnel almost as much as it did anyone else. In fact, he was seeing the clump of anchor chains and cables. It wasn't until Frank Hall, spotting the Zodiac momentarily silhouetted atop a monstrous wave, began shouting, that the commandos saw him. He was clinging to a twist of heavy cable beneath one of the buoys that, through fierce wave action, had separated itself from the main clump and was independently dipping and rising wildly in the gale force winds.

The Green Beret at the tiller cut the big twin Mercury outboard to near idle. He swung the fifteen-foot Zodiac beam onto the steel stalks of cable. Aussie Lewis, relishing the fact that he would be the last person Hall would expect, tossed him a line.

"Hey, Hall, stop fucking around and get in the friggin' boat!"

Frank leaped from the buoy's cable, but his muscles were so cramped he missed the crazily rocking Zodiac completely, splashing into the sea at least three feet short.

"Swim, you bastard!" Aussie shouted.

Hall, though exhausted, might normally have appreciated recognizing the broad, flat accent of his comrade-in-arms. Instead, having missed the Zodiac and gasping for air, he swallowed a mouthful of seawater which he promptly threw up. Aussie dragged the sodden oceanographer aboard. Frank reached out, taking his hand, and Aussie. "Have you picked up anyone—" He threw up again.

"No," Aussie answered him. "No one."

"*Petrel*'s mate saw something," Brentwood told Frank.

The Green Beret gunned the engine, and the rigid craft came about and headed back toward the pitching, rain-smeared white blurs that were the deck lights of the *Petrel*. Frank told the commandos that he hadn't sent any message to Brownlee about the transfer of the "gift" to the *Burkhanov*, and Brentwood radioed Tate to prepare the *Petrel* to haul up whatever was suspended by the cables below the now free-floating buoys. Then, in a heart-stopping moment of doubt, Frank realized that while he'd seen a trunk on the *Star*'s deck, he hadn't actually seen it lowered. What if it had just been a ploy?

As the oceanographic ship approached the Zodiac, Frank caught a glimpse of small yellow figures. Tate's crewmen were dressed in canary-colored weather gear and were busy about the research ship's A-frame. The whine of the stern's Swann winch was faintly audible through the howling of the gale.

Aboard the *Petrel*, through his binoculars, Tate noted that despite its infrequent appearance on his radar screen, the ship that he and Redfern had now identified as a Whalekiller was closing on the buoys.

* * *

The windshield wiper of the Whalekiller's crow's nest whined loudly, trying to keep the rain at bay. The lookout, in the wildly gyrating nest, peered intently through the glass, trying to pick up the *Petrel*, now only a few miles off on the starboard quarter. A squall, however, preceding the storm's center, was completely obscuring the enemy vessel. "Nothing in sight," he told Li through the intercom.

"Keep looking," Li instructed him lamely.

General Chang, feeling queasy in the increasingly violent weather, grew more anxious with the disappearance of the *Petrel* from the radar screen for minutes at a time due to heightened wave action and rain. What was the American ship up to? It was one thing to slow down when he could still observe them, but now . . .

He ordered Li to increase speed.

Li made a face in the "redded-out" bridge. "It'll be a rough ride."

"It'll be rough for them too," Chang countered. "Besides, we must know what they're doing at the buoys."

"Increase speed to fifteen knots!" Li ordered. Within seconds the Whalekiller plunged headlong into the oncoming waves, its bow lost in enormous billows of spray, the boat shuddering under the impact.

As Frank gripped the *Petrel*'s rope ladder, the vessel rose on a swell. The ship's wash sucked the Zodiac down and away, leaving him alone on the ladder, which, despite its heavy weight, was sliding forward and aft of midships like some arthritic pendulum. Redfern climbed over, easing himself down a few rungs, and extended a hand. But Frank, pausing to catch his breath and hearing Aussie Lewis shouting obscene encouragement from the Zodiac below him, climbed the remaining rungs without assistance. Breaching the swing-door section of railing, Frank stepped aboard. His legs, to his disgust, shook from the effort as the Zodiac, with the commandos still aboard, turned about and battled the seas again, running a line from the *Petrel* to the nearest buoy.

"You all right, laddie?" Redfern asked.

"Dave Brentwood—" Frank began. He had to start again, the wind having whipped away his first attempt. "Dave said you saw someone in the water?"

"Some*thing*," Redfern corrected him as they passed through the wet lab to the galley. "While you were being picked up. But when we got there, the bloody rain had started—couldn't see a damned thing." He saw the jaw-flexing concern on Frank's face and added quickly, despite his own reservations, "Well, 'least this isn't the Atlantic."

Frank knew what the Scot meant. The Pacific Ocean was considerably warmer, but the temperature here would fall drastically with the windchill factor. And panic never helped. Frank told him about Angela, describing her, which struck Redfern as idiotic, as if anyone would need a description. But the first mate could see Hall wasn't thinking clearly, obviously exhausted from having been in the water for hours and knowing he was responsible for the woman's disappearance. They heard a loud thump. It was the brake on the *Petrel*'s stern winch being suddenly applied while the commandos, fighting Force Ten swells, went in close to the buoys once more.

It was a tricky business unshackling the buoys from horseshoe-sized U-bolts, in order to shackle them to the *Petrel*'s line. The Green Beret at the tiller had to judge the swells, know when to reverse the twin Mercury props in order to keep the Zodiac from crashing into the buoys, but not reverse so much as to prevent the Zodiac from getting close enough for Brentwood and the others to unshackle the lines. The commandos made several failed passes, one during which they almost capsized. Finally, Aussie Lewis threaded the bosun's spike through the eye of the U-bolt's shank, and, as Brentwood and Salvini grasped the buoy's cable, he turned the spike counterclockwise. It took two more attempts until the shank was out, releasing the first buoy. Another twenty minutes later they released the other two, and then the *Petrel*'s stern winch started hauling in the cable.

The A-frame's block cracked with strain as the weight,

which, from the acute angle, Tate estimated must be at least that of a small car, was taken up by the winch's five-eighths-inch cable. As the cable passed through the block down to the winch, it spat water droplets into the rain-slashed cone of light that spread down from the A-frame's arc lamp. The penumbra of light slid crazily up and down the swells like a huge, undulating sheet. To add to the difficulty of the job—one Tate would never have undertaken in gale conditions if Brownlee hadn't explained that vital national interests were at stake—the winch's wire guider was malfunctioning, which meant they periodically had to stop the winch to reset it.

In the galley, Redfern, passing Frank another coffee, was trying to assuage the oceanographer's concern. "We'll keep looking for her," he assured Frank, both men knowing that with the *Petrel*, her crew, and the commandos all crucial to a successful haul-in, it would be at least a half hour, maybe more, before the *Petrel* could hope to leave station.

Except for the *Petrel*'s engineer, who, by virtue of his temperament as well as training, preferred staying in his diesel-polluted domain, everyone gathered on the afterdeck for the final ten minutes or so of the haul-in. As a rain-lashed crewman, standing off to the port side beneath the A-frame's block, continued to count off the meters, "Fifty . . . forty-five . . . forty . . ." Frank was seized again by what he knew Gloria would have called an "Oh my God" moment of doubt: the possibility that after all this, there might be nothing but a huge clump of heavy chain or sea anchor at the end of the cable now straining the block. He took a deep breath—it didn't help against the coffee's caffeine. He heard the winch drop gears, the A-frame crewman call, "Ten meters to go," and watched as a group of four crewmen, having sought shelter from the rain beneath the overhang above the winch, now moved out on deck, armed with long, lancelike grappling poles.

"Five meters!"

Everyone was watching the angry swirl of water aft of the

Petrel, the deck's hydraulic arm extended to take over the final lift from the A-frame should the latter's width not be able to accommodate whatever was coming aboard. This, Frank knew, was the most dangerous moment. Once free of the water, the load, subject to the roll, pitch, and yaw of the vessel, could swing out into the darkness beyond the apron of arc lights and come crashing, pendulum-like, back into the stern before the crew could manage to grapple and winch it safely down on deck.

"In sight!"

The winch thumped to a complete stop, then began a slow, tortuous whine as the biggest aluminum trunk Frank had ever seen broke surface, the seawater streaming off it in torrents. Tate, taking the computer assist helm himself, used all his seagoing experience to keep the *Petrel* headed into the gale, to mitigate the pitch and roll of the ship. It wasn't enough, for just as the container was no more than six feet above the roiling ocean surface, the *Petrel* rose high on the next wave, and before the winchman could "dump" his load back into the sea to stabilize it, the huge trunk rushed forward on the wave's downslope, the container smashing into the *Petrel*'s stern, sending the deck crew fleeing into the after lab.

"Jesus Christ!" Frank shouted, his knowledge that the Rone was worth over a billion dollars fueling his alarm.

For a moment the winchman's profanity threatened to equal that of Aussie Lewis as he quickly shoved the winch's gear to High. Its motor screamed as he quickly played out cable, dumping the container back into the sea to keep it from swinging, while cursing Tate for not having advised him of the rogue wave that had caused the mayhem.

"Shut your cakehole!" Redfern shouted, rain and salt spray enveloping him. "Don't blame the old man. You canna tell the height of a wave coming at you in the bloody dark, mon!"

Down below, the *Petrel*'s normally phlegmatic engineer was furious with the winchman. "If that bastard damages my props," he told Redfern on the intercom, "I'll have his guts for garters."

"Everybody settle down!" It was Tate, his usually quiet voice booming on the PA in the howl of the storm. "We'll try again. Regroup on the stern."

"Cranberry jelly?" Orloff inquired solicitously, holding up a sterling silver dispenser, watching its spoon swing with the ship.

George Lynch shook his head, electing to take his roast turkey sandwich straight. "Just salt and pepper," he told Orloff. An unsecured tray just brought in by one of the room service stewards slid as the *Southern Star* rose, paused, momentarily suspended in space, then crashed full-bore into the next trough. The collision of hanging pots and pans in the all but deserted kitchen was so loud George had to repeat himself.

"So." Orloff handed him the condiments. "About the shoe?"

"You had a jumper, right?" George said. "I didn't see anyone besides you guys, so I guess she made it all the way?"

Orloff sipped his drink from a crystal tumbler, his other hand on the counter. "You mean," he proffered, "that she—"

"Bought it," Lynch said, taking a bite from the sandwich, talking with his mouth full. "Kaput. Drowned."

Orloff was swirling the ice cube in the cut crystal glass. The swing doors burst open and one of the drunks appeared, bellowing for Orloff to rejoin them.

"In one moment!" the colonel promised.

When the drunk withdrew, Orloff was still studying the ice cube. "You must understand, George, such a tragedy—accident—it puts the cruise line in a difficult position."

Lynch nodded understandingly. "You betcha," he said, munching his sandwich. "Don't worry, chief, I won't say anything."

But Orloff *was* worried. The alcoholic Lynch had blurted out his suspicion in the restaurant bar. Luckily, most of the drunks hadn't paid attention. But the redheaded American Treasury agent, Sheila Moffat, would sooner or later be officially missed. In the middle of the current Russian-American arms limitation talks, Lynch was a walking, talking time bomb. Orloff glanced down to the far end of the kitchen at a lone room-service steward—room service being in little demand, given the rough weather—and spoke to him sharply. The steward dumped a fistful of cutlery in the dishwasher tray and left the kitchen.

Orloff turned to George Lynch. "How are your sea legs, Mr. Lynch?"

"I told you, *George*."

Orloff smiled. "I forgot. How are your sea legs, George?"

"Hey, no problem. Crappy weather doesn't bother me."

"Good. I want to show you something."

"Lead on, McDuff," George answered, clearly proud of the only Shakespeare he could remember.

Following Orloff, stepping over the promenade's outer door's sill onto the deck, Lynch was initially blown back by the gale-force winds. But fortified by his Jack Daniel's and turkey sandwich, he lowered his head and determinedly launched himself once more over the sill onto the water-slicked hardwood of a pitch-black and deserted promenade deck.

"Seychas!" Orloff said. Now! A clutch of hands descended, lifting Lynch up and over.

"Alcoholics," Orloff would explain gently and "off-the-record" to any reporter in Suva who asked, "should never venture out alone on deck." Everyone knew that violent storms at sea had claimed many a foolhardy soul on merchant and cruise ships alike. Yes, even navy personnel. Especially at night.

CHAPTER THIRTY-NINE

DESPITE WAVE-INDUCED CLUTTER, the Whalekiller, barely a mile away from the *Petrel*, all its lights out, was now close enough for its radar to pick up the enemy ship. The Chinese lookout in the crow's nest was able to make out the rain-smeared blob of light that was the *Petrel*'s stern.

Now and then, through his binoculars, Li could distinguish figures moving across her stern deck. But as yet nothing else had appeared, though he couldn't be certain because at times the American ship was bow on to his wildly gyrating field of vision. That position obscured any view of her stern in seas so wild that one lookout had already been relieved of duty because the motion of the crow's nest made him violently ill.

It was sheer luck, a seasick Chang would contend, but Wu Ling—who, to Chang's chagrin, was apparently impervious to motion sickness of any kind—holding to the ancient belief of her ancestors, claimed that what happened was predetermined. In any event, after the Whalekiller's replacement lookout had given his eyes a rest for a few minutes, he raised his binoculars to observe the mile-long expanse of spindrift between him and the American ship. He saw something sliding down the precipitous side of a wave, and saw it again on the crest of the next wave. Instantly recording his heading, he reported the sighting to Li, who in turn ordered all hands on deck and inquired of the crow's nest, "Is it one of the buoys?"

"No, Captain," the lookout responded. "A body, I think."

Li increased speed, which, running with the sea, brought the Whalekiller to eighteen knots, giving Chang the alarming

342

impression that Li was about to drive the ship under. But Li waved all protestations aside. Perhaps the lookout had been mistaken, but if it *was* a body, there was a possibility, no matter how slight, that whoever it might be was alive, the rain itself providing the one thing a body could not do without: fresh water. Li was following the ancient law of the sea—to aid those in distress. It could have been him or one of his men in peril.

The crow's nest intercom crackled again. The object did indeed look like a body, now no less than six or seven hundred meters distant, five points off the starboard quarter. Li adjusted course to three points off the starboard quarter, giving himself a margin for error in the turbulent seas.

At David Brentwood's suggestion, Tate had borrowed one of the commandos' night vision goggles and now could see the walls of water before they hit the bow, enabling him to at least "guesstimate" the frequency of the relatively calmer troughs that would follow. These still packed considerable punch, though. But it did give Tate and, via the intercom, his winchman a window of ten seconds or so during which to give the winch its head. They were hauling the already dented container well clear of the sea's surface, high up near the A-frame's block, substantially reducing the arc of its swing. While it might smack the sides of the A-frame, it couldn't crash against the ship's props, which was Tate's primary concern.

"She's in the frame!" the winchman told Tate excitedly. "Tight as I can get her."

"Very well," Tate acknowledged, asking quickly, "Will we need the arm or can the A-frame bring her in?"

Redfern's voice came on the line. "We'll lower her using the frame," his comment assuring Tate that the container wasn't too wide to fit through the A, the latter capable of being moved through an arc of fifteen to twenty degrees. It meant that the container, still streaming with water, could now be lowered straight down to the deck.

It wasn't as easy as Redfern's self-assured tone made it

sound, for as the winch lowered away, a half-dozen men had
to bully it to prevent it from swinging. As it was, one man's
pike was smacked from his hands by the container, the pike
striking another man in the face, breaking his nose. He yelled
in pain and fell to the deck, dangerously close to the spot
where a moment later the container, its weight continuing to
strain the winch, dropped the last six inches to the deck with a
resounding thump.

Immediately, a man approached with an iron bar, his obvious intent to snap the lock.

"No, no," Frank warned him. "Christ, it's computer electronics. They'll have packed her watertight but don't open it
here. We'll have to get it into the stern dry lab."

"It won't fit in the dry lab," Redfern told him. "It's too
wide, mon!"

Beneath his yellow wet gear hood Frank's face was creased
with fatigue. "All right, fuck it—go get a tarpaulin."

The easiest, if riskiest, way to get the body aboard, Li decided, was to put a man over with a safety line and life jacket
attached. He asked for volunteers. Three men came forward.
Li indicated the first man. "Over you go!"

On the Whalekiller's bridge, the officer on watch dropped
the speed to less than two knots, but told the crow's nest to
keep an eye on the *Petrel*, barely a quarter mile off.

"I'll have to put on deck lights and the bridge's searchlight," Li told Chang.

Chang wanted to argue against it, but by now he was so
violently seasick he was in no mood to press the point. Li
handed him two tablets. "You'll feel better."

As the Whalekiller's lights came on, Tate started in alarm.
He'd seen the ship intermittently on the radar, but during the
time the Chinese ship had increased speed, he'd been preoccupied with the retrieval of the container. The fact that the
Whalekiller was now no more than a quarter mile away took
him by complete surprise.

"Bloody hell!" It was Redfern's voice, equally taken aback,

but not by the Whalekiller's proximity. "It's empty," he declared. "The bloody thing's *empty*!" He wasn't strictly correct. What he meant was that there was nothing in the trunk but seawater.

Frank had slumped down on a bollard by the winch. "Jesus Christ!"

"You've been suckered!" Aussie declared unhelpfully. "A fucking trap, mate. Fucking computer's still on the fucking cruise ship." He kicked the container. "Fuckers tricked you, sport. Bought 'emselves time."

And now Redfern realized why the Whalekiller hadn't closed on the buoys ahead of the *Petrel*. "Wily bastards!" he told Frank. "They *knew*. Roosians used 'em as a come-on to divert our attention from their bloody *Southern Star*."

Later, in the dry lab, Frank used the blackboard to draw up the plan of attack on the *Star*. His brain was racing, his fury at having been so adroitly outmaneuvered by Orloff overcoming his fatigue, his thirst for revenge intensified by his conviction that had it not been for Orloff and his machinations, Angela would still be alive.

Abruptly he got up and, eyes ablaze, feet braced hard against the swells, asked Redfern to plot the shortest course between the *Petrel*'s present position and the *Southern Star*.

"Mon," Redfern objected, "*Petrel*'d never catch her in time. In this weather—"

"Do it!" Frank shouted.

Aussie Lewis turned to Brentwood. He knew the Frank Hall of old was back in action and, as was common among SpecWar types who had served together, the two men had already divined what was on Frank's mind.

"He doesn't mean the *Petrel*," Aussie calmly informed Redfern. Turning to the other four commandos—with Frank, it would make a team of seven again—he zipped up his wet suit and told them, "Load the Zodiac, gentlemen. We're about to rattle the kidneys." It was SEAL lingo for the expectation of a terribly rough ride on the *Petrel*'s rigid inflatable boat— "full-bore" against the gale and "before," as he so eloquently put it, "the fuckers reach Suva."

* * *

When the woman's body that the crow's nest lookout had spotted was brought aboard the Whalekiller, it was limp. The sodden clothes were wrapped about her like Saran Wrap, her hair matted, her lips dark blue. Li himself knelt beside her, listening for any signs of life, but could hear none, though he knew that this might be because of the crashing of the sea against the Whalekiller's side.

"Take her to my cabin," he ordered, "and inform General Chang."

The last action the NVG-equipped and balaclava-hooded "Team Seven," as Aussie had dubbed them, performed before they boarded the rising and falling Zodiac was to load their submachine guns and sidearms—everything except David Brentwood's shotgun—with hollow-points, replacing their standard hardball, full-jacketed rounds.

Redfern, though no commando, had done his National Service—the draft, in the U.K.—and knew enough about the Geneva Convention to voice an objection. "Aren't those bullets illegal, boys?"

"Yeah," Frank answered. "So's murder." He was thinking of the three dead Pave Low crewmen, Michaels's decapitated body, and Reese, killed in the tunnel. He realized he'd been a bit sharp with the Scot, who probably hadn't been filled in on all the details by Brownlee or anyone else, but he didn't care. He was too busy to go into details except with his fellow commandos, who, fighting against the ferocious pitch and roll, were now strapping on their Kevlar vests against their black neoprene wet suits. They checked the rest of their equipment, including first aid kits, Arpacs, Emmerson knives, grappling kits, and night vision goggles. In addition to the Petrel's antiriot BB gun, which Frank was borrowing as a main weapon, the oceanographer was checking out the Glock Aussie Lewis loaned to him.

"Cruise ship's pretty big," Salvini reminded Frank. "Where d'you think the computer'll be?"

Frank had been thinking a lot about that since seeing the

empty trunk. "I don't know," he admitted. "But Orloff'll know."

"We need a good description, Frank," David Brentwood told him, handing Frank the *Petrel*'s stubby, antiriot beanbag gun. "So don't shoot the bastard before we find out."

"First," quipped one of the *Petrel*'s crewmen to another, "they have to board her."

"No," his companion said. "First they have to *reach* her. It's damn near Force Ten out there."

"Isn't that the truth."

Getting there was hard physically, the rigid fifteen-foot rubber boat bashing its way through, up, and over the waves. The seven commandos huddled together against the gusts of howling wind for body warmth, holding onto the gunwales' ropes with both hands, their weapons, condom-tipped, slung across their backs. Other gear, including cartridge-loaded grappling hook lines and portable squeeze-pump gas tank, were stowed amidships. The Green Beret working the outboard flipped the cover of his luminous wrist GPS from time to time. The GPS was the undisputed godsend of Special Ops missions; commandos knew that even in the foulest weather a GPS unit could take them to within ten feet of any given spot on earth.

By Brentwood's GPS reckoning, the *Southern Star*, even at her reduced speed, would be at least forty kilometers away, a minimum of two hours of what Aussie Lewis called "ball-breaking, boat-banging boredom." They could count on the rigid Zodiac inflatable being constantly awash.

The one overriding advantage of the atrocious weather, however, was that, added to the darkness, its sound and fury would prevent Team Seven's approach being either heard or seen. They also assumed the Whalekiller had neither heard nor seen their departure.

Li's ship, though under strict orders from Kornon via Chang to shadow the *Petrel*, had unexpectedly slowed because of Li's on-the-spot decision to retrieve the body his lookout had seen. Because of this, most of his crew and several of Chang's Guo An Bu agents aboard had gone on deck to watch, and so they were there when the crow's nest lookout saw a fast, small craft, evidenced by its phosphorescent wake, plowing up the side of one wave and into another, leaving the *Petrel*. Li had switched his radar to high resolution/short range mode, but because of the sea clutter, all he saw was amber snow on his screen.

"Are you sure?" Li pressed the lookout.

"Positive, Captain. I saw it through the binoculars."

"How many aboard?"

"Couldn't say for sure. Six, maybe seven."

A frantic, raucous twenty minutes later, the Whalekiller's own rubber boat with a heavily armed component of six Chinese Guo An Bu agents and crew was launched. The main weapon aboard was the ship's powerful .50-caliber antitank gun, normally used to finish off a harpooned whale—despite being specifically prohibited by the International Whaling Commission. The men in the rubber boat, another of the ubiquitous rigid inflatable Zodiacs that had replaced the wooden and fiberglass boats, took up the chase eagerly. There was no doubt that the American Zodiac's intended target was the *Star*.

But Tate's lookouts, once the Whalekiller's deck lights had again been extinguished, immediately suspected some nefarious action and closed on the Whalekiller, no more than a quarter mile off her port quarter. It could hardly have missed the Whalekiller's Zodiac launching, a rather clumsy one, during which the Chinese inflatable, dropped into a trough, smacked the water, immediately sending out an iridescent apron of plankton-thick foam. Both of the *Petrel*'s bridge lookouts and Dr. Shalit had spotted it. Shalit, unable to resist her curiosity once the tank had been winched aboard, had come topside to see what all the fuss was about.

"Radio Team Seven," Tate instructed his radioman, "and tell them the opposition are on their tail."

The radio officer tried and failed, atmospheric conditions sabotaging all analogue radio transmissions, though leaving the nonvoice digitally transmitted GPS signals inviolate.

"Well, at least the Whalekiller won't be able to contact the *Southern Star*," the radioman told Tate.

This was little comfort to Tate, however, for it meant Team Seven was on its own, unaware it was being chased.

When the phone rang in her apartment, Gloria was first to it, but with disappointment handed the receiver to Andrew, who did little other than "Yes, sir" and "No, sir" whoever from the White House was on the other end. Finally, he put the phone down. "Nothing yet."

Gloria slumped in the love seat and stared up disbelievingly at the white-stuccoed ceiling of her apartment. "They don't tell us anything for hours, and then they call to tell us they don't know anything?"

"I've got a hunch we'll know by morning," Andrew replied.

"Know *what*?" Gloria asked him.

Andrew was silent for a few moments, then, by the window now, watching the river of traffic lights flow by through the binoculars, responded, "This guy, Larry, who grabbed you in Vancouver. You'd recognize him no problem, right?"

"Yes," Gloria said.

"You said you scratched him?"

"Left cheek," Shirley chimed in. "She's already given the sketch artist a detailed description."

"What I mean," Andrew explained, "is how noticeable is it?"

"It drew blood," Gloria said, the memory sending a shiver through her.

"Come over here," Andrew told her. "Across the street. Guy by the mailbox."

He handed her the binoculars, and she had difficulty focusing, seeing two mailboxes instead of one.

Andrew guided her fingers—they were stone cold—onto the serrated focus wheel. "Adjust this . . . have you got him?"

"With the briefcase?" Gloria asked.

"Yes."

"I don't . . . think so, but it's hard to tell. Not enough light."

"Well, don't worry about it," Andrew answered. "I'll keep an eye on him."

Gloria went back to the love seat, a heavy gloom descending over the apartment, as on those childhood days when she knew vacation was over. Back then, her stomach tightened just thinking about going back to school. The end of the world.

CHAPTER FORTY

THE RAIN WAS now a downpour, the darkness thick about Team Seven, with only breaking wave crests visible, the moon long since overcome by battalions of cumulus that had advanced in a never-ending line from the west. The rain about them was so intense the ocean sizzled. Green Beret's balaclava, like those of the others, was sodden through. He gripped the tiller with both hands as the RIB climbed yet another mountainous wave before crashing into the next trough, the seven commandos enveloped in foam.

"She should be visible!" the Green Beret shouted.

"Well she isn't!" Aussie returned with equal intensity. "Can't see a friggin' thing."

"What's that?" Choir Williams shouted, pointing port side midships.

Then Brentwood saw it through his infrared goggles, a blob with a V shape attached, the V, Choir now saw, formed by two trolling masts.

"What the hell's that?" Aussie shouted.

"Don't know," Brentwood answered. "But it hasn't got any running lights, and—" He saw the wink of a light about three hundred yards away, and a second later there was a high, whistling sound, an explosion, the wave ahead of them erupting in a gigantic spume of water.

"Son of a—" Aussie began, almost falling overboard, the Green Beret turning the RIB around so sharply it almost capsized.

"Antitank round!" the Delta commando bellowed.

"Arpacs!" Brentwood yelled. "Aussie and Choir first, Salvini and Delta second."

It was easier said than done, for despite their training in all kinds of conditions and the Arpac's length—less than ten inches long—it was still quite a feat for each of the four commandos designated by Brentwood to unstrap their Arpacs while having to use one hand to steady themselves on the gunwales.

Aboard the *Push 'n' Shove*, the backblast of the first AT-4 round, the wink of light Brentwood had seen, had blown Cawley back against the winch drum and frightened Brenda Fowler in the wheelhouse.

McBride steadied the protective bumper of the next AT-4 launcher on the trawler's starboard gunwale. He pulled the caulking lever back, put his eye snug against the rear sight, the carrying sling tight against his left arm, and pushed the firing button. This backblast lit up the winch drum. The AT rocket shot out at over 270 meters a second, but again the sea's turbulence sabotaged the militiaman's land-trained aim, the rocket detonating this time a hundred yards aft of the RIB.

He had only two more AT-4s. Dumping the used launcher over the side, he retrieved the next one from its case. Brock had already steadied his against the wheelhouse.

By now Aussie and Choir had their Arpacs ready. They rested the small, three-pound launchers against their shoulders. The Delta commando and Brentwood held them about the waist to stabilize them and kept to one side to avoid backblast.

"Run straight at the whores!" Choir yelled at Brentwood, who was now at the tiller.

Choir and Aussie flicked up the circular peep sight on their respective Arpacs, aimed and fired. Wisps of smoke rose as the propellant shot out of each of the six-nozzled soup-can-size rocket motors. The shaped charge from each Arpac approached the trawler at a relatively slow seventy-five meters per second but they were capable of penetrating ten inches of armor plate.

Only one of the Arpacs hit the trawler, but one was enough. The explosion was small, barely visible from the RIB, now less than a hundred yards away. The *Push 'n' Shove* had turned sharply as Brock and McBride fired at it, but the hole the Arpac made in the wooden side was over a foot in diameter. The water rushed in with the force of a burst fire hydrant.

"Fuck! Fuck! Fuck!" was all Neilson could say, Brenda Fowler screaming at the militiamen to help the crew man the hand pumps, the trawler's two-stroke gasoline pumps too small to deal with the catastrophic implosion.

"Right!" Aussie yelled. "They're done."

Brentwood swung the RIB back onto its original course.

"I hit 'em midships!" Aussie shouted. "What a terrific shot!"

"Ballocks!" Choir yelled. "Yours went to hell and gone. I hit 'em, boyo."

"Balls!" Aussie retorted. "You couldn't hit the broad side of a barn."

It was Salvini, clinging to the RIB's starboard portside rope, who saw the string of dancing white dots on the green background of his night vision goggles, the dancing motion caused not so much by the huge cruise ship but by the ferocious pitching of the Zodiac. "Two o'clock!" he shouted. "A click down the road."

The Green Beret, back at the wheel, signaled that he'd heard, and adjusted course.

" 'Bout fucking time!" Aussie said. The RIB decreased speed as the six who planned to board the *Southern Star*—the

Green Beret to remain with the RIB—limbered up isometrically as best they could in the tight confines of the fifteen-foot boat. Despite their fitness, their muscles needed to be flexed before attempting the boarding. Three of the commandos, Salvini, Delta, and Choir Williams, reached behind their necks and slipped the condoms off their weapons; Aussie and Dave Brentwood left theirs on the MP-5 submachine gun and the twelve-gauge Mossberg. Frank Hall was armed with the *Petrel*'s sanitized antiriot BB pistol, its two-and-a-half-inch-diameter barrel clipped to his vest load, which also held grenades and Aussie Lewis's seventeen-shot waterproof Glock.

"Know how to fire that thing?" Aussie joshed Frank, pointing at the Glock.

"No," Frank said, checking its slide. "Do you?"

"Cheeky bastard!" Aussie riposted. "No fucking respect for your elders."

"Cut the chatter," Brentwood said. He waved the Green Beret to proceed slowly into the boiling wake of the rain-curtained leviathan that was smashing its way into the gale. Rivers of foam raced in torrents down its side, the sea so turbulent that now and then one of the ship's three giant props would tear through the wind-lashed surface, which to the commandos appeared as a heaving cauldron of boiling white on the green background of their NVGs.

As they closed, all senses alert, Frank was acutely aware of the invigorating tang of the sea being replaced by the heavy nose-stuffing stench of diesel fumes blown back toward the RIB from the *Southern Star*'s stack. It filled him with an irrational hatred for the ship, which he used to further pump himself for the precarious climb they intended to make up the sheer clifflike side of the vessel just forward of the stern.

"Hope no one's on deck," Salvini voiced.

"If they are," Aussie responded, "they're going down. It isn't the movies, mate."

Through his NVGs Brentwood could tell from the flecks of foam, which looked like the thermal spots of small white birds against the ship, that the wind gusts weren't as strong on the starboard side, and so he instructed the Green Beret, "Right side."

He then turned to the others. "Ready?"

In calm weather, firing the fist-sized, spring-loaded grappling irons that expanded into four hooks upon release could be tricky. But aiming them in a full-blown gale was something you could do only with what Aussie Lewis's SEAL instructor at Coronado described as "lots and lots of ballbreaking practice." Like skeet shooting, it was nowhere as easy as it looked to the casual observer, especially when the top of the cliff you were aiming to breach was in constant motion.

"On my call!" Brentwood shouted as their RIB pulled abreast of the cruise ship's stern quarter. His voice was all but drowned in the maelstrom of prop wash, wind gusts, and the never-ending advance of the monstrous crests. The latter, striking the bow, were immediately split into two raging rivers. The one on the starboard side carried the Zodiac astern the moment it had nosed out from the big ship's protective wake for a flank run. The Green Beret quickly turned the Zodiac to run with the rush of water rather than risk a capsize by trying to fight it, until he felt the wave running itself out, its energy dissipated in a cross swell.

The Green Beret turned the Zodiac into the relatively smoother water. Brentwood strained his eyes through the saltcrusted NVGs, trying to anticipate a less risky flank run. The Zodiac veered wildly in a gust, its bow rising high, threatening to tip everyone out. Only Aussie's quickly diving forward to shift the RIB's center of gravity saved them, but the Green Beret was gone.

They circled, or tried to, for five minutes, an eternity in the atrocious conditions. A SEAL never leaves his swim buddy, nor do the Deltas or the Green Berets. But they couldn't find him. The night sea had claimed the second member of the team lost in the last four hours.

"C'mon," Brentwood yelled. "Work to do." He knew that if nothing else, another loss of a team member would harden what was already a firm resolve. Besides, they were supposed to be the toughest in the world.

Finally, after what Aussie would have called "an ice age" of cold, screaming, salt-stinging wind—never mind that it was supposed to be the subtropics—Brentwood saw a lull. "Go!" he screamed at the Delta commando, who, without being told, had taken over the tiller, evidencing the benefit of cross-service training. In fact, the Delta trooper was better at the tiller than his predecessor, or perhaps it was the lull between swells, as the Zodiac, ten feet off the starboard side aft, drew abreast of the massive ship. The commandos fired, the explosive in the grappling irons' handles shooting the spring-loaded claws high into the night. The nylon rope ladders, equipped with pencil-thin, high-tensile aluminum rungs, uncoiled behind them like long, airborne snakes. One of the grappling irons fell impotently back into the sea, but the other three locked onto the ship's railing by the afterdeck's wildly slopping swimming pool. Leaving the Delta commando to man the Zodiac, and Choir to provide covering fire in the event of a snafu, Aussie, Frank, and Brentwood quickly wiped the salt particles from their NVGs. Salvini pull-tested the ropes. Then they were scrambling up the ship's side in a display of upper body strength that would have shamed all but the fittest gymnasts.

The four paused at the rail before the final "heave ho" to the deck—Aussie and Brentwood on Frank's left flank, Salvini to the right. Frank, knowing the ship's layout best, dashed forward to the steps leading from the main to the upper four decks. Brentwood, Aussie, and Salvini followed.

Except for Orloff, there would be no shooting to wound. Besides, with Hydra-Shok hollow points, more often than not a hit was a kill, a 9mm slug splaying as it hit.

But Murphy's law was operational this night, two team members already lost, and now, unbeknownst to the four commandos, a *Southern Star* lookout, a committed smoker, was braving the weather for a cigarette away from Mendev's "No Smoking" bridge. He saw something moving in the spill of light aft of the radio room. He hesitated. It could be some crazy passenger, what the crew called a *lyubitel'svezhogo vozdukha*—a "fresh air freak," unlikely though it was, given the gale. But then, lighting the cigarette, he saw a black-clad figure step out from behind the lifeboat. It was Frank, taking quick aim with the Glock, its red laser dot just below the cigarette lighter's flame. He fired twice. The first shot hit the man in the neck, severing the jugular, knocking him back up against the radio room's bulkhead. A white jet appeared on Frank's NVGs—the man's blood spurting out. The second shot went wide in the ship's roll, passed through the bridge's port wing window and sent a milky spiderweb fracture radiating through the glass.

Orloff, in another manifestation of Murphy's presence, happened to be on the bridge, and, knowing immediately that the ship was under assault, drew his 9mm Makarov—a heavy, old-fashioned, but reliable weapon, and awesome at close range. Standing directly behind the radar console, flat against the windowless aft section of the bridge, he shouted instructions to alert his FSB men throughout the ship. In seconds a PA call was made for a Mr. Fritz Borcha, a nonexistent passenger—the signal for a Code Red, armed terrorists aboard.

As Frank reached the bridge's portside sliding door, Aussie Lewis was a foot behind him, Salvini on the bridge's starboard side with Brentwood, but not on the bridge proper because of the danger of blue-on-blue—"friendly" cross fire—instead covering it from a vantage point by the starboard rail.

Crouching beneath the port door's window level, Frank tried the handle. Locked. He moved left, and Aussie, also crouching, fired a burst, wood chips flying, then fired another burst through the glass. Frank tossed in a flash-bang; both he and Aussie hit the deck, the flash blinding the helmsman, Mendev, and the starboard-side lookout, the gut-thumping bang momentarily concussing them. There was panicked confusion on the bridge, except for Orloff, who, having heard the grenade rolling, had adroitly stepped back into the bridge's chart room. He slammed its door shut, closed his eyes and muffled his ears. Even so, the flash-bang shattered the chart-room door's glass panel, a cloud of shards cutting his face. Recovering quickly, he fired at the dark shadow he saw entering the bridge. The shadow, Frank, fired the BB pistol, its beanbag hitting the Russian full in the chest, punching him, winded, back into the chart room. Aussie's MP-5 spit fire in two two-second bursts, the first burst's Hydra-Shoks took out the lookout's face, the second hit the helmsman, blowing a gaping hole where his stomach had been. Mendev had his hands up high, his voice rising, pleading. He almost fell in the next roll, the stink of feces blown about the bridge by gusts coming through the opened portside door.

The radio room door flew open, and the radioman ran for it, out the starboard side. Aussie and Frank held their fire—fear of blue-on-blue. David Brentwood's shotgun roared, cutting the radioman in half. Before taking over the helm, Brentwood stepped into the radio room and discharged four number 4 shot cartridges at point-blank range, blowing out the communication electronics.

Orloff was on the floor, doubled up in pain, his Makarov having slithered across the honeycombed wooden platform behind the steering console when he was struck by the beanbag. As Brentwood took the helm, Aussie gave two sharp "okay" knocks on the starboard bridge door. Salvini came in to cover the port side.

Frank, stuffing the Makarov in his belt, stuck the Glock's barrel against Orloff's throat. "Where's the Rone?"

Mendev, half blinded, in shock, was still yelling for mercy.

"Shut up!" Aussie told him, Salvini warning them to hurry it up. "Japs'll be here any minute!"

"Where's the computer?" Frank shouted. He pulled back the Glock's hammer, his left leg extended against the shrapnel-pocked chartroom as the ship yawed hard to starboard.

Aussie grabbed Mendev and threw him hard against the console. "Where's the computer?"

Orloff shouted at Mendev in Russian as the gale howled in from the shattered port window. Mendev stared at Aussie, then back at Orloff.

Aussie, legs braced on the wooden honeycomb, the MP-5 cradled in his left arm, drew his Beretta, put it against Orloff's temple, and fired.

Mendev gasped. Aussie swung the Beretta on him. "Where's the fucking computer?"

"His—His cabin—Orloff's cabin."

"Where?"

"Japs!" Salvini shouted. "Left and right."

"Next to mine!" Mendev answered. "Aft of the radio room."

Frank was already storming through the radio room toward its rear door, which led into an L-shaped corridor.

Standing flush against the corridor, he turned the knob, opened it six inches, tossed in a flash-bang for insurance, and closed the door. He heard the explosion, waited a second and went in through smoke, the carpeting afire. Again flush to the wall, he tested the knob on the double door next to the captain's cabin. No go. He fired twice and kicked the door, which slammed into a webbed luggage support, sending it flying.

Inside he saw a long, sealed, olive-green freezerlike container, about twenty-two feet long and eight feet wide, bigger than the specs Brownlee had given him. But he thought it was supposed to be white—or had he just imagined that? Smoke from the corridor was filling the cabin, blown in by gusts through the bridge's shattered door.

He heard the stutter of MP-5s through the storm's wailing, the thumps and momentary lightning of two, three flash-bangs, a scream and more firing. He used the BB's barrel to scratch the lid of the green housing. It *had* been white— they'd painted it over. He tried to lift the lid. It wouldn't budge, sealed with four-inch-wide waterproof tape. Christ, *was* there a computer inside?

Shoving the Glock into his thigh holster, Frank used his Emerson to cut the tape. He then unclipped two of the four H.E. grenades from his load vest and opened the lid. Foolish, he told himself a second later—it could've been booby-trapped. But it wasn't—a neat maze of circuit boards and a digital counter window showed the unlit ghosts of numeral filaments beneath it. The Rone sat on rubber shock dampers and side panels, explaining why it had looked bigger than he'd expected.

You're in deep shit, Hall! he told himself. He pulled the grenade's O-ring pins, dropped them in, closed the lid and exited the corridor. In the confined space the bang of the high explosive grenades produced an ear-ringing sensation almost as bad as that of the flash-bangs. When he looked back into Orloff's cabin, the container had blown apart. Smoking pieces of what had been circuit boards were strewn about the cabin, fires raging in the container, toxic fumes pouring forth and mixing with the smoke of the corridor's burning carpet.

Only four minutes had elapsed since the commandos had gone into action, but already Orloff's FSB men, sixteen in all, were in the process of trying to reach the bridge. They were hampered by the gale force winds and rain and the fact that apart from the two outside stairways leading up to the bridge deck from the salon deck below, which Salvini and Brentwood now had covered, the only other entry point was by means of the interior stairway from the salon deck below. The latter was amply covered by Aussie, who had rolled two flash-bangs and a smoke grenade down the stairwell followed by a three-round burst from his MP-5 to discourage any would-be intruder, then slammed the watertight stairwell door shut to keep the smoke grenades' fog from enveloping him.

"Done!" Frank shouted, exiting the radio room.

" 'Bout fucking time!" Aussie shouted. He then heard, rather than saw, the stairwell door open. A face appeared in the fog, a green cravat below it, a handgun at his side. Aussie fired. Healy's arms flew out, grabbing air, his body crashing back down the stairwell—dead before he hit the bottom. "Tell Dave to put this tub on automatic pilot!" Aussie yelled. "I'll get Sal."

Their exit plan had been simplicity itself: over the bridge's starboard wing, fast-roping it below to the restaurant level two decks down, bypassing any opposition on the salon deck, which would now be one deck above them, then out over the stern. They'd come aboard there, and now would shimmy down the rope ladders to the RIB, wasting anyone unfortunate or crazy enough to be strolling around the ship in the gale.

The commandos, firing bursts and rolling two H.E. and smoke grenades astern of the bridge to keep any FSB at bay, were over the bridge's starboard wing within six seconds, fast-roping to the salon level. Sal and Brentwood, descending a few seconds after Aussie and Frank, were caught at the apogee of a roll, their bodies, like the end of a pendulum, crashing into the ship's superstructure, dislocating Salvini's left knee. Brentwood tried to brake the impact with his assault boots pivoting; instead, his right shoulder took the jolt. The stock of his shotgun rammed hard into his kidney, rattling his load vest so severely he imagined the collision would be heard all over the ship. It wasn't, and even if it had been, no one save Orloff's men topside were venturing out of their cabins into the commotion. The purser's switchboard, however, was jammed with panicky calls. While Orloff had nominally been the purser, the officer who in fact fulfilled the purser's functions was rudely awakened from sleep. Ineffectually, this assistant purser responded that the ship was experiencing "minor mechanical difficulties." It was a response greeted by outraged callers with a combination of contempt, anger, and bone-chilling fear. Machine guns firing didn't sound like "mechanical difficulties," muffled though their noise might be by the nerve-wracking fury of the gale.

The assistant purser, frantic himself, had called the bridge. No answer. The radio room. The same.

As Aussie and Frank reached the salon deck's stern quarter, Brentwood and Salvini following, they saw that the grappling ropes were gone. *Shit!*

Brentwood grabbed the nearest life preserver tube and line by the pool at the salon deck's stern, but as he dropped it overboard he was flung into the wildly turbulent pool. The crack of the shot that hit him mid-back on his Kevlar body armor came from the stern of the bridge deck directly above. Aussie

Lewis and Salvini were already spraying the area, unsure of whether they'd gotten the FSB shooter, but at least he now had his head down. Frank squeezed off four quick rounds from the Glock as Aussie changed mags on his MP-5, yelling at Brentwood to stop "fucking around in the pool."

Salvini was already over the side, fast-roping down the life saver line, buffeted by the gusts, again fighting the pendulum effect, quickly glancing through his NVGs for the RIB. It was nowhere in sight. As he hit the water, or rather, as a huge swell rose and snatched him from the rope, he jerked his two Mae West lanyards. He felt them inflating, his body momentarily submerged, numbed by the ice-cold rain on the surface of the usually warmer ocean. As he rose quickly back to the surface, Frank bobbed up nearby. Then he and Frank were firing up at the rocking rail of the ship's salon deck. They couldn't see anyone, but covering fire allowed Brentwood and Aussie to fast-rope without a rain of lead coming down on them.

But where in hell was the RIB? Before he pulled the flare from his vest load, Sal had answered his own question: Choir and Delta had no doubt been forced to stay well clear of the trigger-happy FSB, who, despite the foul weather, must have spotted them tailgating in the ship's wake.

Aussie, though last down, had already fired his flare. The normally loud *bump!* was muffled by the sounds of the heaving sea and wind. Then Brentwood, ignoring the pain down his back, fired his flare. The FSB men would no doubt see the flares, as well as Delta and Choir, but to bring the big ship about in these conditions, even if the Russians wanted to, would require a laborious quarter mile turn at least. Ample time for the RIB to hightail it out of Dodge.

" 'Bout time!" Aussie shouted, his voice whipped away by a seventy-kilometer gust, the RIB emerging from a maelstrom of wind-driven spray and rolling whitecaps.

Within ten minutes Brentwood, Sal, and Frank had been picked up as well, the rigid inflatable turning and, thanks to the heavenly GPS, heading back, this time with the sea running behind them, toward the *Petrel*.

* * *

All six men were among the highest trained SpecWar shooters in the world, and they should have been alert for the unexpected, but now, their mission done—however the powers-that-be in Washington might react to the destruction of the billion-dollar computer—the edge was off, the adrenaline subsiding. They didn't see the other Zodiac until it crested a wave fifteen yards away, a wink of orange at its bow, the Chinese firing at them.

"Holy shit!" It was Aussie immediately returning fire and inquiring of no one in particular, "Who the fuck's this?"

"From that Whalekill—" began Delta, who never finished. He was screaming, his hands clasping his head, blood spurting over the Mercury's shroud. He was dead a second later, toppling into the sea. Frank lunged for the tiller, Sal returned fire. If the .50-caliber burst from the whale-killing gun, however, was a fluke, given the appalling weather conditions, the commandos' return fire was not. Unlike the Whalekiller's crew, who knew only how to kill the biggest mammals in the world, the five ex-SEALs, trained in every conceivable shooting configuration in every conceivable condition in sea, land, and air, delivered a punishing enfilade of fire. In fact, the Chinese Zodiac had appeared only once more, coming out of a deep trough, but as it crested, the concentrated two-second onslaught of HK and AK-47 submachine gun fire from the ex-SEALs chopped it and its occupants to pieces. All were dead except for one man floating in the water. The law of the sea dictated rescue; the law of antiterrorist missions dictated no prisoners, since the one you let live today could kill you tomorrow. Brentwood's shotgun blew his head off.

"We're leaking!" Sal shouted, pointing at a bullet hole midship on the port side, his voice not panicked but merely loud to overcome the feral rage of the gale.

"What next?" Aussie said in a deadpan Laurel and Hardy tone, while Frank, who'd spent more time at sea than any of them, calmly flipped up the snap-down clasps of the inflatable's first aid box, taking out the roll of two-inch-wide surgical tape.

"That won't hold it!" Aussie opined.

"What do you know?" Frank countered. "I've done this before."

They were both correct. The tape held, but a partial leak continued, compensated for by each man taking a turn in working the RIB's dessert-bowl-size pump with his hands, as if performing CPR massage. Brentwood, in the mad reverie that he knew could take you over immediately following a dangerous mission, was complaining in the most un-SpecWar way that he should be excused from such exertion because of "my bad back," everyone else telling him to "shut up and keep pumping."

Yes, they'd lost another man in Delta, but the brutal truth was, he hadn't been one of Freeman's original SEAL/ ALERTs, and there was no close personal tie.

Approaching the *Petrel*, Aussie Lewis was tired, cold, and thoroughly fed up with the gale's hard-driving winds. He thought he glimpsed another burst of fire, this time from the oceanographic vessel. He was mistaken; it was the high in- tensity thousand-watt electronic semaphore bypassing the at- mospherics. No longer "manned," as in its heyday, the lamp was being automatically operated via a computer-programmed tape from the *Petrel*'s bridge. Tate's alphabetized message was "digitized" by the bridge's navigational computer into a series of "winks" inside the louver-shuttered lamp. Its insis- tent and repetitious winking this early morning informed what remained of Hall's team of a message the Whalekiller's cap- tain, his ship standing off no more than a quarter mile, had given the *Petrel*. By making a series of passes within megaphone- hailing distance, and through gestures as well as barely un- derstandable English, the Whalekiller had informed the *Petrel* that a woman, an American, suffering from severe hypo- thermia and exposure, had been taken aboard the Chinese vessel. The Chinese Zodiac had been so "badly damaged" by the storm it could not be used to transfer her to the *Petrel*. Would they send someone for her?

A trap? Frank wondered. But what choice did he have? He and he alone had gotten her into this. It was his job to get her out. What's more, he had no right to involve his three comrades.

He told them he'd take them back to the *Petrel* first, then go to the Whalekiller alone.

"Screw you!" Aussie replied and, looking at Salvini and Brentwood, asked, "How 'bout you guys?"

"Let's go," Sal said.

"Roger that," Brentwood added. "Avanti!"

"Could be a trap," Frank warned them. "The Whalekiller must've sent those Japs after us. That's why the bastards have a 'badly damaged' Zodiac. We *sank* the goddamn thing!"

"So?" Aussie countered, ducking to avoid the worst of a breaking wave. "We've all been out of radio contact— Chinese captain won't know we shot it to rat shit. We'll play it close to the chest. *What Japs?* He's not going to admit he sent anyone to wax us. Anyway, maybe he thinks they're just overdue!"

That brought a gust-drowned chuckle from Sal, who shouted, "Aussie may be right. 'Sides, they won't want a shoot-up with the *Petrel* as witness. There'd be hell to pay when Tate gets to Suva."

General Chang's face was a light shade of green. The anti-motion medication he'd taken with a large amount of whiskey was clearly not working, and angered rather than comforted by Wu Ling's sympathy, he banished her to the galley. Meanwhile, between episodes of dashing out to throw up over the Whalekiller's leeward side, he told Li that they should use the blanket-wrapped American woman as a hostage.

"Hostage?" Li queried. "Against what?"

"The supercomputer."

"What computer?" Li asked, his binoculars fixed on the approaching Zodiac with the four American commandos aboard. "I don't see any computer."

Chang, wild-eyed from the ill-advised combination of the anti-motion-sickness pills and booze, was obviously not thinking clearly. "The computer—" he began, saliva dribbling from him like a baby, "on *Southern Star.*"

"Well," Li said, his tone markedly unsympathetic to anyone who, unlike him, suffered from any kind of motion sickness, "where *is* the computer? We haven't heard anything from the *Star*. I'm not about to hold an American hostage or fire on an American vessel, inflatable or otherwise, without a shred of evidence."

And Li didn't bother to add that any such action would certainly scuttle the delicate arms limitation talks between China and the Americans. Chang rushed once more to the leeward side.

Suddenly, panicked by the prospect of failure, of having nothing to deliver to Beijing, Kornon, or Swiss Rhine Petrochemicals, Chang, in a Herculean effort, given his weakened condition, forced himself away from the rail and, going down the few steps to Li's cabin, stumbled in and, drawing his gun, ordered Angela to sit up on the bunk. At first she didn't move, but seeing his wide-eyed madness, she managed to raise herself. She was still shivering violently from the hypothermia, and sat cowering against the bulkhead, whereupon Chang, his back also to the bulkhead, grabbed her in a headlock, pressing the Walther against her temple.

Topside, the Whalekiller's deck lights ablaze, the conversation between Frank and Li—neither knowing more than a few words of the other's language—was carried out primarily by shouts and hand gestures. The Zodiac rode high on a crest then dipped out of sight.

Despite the experienced team aboard the nimble Zodiac, however, it took several more minutes to come alongside and secure a line to the Whalekiller.

As Frank grabbed the rope ladder his nerves were taut, alert to the fact that anything could still happen, alert to Aussie Lewis's mantra that "it isn't like the movies, mate," that sooner or later, one way or the other, the world kills you and yours.

"She's down below," Li informed him, leading the way. He

entered the cabin behind Li with the Glock ready, safety off. But simultaneously he realized he'd lost count of how many rounds he'd fired on the Russian ship and against the Chinese Zodiac. The Glock was likely on empty, or damn close to it.

Li stopped in his tracks when he saw Chang holding the girl, and said something in Chinese. Chang, his voice near hysteria, waved the gun at Li to stand aside. Li did so.

"*Where* is the computer?" Chang shouted at Hall.

In the sea-crazed Force Ten it happened in a nanosecond, Frank's realization that with no computer to trade, even if he'd wanted to, it was a no-win situation. The ship rolled as both men fired. Chang's shot exploded past Angela's ear. Frank's hollow point hit Chang much lower than he'd aimed, knocking the general off balance onto the bunk. Angela locked her hands on his wrist, giving Li time to disarm him. Chang screamed obscenities, Li's crewmen and Wu Ling gathering excitedly outside the cabin. Several grabbed Frank, and Li told them to release him. Angela, splattered with blood, trembled as much from sheer terror as from hypothermia.

Frank went to her, comforting her as best he could. Sal, Brentwood, and Aussie in the RIB—not having heard the two shots over the rage of the gale—were waiting to help lower her into the Zodiac for the rough ride back to the *Petrel*.

"I've been shot," she murmured.

"No," Frank assured her, "you're okay." The blood had come from Chang who, witnessed by Wu Ling, was now writhing and moaning on the bunk, being given a morphine shot, holding his buttocks where Frank's shot had gone astray.

It was a shot that neither Sal, Brentwood, nor Aussie Lewis would ever let Frank forget, henceforth dubbing him "Assman." Frank suspected they'd hijacked the monicker form one of Sal's favorite episodes of the old *Seinfeld* show.

"Shit," Frank protested, "the ship was pitching like hell."

"Oh yeah," Aussie said in a plaintive, whining tone, "it was all the ship's fault," adding roughly, "Shoulda nailed him, Frankie."

"He *did*," Sal offered. "In the butt!"

Frank had the feeling his comrades' laughter would be repeated as they mercilessly retold the story among Spec Op warriors.

EPILOGUE

GLORIA'S PHONE RANG.

"Yes?"

"He's all right." It was Andrew, calling from his office. He and Shirley were no longer on duty in Gloria's apartment, since Larry had been caught and detained, thanks to the police sketch, at SeaTac Airport. He'd been about to board a United Airlines flight to Albuquerque.

"Frank's coming home," Andrew told Gloria, "flying out from—" He stopped. In his haste to relieve her of her anxiety he'd almost blurted out, "Suva," but remembered just in time that the White House had strictly forbidden him to give out the location. Meanwhile, should the Russians kick up a stink, the game plan was for the State Department to issue a vigorous denial that any Americans had been involved in the "horrendous" act of piracy, obviously perpetrated by "terrorists," against the *Southern Star*. And indeed, if the Russians made such a charge, they would have to explain what it might have been that the terrorists were after. Certainly no passengers had been attacked or robbed by the marauders.

As it transpired, the Russians did not accuse the Americans of anything. The arms limitation agreements were about to be signed, and, concomitantly, huge American loans to Russia and China were at stake.

Angela Chabot was offered and accepted a three-million-dollar, tax-free transfer to a Bahamian bank. She insisted, however, it be changed to a Swiss account. It was done.

Recovering in a private ward of Suva General, she was apologized to profusely by Frank Hall, who suggested that when she returned to the States perhaps she might like to visit him and Gloria in Portland.

She looked at him long and hard and replied, "I don't think so."

In Zurich, at his usual table in the Bauschantzli café, Reinhard Klaus was sipping his latte, pausing now and then for another slice of Ruëblichueche, the local carrot cake, when he felt the slight tremor of his cell phone in his inside pocket.

It was his secretary. There was a long distance call from Beijing, from a Colonel Chang.

"*General* Chang?" Klaus commented.

"No, sir, a *Colonel* Chang."

There was a pause.

"I know no such person," Klaus said, snapping the cell phone shut and gazing out on the lake, a cold breeze out of nowhere rustling the Chinese lanterns. There was a searing pain in his stomach. Grimacing, he pushed the cake away.

Morton Dalgliesh was not pleased. He was apoplectic.

"You *blew it up*?" he charged Frank, who was on scrambler from Suva.

"Better that than the bad guys get it," Frank replied.

"But we'll—we'll have to build another prototype!"

"I guess so. I had no option."

There was an outraged explosion of air on the other end, Frank thinking Dalgliesh had farted. You heard everything on these digitals.

"You *guess* so!" Dalgliesh blustered. "You, my friend, are in a lot of trouble. When you get back here to Washington I'm going to personally tell the President to—"

"Do what?" Frank cut in. He was tired, and they were calling his flight. "Listen, *Morton*, you return that spoon you stole and I won't tell the FBI." He slammed down the phone. He was so bone weary that it wasn't until he gave the check-in

attendant his ticket that he realized the U.S. consulate in Suva
had booked him first class.

He'd take it.

IAN SLATER

Don't miss one explosive novel!
Find out which Ian Slater
blockbuster you need.

WWIII

In the Pacific, Russian-made bombers come in low. In
Europe, Russian infantry divisions strike aircraft and
tanks begin to move. All are pointed toward the Fulda
Gap. And World War III begins....

WWIII:
RAGE OF BATTLE

From beneath the North Atlantic to across the Korean
peninsula, thousands of troops are massing and war is
raging everywhere, deploying the most stunning arma-
ments ever seen on any battlefield.

WWIII:
WORLD IN FLAMES

NATO armored divisions have escaped near defeat in the
Russian-ringed North German Plain. The once formidable Russian assault falters and NATO forces struggle to
end this worldwide conflagration.

WWIII:
ARCTIC FRONT

In the worst Siberian winter in twenty years, blizzards are
wreaking havoc with U.S. cover, and it is up to the
unorthodox U.S. General Freeman to hold this arctic
front.

WWIII:
WARSHOT

General Cheng is massing divisions on the Manchurian border while Siberia's Marshal Yesov readies his army on the western flank. If successful, this offensive will drive the American-led U.N. force into the sea.

WWIII:
ASIAN FRONT

At Manzhouli, near the border of China, Siberia, and Mongolia, the Chinese launch their charge into the woods. It's all-out war, and only the brave and ruthless will survive.

WWIII:
FORCE OF ARMS

Four sleek Tomahawk cruise missiles are headed for Beijing. It is Armageddon in Asia.

WWIII:
SOUTH CHINA SEA

On the South China Sea an oil rig erupts in flames as AK-47 tracer rounds stitch the night and men die in pools of blood. From Japan to Malaysia, the Pacific Rim is ablaze in a hell called WWIII.

The World War III series
by Ian Slater
Published by Fawcett Books.
Available in bookstores everywhere.